RECKLESS *Invitation*

samantha christy

Athena Books Publishing Group

Saint Johns, FL 32259

This is a work of fiction. Names, characters, places and incidents are either the product of the author's imagination or are used fictitiously, and any resemblance to actual persons, living or dead, business establishments, events or locales is entirely coincidental.

Cover designed by Letitia Hasser | RBA Designs

Cover photo by WANDER AGUIAR

Cover model – James Clippenger

ISBN: 9798673790380

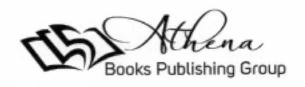

For Bruce.

I could listen to you play guitar for the rest of my life.

Please let me.

RECKLESS *Invitation*

Samantha Christy

Chapter One

Liam

My head hurts. I squeeze my eyes tightly to stave off the morning light, turn over in bed, and breathe deeply, hoping my hangover won't be bad. My eyes open abruptly when I smell perfume. Staring at the pillow next to me, I realize I'm not in my own bed.

Motherfucker. I did it again.

I sit up too quickly and rub my eyes. My skull pounds to the beat of my heart. I glance around the room for clues but don't find any. Expensive-looking art adorns the walls. I peer through an archway into the bathroom, raising a brow at the size of it. My clothes have been stacked in a pile on the dresser. Whoever lives here is very neat. And well off.

On the nightstand I don't find Advil, which is usually the first thing I reach for in the morning. Instead, I see what's left of a bottle of whiskey, and next to that is the flyer from Mom's funeral. I really have hit an all-time-low, going home with a stranger on the day I buried my mother.

She's better off.

That's what I keep telling myself anyway. For the past thirteen years, she's been living in her own hell. I tried to tell her what happened wasn't her fault, but it fell on deaf ears. At least she didn't feel any pain. That's what the doctor told me. He said she was most likely knocked unconscious the minute her head hit the shower floor. There wasn't even any blood. By the time the housekeeper found her the next morning, the running water had washed it all away.

Kind of ironic that I tied one on shortly after she died as a result of being too drunk to take a fucking shower.

Like mother, like son. I twist off the lid to the bottle and take a swig.

I grab my jeans off the dresser, jamming first one foot in and then the other, then throw on my shirt and leave the room. I stop when I see whose back is turned to me as she cooks at the stove. Dark-as-night hair falls to the middle of her back. A short robe barely covers her ass. I must make a sound because she turns.

"Eggs?" she asks.

"Sure. Whatever." I sit on the couch in the living room and put on my shoes, wondering what the hell happened last night that would have me hooking up with one of the people I despise most in this world: Veronica Collins.

She raises the spatula. "How about a thank you?"

I snort. Even half-naked, she's still a raging bitch.

I must have been particularly shit-faced to have gone home with her. I don't remember a damn thing. I search my memory but come up blank. The last thing I recall is leaving my uncle's place after the reception. If I remember correctly, I required help to navigate the steps outside the front door.

A few minutes later, Ronni puts breakfast on the table. I get up slowly, so I don't jar my throbbing head, and join her.

"What happened last night?" I ask, then shovel a forkful of scrambled eggs into my mouth.

"Wow. I knew you were wasted, but you really don't remember?" She laughs. "Don't worry, it was nothing to write home about."

I cringe. I've wondered if I'm a better lover when I'm piss drunk. Guess not. "So we…?"

"You woke up in my bed, didn't you?"

I rub a hand across my jaw. "I hope you don't expect—"

"Let me stop you right there, Liam." Her lips curve into a nasty smile. "I don't expect anything from you. I don't want anything from you. And I certainly don't need anything from you. It was sex. That's all."

I finish what's on my plate. "As long as we're clear on that."

She studies me. "You're a lot more fucked up than I gave you credit for."

"Yeah? Well, we can agree on that too."

She shakes her head. "Not to sound too cliché, but you're reckless. You didn't even offer to use a condom."

My eyes snap to hers. I *always* use condoms. I thought.

"We did," she says. "But only because I mentioned it. Listen, I'm about to make you and the rest of Reckless Alibi rich and famous, and the last thing we need are a dozen paternity suits. If you can't keep it zipped, then at least find someone who won't trap you."

"You mean someone like you?"

"I told you, I don't need or want anything from you. But, yeah, if you need to get your rocks off, you can always call me. I'm safe, discreet, and I'm used to quirky musicians."

My eyebrows shoot up. "Just how many of us are you sleeping with?"

"Does it matter?"

I get up from the table and rinse my plate. "Guess not." I think about what she said. I turn and lean against the counter. "On a scale of one to ten, exactly how quirky am I?"

"About three hundred and fifty," she says without hesitation.

My stomach clenches. "Sounds about right."

She motions to the door. "You'll be leaving now, won't you?"

"Can I use your shower first?"

"I'd prefer you didn't. That's my personal space. You understand."

"Ronni, my dick was inside you last night."

"That's the *only* part of me it touched," she mumbles in amusement.

"You are a prize," I say sarcastically, striding over to pin her to the chair. "Just so we're clear, this stays between us."

"You think I want anyone knowing about this? Like I said, I'm discreet."

I back away. "Okay then. I'm outta here. I've got stuff to do."

"Like working on those songs?"

Damn. She's not pulling any punches. I shoot her a furious scowl.

"What?" she asks. "Brianna and Crew can only carry you so long, you know. You're the one who writes the music, not them. They're the lyricists. But you've had them pulling double duty for months."

"Seriously, Ronni? My mom's body isn't even fucking cold, and you're bringing this shit up?"

"Someone has to."

I pick up my jacket and cross to the door.

"Check your bank account," she says. "Your royalties from the first album have started rolling in. I think you'll find a sizeable amount was deposited this morning. Soon you'll be getting even more from the second album. I meant it when I said I was going to make you rich. But you have to do your part, too, and get back to writing music."

I wave dismissively and walk out, hearing nothing after she started talking about royalties. On the elevator, I pull out my phone and check my account. My eyes go wide and excitement courses through me when I see a balance with so many numbers I have to read it twice. I send a text.

Me: Check your bank account, then meet me at Dirk's ASAP. I'm moving out.

I wait a few minutes for his reply.

Crew: Holy shit! I'll be there by noon, brother.

I text Garrett and Brad, too, asking them to meet me at my uncle's.

On the hour-long train ride from New York City to Stamford, I fantasize about being out from under Dirk's thumb. For thirteen years he's controlled everything in my life. Not anymore.

Guilt washes over me. If I'd gotten the money a week sooner, I could have moved Mom out of his house. Maybe then she wouldn't have been so depressed all the time. Maybe then she wouldn't have fallen and hit her head.

At the train station, I kick a brick wall waiting for my Uber, mad as hell at Dirk. He'll get his due. Somehow I'll make sure of it. I've got the ace in the hole to make it happen—when the time is right.

When my ride pulls up to his palatial estate, I'm happy to see my car parked around the side of the house. At least I didn't drive in the state I was in. Crew and Bria arrive, and I greet them. Crew's smile is huge. He knows what this means to me.

He pats me on the back. "I'm still sorry as hell about your mom, but damn, I'm glad you can finally get out of here."

"Me too."

Crew is the only person who knows about my past. The shitstorm that was my childhood. I was always there for him, and he's there for me. Has been since we were kids.

"What happened to you last night?" Bria asks.

I'm relieved they don't seem to know anything about Ronni, but I still have no clue how we ended up at her place. "Took a cab home. Slept it off." That seems to placate both of them.

We go inside. The only person who sees us is Helen, the housekeeper. She smiles and keeps wiping Dirk's plaques on the parlor wall. He loves to remind everyone how important he is. As the mayor and the owner of the largest car dealership in this part of Connecticut, his narcissism knows no bounds. If he has his way, he'll be governor in a year, but not if I have anything to say about it. My life's mission—other than being part of a successful rock band—is to bring him down.

We stroll down a long hallway in the east wing to where Mom and I had lived, along with a few of the staff. Crew and Bria stop at her door, looking sad. "Come on, let's get this over with," I tell them.

"Don't you need a U-Haul or something?" Bria asks when we get to my room.

I look at the ornate furniture. It's not as nice as the rest of the house but fancier than what most people can afford. "None of this shit is mine. I only need my clothes, guitars, and a few other things."

"Do you have any boxes?" Crew asks.

I shake my head and lean against the wall. "I don't even own any fucking suitcases. Everything here is Dirk's."

Crew sends a text to Garrett, asking him to pick some up on the way. "Stack what you're taking on the bed, and we'll pack it up when Garrett gets here."

A half hour later, I realize I have more stuff than I thought. The bedroom door opens. I expect Garrett and Brad, but it's not them.

"What's going on here?" Dirk asks.

"What does it look like? I'm moving out."

He looks surprised, or maybe taken aback.

"Did you think I'd live here forever? Thanks to you, Reckless Alibi is on the fast track to being one of the hottest bands around. With that comes money. Lots of it. I don't need you anymore."

He takes a purposeful step toward me. "That's where you're mistaken. You'll always need me, and I'll always have a hand in what you do."

I set my jaw obstinately. "You're wrong. I'm on my own now, and that's exactly how I want it."

He chuckles. I'm all too familiar with that devious laugh. He's got something up his sleeve. "You underestimate me. Do you really think I'd give you all the opportunities you've had and not make sure I'd profit from it?"

Garrett and Brad walk in. The air is thick with tension.

"Bad time?" Garrett says, dropping an armful of boxes on the floor.

I turn to Dirk. "What did you do?"

"I guess it's time I told you. Two months ago I bought Indica Record Label."

I swallow incessantly to keep the bile from spewing from my mouth. He owns the recording company that puts out our music. "You fucking prick."

He smirks. "Is that any way to talk to your new boss?"

I get in his face. "You won't be for long."

"I know you recently got a fat check, but it's a far cry from being able to buy yourselves out of the contract. You're stuck with IRL, and you're stuck with me whether or not you live under my roof."

"Get the fuck out."

"You can't order me out of what's mine, son."

"Do *not* call me that, you son of a bitch. You aren't even my real fucking uncle."

Bria whispers to Crew behind me. "Dirk's not his uncle?"

"No."

"Wrong again, son. My brother adopted you. I'm your uncle legally and otherwise."

My face contorts. "Otherwise? As if you've ever acted like family. I've had enemies who were more compassionate than you."

"Look around," Dirk says. "You'd do well to remember everything I've done for you."

I laugh gruffly. "Everything you've *done* for me? You're delusional. You think putting a roof over my head, over Mom's head, somehow exonerates you from all the shit you've done?"

"Careful," Dirk warns. "Best not to air dirty laundry in mixed company. It might make your friends view you a whole lot differently."

"Go to hell, Dirk."

"Get your shit and get out then. And leave the keys to the Mazda." He leaves.

No one knows what to say. The silence is deafening.

I view the boxes on the floor. "You brought tape, right?" I ask Garrett.

He holds up a thick roll.

"Let's get going. I don't want to be here a second longer than I have to."

Crew starts filling a box. "You can crash on my couch if you want."

"I can stay at a hotel."

"Don't waste your money," he says. "I'm at Bria's half the time anyway." He turns to her. "Babe, you mind if I stay at your place? That way Liam can use mine."

Bria tries to mask her excitement. They've been together since last year. I'm surprised they haven't already shacked up, given that Crew hates where she lives. "I suppose I could put up with you for a few days."

He wraps his arms around her and whispers something that makes her cheeks flame.

I throw the tape at him.

We carry the boxes into the hall. Dirk waits in the hallway, presumably to make sure I don't take anything that's not mine. He doesn't have to worry. I want none of it.

I stop in front of Mom's door, wondering what Dirk will do with her stuff. It occurs to me I might want some of it. "Give me a minute," I say to my friends.

"We'll take these to the car," Brad says. "Take your time."

I open the door and stare into her room. I haven't been in here since she died, but Helen obviously has. It's as clean as the day we moved in, with the exception of several boxes stacked against one wall. All her things have been packed.

"Didn't take you long, did it?" I ask Dirk, who's standing behind me.

"Her things are being donated to charity."

I step inside her room and close the door in Dirk's face to keep myself from throwing a punch. Leave it to him not to tell me.

I examine the boxes until I find the one I'm looking for. I drag it over next to the chair by the window and remove the tape. Inside are framed photos. There are far too many for me to take. There's really only one I want anyway. I dig until I find it.

A knock startles me. Crew pokes his head inside. "We're ready when you are."

I raise my chin in acknowledgement. He shuts the door.

I trace the faces of the two people in the picture with me—Mom and Luke—and my throat thickens when it occurs to me that of the three of us, I'm the only one still alive.

Chapter Two

Ella

Jenn pulls me along as we trail behind Krista. "Come on," she whines. "We'll get nowhere near the stage if we don't hurry."

"I don't know what the big deal is," I say, shaking glitter off my clothes. Why I let them put it in my hair is beyond me. And they overdid it, by a lot, but there was no time to wash it out. I feel like Lady Gaga. "I've never even heard of them. Ruthless Alibi. What kind of name is that for a rock band?"

"It's *Reckless* Alibi, and it's a great name. I promise you'll download all their music after tonight."

I give her a sideways glance. I haven't seen her this worked up since junior year when Zac Efron signed an autograph for her outside one of his movie premieres.

Several women push past us on the sidewalk leading to the club—*grown* women, who act like they are kids going to meet Mickey Mouse. Krista turns around and takes my other arm. Now they're both pulling me. We get in line behind the crazy women.

"How is it that the two of you are going bat-shit crazy over this Ruthless Alibi band, and I don't have a clue who they are?"

"Reckless!" they both shout.

"Whatever."

Krista says, "You've had your head in the sand since you and Corey—"

I give her the evil eye.

"Sorry." Her bottom lip juts out. "I forgot we weren't mentioning the bastard's name. What I meant to say was that since you broke up with Dickhead, you've been MIA. That all changes starting now. Two weeks is long enough to mope around."

We inch closer to the door. I glance behind us; the line goes down the street and around the corner. "Exactly who are these guys?"

Jenn taps on her phone and shows me a picture. "They aren't just guys. One of their singers is a girl. Their songs have been on the radio for months. I'm sure you've heard them. Here." She puts her phone against my ear.

I nod, familiar with the song.

"Twenty bucks cover," the man at the door says.

"Twenty dollars? Really?" I try to step out of line.

Krista takes my hand. "Oh, no. We're doing this. It's our treat."

They each pay their way and split mine. "I'm buying the drinks then," I shout over the crowd.

"Who cares about drinks?" Jenn says. "Let's go find a good spot."

I check the time on my phone. "But the sign says they don't start for an hour."

"Spot first, then drinks," she says. "Trust me."

I follow them as they weave through a hundred people. Jenn has no problem blazing a path through the throng. "Sorry," I tell a few when we bump into them as we pass.

She drops my arm and runs ahead, laying claim to a high-top seconds before another woman gets there. The loser pouts, then runs for a table farther back.

Jenn gloats. "You gotta be faster than that. This is a great place, don't you think? Close to the dance floor, and we'll still see the band."

"Dance?" Krista says, surveying our surroundings. "I don't know. Someone will steal our table."

"We'll dance *on* the table," Jenn says.

Krista squeals. "Yes!"

I take a seat. "You guys are crazy."

"Ella, you need to loosen up. When was the last time you really let your hair down?"

"You mean my hair full of silver glitter?" I say sarcastically and chew my lip. "Well, let's see—I dated a tax attorney for eighteen months, so I'd say about one day longer than that."

"Your hair looks great. It really sparkles under the lights. You're due for a fun night out," Jenn says. "We'll even give you first dibs." She pounds the high-top.

"I am not dancing on the table."

"Not yet maybe. But after three or four drinks …"

"Not *ever*."

A waitress comes by, and I order three margaritas.

"Make it six," Jenn says. I give her a hard stare. "What? She might not get back for a while."

I hear screaming coming from the front door.

"Looks like the band is here," Krista says.

I crane my neck. "Where?"

"They probably won't come in through the front. Hopefully they'll stick around after." She pulls up her lightweight sweater, exposing a tight tank top. "I want all the guys to sign this."

I shake my head at both of them. "What have you done with my best friends?" They laugh and hug me.

Krista gets out her phone. "Which one do you want? You can pick anyone but Liam. That sex god is mine. Interesting fact. You two have the same last name."

"I think Ella would look good with Garrett," Jenn says.

"Which one is he?"

"Tats."

My eyes widen. "That's a lot of tattoos on his arm."

Krista giggles. "Makes you wonder where else he's got them."

I study the men in the picture. "If I were forced to choose, I'd take this one."

"Good choice. His name is Crew. Singer. Hot." She fans herself.

"What about you, Jenn? Who would you choose?"

"Brad, for sure." When Krista isn't paying attention, Jenn leans close. "I lied. It's totally Liam, but I can't say that in front of her."

Half a dozen drinks are placed on our table. We all reach for one.

"To Reckless Alibi," Krista says. "May we all be lucky enough to take one of them home tonight."

I clink my glass to theirs and drink, even though that's not at all what I want.

It's been fourteen days since I left the cheating bastard. I'm not about to invite another train wreck into my bed. I'm done with men. I'll focus on the three things most important to me: friends, work, and running. At twenty-three, I don't need or want to be tied down. I plan to enjoy the freedom Rat Bastard afforded me by screwing his nineteen-year-old neighbor. I'm too young to be in a long-term relationship. I wasted enough time as it is.

"Ella!"

I turn to see both of them staring. "What?"

"Where'd you go?" Krista asks.

Jenn's smile fades. "You're thinking about *him*, aren't you? Stop it." She pushes my drink closer to my lips. "You promised you'd try and have a good time. You deserve to have fun."

I sigh heavily. "You're right. I'm sorry." I down a few gulps, making a face at the tartness.

Half an hour and two drinks later, the crowd goes ballistic as the band takes the stage. I again gape at my friends as if aliens have invaded their bodies.

Now that I'm feeling a bit tipsy, however, I get into the music as they play. They're good. It's hard not to swing my hips to the beat. The male singer—what's his name, Crew?— and his female counterpart are stunning together. I wonder if they're a couple. Krista and Jenn don't seem to notice what I do, or maybe they don't care. They're too busy drooling over the men on stage.

Occasionally the one playing guitar glances at our table. Every time he does, Krista screams, "Oh, my God, he's looking at me!"

When he does it again, I watch him closely, unsure what he's looking at. I turn to see what's behind me—it's a wall. When I look back at him, our eyes lock, and he rewards me with an irresistible and devastating smile. Oh, gosh. It's not her he's looking at, it's *me*. I'm sure it's the hair. Jenn said it sparkles when lights hit it.

Shortly after the band takes a break, a tray of drinks arrives. "From the guitar player," the waitress says. "You lucky girls."

Jenn and Krista squeal like teenagers.

"Do you think this means he wants to take me home with him?" Krista asks.

"He's probably got herpes," I say. "Rock stars sleep with everyone."

"So he'll wear a condom," she says.

I cringe. "Gross."

"Oh, come on, El. Don't be so uptight."

The band comes back, and Krista goes wild. When it appears they're winding down, she does the unthinkable. She gets up on the table and dances—until a very large man comes over and pulls her down. Then he puts her over his shoulder and starts for the door. He turns. "If you want to get your friend home safely, I suggest you follow me."

Embarrassed, I take Jenn by the elbow and we follow.

Outside, someone is setting up a roped-off area by a second door. Krista eyes it. "I'll bet that's where the band will come out. You guys, we have to stay. If we wait here, we'll be in front. They'll see us. Please. Oh, God. Does my hair look okay? Brutus back there messed it up when he went all Tarzan on me."

Jenn and I peer at each other. Krista has gone off the deep end. She's had more to drink than the two of us put together. I shrug. "Fine by me," Jenn says.

Krista takes off to position herself in what she deems to be the best spot. Other people see us and gather around, speculating on when they will come out. Someone exits the main door, and I can no longer hear the band play.

"Shouldn't be long now," I say. "Sounds like they're done."

"Unless they stay for drinks," Jenn adds. "We could be here for hours."

"Wonderful."

My feet start hurting from standing in one place. More and more people gather behind us. A few times, I have to ask the drunk women behind me to please stop crowding us. One of them is telling me off when the door opens. Screams and cheers erupt as the members of Reckless Alibi step out on the sidewalk. There is a huge man in front of them and a few others in the rear with SECURITY printed across their T-shirts.

Autographs are signed. Pictures are taken. Krista is about to come out of her skin waiting for them to get to us. "We should have stood right by the door. What if they stop signing before they reach us?"

"I'm sure they'll be happy to autograph your boobs," I say.

Suddenly I'm pushed from behind. I fall through the ropes, my heel catching on the pavement. As if in slow motion, I see Jenn reaching for me. I try to take her hand but miss. Then everything goes black.

Chapter Three

Liam

The ropes are breeched, and the first thing I see is Crew protectively putting his arms around Bria. Thor lunges forward to keep bystanders from trampling over the girl who fell down.

I see silver sparkles. Shit. The girl from inside. I rush over and pick her up. She looks at me in a daze as I carry her to the limo. Once inside I flip on the light. Blood trickles down her temple and a large goose egg is forming.

Crew, Bria, Garrett and Brad slip in behind us.

"What happened?" the girl slurs. I can't tell if she's drunk or stunned from the fall.

"Looks like you were pushed from behind. You fell on the pavement and were about to get trampled to death." I'm more than a little concerned at the sight of her head. "I'm afraid you may have a very bad headache tomorrow, but right now I'm taking you to the hospital."

She touches her head then stares at the blood on her fingers. She seems embarrassed. To be hurt? To be in my lap? "Uh, I'm fine. I should go. Krista and Jenn are probably wondering where I am." She tries to sit up but cringes in pain.

"Don't move." I crack the window. "Tom, can you please find two women, Krista and Jenn, and tell them we're taking …" I glance at the woman in my lap.

"Ella," she says, looking mortified.

"Tell them Ella is going to the hospital. She's got a possible head injury. Give her friends your contact info so they can call later."

"I'm on it," he says, turning away.

I close the window as fans swarm the limo and try to peek inside. "Take us to the nearest emergency room," I tell the driver.

She touches her head again, but I remove her hand. "You shouldn't. Your hands could be dirty." Bria gives me some wadded-up tissues, and I press them gently to her temple. Ella tries to wiggle off my lap. "Stay still. You could have a concussion."

Her eyes close. "This is not happening."

It's hard not to smile. If she's aware enough to be embarrassed, she must not be injured too severely.

"Is there anyone we can call for you?" Bria asks.

Ella retrieves her phone from her back pocket. The unexpected squirming causes pangs of pleasure to shoot through me. Douchebag, I tell myself. She's hurt, and you're getting a fucking boner?

She moans in pain. "I can do it. Thank you."

The limo comes to a stop, and the driver tells us we're there.

Everyone starts to get out. "It's okay," I tell them. "You can head back. I'll handle this."

"We should stay," Bria says. "How will you get home?"

"I'll figure it out later. Right now I need to get Ella inside."

They move aside, and I remove Ella from my lap and get out. She takes my hands as I help her onto the sidewalk. "Go slow," I say, ignoring the softness of her skin.

"Don't worry. I doubt I'll be running marathons anytime soon." She almost laughs but stops. She must be in pain.

I shut the limo door and give the roof two pats. It drives away as I slowly escort her inside. "Sit here," I say, finding an empty bench in the crowded waiting room. I hand her the bloody tissues. "Hold this on your head if you can. I'll be right back."

I cross to the counter. Pointing at Ella, I tell the person at the desk, "She hit her head on the sidewalk."

The nurse cranes her neck to get a look. "She seems stable. You'll have to wait. Name?"

"Liam Campbell."

She eyes me like I'm stupid.

I mentally smack myself. "Oh, *her* name. Uh, Ella …" I don't know her last name, so I stop.

"Okay, Mr. Campbell, keep her awake, and we'll get her seen as soon as we can."

I return to Ella. Her head is leaning against the window behind her. She looks tired. "The nurse said it could be a little while. She said you shouldn't go to sleep."

Her eyes dart around the room. "Not likely, with all the crying."

There is a woman with three little kids, and one of them holds his arm as if it's broken. "Sorry," I say. "I bet the noise isn't helping your head much."

"I'm fine."

I laugh. "You are not fine. You have a second head growing out of your temple."

Her hand covers her mouth. "I'm so embarrassed. I don't know what happened. One minute I was standing there, and the next you're putting me in a car."

"You blacked out?"

"I don't know. I remember falling and then you were looking down at me."

"Shit. If you blacked out, it might be more serious than we thought. Hold on." I go over to the counter again and wait for the person in front of me to clear.

"You again?" the nurse says. "I promise we're working as fast as we can to get everyone seen."

"Yeah, but I have new information. She might have lost consciousness when she fell. That's bad, right? Don't you think she should be seen now? You know, in case she has a brain bleed or something? I mean, you wouldn't want to be sued for leaving a woman to die."

This gets her attention. She looks up from her computer and over at Ella. "I'll move her up the list. Should only be ten more minutes or so."

"Thank you."

Walking back across the room, I see Ella's eyes flutter closed. "Oh, no. You can't go to sleep."

She strains to open them. "Then find me some coffee."

There's a coffee vending machine on the other side of the room. I race over and get her a cup.

She makes a face when she tries it. "This isn't coffee, this is brown water." She shoves it back at me.

I glance out the window. "I did see a Starbucks outside, but I'm not sure—"

"Please? I'd kill for a mocha latte."

She reaches into her pocket, but I stop her. "This one's on me under one condition. You promise to stay awake."

"Yes, sir."

"Ma'am," I say to the lady on the other side of her. "Please make sure she doesn't fall asleep."

Her finger is wrapped in a bloody bandage. "You're leaving her here?"

"The woman wants coffee. In fact, do you like Starbucks? I'll get you one as well."

She gives me her order and then I'm crossing the street. The line isn't too bad, but I keep looking back at the hospital. I can't see the ER windows from here. What if she falls asleep?

My name gets called, I pay, and then I'm racing back to the hospital. Ella's gone. My heart pounds, thinking she got up and walked out.

"They took her back a few minutes ago," the bloody bandage lady says. I hand her the coffee and thank her.

I contemplate my next move. I got her here. She's being seen by a doctor. Maybe I should leave. I don't know her. She didn't seem confused.

I turn for the door then remember the latte in my hands. I go to the desk, using the coffee as an excuse to stay. The truth is there's something about Ella that makes me want to stay and see if she's all right.

"Remember me?" I ask the nurse. "Liam Campbell. Ella was just taken back. I was getting coffee. Do you think I could join her?"

"Of course. I'll buzz you through." She turns and calls to a young woman in a red vest. "Stephanie, please take Mr. Campbell to bay seventeen."

"Right this way, Mr. Campbell," Stephanie says.

"It's Liam."

Her steps slow and she gives me a second look. "As in Liam Campbell from Reckless Alibi?"

I smile. There's no better feeling in the world than when someone recognizes me by name. It's been happening more and more these past few months. "Guilty."

Her jaw goes slack. "Oh my God, I love your songs. I listen to them all the time. I play guitar too, and hope to be in a band when I graduate high school in May."

"Well, thanks for listening to our music, and good luck with yours."

"I can't believe I'm walking with you. My friends will freak when I tell them. They'll never believe me." She looks around. "Hey, I'm not supposed to have my phone out, but no way can I miss this opportunity. Can I snap a quick picture with you? Please? It would mean everything."

"Do it."

Faster than lightning, the phone is in her hands and our heads are close for her selfie. She squeals. "Thank you, thank you, thank you! Oh gosh, you probably want to check on your wife. She's right behind the curtain. It was so nice to meet you." She walks away.

Wife?

I peek around the curtain. There's a doctor with Ella. He sees me. "Mr. Campbell?"

How does he know my name? "Uh, yeah."

He offers his hand. "I'm Dr. Stone."

After we shake, I notice Ella has changed into a hospital gown and the blood on her face is gone. There's a bandage on the left side of her head. I can't help but stare, glitter hair and all. She's fucking gorgeous. Onstage I couldn't figure out why I was drawn to her. A melody plays in my head, and I pat my pockets, wishing I had blank sheet music.

"Ella most likely has a concussion. Due to the late hour, I'd prefer she stay the night for observation. Her blood pressure is higher than I'd like. She'll be taken up for a CT scan. Assuming there's no further damage, which I don't expect, she'll need to rest for a few days, then ease back into normal activity. I suspect with a little TLC, your wife will be back to normal in no time."

I cock my head, confused. The doctor leaves.

I step over to the bed. "You told them we're married?" I say a little harshly.

"Of course not."

A nurse comes in before I can get out another question. "Ms. Campbell?" She checks Ella's wristband and then hands her a small cup with pills in it and a glass of water. "The doctor prescribed this for the pain."

As soon as she leaves, I resume my position at Ella's side. "Then why is everyone calling you Mrs. Campbell?"

"The nurse didn't call me Mrs. Campbell, she called me *Ms.* Campbell. Big difference."

"Who gives a shit about that? Why do they think we're married if you didn't tell them?"

"Listen, if you think this is all a big ploy to get you in my bed, you're sorely mistaken. I don't know who you think you are, but you obviously think highly of yourself if you assume women will fall at your feet and pretend to be your wife."

"But … what the hell?" I think back to when we first entered the ER. "Oh, shit. It's my fault. I didn't know your last name. They probably assumed it was the same as mine."

She laughs, then cups her head in pain. "I almost forgot; Krista told me we have the same last name."

My face slackens in surprise. "Your name is Ella Campbell?"

She nods.

I chuckle, wondering what the odds are. Then I stiffen. "You're not related to Dirk Campbell or" —I swallow— "Don Campbell, are you?"

"Not that I'm aware of."

Relief courses through me. "Good."

I hand her the coffee. She looks at it thoughtfully, then regards me for a few moments. "You should know I'm not going to sleep with you."

My brows shoot up at her bluntness. "What makes you think I want to sleep with you?"

"Oh, come on. The drinks you sent to my table. The fuck-me eyes you were giving me."

I try to look innocent. "That was *you?"*

"The knight-in-shining-armor act after my fall."

"It wasn't an act. I was being a good Samaritan. And for argument's sake—not that I want to sleep with you—but why *wouldn't* you?"

She looks me up and down. Parts of my anatomy tingle under her perusal. "Look at you. You're in a rock band. You probably have syphilis or something, not to mention I don't do one-nighters, nor do I sleep with arrogant men I've just met."

"Arrogant? Who says I'm arrogant?"

"Okay, fine. Maybe you're not. But you'd be one of the few who aren't."

"You know a lot of guys in rock bands, do you?"

"No, but they have a reputation."

"You mean a stereotype. Not all musicians are narcissists."

"Are you saying you aren't?"

I shrug. "If I'm being honest, maybe I am a little, but it's only because I'm confident in my abilities."

Her lips curl in disgust. "You think an awful lot of yourself, don't you?"

I realize what she must be thinking. "I'm confident about my *guitar-playing* ability. Get your head out of the gutter, *Mrs.* Campbell."

She laughs again, then cringes.

I feel guilty causing her pain. "Sorry."

"I might have lied to you a minute ago. The real reason I don't want to sleep with you—or anyone—is because I recently got out of a long-term relationship. So, no offense, but I won't be getting in anyone's bed for some time. If that's why you're here, you're wasting your time."

Someone comes around the curtain with a wheelchair. "I'm here to take you up for your CT scan, Mrs. Campbell."

We glance at each other in amusement.

Before they wheel her away, she stops the man pushing her. "Liam, I'm not sure I ever thanked you for everything you did for me tonight. It was very nice meeting you. I enjoyed your music, and I plan on downloading more, but I've got it from here. Goodbye, Mr. Campbell."

She is taken away, and I have to lean against the wall because of all the fucking noise in my head. I go to the nurse's station. "What time do patients usually get discharged after staying overnight?"

"If she's transferred to another floor, it'll probably be late morning or early afternoon, but it depends on how backed up they are."

I check the time. Eleven thirty. That gives me nine or ten hours. I do a quick google search before racing out the door.

Chapter Four

Ella

I am wheeled back to the ER after my CT scan. The chair in the corner is empty. I'm not sure why it makes me sad that Liam isn't here. I told him to leave, and I meant what I said. I'm not interested in a romp in the hay. Still, I feel the corners of my mouth turn down. I guess it was nice to have someone famous giving me attention, that's all.

Dr. Stone comes in. "As I said before, I'd like to keep you overnight for observation."

I glance at the curtain. "I have to stay here?"

"We'll admit you, and you'll be moved to another floor."

"But I can leave tomorrow?"

"More than likely. I didn't find anything significant on the scan. However, there's still the issue of your hypertension. We'll observe you tonight, but my best guess is it'll resolve itself by morning, and you'll be good to go."

"When can I get back to running?"

"Take a few days to rest, but after that it's largely dependent on how you feel. Take cues from your body. Start slowly and work up from there. Having a running partner might help keep you from overdoing it."

I lost my running partner two weeks ago. "Okay, thank you."

"Someone will be in to move you shortly."

He pulls back the curtain to leave, and familiar brown eyes are staring at me. I turn away.

"Looks like you have another visitor," Dr. Stone says. "I'll leave you to it."

"Jesus Christ, Ella. What happened?"

"How did you get in, Corey? I thought they only let family back here." I momentarily think of Liam and how everyone thought he was my family.

"I saw something Jenn posted on Instagram about you being rushed to the hospital. I tried to call you. I got worried. This is the third hospital I checked. I told them I'm your brother."

"I need to talk to this place about their security," I grumble under my breath, then I realize I haven't checked my phone in a while. I should let Krista and Jenn know I'm okay.

"Come again?"

"Nothing. I'm fine. I think you should leave."

He pulls up the chair. "I'm not going anywhere while you could be dying."

I point to my head. "I'm far from dying. I fell. I have a concussion. No biggie."

"Then why are you still here? Shouldn't they be discharging you?"

"They're keeping me overnight for observation."

Concern wrinkles his forehead. "Sounds serious."

"It's not. Like I said, observation. Corey, we broke up. You should go."

He takes my hand. It feels so familiar. "I think I should stay. When you get out tomorrow, you should come home with me so I can take care of you."

My jaw drops. "You cheated on me. Two weeks ago you cheated on me, and you want me to stay at your apartment?"

"I didn't cheat on you two weeks ago, Ella. That's just when you found out."

I rip my hand away. "I don't care if it was two weeks or two months. You slept with another woman."

"I was drunk. I told you it will never happen again. I love you."

He's said the words a thousand times. I've said them back just as much. This is what I was worried about. Corey has always had this uncanny ability to make me want what he wants. It's why I locked myself in my apartment for two weeks. I was afraid if I saw him, I'd take him back. I need more time away from him so I can build my walls and become stronger.

"I can't be with a man I don't trust. It's hard for me to believe she was the only one, and I can't be sure you'll never do it again."

"You have my word. I promise."

"Have you quit drinking?"

He looks like I asked him if the sky is green. "No."

"Then you can't promise it won't happen again."

"You want me to stop drinking to prove how much I love you? Is that what you want?"

"I don't doubt that you love me. I still love you. Those feelings don't go away overnight. But I can never be with you."

He traces my jaw. "You still love me. I knew it. We're meant to be together, Ella."

I reach around on the bed, find the call button, and push it. A moment later, a nurse comes around the curtain. "Is there something I can do for you?"

I nod. "You can escort him out. I don't want any more visitors."

"Ella. No."

I turn away.

"Come now," the nurse says. "It's late, and she needs her rest."

He leaves without another word.

My head slumps into my hands, and I cry until my forehead throbs.

~ ~ ~

"Knock knock," someone says at the door. Krista and Jenn walk in with balloons.

I smile. "You didn't have to come. I'm being released this afternoon."

"Yeah, but hospitals are boring, and we feel guilty about dragging you out against your will last night."

"I wish I knew you were coming. I'd have asked you to bring—"

"Ta-da!" Jenn reveals the Starbucks cup hiding behind her back.

My eyes mist. "I love you guys."

Jenn pulls the tray table over and puts down my latte. She hugs me and eyes my bandage. "Seriously, though, are you okay? You took one heck of a fall."

"More importantly," Krista says, "you got to ride in a limo with Reckless Alibi."

I chuckle.

"Come on, sister, spill!"

They take a seat on either side of the bed.

"I don't remember much more than being morbidly embarrassed. I mean, the guy picked me up and carried me to the car like a baby."

"Eek!" Krista squeals. "Not just any guy. Liam fucking Campbell."

A smile spreads across my face.

"What is it?" Jenn asks.

"They thought we were married."

They are both about to jump out of their skin. "Tell us everything," Krista says. "Don't leave out a single detail."

They hang on every last word as I tell them what happened.

"You got pictures with him, right?" Jenn asks, glancing around the room. "What did he sign for you?"

"Uh …"

Krista's biting stare scolds me. "El, tell me you got some swag out of this."

I shake my head.

Krista feigns heart failure. "And you just let him leave?"

"Weren't you listening?" Jenn says. "She *told* him to go."

"You're crazy!" Krista shouts.

I cringe, because I still have a pounding headache.

"Sorry, but you really missed an opportunity there."

"Blame it on the head injury," I say.

There's a knock on the door, and Dr. Stone walks in. He has my chart in his hand. Flipping through it, he says, "I know you saw Dr. Su this morning, but I like to follow up once my patients leave the Emergency Department. Looks like my prediction was accurate. Your blood pressure is right where it should be. You feeling okay?"

I touch my head. "Only a little throbbing."

"That will go away sooner rather than later. Try not to overdo it when you get home. They've issued discharge orders so you should be good to go in a few hours." He glances at Krista and Jenn and then back at me. "I also heard there may have been an unwanted visitor last night. I apologize. We're training new staff, but that's no excuse. It never should have happened."

"It's okay. Thanks for all your help, Dr. Stone."

"You're welcome. Good luck, Ella."

After he leaves, Krista and Jenn go into full swoon mode again.

"First the gorgeous rock star and now the hot doctor," Jenn says. "Some girls have all the luck."

"Was he serious about the unwanted visitor?" Krista asks. "Did you actually make them throw Liam Campbell out?"

"No, not Liam."

"Then who?" Jenn asks. She sees my apprehensiveness. "Oh my God, it was the dickhead, wasn't it? Shit, Ella. I should have known when he commented on my Instagram post. I'm so sorry."

"It's not your fault. He seemed genuinely concerned about me. Even asked me to go home with him so he could tend to me. He said he still loves me."

"Stop it," Krista says. "He's a lying, cheating bastard."

"I know, but it was hard seeing him again. I guess I miss him more than I thought I would."

"Nope," Jenn says. "No way. I see the look on your face. You are not getting back together with him."

"Why do you think I had him kicked out? I don't want him back. But that doesn't mean I don't miss him."

"Maybe it's not him you miss," Krista says. "Maybe it's sex."

Jenn swats her arm. "Maybe it's being in a relationship. Being in love. Knowing someone has your back."

I drop my eyes. "He didn't have my back. He cheated behind it." I sink into the pillow. "I wish I could, I don't know, disappear for a while."

Krista offers a sad smile. "Hey now, that's why you have us. We're your people. We'll always have your back, no matter what."

A nurse pops in. "I have the discharge papers for you to sign."

"We should go," Jenn says. "Call me later if you want a ride home. Or if you need ice cream. Or alcohol. Or anything."

I hug them both before they leave. Then I fill out the twenty-five forms the nurse left. "All this for one night in the hospital?"

"Need help?"

My heart flips when I see who's in the doorway.

"I mean, who better to help you fill out all that shit than your husband?"

Chapter Five

Liam

"Come in," she says.

I cross the room and hand her a vase of flowers so big, she almost drops it.

"Here, let me." When I take them back, her hand brushes mine and our eyes meet. It's easier to see hers clearly today, as the large bandage from last night has been replaced with smaller Band-Aids. She has the most incredible brown eyes—lighter in the middle and several shades darker around the outer edges. They're exotic. I can't shift my gaze away.

She pulls back. "Why are you here?"

I get the papers from my back pocket and hand them to her.

"What's this?"

"It's a song I wrote. Or rather, it's a melody. Crew and Bria write the lyrics. I write the music to go with them."

She seems confused. "Sorry, I can't read music. I'm not sure what I'm looking at."

"It's the first Reckless Alibi music I've written in months."

"Okay." She pretends to be interested in the sheet music that probably looks like a foreign language to her.

"You don't get it. I haven't been able to do this since last fall. My bandmates have had to step up and compose music for me. I've been in a slump—the biggest one I've ever had. Then you fell into my life and *voila*, a new song."

"You're right. I don't get it."

"Last night after I left, I found a music store and bought blank sheet music and a used guitar. I got a cheap hotel room down the street, because my place is back in Stamford. Well, Crew's place is. Anyway, the point is, instead of staring at blank sheets, I *filled* them. It took me less than seven hours to score a complete song. That might be a record for me, and I have you to thank."

She narrows her brows. "Uh … you're welcome?"

"That's why I came back. I need all the inspiration I can get."

Her expression flattens. "Liam, I'm not sleeping with you."

"I know. You said as much last night. The amazing thing is—I knew that, and I wrote music anyway." I chuckle, because the funny thing is, I *don't* want to sleep with her. Not this girl. I don't want her to know how truly twisted I am. "Some would say you're my muse, Ella."

Her eyes widen. "Your *what?*"

"My muse. My inspiration. And just so you know, once a musician finds his muse, that's it."

She pulls her bottom lip in, then releases it. "What do you mean, that's it?"

"I don't know. I'm just glad we met, that's all."

"All finished?" a nurse says, popping her head in.

Ella hands me back the sheet music. "Almost."

"You're free to get dressed. Someone will be by soon to wheel you out."

"Wheel me?" Ella asks. "But I can walk."

"It's standard procedure. All patients leave in a wheelchair." The nurse glances at me. "Is this your ride home?"

"Yes," I say before Ella can answer.

"Good. I'm glad you have someone to look after you."

Ella signs the last form, and the nurse gathers the papers and leaves.

"I can take the subway. My legs work perfectly fine."

"Or I can give you a ride home in a cab. You don't want to take the subway with a head injury. Who knows what can happen?"

She gets out of bed and picks up her clothes off the chair. "Fine. But you're only dropping me off. You're not coming in."

I hold up my hands. "I'll be a total gentleman."

While she's in the bathroom, I spy her phone on the tray table. I pick it up, surprised to find it unlocked, and call myself. When she returns, it's back where it was.

"I can't wait to get home and wash this glitter out of my hair," she says.

"I kind of like it. It's what made you stand out among the rest."

"It makes me look like a streetwalker."

"Maybe at eleven in the morning. But last night, it worked. You met me, didn't you?"

"As if that was my intention."

"What was your intention?"

She sits and rubs the side of her head. She's obviously still in pain. "It was supposed to be a fun night out. A way for me to get my ex out of my head."

"The ex. Right. What's his name?"

"Dickhead. Rat Bastard. Cheating Cradle-robber—take your pick. He showed up last night after you left."

My spine stiffens. "Is he stalking you?"

She shakes her head. "He was worried about me. Says he still loves me."

"Are you thinking about getting back with him?"

"I don't want to. What would keep him from cheating again? But I still love him. I'm embarrassed to admit I hid in my apartment for two weeks in hopes I wouldn't run into him. He has a way of convincing me to do stuff I don't really want to do."

I ball my hands into fists and tighten my jaw. "What kinds of things?"

She sees my reaction. "It's not what you're thinking. It's things like going to hockey games when I hate hockey, and taking cooking lessons when I'd rather be shoving bamboo shoots under my fingernails. He made his hobbies my hobbies. The only thing he got me into that I love is running."

Her phone vibrates. She types a text.

"That's not him, is it?"

"It's Jenn. She wants to know if I need a ride."

"You told her you're good, right?"

"I did."

A smile tugs at the edges of my mouth. "How come?"

"Because you're here. You offered. Because I listened to more of your music this morning, and it would be a shame if you were unable to compose more often." She glances at her phone. "My friends are mad at me for not getting a picture with you. They thought I should have at least asked for your autograph."

"Why didn't you?"

"I'm not a crazy fangirl, like they are. I don't drool over famous people."

I hold my chest. "Damn, Ella. Way to deflate a guy's ego. I thought you'd say it was because you had a head injury."

She smiles. "That, too."

"What do you want me to sign?" I look around the room. "How about one of those balloons?"

"Can you make it two? One for each of them?"

"You don't want one for yourself?"

She shrugs. Her face pinks up, like maybe she does want one but won't admit it. I take the marker from the white board on the wall and sign all six balloons.

"Thanks. They will be beyond excited."

"Now for that picture." I crouch next to her chair and lean close, snapping a photo of the two of us with my phone. When she turns to speak, our mouths are inches apart. I resist the urge to kiss her, knowing she'd deck me.

"*I'm* supposed to take the picture," she says.

"Right. Go ahead."

I plaster on my best smile as she takes one.

A young man comes through the door with a wheelchair.

"Your chariot awaits," I say. On the way out, she reminds me I'm only to drop her off. "Fine by me. I've got somewhere to be. I can't wait to show this new song to the rest of the band."

"What's it called?"

"That's for Crew and Bria to decide. But I was thinking something along the lines of 'Ode to a Goose Egg'."

Jesus, her smile has more melodies bombarding my head.

~ ~ ~

After leaving Ella's, it's a short subway ride to Bria's place. Crew comes downstairs to let me into the building. I immediately shove the sheet music at him.

He follows me up the stairs, taking twice as long as me because he's preoccupied with what I gave him. "When did you write this?"

"Pulled an all-nighter last night."

He's confused. "Back in Stamford?"

"Locked myself in a hotel room here in the city."

"Why?"

"I was inspired."

A smile splits his face. "The girl you took to the hospital?"

I shrug, not wanting to admit it took a woman to get me out of my slump.

He shows it to Bria when we walk through her door. She runs to fetch her notebook. "I think I have some lyrics that will work perfectly with this. Maybe we can even start rehearsing it this week."

I sit heavily on her couch. "About that. I'm not sure we'll be welcome to keep practicing in Dirk's barn. Not after what happened."

"But he owns the company," Crew says. "Surely he wants us to have a place to practice."

"Do you think we can afford to rent another place?" Bria asks.

"We should talk to Jeremy and Ronni about it," Crew says.

Ronni. I almost dread all of us being in the same room. Will they be able to tell something happened between us? But she's our IRL rep, and there will be no avoiding her.

I glance around Bria's tiny apartment, guilty because I'm staying at Crew's much larger one while they are crammed in here.

"The two of you should be living in Stamford. I could stay here; it's more suitable for one."

"Musical apartments?" Bria asks. "We're fine here. Plus, I love living in the city."

"I think I'd like it, too," I say. "In fact I think we should all live here."

Bria eyes her bed and the couch. *"Here?"*

I laugh. "Not here. The city. We play in New York more than we do back home. It makes sense."

"Rent is expensive," Crew says.

"But we're starting to make money. We'd be able to afford it if we have roommates."

Bria looks at Crew and back at me. "Are you trying to shack us up?"

"Like you don't practically live together anyway. I bet if I check your closet, I'll find a shit ton of Crew's clothes. Hell, he probably has a toothbrush here."

"He doesn't," she says with a smile. "He uses mine."

I cringe. "That's fucking gross."

Crew pats me on the back. "Someday, brother, you'll want to share a toothbrush with someone and then you'll know."

I have the urge to hit him with a snarky comeback, but images of Ella float around in my head. I push them away, knowing I could never have what they have—a normal, healthy relationship. Fucking Ronni—that's what I get. That's what I deserve.

"Say we all agreed to live in the city," Crew says. "You'd have to bunk with Garrett or Brad."

Bria shakes her head. "Brad is moving in with Katie."

"Really?" I say. "But she doesn't even like us. And she lives in Stamford."

"So live with Garrett. He won't want to stay in Connecticut if the rest of us are living here."

"I wouldn't even begin to know where to start," I say. "I'm not familiar with the city except for the bars."

"My stepdad, Gary, works in building management," Crew says. "I'll talk to him when we return from Florida and see what he knows."

Florida. Right. With everything that happened last night, I almost forgot we go on tour in a week. "Can you talk to him now? Maybe then we can set something up for when we get back?"

"Sure thing."

"And we'll meet with Jeremy to see about a new rehearsal spot."

"And Ronni," Crew says.

"Yeah, that's what I meant." I put my jacket on. "I'm taking off."

Crew looks at me sideways. "You got somewhere to be?"

"I do." I tap my head. "The flood gates have opened, my friend. I've got some composing to do."

Chapter Six

Ella

My trashcan is filling up with cards, candy, and flowers. None of which I want. Corey seems to think that after he lied his way into seeing me at the hospital last Friday, he's free to start courting me again.

I can't even get away from him in my own apartment.

I wish I had work to keep me busy, but I'm between jobs. I have a meeting next Monday with an author who is looking for someone to illustrate an entire series, not just one book. I skim my hand across the shelf where I keep all the books I've worked on since I graduated two years ago. Twenty-one. That may not seem like a lot to some people, considering the average children's book is only thirty-two pages long, but there is an illustration on each page or two, and it's pretty much taken up most of my time.

The nature of my job means I'm not always sure where my next paycheck is coming from. Getting a ten-book contract would set me up for the entire year.

I sit at my art table, doodling and listening to my playlist. A Reckless Alibi song comes on. I sing along with it. I know a lot of the songs now. I've played them many times since I came home from the hospital. Krista and Jenn were right—they are crazy good.

I've since found out the band has only recently come to be on the radio. No wonder Liam didn't get recognized by anyone in the hospital or on the street as we waited for a cab. I wonder how long that will last. Seems to me a band that good won't be playing in clubs very long.

I study my drawing. The character I've sketched looks surprisingly similar to Liam Campbell. I draw a girl with a bump on her head next to him. Then I glance in the mirror. My goose egg has flattened out, and all that remains is a greenish-yellow circle.

I haven't had any headaches in twenty-four hours. That's my cue to get out there and run again. I put down the pencil and reach for a jacket, deciding there's no time like the present to go for a walk. Maybe even a jog, depending on how I feel.

Before I get out the door, my phone rings. I don't know who it is. The number is not from around here. "Hello?"

"Hello, Mrs. Campbell."

My lips curl in surprise. "How did you get this number, Mr. Campbell?"

"We're married. It only makes sense I'd have it."

"Very funny."

"Okay, so I may have called myself from your phone when you were changing. You really should keep your phone locked, you know."

"Maybe you shouldn't go around snooping in random girls' phones."

"You're hardly a random girl. Are you doing all right? How's the head?"

"Good. In fact, I was heading out for my first run—or at least a walk—to test the waters."

"I was hoping we could meet up."

"Why?"

"I have something to show you."

"What could you possibly have to show me?"

"You'll see. Can you meet me? I'll come to your place."

I hesitate. He knows where I live, but I'm not sure it's a good idea.

"So not your place," he says in response to my silence. "How about I meet you where you run?"

"You want to go to Central Park?"

"It's as good a place as any. I can be there in ninety minutes. Text me and let me know where to find you."

"Fine."

"See you then, El."

My pulse quickens when he calls me that. Krista and Jenn use the nickname all the time, but Corey never did. He was too formal for nicknames. I try to quickly come up with a nickname for Liam but can't. I may be artistically creative, but I have zero wit. "Bye, Liam."

I return to my bedroom and change into my best, most flattering, running pants. Then I roll my eyes at myself in the mirror.

~ ~ ~

I see him across the lawn. He hasn't spotted me yet, and I take a minute to look him over.

He's handsome. His thick, dirty-blond hair barely reaches his collar. It's currently under a knit cap, somehow making him look sexy and roguish. At least he's wearing it because it's cold and not as a fashion statement. Something is slung over his shoulder. A guitar case. He's tall. Much taller than I am. And strong; he picked me up off the ground and carried me to the car.

He's the opposite of Corey. My ex has dark hair, dark eyes, is well under six feet, and can't be over a hundred-and-fifty pounds, soaking wet. My heart hurts thinking about him. How can someone still love a man who cheated on her?

Liam spots me and waves. I move toward him. His long legs eat up the distance in a few strides.

"How's the little Mrs.?" he asks with a smirk.

I give him the stink eye.

"What? I'm joking. But you have to admit, it was pretty funny they thought we were married."

"I thought for a minute you believed I was some crazy fangirl when you asked if I told them I was your wife."

He looks guilty. "I may have thought that, but that was before I got to know you."

"Oh, so you know me now? After two conversations?"

"Are you kidding? You're my best friend, El."

I'm confused by his behavior.

"Since we met I've composed two songs. Two songs in four days! At this rate, I'll have our fourth album finished by late spring."

"Oh, right. I'm your muse," I say, unconvinced. "Tell me something. How does a girl who fell flat on her face in front of you, and in your own words, grew a second head out of my temple, inspire you?"

"Beats the hell out of me. But who am I to question the inner workings of the universe?"

"You think meeting me was destiny or something?"

He shrugs.

"But I'm unavailable, Liam, emotionally and physically."

"I get it. And the thing is—so am I. That's why I have a proposal for you."

I step back. "I'm not being anyone's fuck buddy, if that's what you're thinking."

He laughs loudly. "I assure you, that's not what I want." He motions to a bench. "Can we sit for a minute?" He carefully places his guitar case next to him.

"Do you carry it everywhere?" I ask.

"No. What do you do for a living, El?"

"What does it matter?"

"Are you a waitress? A teacher? Lieutenant governor?"

I chuckle. "Wrong on all counts. I'm a children's book illustrator."

He cocks his head. "Well, that I didn't expect. I've never known a book illustrator before."

"I've never known a rock star."

"Touché," he says, amused. "This job of yours, is it flexible?"

I nod. "That's part of the reason I love it so much. I make my own hours, take on as much or as little as I want, and I work from home."

A smile the size of New York City splits his face. "I was hoping you'd say that." He unzips the guitar case and pulls out a shiny brown twelve-string guitar, handling it as if it's a newborn baby. "I want to play something for you."

Suddenly I'm excited. "I'm all ears."

He fishes a guitar pick out of his pocket and strums. I'm mesmerized by the sound and entranced by the way his fingers grace the strings. The way he plays is elegant and passionate. It's like the guitar is an extension of him. His eyes close, and he plays without looking.

I'm amazed at his talent. Before this moment, I was sure there was no one in love with their job more than me. Looking at him, I know I'm wrong. He was obviously made for this.

It's only a melody, and it doesn't sound like a love song, yet it makes me feel so much emotion. If I weren't hung up on the rat bastard, I might even be aroused by what I'm hearing, what I'm seeing. By the sheer intensity exuding from his every pore as he gives it everything he has for his audience of one.

His eyes open as the song winds down. It's not until he stops playing and people start clapping that I realize onlookers stopped to listen. He gives them a nod and puts his guitar away.

"Wow," I say. "That was … I actually don't have the words."

"*That* was because of you," he says, weaving the guitar pick between his fingers so quickly, it's hard for me to follow it.

"But how? I didn't do anything."

"Like I said, I'm not about to question it. But I'm sure as hell not going to ignore it." He stops the thing he's doing with the pick and looks up. "Ella, I'm just going to come out and say it. I know it sounds completely ludicrous, and maybe it is, but I've thought about it for days. I heard what you said about your ex. You want to get away from him, and I need you to keep me from sinking back into the slump."

"What are you saying?"

"Reckless Alibi is heading to Florida on Friday. We're touring there for six weeks. I'd like you to come with me."

My eyes narrow and my mouth falls open as I replay his words in my head, then reach a conclusion. "Are you crazy?"

"I know it seems like I am, but I'm dead serious."

I shake my head vehemently.

"Before you say no, I'm not asking you to sleep with me. I know it's off the table. You'll have your own hotel room and everything. You can take mine, and I'll bunk with Garrett or Brad. You can bring your work with you. You can run. I hear the beaches are great for that. You'll get a killer tan. You don't even have to come to all our shows. I just want you to be there. We can talk, hang out. Nothing more, I promise."

I start laughing. I can't stop. This whole thing is so far out of left field, I don't even know what to do with it. I calm down and take a breath. "Liam, you don't even know me."

"I don't, but I can't deny what I've been able to do since meeting you. I'm asking you to come and be my friend. I swear I won't touch you. It will be strictly platonic. I've even cleared it with my bandmates. You have no idea how stoked they are that I'm writing music again."

I get up and pace. This is crazy. It's ludicrous. But why, in the back of my mind, is a voice telling me to do it? Six weeks without any possibility of seeing Corey. Surely that would be long enough to get over him.

I stop. "You swear there's no ulterior motive? Because if this is all some ruse to get in my pants—"

"Ella, from what I can tell, you might be one of the nicest women I've ever met, aside from Bria. There is no way a girl like you would want to be with a guy like me, so believe me when I tell you I'm not even going to try. You're normal, and I don't mean that in a boring, unexciting way. You're normal in ways I envy."

"Why do you think I'm so normal? You can't possibly know that."

"You're a children's book illustrator. Your friends fangirl over my band. You run in Central Park. You're the very definition of normal. Am I wrong?"

I snort. "Well, no, but—"

"Come with me. Please."

"Tell me why you think *you're* not normal."

He laughs bitterly. "It's not something I discuss with anyone. Not even my muse. Let's just say I'm fucked up in ways a girl like you could never imagine."

The distance I see in his eyes makes me feel sorry for him, and I'm more than a little curious about who Liam Campbell really is. I sigh deeply.

"You're thinking about it, I can tell," he says with a sly grin. "Say yes, El."

I glance around the park where I used to run with Corey every day. There are so many memories. Memories I want to forget. "On one condition."

"Anything."

"You run with me when we're down there. Running alone sucks. I need a partner."

"But I don't run."

"I'll teach you. At the end of the six weeks, I'll have you ready for a 10K."

"What's that?"

"Just over six miles."

He rubs his jaw. "I don't know if I can do it. I drink a lot."

"Do you smoke?"

"No."

"Then you can do it. That's the only way I'll say yes."

He gets off the bench, slings his guitar over his shoulder, and smiles.

Me—I'm standing here wondering if I just made a deal with the devil.

Chapter Seven

Liam

Eighteen years ago

Luke tosses me the football. I run around Mom and Donny all the way to the orange cone. I jump up and down, pleased with myself for scoring a touchdown. Large arms pick me up. "Way to go, sport."

I smile at Donny. "I won!"

"You sure did," he says, putting me down and giving me a tickle.

Luke joins us, and we're both pulled into a great big hug. We end up on the ground, wrestling. It seems like we're always wrestling. It's fun. We never used to wrestle. Not until Mom started going on dates with Donny.

Mom sits down in the grass next to us. "This is nice," she says, gazing into Donny's eyes.

She's happy now. She sings in the shower. I can hear her because the bathroom is on the other side of the wall where Luke and I sleep in bunk beds. And she makes pancakes a lot. We used to only get cereal, but not anymore.

Mom pulls me into her lap and draws Luke close. "Donny and I have something we want to talk to you about before we rejoin the others."

For a second, I feel sick. When she sits us down and talks to us, it's usually because we have to move again. I hate moving. We do it a lot. Luke told me every time we move, we end up in some place smaller. I don't remember like he does. He's ten and knows more than me.

"It's okay, Liam," he whispers and gives me our secret handshake, the one he said will always protect us.

I turn in Mom's lap and ask, "Are we moving?"

"Yes, but this time it's not because I have to change jobs." She glances at Donny, and they smile at each other. "Donny and I are getting married. We're going to live with him."

I look around at the huge yard that's big enough for lots of football fields, at the pool that has a slide *and* a diving board, and at the great big house Luke and I got lost in earlier when we went looking for a bathroom. Excitement makes me jump off her lap. "We're going to live here?"

She laughs. "Well, not here. This is Dirk's place. Donny doesn't live with his brother, you know that. You've been to his townhouse before. But guess what? He just bought a house a few miles away. It's not quite like this one, but it's much bigger than our apartment. You will each have your own room, and there's a yard with a swing set."

"A yard? Can we put a tent up and have sleepovers out there, like Will?"

"Who's Will?" Donny asks.

"My friend from school. His dad puts up a tent in the backyard, and they eat hot dogs and cook mores."

Donny chuckles. "I think you mean s'mores, sport."

"Yeah, s'mores. Can we do those?" Excitement overcomes me. "Are you going to be our dad?"

Luke perks up, eagerly awaiting an answer. He really wants a dad. He's the only kid in fourth grade that doesn't have one. He says that even though some of his friends don't live with their fathers, they get to see them and go out for ice cream or pizza. I always wanted a dad to take me out for ice cream.

"There's something else we wanted to talk to you about," Donny says. "When your mom and I get married, I'll be your stepfather. That's kind of a dad, but not really a dad. We've talked about it, and if it's okay with the two of you, I'd like to adopt you."

"What's that?"

Mom pulls me back on her lap. "It means a judge will sign papers, legally making Donny your father. It means he will make you pancakes, like I do. He'll take you to baseball practice. We'll go on vacations together. He'll keep you safe—keep *us* safe—always."

"I'll get to call you Dad? And so will Luke? And we'll live with you forever?"

"That's exactly what it means," Donny says. "Assuming it's okay with you."

"Can we get a dog?" Luke asks.

Donny laughs. "I think a dog would be a fine addition to our family."

Our family. Suddenly tears prick my eyes. Backyard campouts, vacations, a house, a dog. Luke and I are about to get everything we've dreamed of.

Donny grabs me and then Luke, tackling us to the ground, tickling us again. "What do you say?"

"I say yes," Luke says.

Donny turns to me. "What about you, sport?"

"Can we name our dog Sally?"

Mom and Donny laugh and then the four of us have the biggest tickle fight of all time.

Someone comes over. "Excuse me, lunch is being served in the tent by the pool."

Mom helps Luke and me wipe the grass off our clothes. Heading to the tent, I spy Donny's older brother standing by a tree, watching us. He's been doing it all day.

Luke sees what I see. When Mom and Donny walk ahead, Luke says, "I'm glad we're not going to live here. That Dirk guy gives me the creeps."

"But he has a pool."

"I'm sure Donny will bring us over to use it," he says. He stops walking. "You know if Donny is our dad, Dirk will be our uncle. It will be kind of strange calling Donny *Dad*, don't you think?"

"But you want to, right?"

"Yeah, I want to."

"Good, because I want to, too. Luke, this is the best day of my life."

He smiles. "I'm glad you'll have someone else to protect you."

We do our secret handshake.

I wonder if we'll teach it to Donny.

Chapter Eight

Ella

I stare at my phone, knowing what I need to do. It was stupid to think I could run away, and that would somehow make everything all right. I have to put on my big-girl panties and deal with my life.

I pick it up and dial. Liam answers, "Hello, wife."

"I'm sorry, I can't go with you."

"But you said you want to get away from him. This is the perfect opportunity."

"Leaving now would be avoiding my problems. It would be wishing them away, and for what? To return in April, knowing nothing has changed?"

"But what could it hurt?"

"I have a big meeting on Monday."

"Fly down after."

"It won't work. The hotels wouldn't have an art table."

"I'll buy you one. We'll pack it in with our equipment."

"I've heard running on the beach is hard on the ankles."

"So we'll run on the sidewalk."

I close my eyes and lean back on the pillow. "I can't."

"None of those are good reasons, El. Unless you still love him."

"Of course I do. It doesn't just go away."

He's silent for a beat. "Just because you love someone doesn't mean they're a good person. It doesn't mean they know what's best for you, or that …" There is a long, drawn-out pause. "Or that they aren't a monster."

My eyes shoot open, and I wonder who he's talking about. "Corey's not a monster. He's just a guy who cheated on me."

"How about I come play you another song? Maybe if you see how much you inspire me, you'll change your mind."

"My decision is final, Liam. I'm happy to be your friend, but I'm not going to Florida."

He sighs deeply.

"I think you'll find I'm not really your muse. You most likely came out of your slump because you're excited about going on tour. You'll get down there, see the crowds and the fans, and you'll forget you even asked me."

"If that doesn't happen, can I call you? Can we Facetime or something?"

"I can do that."

"Call me if you change your mind, even if it's weeks from now."

"I won't."

"Way to kill a guy's hopes and dreams, El."

"I think all your dreams are about to come true, Mr. Campbell. When you get back to New York, you'll be so famous, you won't even remember who I am."

"Not gonna happen."

"Good luck, Liam."

"Bye, Mrs. Campbell."

~ ~ ~

I play Krista and Jenn the new music file Liam sent me. It's him playing the guitar. No singing, no drums, no keyboard. It still astonishes me how there can be so much emotion without lyrics. I've never known any musicians before, but I imagine this kind of passion has to come from pain.

"Holy shit," Krista says. "He wrote that because of you?"

"Tell me again why you changed your mind?" Jenn asks.

"Because I can't do it."

Krista gives me a hard stare. "Because you *won't* do it."

I sip my coffee and turn to watch the passersby outside the café. "It was crazy to even consider it. I don't know him. I don't know the band. They could be in a cult. He could be a serial killer."

"Last fall, Crew sang a song in front of a thousand people, declaring his love for Brianna," Krista says. "Does that sound like something someone in a cult would do?"

"If this were a random person asking me to accompany him to Florida for six weeks, you'd tell me not to go."

"Yeah, but this isn't some rando," Jenn says. "This is Liam Campbell. You'd be on tour with Reckless Alibi. He already said you'd have your own room. He even said he didn't want to sleep with you."

I laugh. "That's exactly what men say when they want to get you into bed."

"Maybe you *should* sleep with him," Krista says. "What better way to get over the dickhead than to bag a rock star?"

"I'm not sleeping with anyone."

"I'm just sayin'. There could be worse rebounds."

"I don't need a rebound. I don't need a man at all."

Krista flops back on the couch cushion and screams in frustration. "I can't believe you're going to pass on the opportunity of a lifetime. Hey, you should introduce us. Maybe I can become his muse."

I check the time. "I have to go. If I don't get out there now, the park will be too crowded."

It's not altogether a lie. I like running when there aren't as many people around, but there's only one person I don't want to bump into. I know his running schedule like the back of my hand.

I zip up my jacket and put on my hat and gloves.

"You could be running on the beach in a few days instead of freezing your ass off here," Jenn says. "Think about that."

"Bye," I say, leaning over to give them each a quick hug.

Stepping outside, I inhale the crisp air. "It's probably too humid down there," I tell myself. "And running in the sand may be difficult."

"Excuse me?" a lady says, thinking I'm talking to her.

"Oh, sorry. I was …" I twirl my finger in the air by my ear and then take off across the street.

I put my earbuds in and listen to music. Halfway through my run, a Reckless Alibi song comes on. It makes me think of Liam and how he played his guitar for me right here in the park. He seems normal enough. Then again, he went to great lengths to tell me how *not* normal he is. It makes me wonder about him. Why does he think someone like me wouldn't want to be with someone like him? As my friends would testify, any girl in her right mind would want to be with him. Any girl but me.

Is that what it is? The chase? Wanting what he can't have?

Someone takes hold of my elbow. I jerk away, on high alert. I turn to see my ex running alongside me. I stop and pull out the earbuds. "It's only eleven. You never run until lunchtime."

He shrugs. "I've changed my hours."

I consider him suspiciously. "Have you been waiting for me?"

"Every day," he says. "I've been coming at different times, hoping to run into you."

"So you're stalking me now." I shake my head and walk away.

He comes up next to me. "Jogging in the park is not stalking, Ella. I wanted to see you again—make sure you were okay after your fall."

I raise my cap and show him the faded bruise. "I'm fine. I'm running, aren't I? There, now you know. You can go now."

I turn on my music and run. A second later, one of the earbuds is yanked out. "All I'm asking for is a chance."

"You had your chance, Corey. For eighteen months. And you blew it. It's not like what you did was some kind of forgivable offense, like forgetting my birthday. Your dick didn't accidently slip into that girl. You wanted someone else, and you had her."

"I made a mistake. You've made them too."

I look him straight in the eye. "I've never cheated."

"I love you, Ella."

My heart flutters when he says it. His eyes are full of guilt. I remember the first time he said those words. We'd only been together three weeks. He took me to Coney Island. We ate hot dogs and then went on a roller coaster. I got sick right after, losing my lunch into a trash can. I'd never been so mortified. That's the moment he chose to say he loved me.

We laughed about that moment for the next seventeen months. I was sure I'd end up being Mrs. Corey Gorman. Even with all the boring stuff he made us do together, I thought he was the one.

Tears come to my eyes. I turn away and wipe them, but not soon enough for him not to notice.

"You still love me, and not just because it takes time for those feelings to go away. You love me because we're meant to be together. You love me because I make you laugh. You love me because I always remind you to take your keys so you never get locked out of your apartment, like you did the first day we ran together. You love me because I'm nice to homeless people."

I'm trying not to listen, but him saying these things are merely a reminder of everything I'm trying to forget. My heart can't take it. Everything he's saying is true. I swallow hard.

He steps closer. "You love me because we're soul mates, Ella."

He wraps me in his arms. My walls begin to crumble. He feels so familiar, like coming home after a long journey. I sink into him.

A Reckless Alibi song starts playing in my right ear, and I hear Liam's voice in my head. *"Just because you love someone doesn't mean they're a good person."*

I push Corey away. "We're not soul mates. We never were. You proved that the day you screwed another woman. Goodbye, Corey."

"Ella!" he calls after me. But I don't stop running. I move fast and go far, until my head pounds. I run until I find the bench where Liam played the song.

I sit and get out my phone, trying to slow my rapid breathing.

He answers on the first ring. "Tell me you changed your mind."

My eyes close. "Email me the plane ticket."

Chapter Nine

Liam

I strain my head around the seat in front of me to see Ronni coming down the aisle. It's the first time I've laid eyes on her since the day after Mom's funeral. She stops in business class. Not only did they have to hold the plane for her, she's not even sitting with us. The flight attendant helps her with her carry-on and then Ronni catches me watching. In usual Ronni fashion, she ignores me.

"Why is she even going with us?" Bria asks.

Jeremy leans over the seats in front of us, where he's sitting with Garrett and Brad. "She's only coming to make sure you get settled. She'll stay for the first few shows and then fly back."

I raise a brow. "She doesn't think our manager can handle it?"

"You know how she likes to micromanage," he says with a snarl.

"Thank God she'll only be there a short time," Bria says. "I do not need her breathing down my neck." She does her best impression of Ronni. *"'Cut your hair. Highlight your hair. Change your eye color. Can you grow taller?'"*

Everyone laughs.

Bria and Ronni do not get along. They haven't since day one, when Ronni was introduced as our IRL rep last summer. At first we all thought it was because Ronni was after Crew. Now we know better. Ronni is a self-centered bitch on wheels.

Crew takes Bria's hand. "What's the first thing you want to do when we get there?"

"The beach. No—Disney World. Do you think we'll have time to go to every theme park?"

Crew laughs. "Probably not."

We take off. It's exciting, but a little terrifying. I've never been on a plane before. Neither has Crew.

"Better get used to this, boys," Bria says, taking our hands. "We'll be flying all over the country soon. Maybe even the world."

"A world tour?" I muse aloud. And then, before any other thought enters my head, I wonder what I'd have to do to convince Ella to go with us.

I'm still not positive she'll come *this* time. I forwarded her ticket to Jacksonville, but that doesn't mean she'll use it.

When the flight attendant comes by with the drink cart, I order a half-dozen tiny bottles of whiskey and one Coke. "Anyone else want something?"

The seatbelt sign is turned off. Jeremy stands and turns to address us. "Check your email. I sent you the finalized schedule Ronni gave me yesterday. We're starting in Fernandina Beach tomorrow night, where Bruce will meet us with the van. We'll work our way down the east coast of Florida, then up the west coast through Ft. Myers. We'll spend a lot of time in the Tampa area before cutting over to Orlando and then up to Gainesville, where you'll play on the massive campus at the University of Florida. We made sure to schedule you after their spring break, so hopefully those who vacationed at the east coast beaches will have seen you and told all their friends. We'll finish the tour by going to Tallahassee and Panama City, then over to the naval air station in Pensacola, where your last concert will be for the armed services."

Crew puts an arm around Bria, who looks kind of green. "What is it?"

"That's a lot of performances with few days off."

Garrett laughs. "You of all people, Bria, should be prepared for this. You toured with White Poison."

"That was different," she says. "All I had to do was show up and sing twenty feet behind them. Nobody would have noticed if I wasn't there. I didn't have to worry about screwing everything up. What if I trip over something onstage?"

Crew kisses her temple. "I'll catch you."

They share a moment. I can't turn away. Crew and Bria have lived their romance in front of us, most of it onstage. In some strange way, I envy them. I toss back a shot of whiskey.

Jeremy leaves to use the bathroom. Shortly after, Ronni takes his place. "I trust Jeremy has given you the schedule. Anyone have any questions?"

"Yeah," I say, trying not to spit in anger as I talk. "Why in the hell didn't you tell us Dirk bought the label?"

"Because it doesn't change anything, and because Dirk asked me not to." She glances at me. "I'm good at keeping secrets."

I empty another one of the tiny bottles, shaking every last drop down my throat. "It's not going to work, you know. He'll want to control everything and everyone."

"I don't think so. He's more like a silent partner. Niles is still the president and the boss as far as I'm concerned. I suppose he has to report to Dirk, but Dirk is leaving the day-to-day operations to us. And speaking of day-to-day operations, Niles and I have been able to procure you a new rehearsal space at IRL."

"You want us to rehearse in New York?" Brad asks. None of us seem as bothered by it as he does. In fact Bria and Crew appear downright excited.

I suspect it's another way for Dirk to keep me close, but it's better than his barn. It's also more than an hour away from his house.

"As you know we only have the one studio. We reserve it for our best clients. Right now, you're our best client."

Crew snorts. "What happens when we're not?"

Ronni studies her manicured nails. "Then I guess you'll be out on your asses. So do yourselves a favor and remain at the top." She eyes the empties on my tray table and returns to business class.

"New York?" Brad says. "That's a long way from Stamford. Isn't there someplace closer to home?"

Crew, Bria and I look at each other. Guess it's time to tell Brad and Garrett what we talked about.

"I was thinking I'd move to the city," I say. "We play more gigs there than anywhere else. Now that we'll be rehearsing at IRL, it makes sense. I asked Crew to have his stepdad check into some places." I turn to him. "Has he had any luck?"

"That depends. One-bedrooms in decent locations are off-the-chart expensive. Maybe if it were a year from now, you could afford it. The two-bedroom apartments he found didn't hold much promise. I know you talked about living with Garrett, but what if three of us live together? Gary found a modest three-bedroom on a great street. It's about two miles from Bria's."

"Three of us?" Garrett asks. "As in you, me and Liam? What about our boy, Brad?"

Brad grins. "I told you Katie and I are moving in together."

"So both of you move to the city."

"She works in Stamford. That wouldn't be fair to her."

"Sorry, man," Garrett says. "That would have been sick if we all lived together. Well, everyone but Bria."

Crew studies his girlfriend. "It could still work you know." Bria questions him with her eyes. "Brad's out. That's three bedrooms and four of us. You and I could share one."

Her lips form a flirtatious grin. "You want to live together?"

"Hell yes, I do. I've been asking you for six months. We sleep over at each other's places half the time anyway. What do you say?"

Her smile fades. "I don't know. I don't think I could share a bathroom with three men."

"There are two bathrooms. We get one, Liam and Garrett use the other."

"Can we afford it?" she asks.

"With all four of us making money now, yes."

"It could work," I say, turning to Garrett. "You in?"

"I'm in. Just say when, and I'll give notice."

"Gary said the place is available in two weeks. I'll see how far he can push them out. Obviously May would be best for us, but we might have to start paying rent sooner."

"We're really doing this?" I ask.

"I guess we are," Crew says.

I flag down the flight attendant and order more drinks to celebrate.

For the next hour, the four of us talk about how great it will be to live together in the city. We go over what furniture we have. Well, what furniture *they* have; I have none. Crew can't stop smiling. He hates where Bria currently lives.

Brad stares out the window.

"He's feeling left out," she whispers.

"It's his choice," I say. "Katie has him so far up her ass, he can't see daylight."

"But he's a part of RA," Crew says, "and Katie is a permanent fixture in his life. We'd better get used to it."

"Maybe *she's* the one who needs to get used to *us*," I say. "Who doesn't like to be around rock stars?"

I'm thinking of Ella again, the woman who thinks I have syphilis because I'm in a band and believes I'm a narcissist who sleeps around. Who's convinced I have ulterior motives for wanting her near me.

I can't stop picturing her sitting on the bench next to me when I played. The way she looked at me. Nobody has ever looked at me that way before. Girls and women scream and throw themselves at me, but they never just *look* at me. Not like that. If I thought she was my muse at the hospital, it was only the tip of the iceberg. Back then, I couldn't even begin to imagine how she would live in my fucking head twenty-four-seven.

I pull out my phone and gaze at the picture I took of the two of us. I start to get hard, stash the phone, and unbuckle my seatbelt. "Be right back."

A woman is waiting for the bathroom, and I line up behind her. Ronni flashes me one of her fake smiles.

A few minutes later, the woman exits and it's my turn. Someone pushes me from behind and then there's two of us in the tiny lavatory. Me and Ronni. She shimmies against me.

"Seriously, Ronni? There's like two inches of space in here."

She rubs my semi-hard dick and then grabs it through my pants. "I'd say more like six or seven."

I flinch and push her hand away. "What the fuck are you doing?"

She puts my hands on her tits. "Just testing the limits."

"Well, that's a hard fucking limit, Ronni."

She unbuttons her blouse and unhooks the front of her bra. "Let's make this quick. There's a line." She turns away. "And you reek of booze."

I unzip my pants and push them down a few inches. I'm not fully hard yet. I stroke myself until I am.

She squirms, watching. "That is so hot."

"Are you ready for me?"

"Why don't you find out?"

I put a hand under her skirt. No panties. I easily stick a finger inside her. Oh yeah, she's ready.

"Do you have a condom?"

"Fuck."

She gets one out of her skirt pocket and hands it to me. I put it on. She leans against the counter and perches a leg up on the toilet, giving me access in the small space. I close my eyes and fuck her. She doesn't talk, which is good, because then I couldn't pretend she's someone else. Someone who would never in a million years let me do this to her. Someone who deserves so much more than I'm capable of giving.

Ronni reaches between us; she's rubbing her clit. That helps me come, and I bite my cheek to keep from grunting loudly. Ronni's moans, no doubt, are heard by anyone in earshot. I pull out and toss the condom.

She doesn't even seem embarrassed. She washes her hands. "See you on the ground," she says and steps out.

A man tries to enter but sees me. I quickly buckle my belt and wash up. He smirks as we pass each other. I ignore him. I'm not exactly proud of what just happened, and for some messed-up reason, I feel guilty about it. I push the thought out of my head. Because I know this is all I get. A sick fuck like me deserves nothing more.

Chapter Ten

Ella

Coming in for the landing is exciting. There isn't a cloud in the sky. I can see the coastline perfectly, including tiny people dotting the beach. Even at six o'clock in the evening, people go to the beach. In March, no less. I still can't believe I'm doing this.

I'm not sure if the feeling in the pit of my stomach is from the plane landing, or my continued uncertainty. Getting away from Corey is good. And even though I'll be working, this will seem like a vacation.

In baggage claim, I wait for my one large suitcase to come around and that's when I see him. Liam is searching for me. His eyes dart from one woman to the next like a boy looking for his long-lost mother. He sees me and smiles in slow motion. Then his teeth appear. He's genuinely happy I'm here.

The kid in front of him moves, and I notice the sign he's carrying: **Mrs. Campbell**

I laugh as he trots over. "I wasn't sure you were coming."

"Me either."

"What finally made you do it?"

"Maybe I thought I needed to celebrate."

His eyes brighten. "You got the job?"

I'm still absorbing the news myself. "Ten books. It's a dream come true."

"Congratulations!" He hugs me, the kind you give a friend, and I relax.

My suitcase is coming toward us, and I reach for it. "That's mine."

He gets to it before I can.

I put my backpack on and start for the door.

"Don't you have anymore? We'll be here six weeks."

"Bikinis don't take up much space."

His jaw goes slack, but he recovers quickly. "What about all your art stuff?"

"In the backpack, along with my laptop and supplies. I've got almost everything I need." I don't mention the art table. I resist the urge to ask him if he's still planning to get me one. He's doing so much already—giving me his hotel room, paying my expenses. If I have to work on a desk in a hotel room, it'll have to do.

A large van is waiting outside. The driver helps put my suitcase inside.

"This is Bruce," Liam says. "He gets us where we need to be and sets up our equipment."

"Nice to meet you. I'm Ella."

"It's my pleasure, Ms. Campbell," he says. "I'm at your disposal. If you need a ride anywhere—shopping mall, grocery store, beach—just say the word."

We climb in back.

"This is how we'll travel between cities," Liam says. "Bruce drove down from New York with our head of security."

They have their own security? Maybe they're bigger than I thought.

I bounce up and down in my seat. "It's pretty comfy. You guys must be doing well to afford a roomy van like this."

"It's not really ours. It's what we always use, but it's my uncle's. Anyway, forget about that. What do you want to do first?"

I shrug, not knowing what my choices are.

"We're playing at a bar in Jacksonville Beach from nine until midnight, but like I said, you don't have to come to every gig."

He flew me down. I should go, but I'm exhausted. "Liam, would you mind terribly if I passed on this one? I was up at six this morning to prep for my meeting. My day was pretty stressful, and I just want to eat, shower the plane grime off, and go to bed."

"I don't blame you. It's fine. Bruce can drop you off on his way to set up."

He tells me about the two times they played in a town north of here. I ask him to tell me what our days will be like.

"With the exception of weekends, we play about every other day, so there's time off to do other stuff. We'll change hotels every two or three days, depending on how far away the gigs are. Mostly we play at night, but there will be some daytime concerts—most of those are beachside."

"Sounds like you'll be busy."

"We will, but not so busy that we can't have some fun. I bought running shoes at the mall yesterday—not that I call running fun—it's more like torture—but I did promise."

I remember when I was a novice runner. "It'll only seem like torture for a week or two. After that, it gets easier."

"How often do we have to do it?"

"Daily would be ideal, but for a beginner, three times a week."

He regards me thoughtfully. "I guess I can agree to that."

"We're here," Bruce says.

I look at the hotel. Something-or-other Suites. It looks decent enough. Not the Waldorf Astoria, but it's no Motel Six either.

We get out, and Bruce hands Liam my suitcase, then checks his watch. "We'd better get going."

"You go," Liam says. "I'll get Ella settled and catch an Uber."

I think I see a sliver of water between the buildings down the street. "Wow, is the beach right there?"

"It is. I went earlier. Garrett and I tried surfing." He rolls his shoulders. "Got the shit beat out of me."

"Is it safe? You know, if I wanted to go for a walk later?"

"Should be," he says, leading me to the elevator. "Crew insisted all our hotels be in nice areas. He's kind of hung up on protecting Bria. I'm sure you'll figure that out by the time this is over."

"Speaking of your bandmates, when will I get to meet them? Are they here?"

"They went to a fancy seafood restaurant at the beach."

"I'm sorry you couldn't go. I could have caught an Uber from the airport."

"Don't be ridiculous. You're here because I asked you, El. I'm not going to make you fend for yourself."

Up on the fourth floor, he pulls a keycard out of his wallet. "It's the only key, and it's yours."

I take it and open the door. He follows me in, dragging my suitcase behind him.

The room's not huge, but it has a king-sized bed, a couch, a desk, and a small fridge/microwave unit. There's a large box in the corner, and I stride over to it. "You got me an art desk?"

"I had no idea what kind you wanted, but this was one of the few desks that was easily moveable. It collapses and can be carried with a handle, see? I hope it's okay."

"Okay? It's great. And very thoughtful. I wasn't sure you'd remember."

He gestures to the suitcase. "Where do you want it?"

"On the rack thingy, I guess. It doesn't make sense to unpack if we're only here for a few days."

"After this we go south to St. Augustine. I'll text you the schedule."

"Are you off tomorrow?"

"No. We play two gigs here. We're opening for another band at an amphitheater by the football stadium. It seats over five thousand. It'll be our largest gig here but the only one where we're not the headliner."

"I'll for sure have to go to that one. Uh, if you can get me a ticket."

"You don't need a ticket, El. You're with us. You can come backstage."

"That could be fun."

"I should warn you about Ronni."

"Who's that?"

"She's our rep from our record label. Veronica Collins. She's kind of like a manager, except we already have one of those—Jeremy. He's cool. She's a bitch. Might want to steer clear of her. She hates Bria. To be honest, I think she hates all women."

"Got it. Stay away from the Queen Bee."

He laughs out loud. "That's exactly what she is. She'll sting you if you let her. Don't let her."

"I can take care of myself."

"She'll only be here a few more days. She has to get back to her other clients in New York."

"And everyone else? Anything I should know about them?"

He thinks on it and shakes his head. "Nope. They're all good."

I sit on the end of the bed, the day weighing on me. Being here is surreal. I gaze at Liam. He's perched on the arm of the couch with an easy smile on his face. "Liam, what are we doing? This is all so strange. I don't know you, but I'm sitting in your hotel room. The room you gave me so I can be here and what—inspire you in some way? I don't even know how to do that. I mean, what am I supposed to do?"

"Just be here—at the hotel, the beach, and a few of our gigs. Doesn't matter as long as I know you're close."

"But why do you need me here?"

"I don't know. I just know I do."

"I'm not sleeping with you."

"God, El, you're beginning to sound like a broken record. I told you that's off the table. I'm not blind. You're hot, and any guy should be so lucky. But that's not why you're here. There are plenty of women I could get off with if I wanted to. But none of them have inspired me the way you do. I told you, you don't want someone like me. You deserve …"

"I deserve what?"

He goes to the door and opens it. "You deserve better," he says, right before stepping through and letting it shut behind him.

Chapter Eleven

Liam

Thirteen years ago

Dad, Crew, and I are sitting in the stands at Luke's baseball game. Dad and I only miss a game when I have one of my own. Dad coaches my team this year. He can't coach Luke's anymore, now that Luke is fifteen and plays on the high school team. He alternated coaching our teams every other year, because he didn't want to play favorites.

Luke is on deck. He runs behind the dugout for a second. It's because he has to throw up. He does it every time he's going up to bat. He also throws up before taking a big test. Sometimes he throws up at home for no reason at all. Dad calls him Nervous Nelly.

Luke steps up to the plate and whacks the ball over the fence. Everyone stands and cheers. "You see that, son? That's how a real man plays ball."

I pout. "I'm a real man. I'm eleven."

He laughs. Then he looks at me in a way he never has before. "You know, maybe you're right. Maybe you're becoming a man."

For the rest of the game, I feel him staring at me. I'm proud of myself for bringing my maturity to his attention. I *have* noticed a few hairs down there recently.

"Your brother is really good," Crew says.

Crew is my best friend. He comes to a lot of Luke's games. I think he likes hanging out with Dad and me. His parents got divorced last year. I feel bad that he doesn't see his dad much anymore. It makes me think back to when I was little and didn't have a father. Now my family is the one everyone envies.

When the game is over, Dad takes us out for pizza and ice cream and then to Uncle Dirk's for a swim. Mom almost never joins us. She works the second shift as a nursing assistant. But Dad's hours have always been flexible. He's a manager at Uncle Dirk's car dealership. He's related to the boss, so he gets to do whatever he wants. He says maybe someday Luke and I can work there. Uncle Dirk is a lot older than Dad, and he and Aunt Sylvia don't have any kids. I guess it's why he always lets us use his pool.

Crew and I do cannonballs into the deep end, splashing Dad. He jumps in and dunks us. Luke sits at the side of the pool on his phone. He's always on his phone.

"Aren't you coming in?" I ask.

He shakes his head.

"You're missing out," Dad says.

"I'm good here," Luke says without looking up.

An hour later, when we're drying off, Crew nods to the house. "Why is your uncle always watching?"

I study the house. It takes me a second to find him among the many windows. He's standing in his office, sees us staring, and moves away. "Maybe he's jealous that he doesn't have kids."

"He's weird."

"That's what Luke used to say."

"Used to? Luke doesn't think he's weird anymore?"

"I don't know. He never really talks about him."

"Weird or not, you guys are lucky to be related to someone who lives here."

"Yeah, it's kind of cool."

"Come on," Dad says. "We need to get home and walk Sally."

We drop Crew off at his mom's and head home in our decked-out Mazda SUV. Another perk of working for Uncle Dirk is that Dad gets to drive all the great cars.

We pull up to our house. Sally's furry face is in the front window. She tackles me when I go inside. "Hey, girl. Did you miss me?"

She licks my entire face and neck. I think she loves me the most because I'm the only one who will let her do it.

"You two hit the shower before bed," Dad says.

"Me first!" I yell, racing to the bathroom I share with Luke.

Hair wet and a towel around my waist, I go to my bedroom. Dad is sitting on the bed, waiting for me. He has a magazine in his hand. Maybe he's going to give me his old Sports Illustrated.

I duck into my closet and put on pajama pants. He pats the bed beside him. I sit.

"You got me thinking," he says. "Today at the game you said you were a man. I guess it's only fitting you find out what it takes to become one."

"Okay." I scoot back against the headboard, expecting a life lecture.

"Mom hasn't talked about this with you. She said it's a father's job. Like all women, she's embarrassed to talk about what goes on down there." He nods to my lap. "And it's really none of her business, is it?" He puts a hand on my knee. "You've probably been touching yourself for a while, right?"

My cheeks flame. How does he know?

He offers me an understanding smile. "It's okay. All men do it. Even me. It's perfectly normal. Healthy even. You shouldn't be ashamed of it. But that doesn't mean we go around talking about it. A man never tells what happens in his bed. Understand?"

I nod, still embarrassed.

"Have you ejaculated yet?"

My face heats up again. It's something I've heard about, but I don't really get it. I shrug.

He squeezes my knee. "Don't worry, it'll happen soon. And when it does, your whole world will change."

I can't speak. This whole thing is mortifying.

"You can talk about it with me. I'm your safe place. Whatever you tell me will never go beyond these walls. I'm here to protect you. I brought you and Luke and your mom into my home. We have a good life. Lord knows what would have become of you if I hadn't married your mother. I hate to think of you back in that tiny apartment, wondering where your next meal is coming from. You wouldn't want to go back to that, would you?"

"No. I love it here."

He grins. "I love having you here. I love you and your brother. I love you as if you were my own flesh and blood. We're family. Nothing will ever change that."

"I love you too, Dad."

"You know I don't like to play favorites." He slaps the rolled magazine on his leg, then hands it to me. "I gave one of these to Luke when he was about your age. When he, too, became a man."

I check out the cover. It has a half-naked woman on it. I gulp.

He leans over and opens it to a picture of a woman touching a man's penis. I'm shocked, but at the same time, I feel hot and tingly.

"This is yours now," he says. "It makes it better when you touch yourself down there. Just make sure you hide it where Mom won't find it. It would only embarrass her."

He gets off the bed, then leans down and puts his hands on my shoulders. "I envy you. If only I could go back and relive those fine moments of becoming a man."

My eyes stray to his crotch. His sweatpants are bulging. I wonder if he gets hot and tingly, too, when he sees the women in the magazine. I guess what he says is true—that it's normal.

"Goodnight, big man," he says, crossing to the door.

"Night, Dad."

After he leaves, I thumb through the magazine, feeling all kinds of zings through my body. I reach under my pants and stroke myself. He's right. It is better this way.

Chapter Twelve

Ella

I've been to my share of concerts, but I've never had the privilege of going backstage. It's a whirlwind of activity. Liam and his bandmates are being treated like royalty. If I'm honest, so am I—by association.

Bria sees me standing alone. "What do you make of all this?"

Even though this amphitheater is a relatively small venue in the overall scheme of concerts, it's still more exciting than anything I've ever done. "It's kind of surreal."

"I'm still getting used to it myself."

"But Liam said you used to be a backup singer for White Poison. This must be like small potatoes compared to that."

"It's different when you're out in front," she says. "I was invisible back then."

"Do you get nervous?"

"Every time. But Crew keeps me grounded." She gazes longingly at him. He winks at her.

"You guys are great together."

"We are," she says. "In more ways than one."

"Liam tells me you're all moving into the same apartment when you return to New York."

"Everyone but Brad. He's moving in with Katie."

I glance around, searching for someone who looks as lost as I do. "Where is she? Maybe we can hang out when you're playing."

"She didn't come on the tour. She rarely goes to any performances."

"Why not?"

"She doesn't like rock and roll. Or alcohol. Or crowds."

"And he's dating her? Seems odd."

"They're more than dating. He's going to marry her."

I glance at Garrett. "How about him? Is he attached?"

Bria snorts. "Garrett? No. He's the stereotypical musician. He goes out with a lot of women but rarely more than once or twice."

"What about Liam? Would you say *he's* a stereotypical musician?"

She gazes at me for a long moment.

I met Liam's bandmates this afternoon, and they all seem to know my being here isn't because Liam and I are dating. But maybe she thinks I'm interested.

"I don't care if he is," I add. "It's just that he doesn't say much about himself, and I haven't known him long."

"I hope you don't find this question rude, Ella, but exactly why are you here? If you aren't interested in a relationship with Liam, why follow him to Florida and agree to stay for six weeks?"

"He didn't tell you?"

"He's not exactly a Chatty Kathy. He told us you're his muse."

"I came to get away from my ex."

"Bad breakup?" She looks concerned. "Oh, gosh. He wasn't hurting you, was he?"

"No, nothing like that. We dated for a year and a half, but after we split, he kept showing up—at the hospital after I fell, at the park when I went running. And he wouldn't stop sending me things." My eyes shift to the floor. "In some ways I still love him. I didn't trust myself to be around him and not take him back, so when this opportunity presented itself, it seemed like the perfect solution."

She smiles, satisfied with my explanation. "To answer your question, no, Liam is not the stereotypical musician. He's …" She studies him as he chats with the sound guy.

"Dark and twisty?"

She thinks about my words. "Actually, I think that's exactly how I would describe him. What has he told you? I've known him for a year, and I still can't crack that hard exterior of his."

"Nothing much, but some comments he's made had me assuming he's got a fractured past."

"Dark and twisty. Fractured past. I'd say you're right on point, Ella."

"He's not, I don't know … dangerous, is he?"

She laughs. "Liam? Dangerous? He might have skeletons in his closet, but he's one of the gentlest men I've ever known. They all are, even Garrett the playboy."

"Good to know." I breathe a sigh of relief, even though deep down, I've felt he's one of the good ones.

The woman with black hair keeps staring at me. She's been talking to someone wearing a headset. Someone important, by the looks of it. The man is directing everything and everyone, keeping things moving like a fine-tuned machine.

Bria sees me watching the woman. "That's Veronica. Excuse me—*Ronni*." She air quotes the nickname.

"Liam warned me about her. Said I should avoid her."

"That's good advice. The woman hates me. Has from day one. She gets along much better with the men."

I eye Ronni's long, thin legs, jet-black hair, and inviting cleavage. "Gee, I wonder why?"

The man wearing the headset calls Bria and the others over.

"Gotta go to work now," Bria says. "Enjoy the show."

"Break a leg."

She chuckles, and my cheeks heat. I mentally smack myself. Is that just what you say to actors, or does it apply to musicians as well? I hope she doesn't think I'm stupid.

Bria joins the others, and they huddle together. Then they shout, "Let's get Reckless!"

Liam picks up his guitar, slinging the strap over his shoulder. He seems completely at ease. I'd be throwing up if it were me. I feel a little sick just watching. I peek out at the audience. The seats are almost full. I've never heard of the band they're opening for, but I'm told they're big in the state of Florida.

They start playing, and I'm mesmerized. I've heard all of Reckless Alibi's songs by now, and I've seen them live. But somehow this is different.

Liam glances over at me and gives me a lift of his chin. I return the gesture with a thumbs-up. Then I feel stupid a second time. Who gives a rock star a thumbs-up? Don't they do some rocker "I love you" sign with their hands? I guess I have a lot to learn.

"I wasn't aware RA had groupies yet." Ronni is standing next to me. The music is loud, and I'm not sure I heard her correctly.

"Hi, I'm Ella Campbell."

Her eyebrows hit the ceiling. "Liam's sister?"

"Actually we're—"

"Jesus, please tell me that boy didn't do something monumentally stupid, like get married."

I step back. "It's a coincidence. We're not together." I extend a hand. "Nice to meet you, Ronni."

She doesn't shake it, but she does give me a distasteful once-over. "You probably shouldn't be back here."

"I, uh … I've got this thing." I pull the lanyard out from under my shirt.

"Those credentials are meant to be worn on the outside of your clothes, so people can see them."

"Yeah, sorry."

"Liam brought you here, but you're not together?"

"That's right." I don't offer her any more information than I have to. Based on what Liam, and now Bria, told me, I probably shouldn't even be talking to her. "I'm really excited to hear them play. Excuse me while I watch." I take two steps away. She doesn't follow, but I can feel her stare boring into me. I try to ignore it and enjoy the show.

Thirty minutes and eight songs later, Reckless Alibi leaves the stage. Liam comes over and gives me a quick hug. "Thanks for coming."

"It was incredible. You should have been the main act."

He thumbs at the crowd. "Let's hope some of them think so too, and buy our albums."

We step out of the way to let a bunch of large men move their equipment off the stage.

Garrett slaps Liam on the back. "You were on fire, man. Really top-notch tonight."

Liam smiles and turns back to me. "See, I told you. It's not only the composing. You bring out the best in me *all* the time."

He says it so matter-of-factly, as if he just said the sky is blue. If it weren't for him being the perfect gentleman for the past twenty-four hours, I'd think he had ulterior motives.

"Score another one in the books," a man says, joining us.

Liam steers me over to him. "Ella, this is our manager, Jeremy Halstead. He skipped out on us to take his mom to dinner."

"Nice to meet you, Ella. I didn't miss much," he tells Liam. "Snuck in after the third song. I figured you were in good hands with Ronni. I don't get to see Mom much anymore, since she refuses to travel."

"How is she?" Bria asks.

"Old," Jeremy says. He turns to me. "She retired to Florida ten years ago, after my dad passed."

"It must be nice for her to live here. I mean, beach weather in March!"

"You won't find her at the beach, but she does love it here."

I get the idea Jeremy is more beloved by the band than Ronni. He's older than them, for sure, but he seems nice.

"Jeremy, are you joining us for drinks?" Crew asks.

"Nah, you kids go ahead. Bruce can drop me at the hotel."

"How come you never ask *me?"* Ronni says.

The five band members look at each other as tension mounts.

"I'm kidding," Ronni says. "As if I'd be caught dead." She turns on her heels, dismissing us with a wave of her hand.

"When is she going back home?" Garrett asks.

"Thursday," Jeremy says.

"Not soon enough," Bria mumbles.

I help carry their equipment to the van. "Ronni would have a fit if she saw us," Liam tells me. "She says high-quality bands can't be seen moving their own stuff. 'It sends the wrong message,'" he falsettos.

"I'd say quite the opposite. That you like to help ease the burden on your staff."

Garrett laughs. "Staff? Did you hear that, Bruce, you're our *staff*." The two men share a chuckle.

Garrett comes up behind me and whispers loudly, "The technical term is 'roadie.'"

I flush. "I'm sorry. I don't know anything about this."

"He's teasing you, El," Liam says. "Staff, employee, roadie—it's all the same shit."

We pile into the van, and Liam introduces me to Tom Horton, their security guy. "Ah, Thor," I say, shaking his large hand.

He shakes in silent laughter. I wonder if I wasn't supposed to call him that to his face.

"Tom goes almost everywhere with us," Liam tells me.

"Just pretend I'm not even there," Tom says.

"You?" I say, taking in arms that are the size of, well … Thor's.

"You'll get used to me. I'm like a fly on the wall."

"More like in the ointment," Brad jokes.

The people in this van really enjoy each other. They're always joking around. I've only been here for one day and already I'm having more fun than I anticipated. I scan our surroundings for the one person who doesn't seem to fit. "Why isn't Ronni here?"

Crew snorts. "Veronica? Ride in the van? She wouldn't lower herself. She only rides with us if we're in limousines."

"You get to ride in limos?"

"Sometimes," Liam says. "Like the night we met, remember? It's usually when Ronni's trying to impress someone."

"That whole night is a bit fuzzy," I admit.

"We'll ride in them a lot more after this tour," Garrett says. "When we're more famous than God."

Bria smacks him in the arm. "Nobody's more famous than God."

"Eddie Van Halen is," Liam says.

I give him a sideways glance.

"Oh, come on," he says. "Everyone knows Eddie. Please tell me you know who he is, El. He's like my fucking hero. One of the greatest guitar players of all time."

"I know the band Van Halen. I didn't know it was named after a guy."

He grabs his chest like he's dying. "You're killing me."

"Don't mind him," Crew says. "Besides, we all know the greatest guitar player of all time is Jimi Hendrix."

Liam swipes a drumstick from Garrett and pops Crew on the head. Crew leans over the seat and gives Liam a wedgie.

"Stop acting like toddlers," Bria says. "You're going to give Ella the wrong impression."

I laugh at their antics. "It's actually quite refreshing."

"It is?" Bria asks, looking confused.

I lean close and whisper. "I used to hang out with a tax attorney. *This* is fun."

She giggles, and I can see us becoming friends.

Chapter Thirteen

Liam

"Stop!" My lungs are burning so badly, I feel I can't take another breath. I stand bent over with my hands on my hips, huffing loudly.

Ella runs a few steps ahead and then jogs in place, looking at her watch. "We've only gone a quarter mile."

"No way. It was over a mile, for sure."

She points behind me. "You can still see the red lifeguard stand where we started."

I feel like less of a man because I can't keep up with this one tiny woman. "Shit."

She laughs. "It's okay. This is your first time. Catch your breath and then we'll go again. But you should know, ordering that second bottle of whiskey for the table last night was probably what did you in."

"I thought you said I could do this unless I was a smoker."

"You can. But it will be a lot easier without a hangover. Not to mention people do stupid stuff when they're drunk."

"Speaking from experience?"

She digs her shoe into the sand and shrugs.

"The dickhead?"

She nods.

"What can I say? Guys can be assholes."

She studies me. "Are you an asshole, Liam?"

"You tell me."

"I've only known you for a short time. The jury is still out, but you came dangerously close last night."

Guilt twists my insides. "Shit, Ella, I put the moves on you, didn't I?"

"No, but you ran off a guy who did."

I run a hand through my hair. "Someone tried to pick you up last night?"

"I thought it was kind of ballsy, considering I was sitting at a table with mostly men, not to mention Thor was standing close by."

"Did you *want* to hook up with him?"

"Of course not. I told you I'm down here to forget about a man, not have a fling with one."

"Well, as my friend I give you permission to tell me if and when I cross the threshold to assholery."

"So if we're out drinking, and you get out of control, I have the authority to make you stop?"

I think about all the stupid shit I've done when tying one on, Ronni being the most recent of said shit. Then I think about what Ronni said about me being reckless. Maybe having someone around to keep me grounded is exactly what I need. Plus, it might be refreshing to actually remember everything about my nights for once. "Yeah, that's exactly what I'm saying."

A smile lights up her face. "This could be fun. It'll be like you're my bitch. You have to do everything I say."

I take a step closer. "Let's make this clear. Nobody is the boss of me. I'm only talking about the drinking, Ella."

"I was joking, Liam." She looks guilty, and I feel like a goddamn douche.

"Come on. I'm ready now."

A little farther down the beach, my phone vibrates. I use it as an excuse to stop again.

"You're never going to be able to do this if you don't push yourself," she says.

I hold up my phone. "Text from Queen Bitch of the universe." Ella jogs around me in circles as I read it. "Holy shit!"

"What is it?" She stops and her head brushes my shoulder as she peeks at my phone.

I ignore the shockwave coursing through me. "She's lined up an interview at a radio station in three hours."

"Sounds exciting."

"Hell yes, it does. We should head back to get ready."

She shoots me a scolding stare. "We have three hours, Liam. I'm not letting you bail. I know running isn't fun at first. But if you give it a chance, you may come to crave it. It's exhilarating. It's even relaxing in some ways. It's freeing."

While my body wants me to quit, I can't deny her passion. I'd be a douchebag if I didn't hold up my end of the bargain. "Fine, let's go."

We run. She tries to make conversation, but I'm just trying to fucking breathe.

"Back there, you said *we* had to get ready. You don't really want me to go with you to the interview, do you?"

"You're … going," I huff.

I make her stop several more times before she concedes we're done for the day. "Two miles," she says. "Not bad for your first try."

"Yeah, but I could only run twenty damn feet at a time."

"That's not true. You ran eight quarter-miles. You'll improve quickly. I bet tomorrow you'll run a half mile without stopping."

"We have to do this again tomorrow?"

"At least three days a week, remember? Your legs probably feel like Jell-O right now, and you might wake up sore, but that just means it's working. We're going to whip you into shape in no time."

"You don't think I'm in shape?"

She peruses my body. I'm not wearing a shirt—we are on the beach, after all. She looks at my shoulders, arms, and bare middle. When her eyes track across my shorts to my legs, my dick jumps.

Her eyes snap to mine. Yeah, she saw it.

"I'm, um, talking about making you healthy on the inside."

"Because my outside is already perfect?"

She rolls her eyes and starts toward the hotel. "Narcissistic musicians."

I stand behind her in the elevator as we ride up to our floor. She has an incredible body. I can see every curve of it through her spandex shorts and running bra, and she's one of the most genuine people I've ever met. She doesn't feed me lines to get me into bed, like most women. She doesn't get all nervous around me. She doesn't take my shit. She reminds me of Bria.

I envy the relationship Crew has with Bria. Sometimes I think I could have that too. If Crew could overcome his past, maybe I can overcome mine.

I laugh inwardly. Who am I kidding? No woman like that could ever deal with the fucked-up person I am. It wouldn't be fair to her. In some ways, it might even be dangerous. Ella is too good for me, that's for damn sure.

"Liam?" She's holding the door open for me. "This is our floor. Where'd you go?"

"Just tired from the run, and I need a glass of water. My mouth is drier than the Sahara."

"I've got a bottle in my room."

I follow her in and collapse dramatically on the floor. She gets two bottles from her fridge and lies down next to me. I rise on an elbow, drink, and put my head back down. We lock eyes for a split second before she glances away. Her chest rises and falls slowly. It makes me hard. I turn and look under the couch. "Housekeeping really needs to clean under there. I think I see a used condom."

"Ew," she says, hopping off the floor.

I get up, chug the rest of the water, and try to make a jump shot in the trash with the empty bottle. It misses. When I go over to pick it up, I stop at her art table. I look at one of her sketches. "Is this … me?"

She marches over and gathers all of her drawings into a pile. "Yes and no. Maybe it's the eight-year-old version of you."

I'm intrigued. I hold my hand out. "Can I see them?"

She thinks about it, then gives me the pile and sits on the bed. I go through each one. There are six or seven of me and a few more that aren't. "Is this a monkey?"

"A chimpanzee," she says.

I laugh. "You're drawing me, and you're drawing monkeys. What does that say about me? You think I'm a Neanderthal?"

"Chimpanzees, not monkeys, and don't flatter yourself. Artists often draw likenesses of those who are close to them."

I raise a brow. "So now we're close?"

"In proximity, you dork."

"Why are you drawing pictures of me and monkeys—sorry, chimpanzees. Do you have some kind of simian fetish?"

She hands me a folder. Inside it is a loosely bound manuscript entitled, *The Adventures of Jimmy and Jojo.* "It's the series I'm illustrating. I was playing around with what the kid should look like. Your likeness seemed a good candidate."

I can't contain my smirk. "So you're saying I'm hot?"

"I'm saying your face works well on an eight-year-old."

I cringe. "Ouch, El. Way to emasculate me."

"Nobody is denying you aren't attractive. I think you have that roguish boy look I was searching for."

"You think I'm attractive then."

"Shut up."

I laugh, put the drawings down, and get out my phone to snap a picture of the top one. "Evidence that I knew you before you became a famous illustrator." I aim my phone at her and take another one.

She tries to cover her face. "I'm all sweaty."

I glance at the photo. "Too late, I got one."

She points to the door. "You have to leave. I need a shower."

There are about fifteen comebacks I want to blurt, but I don't. I leave and go down the hall to Garrett's. He's not there. I look at her picture again, and I can't keep thoughts of her taking a shower out of my head. I strip in the bathroom. In the shower, I rub one out. I knew I'd be doing this from the minute I saw her in her running clothes. But what I didn't know is that I'd be thinking about her doing it for me. For the first time in my whole miserable life, I'm imagining a woman tugging on my dick. I'm not thinking about sex or going down on some random girl. I'm not fantasizing about touching a woman's breasts. I'm thinking about Ella stroking my cock. And I come all over the shower wall, shouting while I ride out the most powerful orgasm I've ever had.

Chapter Fourteen

Ella

"My name is Melissa. The three of you can wait out here," she says to Ronni, Jeremy and me. "The band will be in the booth. You'll be able to see them through this window and hear them through those speakers."

"I think I should be with them," Ronni says. "I'm the one who vetted the questions."

"Sorry," she says. "As you can see, it's pretty cramped in there. I'll be out here with you if you need anything."

Liam and the others look amused that Ronni's been put in her place. They are led into the booth and given headphones. They sit around a table with microphones in front of every seat.

Matt, the radio personality, tells the audience he's got something special in store for them. "I just so happen to have five fascinating people sitting with me in the studio today. This will be the first ever radio interview with this up-and-coming band from New York. Listen to this and then I'll be back with Reckless Alibi."

Ronni finds a chair to sit on. "They better not say anything stupid."

"Relax," Jeremy says. "Everything will be fine. This show will be syndicated all over the state and even outside of Florida. You've been trying to make this happen for months. *You* did this."

"Damn right I did. I should be in there."

"You should be happy, knowing you're the woman behind the band."

She picks at a fingernail, then turns her attention to me. "Why are you here?"

"Liam asked me to come."

Her lips curl in disgust. "Are you his flavor of the week?"

I try not to be snarky. "I told you we're not dating."

"But you want to."

"We're friends."

"Right."

"Give it a rest, Ronni," Jeremy says. "You don't have to control everything, you know."

"*Humph*," she grunts and twirls in her chair.

Jeremy points to the booth. "They're getting started. Let's listen."

"Wow," Matt says. "That's as hot as a cat on a tin roof. People, if you could see who's at the table with me, you'd agree that in person they are as amazing as their music. You're a great-looking bunch."

The five of them glance at each other. Crew leans in and says, "Uh, thanks."

Matt laughs. "Humble, too. I like it. Chris Rewey, you're the lead singer."

"Co-lead, and you can call me Crew."

"Right. Sorry. You and Brianna are the lead singers. Give me a rundown of the band. Tell me who you are and what you do."

"Sure. Like you said, Brianna and I are the singers. We also both play keyboards. I play backup guitar sometimes. We write the lyrics to the majority of our songs. To my right is Liam Campbell, lead guitarist. He puts our lyrics to music. Garrett Young is our drummer and backup singer. Next to him is Brad Templeton, who plays bass."

"That's it? You play bass?" Matt says. "Only the one job?"

He's obviously messing with him, but Brad is irritated.

"Playing bass is harder than you think," Liam says in his defense.

"Sure it is," Matt says. "So, Crew, how long has Reckless Alibi been together?"

"About four years. Liam, Garrett, and I have been a part of the band from the start. Brad and Bria joined us last year. Brianna used to sing backup for White Poison."

"Really? Can you tell us about it, Brianna? I hear they're a wild bunch of Brits."

"They sure are. I was fortunate to have the opportunity to sing with them."

Matt nods. "Hmm. A little voice in my ear just told me you used to date Adam Stuart, their lead singer. Is that true?"

Bria appears horrified. Crew grabs her hand and nods. "Yes," she says. "But not for long. I found out where I really belonged when I met these guys."

He notices their clasped hands. "You and Crew are together?"

Crew glances through the window at Ronni, who's making the cutthroat sign and having a minor conniption. "We are."

Ronni stomps her foot and cusses.

"Brianna, are you just with Crew or …" He smirks at the other men at the table.

She laughs off his insinuation. "I'm a one-man woman, Matt."

"On that note, here's another song by Reckless Alibi. We'll be right back after."

Ronni is pissed. "When will they ever listen?"

"Nobody cares that they're a couple," Jeremy says.

"They do care. I guarantee they'd sell more records and have more fans if women thought they had a chance with him."

"I think you're wrong."

"Well, that's why you're the manager, and *I'm* with the record label. Because I know what's best for them." She turns to Melissa. "I want to speak with whoever's in charge. Personal relationships are not a topic I approved."

Melissa gestures to Matt. "You're looking at him."

Ronni stares into the booth, ready to spit fire.

Jeremy pinches the bridge of his nose, catches me watching, and shrugs.

"Why is she referred to as Brianna?" I ask. "She goes by Bria."

Jeremy stares at the back of Ronni's head. "She thought it sounded more professional."

Ronni ignores us, only paying attention to her phone.

"And we're back," Matt says. "Brianna, that was a powerful song. How do you and Crew come up with the lyrics?"

"It's different for every song. Sometimes it's based on an experience we've had, sometimes it's drawn from a feeling. Maybe we saw or heard something, and it inspired us. Crew once wrote a song about helping a turtle. I wrote one about my brother, who's a firefighter. Sometimes Liam gives us music, and we write whatever comes to mind when we listen to it."

"Interesting. Liam, as the composer, you give them the music and they write lyrics for it?"

"Sometimes. It works both ways, like Bria said."

"Composing music must be hard. How do you think up new songs that aren't the same old notes over and over?"

"It's funny you say that, Matt, because music is essentially made up of very few fundamental sounds. There are seven main musical notes in the chromatic scale, twelve musical scales, four octaves on a guitar, and seven on a piano. If you change the pitch of a note, you can alter the entire melody. The possibilities are endless."

"I've often wondered how musicians keep coming up with different melodies."

"Think of all the books in the world. There are only twenty-six letters in the alphabet, yet libraries are full of stories that have been created by combining those letters. By the same token, there are only three primary colors, but mixed together in different proportions, you can make millions of others."

Matt falls silent for a beat. "Well, damn. I'm not sure anyone has ever explained it to me that way. You got a PhD or something?"

"My higher education comes from life."

"And what about your inspiration? Where does that come from?"

Liam catches my eye. Our gazes lock. I bite my lower lip. "Different places, I guess. Glitter, a sidewalk, a hospital gown."

My cheeks heat.

Ronni peers at me suspiciously when she sees the way he's gazing at me. I turn away.

"Those are unusual muses," Matt says.

"Indeed they are."

Matt moves on to the others, who talk about their tour of Florida and where they'll be playing. Liam keeps looking at me and smiling. I think about what he said about music, books, and colors.

It's very introspective. It's like I'm seeing a whole other side to him that's as endearing as it is intriguing.

The interview ends, and Matt shakes hands with them before they join us.

Ronni pulls Matt aside and gives him a piece of her mind.

"This is media, Ms. Collins. We're here to push the envelope. Seek the truth. I hardly think you'd have gotten where you are without knowing that."

In usual fashion, she walks off in a tizzy. "God, I can't wait to get back to New York."

~ ~ ~

After enjoying dinner with the band, I wash my jogging bra and shorts, hoping they'll dry by morning. Liam was right; I probably should have brought more clothes with me. I might be doing laundry every other day.

I get comfortable in my sleeping shorts and tank top, and sit at my art desk. I try to come up with a different version of Jimmy, but I can't. Every kid I draw looks like Liam. After today's interview, I can't get him out of my head. I finally give in and move forward, pulling out the first manuscript and sketching a few ideas for Jimmy and Jojo's trip to the park.

I'll send the author weekly pictures of my progress, and she will tell me if she thinks I'm going in the right direction. Maybe she'll hate the eight-year-old Liam lookalike and make me change it, but I suspect she'll love it.

An hour later, I can hardly keep my eyes open. I put my things away and crawl into bed, dreaming about the adult version of Jimmy.

A knock on the door pulls me from sleep. I glance at the clock. It's after midnight. I get out of bed and stomp to the door, thinking maybe I had him pegged all wrong. He's here for a late-night booty call, isn't he?

I rip open the door, ready to tear him a new one, and see a surprised Ronni in the hallway. She's wearing a hotel bathrobe.

She examines the number on the wall next to the door. "This is 412, right?"

"Yes."

She pushes past me. "Why are you in Liam's room? Where is he?" She turns on the light and peeks inside the empty bathroom.

What the hell? "He's not here."

"Did he go out for more alcohol?"

"He's not staying in this room. He let me have it."

She cocks her head. "Are you homeless or something?"

"It was part of the agreement."

Her eyes widen behind a thick layer of mascara. "What agreement? As their label rep, I should be privy to any agreement one of my clients makes with another party."

"I don't think this concerns you or the record label."

"Is he paying you to fuck him?"

My jaw drops at her crassness. "Of course not."

"Then why are you in his room?"

"He's staying with Garrett. Maybe you should talk to him about this."

When she pulls her phone out of a robe pocket and taps on it, the tie comes undone to reveal she's practically naked underneath. And by practically, I mean she's got on a lacy bra and a garter belt. Not exactly something you'd wear to bed. *Oh, God, she came here to sleep with Liam.*

A minute later, Liam is in the doorway in sweatpants. I assume she summoned him. "What the hell, Ronni?" he shouts.

She pulls him inside and shuts the door. "Why is this girl in your hotel room?"

"This girl is Ella, and she's here because I invited her."

"What am I missing?" Ronni says. "You invited her back to your hotel, but you're not sleeping with her?"

"That's right."

"Explain." She pulls the robe around her and sits on the couch, crossing her legs. "You picked up some local and gave her your room?"

"Ella's not a local. She's from New York. She'll be with us for the entire tour."

Ronni laughs. "You've got to be kidding. You brought along a little fuck buddy, and she won't even sleep in the same room as you? My, you are a piece of work, aren't you, Liam?"

I step forward. "I've told you more than once we're not sleeping together."

Ronni is confused.

"You wouldn't understand," he says.

She stands. "Well, pack her stuff. She's out. IRL is not paying for her room."

"IRL isn't paying for it, RA is paying."

"Look at whose name is on the invoice, genius."

"It's *our* music that makes you money. Our gigs that bring in fans."

"Gigs you wouldn't have if it weren't for me. We have a contract, Liam. My word is final. She's out."

"She's not leaving. It's my right to give her the room that's meant for me."

"But clearly you're not sleeping here. Therefore the room isn't needed. We're not paying."

Liam glances at me, clearly at a loss. I get the feeling Ronni often gets her way. I go to the closet and pull a pillow and sheets off a shelf and toss them on the couch. "Then he's moving back in. I'll take the couch."

Ronni pouts. She knows she's lost.

Liam smirks and opens the door. "I guess you'll be leaving now, Veronica."

She stomps to the door, then turns to get in his face. "Watch yourself. You'd do well to remember I'm the one in charge."

He laughs. "Yeah, it definitely looks like it from where I'm standing."

When she leaves, I realize Liam's bandmates are in the hall. I guess they were kind of loud. Garrett looks at Ronni in her robe, at Liam half naked, then at me, and smiles. "What did we miss?"

"Typical Ronni drama," Liam says. "What's new?"

"You coming back to the room?" Garrett asks.

"Nah. I'll be crashing on Ella's couch."

"Suit yourself." Garrett and the others drift back to their rooms.

"That ought to give them something to talk about," he says with a chuckle, settling on the couch before he turns out the light. "Now go to sleep. I'm fucking beat."

I crawl back into bed, but I certainly don't sleep. I can sense him. I can smell him. I can hear him breathe. I lie here thinking about the half-naked man ten feet away from me, and it dawns on me that today was the first day in three weeks I didn't miss Corey.

Chapter Fifteen

Liam

I yawn on our way to the beach. "Did we have to get up so damn early?"

"It's easier to run in the morning before you get caught up in the rest of your day, plus we're leaving for St. Augustine at noon because you're playing at three o'clock today."

I raise my brow. "You seem to know my schedule pretty well."

"I have to be able to plan our runs."

"Lucky me."

We reach the end of the boardwalk. I start down the stairs. "Aren't you forgetting something?" she says behind me.

I look back to see her stretching against the wooden railing. "Right. Why do we have to stretch?"

"So you won't tighten up during the run."

"Do we have to do it every time?"

"Yup. Before and after." She watches me as I copy her motions. "Are you sore today?"

"I wasn't going to say anything because I didn't want to seem like a wimp, but yeah, my calves are fucking killing me."

"This run will loosen them up."

"Take it easy on me, okay?"

"Easy? We're running farther today. You have to keep pushing yourself, or you'll never do better."

We walk down on the sand. "Maybe some of us don't need to do better."

"You'll thank me one day."

"I doubt it. But a deal is a deal. Let's go."

It's hard to keep up with her. She tries to talk to me, but it takes everything I have to just breathe. My lungs burn. My legs feel like they're giving out. But I make sure I go farther than I did yesterday to prove to her I can. Once I know we're well past that point, I stop and fall to the ground.

"Good job. You made it almost half a mile. But you shouldn't lie down, you should keep moving."

"I can't."

She holds out her hand to help me up. It's ridiculous thinking a small person like her can help up a big guy like me, but I take it. Her hand is soft. It's nothing like mine. I've got permanent calluses from playing guitar. I idly wonder if she cares.

"Walk for a minute," she says. "Then we'll go again."

"You really are a slave driver, aren't you?"

She giggles. "Maybe I get off on torturing you."

I get a sick feeling in my gut and take off running.

She runs up alongside me. "Was it something I said?"

"Can we get this over with?"

I don't make it far before I have to stop again.

"You didn't rest long enough," she says. "Listen to me, I know what I'm talking about. I went through this not too long ago."

"You haven't been running long?"

"About eighteen months."

An unfamiliar feeling washes over me. That's how long she was with her ex. He was the person who got her into it. Something gnaws at my gut when I think of him doing this with her.

"Can I ask you something?" she says.

"Shoot."

"How is it that you hate Ronni, but she showed up for what I can only assume was a booty call at your hotel room last night?"

I wondered if she was going to bring it up and hoped she wouldn't. I'm not exactly proud of what I've done with Ronni. "I'm not gonna lie. We hooked up once or twice."

"But why? Seems to me she treats you terribly."

"She's discreet, or she was before last night's debacle. She doesn't expect anything. And she doesn't ask questions."

"Questions about what?"

"Everything."

She studies me thoughtfully. "Were you in a relationship that ended badly?"

I gaze at the ocean. Nothing could be truer. "You could say that."

"I'm sorry. I guess we're two peas in a pod."

The thought of Ella enduring what I did makes me sick. "No, we're not." I start running again.

We pass the place we ran to yesterday and turn around. On the way back, her phone rings. She checks it and puts it away. It rings again. She doesn't look this time. When we stop again, I have to ask, "Was it him? The ex?"

She nods.

"Does he call you a lot?"

"Yes."

"So block his number."

Her eyes become distant. "I can't."

"Has he left messages?"

"Every day. I don't want to listen to them, but I can't help myself."

"Is he stalking you?"

She shakes her head.

"Did he leave one just now? Let me hear it."

"That's kind of private, don't you think?"

"El, I'd be a douchebag if I didn't worry about your safety. You can't possibly be subjective. Come on, play it."

Reluctantly, she pulls out her phone and plays the message on speaker.

"Ella, please return my calls," he says. "I'm getting worried about you. I haven't seen you running in the park all week. I know you had a head injury. I'm going nuts, thinking something has happened to you. I love you. I know you know that, but I'm going to remind you every day. We belong together. Call me back. Please."

She seems to be on the verge of tears, and I feel like a dick, forcing her to listen.

"You didn't tell him you were going away?"

"And risk him following me?"

I go on high alert. "You think he'd follow you?"

"Probably not, but I wasn't about to call him. Every time I hear his voice …" She turns away and stares out at the water.

"Every time you hear it, you want to take him back."

"I know it's wrong. What he did was awful. Unforgivable."

I kick a shell. "It's amazing how we let people we love treat us."

"So we *are* a lot alike."

"I told you, El. I'm nothing like you, and you should be goddamn grateful for that." I hold out a hand. "Give me your phone."

"Why?"

"Just give it to me."

She places it in my palm. I page through her recent texts until I see his name. He's been doing more than calling. I read a few and then type out my own.

I'm fine, Corey, but I'm gone. Please don't contact me anymore. Goodbye.

"What are you doing?"

"What you should have done."

She takes the phone back and reads the text I sent. I brace myself, expecting her to lay into me, but she seems relieved. "I suppose I should thank you. I should have sent that text long ago."

"You should turn it off. I'm sure he'll reply."

She hands it back to me. "You hold on to it for a while. That way I won't be tempted to look."

I stuff it in a pocket, and we finish our run.

~ ~ ~

It's hot and humid. My shirt is drenched by the time we play our last song at the outdoor shrimp festival in downtown St. Augustine. Despite the heat, people are dancing. Ella stands off to one side, her hips swinging to the beat. I give her a smile. She responds by doing the "I love you" sign with her right hand. I'm pretty sure she thinks it means something else.

After we finish, we pose for pictures and sign autographs. The crowd clears, and Ella finds me. She holds out a T-shirt. "Sign this for me?"

I cock my head. "You want me to sign a Reckless Alibi T-shirt? Are you going to wear it?"

"Why not? It will be good advertising." She gestures to several girls nearby who are already wearing them.

I wasn't even aware they were being sold here, but I admit I love the idea of people having them. I especially like the idea of Ella wearing one.

"I'll sign it, but you have to put it on right now."

"Here?" She glances around.

"Here."

"Fine, but only because I'm all sweaty." She eyes the shirt stuck to my skin. "Looks like you should get one too."

I laugh. "I'm not going to wear an RA shirt."

"There are a lot of booths here selling T-shirts. I'll change into this one if you wear another one of my choosing."

"Deal."

I help the guys pack up our gear as she goes in search of one. Ten minutes later, she hands me a fresh shirt. It says "I'm a shrimp" over a giant picture of a prawn.

"You want me to wear a shirt saying how tiny I am? El, you don't understand men very well."

"It's a huge shrimp. Some might even call it *jumbo*. You said you'd wear whatever I bought you."

I peel off my wet shirt and toss it in a nearby trashcan. I don't miss the way she's averting her eyes. Yeah, she's trying not to look at me. I almost make a snarky comment. Then I remember why she shouldn't be looking at me that way and quickly don the shrimp shirt.

A few girls come over, wanting a picture. "They saw you half-naked," Ella whispers before stepping away. Soon there's a large gathering. One of them gets my shirt out of the trashcan. Gross.

Thor comes over to make sure everything is okay. A few people surround Ella. "Go check on her," I say.

"We're ready to head out, Ms. Campbell," he says loudly.

One of the girls at Ella's side says, "Oh my God, you're married to Liam?"

She's caught off-guard. "Uh, no."

"Liam's *married*," the girl says to her friends as if delivering news that her dog just died.

Someone comes up behind me. Ronni takes my elbow. "Liam is not married. It's an unfortunate coincidence that they have the same last name. Rest assured, not only is he single, he's available."

Several girls scream. More come over and want pictures. Ronni moves aside, obliging them while eyeing Ella like she's a piece of spoiled meat. What's with her? She's not actually jealous, is she?

"Reckless Alibi will be playing in Port Canaveral this weekend," Ronni announces. "We hope you'll drive down and join them."

After the crowd clears, Ronni and Thor leave. Something occurs to me. "Fuck. There are now a dozen pictures of me out there wearing this stupid T-shirt."

"I think it's adorable," Ella says. "Which reminds me, I need to change, too."

She ducks into a porta-potty. When she comes out, I don't think I've ever seen anyone more beautiful. Her long hair is pinned up to keep it off her neck. The makeup she had on earlier has been sweated away. Best of all, she's wearing a shirt with me on it. Well, not just me—it's a picture of all of us—but yes, me.

My pants get tight. I adjust myself and try to think of something else. Anything else. "You want ice cream?"

"Sure. It's hot enough."

"Bria told me about a place called St. George Street. There are lots of shops and restaurants and ice cream places. I think that's where they went. Want to meet up with them?"

"Lead the way."

We make small talk on the way over. A group of young kids are doing sign language. It reminds me of something Ella did. "Give me your hand."

She shoots me a disapproving stare.

"I don't want to hold it, El. I need to show you something."

As I move her fingers into place, bolts of pleasure shoot through me. I've come to crave the feel of her soft hands. The electrified pulse of her touch. But I push the feelings aside. "This is what I think you were going for. It's the 'rock on' sign, or devil's horn to be precise. You don't use your thumb. The sign you flashed me means 'I love you'."

Her cheeks flame, and she covers her face with her hands. "I'm so bad at this."

I laugh. "You're better than you think."

"How can that possibly be?"

"I wrote another song. That's why you're here. For inspiration."

"Are you going to play it for me?"

"When it's finished. I'm putting the final touches on it."

We pass a large fort on the water. I've never been one to sightsee, but suddenly I have the urge. "Want to go inside?"

"This is the oldest city in America," she says. "Might as well see some history while we're here. But first you promised me ice cream."

My phone vibrates with a text. It's a group text from Ronni, telling us she's returning to New York. I read it to Ella, smiling.

"You're happy she's leaving?"

"Of course I'm happy. She's a damn thorn in our side."

"I thought maybe you wanted her to stay."

"What the hell gave you that idea?"

"Her showing up naked last night."

"I don't even like Ronni. She was a distraction, nothing more."

"Was?" she asks.

I try not to read too much into her question, because even if she thinks she's changed her mind about me, I can never allow anything to happen. I like being her friend. If I let it go beyond that, she'll run so far, so fast, I'll never see her again. "Yeah. Was. Now let's get you some ice cream."

Chapter Sixteen

Ella

I've made a lot of progress on my drawings over the past week. You might even say I've been inspired. I pencil in the hair, making it just the right shade, then scold myself when I look at a picture on my phone, making sure it matches his exactly.

I sent the preliminary sketches to the author this morning. She texted only one word: Perfect. I'm destined to draw pictures of him for the next year. Jimmy and Jojo will go on adventures to the zoo, the beach, an amusement park. Art may be imitating life, as those are some of the things Liam has promised we'll do during our time here.

It's Saturday. There's four hours until they play tonight, and I'm getting excited all over again. I thought I'd get bored seeing them play the same songs over and over, night after night, but the opposite is true. With each performance, I get into it more. Ronni was right; I'm a groupie.

I'm not the only one. I've noticed familiar faces in the crowd at the last three performances. Girls who seem to be following

Reckless Alibi down the east coast. The band is becoming more popular with each concert.

I glance at the empty couch in the hotel room. It's a different couch, a different room, but a part of me wishes he were still sleeping on it. He stopped sharing my space after Ronni went back to New York. He's bunking with Garrett again.

My phone rings. I glance at it and see the face I've been drawing the past two hours. "Hey."

"Are you busy?"

I give Jimmy's hair one last stroke of the pencil. "Not really."

"I want to take you to see something."

"What?"

"It's a surprise. Can you meet me in the lobby in ten?"

"Do I need to wear anything in particular?"

"We'll be outside, but we're not going to the beach."

I change into shorts and a halter top and then find him downstairs with his guitar case slung over one shoulder, a beach towel over the other, and a cooler in his hand. He walks me to the van. "Is Bruce driving us somewhere?"

He jingles the keys. "We're borrowing it." He drives in silence.

"Where are we going?"

"Someplace I heard about that I thought would be fun."

Twenty minutes later, we arrive at our destination. I get out of the van. We're at a park on the end of a point by the water. There are other people here, so I assume it's a popular spot. Large rocks are piled up against the shoreline. "What's special about this place?"

He checks his watch. "You'll see in about fifteen minutes."

I narrow my eyes. "Is there a blowhole that erupts when the tide comes in or something?"

"Not a blow hole." He grabs the cooler. "Come on." He finds a spot on the grass and spreads out a towel. Then he opens the cooler and offers me a bottle of beer.

"Anything else in there? Maybe a soda?"

He puts the bottle between his thighs, hands me a Diet Coke, then opens his beer and swallows half of it.

"How come you drink so much?"

He regards the half-empty bottle like he didn't know he gulped that much down. "Habit, I guess. Why do you ask?"

I gaze at the water. "Corey drank a lot. People sometimes make bad choices when they drink."

He looks sad for me. "I don't," he says. But we both know he's lying.

"What about Ronni? Are you saying your 'once or twice' wasn't a product of a drunken mishap?"

"Okay, you got me there."

"What's up with her? I mean, why her when there are plenty of other women out there willing and able?" I think about the girls at the festival today who were throwing themselves at him.

"Didn't we already go over this?"

"You said she doesn't ask questions."

"But apparently you do."

The way he says it makes me feel guilty. "Sorry. I know you didn't bring me here for the third degree."

He takes his guitar from the case. "I promised you a song."

My eyes light up. I lie back on the towel and let him play. As I listen, I realize how little I know about him. The truth is I want to know so much more. What was his childhood like? Who hurt him? Why does he hate questions?

I follow his left hand as it glides between the frets. I stare at his fingers as he expertly strums the strings. I look at his eyes and see the way he's looking at me. The song is incredible. *I* inspired him to write this?

He stops abruptly, and I instantly miss the music. He puts the guitar down and stands, offering me his hand. "Come on."

He helps me up and I finally understand why he brought me here. A humongous cruise ship is coming down the channel. My jaw drops. I've seen them in pictures, on TV, but never in person. We stroll to the edge, along with many others.

The ship gets closer. Cruisers are on the top deck, lining the railings. Some are on lower floors, on private balconies. They wave. I'm startled when someone blows an air horn next to me, then I see why. The ship blows its horn, and everyone on the shore erupts into cheers.

Liam and I get caught up in the excitement and wave emphatically to those on the ship. "Look there," he says, pointing to the front. "I think it's the bridge."

Men in white uniforms are surrounded by glass walls in a section overhanging the side of the ship. One of them waves at the crowd. "Do you think he's the captain?"

"Probably not, but we can pretend."

The ship passes us and goes out to sea. I turn to Liam. "That was incredible!"

He points down the channel, and I see two more ships coming our way. I smile. There are more cheers, waves, and air horns as the second ship comes by. The more boisterous the crowd, the louder and crazier the passengers on the ship become. When the third one passes, a guy on a balcony strips off his shirt and waves it over his head. Girls onshore whistle and clap.

"She's flashing her tits!" a man yells.

A woman on the ship is jiggling her breasts for the onlookers. I playfully cover Liam's eyes so he can't enjoy the show.

He removes my hands and tilts his head back to better study my face. "Is there some reason you don't want me looking at a woman's boobs?"

My insides twist. *Is there?*

Something between us changes. He doesn't release my hands, and I don't want him to. I stare at his lips, wanting him to kiss me. In the back of my mind, a little voice is saying, "Corey who?"

He leans in. I close my eyes.

But I don't feel his lips. He drops my hands and returns to the beach towel. He puts his guitar away, then he rakes his fingers through his hair.

I feel all kinds of awkward. "How did you get interested in playing guitar?"

He doesn't look at me. "You sure do ask a lot of questions." When I don't say anything, he gathers up our stuff and starts for the van.

I don't follow. I'm frozen to the ground, wondering what happened. How did things go from perfect to disastrous in a second?

He turns and blows out a long breath. "Ella, I promise you don't want to hear my answers."

Chapter Seventeen

Liam

Thirteen years ago

"Colleen, don't coddle him," Dad says. "He needs to suck it up and take it like a man. It doesn't hurt that bad, does it, son?" He turns to Mom. "I have half a mind to sue the ball field for having a damn hole in the outfield."

Luke hobbles on crutches to the car.

"It sucks you'll miss the rest of baseball season," I say, feeling guilty because I'll still be able to play. "Will you still come to my games?"

"Sure."

I hold my hand out, wanting him to give me our secret handshake. He rarely does it anymore. I guess going to high school makes such things not cool. He glances at Dad, who's gone on ahead, and quickly does the handshake. I smile.

When we get home, Dad gets something out of the trunk. He follows us inside and waits for Luke to sit down, then hands him a huge box.

Luke looks at it. "What's this?" His leg must really hurt, because he doesn't seem happy to be getting a surprise.

"Go on, open it," Dad says. "When you were getting your cast on, I made a quick trip to the music store. I thought you should have something to do while you can't play ball."

I think I'm more excited to see what's in the box than Luke is. We're lucky. Dad is always giving us stuff, unlike most of my friends, who only get things on birthdays and Christmas.

Mom helps Luke open the gift. They pull out a large black case. I've seen something like this before. He opens it. "You got me a guitar?"

"I had to think of something you could do sitting down. They had keyboards, too, but I think they're more for girls. Guitars are for manly men like us."

Luke cringes when he says that. Maybe his leg is throbbing. "Thanks," he says, setting it aside.

Mom wraps her arms around Dad. "I'm sure he'll play it later, when he feels up to it. What a thoughtful gift, Donny."

"Only the best for my family."

Luke gets up and grabs his crutches. "I'm going to lie down. Today kind of took it out of me."

I follow him to his bedroom, which is across the hall from mine. "Luke?"

"What?" he snaps.

I back off. He usually doesn't talk to me that way.

Luke relents. "Sorry. My leg hurts, is all. What were you going to ask me?"

"I know Dad gave the guitar to you, but do you think I could try it? It's okay if you want me to wait until you've had a chance."

"You can play it. Maybe I'll give it a try later." He turns. "Or maybe not," he mumbles and closes the door.

I run to the living room, eager to get my hands on it.

While I'm strumming, Mom makes all of Luke's favorites for dinner, then heads off to work. She was lucky to get half a shift off to meet us at the Emergency Room. "Put the leftovers in the fridge. I'll eat when I get home. Love you guys."

The three of us eat together, like we always do when Mom's at work—in front of the television. She never allows it when she's home, but Dad lets us get away with a lot when she's not around. As long as we don't tell her, that is.

Luke conks out early after taking the pain medication the doctor gave him. When I go to my bedroom, there's a new magazine on my bed. I close the door, even though I know Mom's not here to see it. I have a stack of half a dozen magazines Dad has given me in the past month hidden behind my dresser.

Something's different about this one. There are no women on the cover. Only men. I open it and flip through the pages, surprised to see men touching each other. They're more than touching each other; they're doing a lot of things. It kind of feels wrong to look at them, but I can't stop. And just like when I look at the other magazines, I get all funny and tingly inside.

I close it, stash it behind the dresser, and pull out one of the others.

~ ~ ~

My bed creaks. I open my eyes to darkness. Maybe Mom's coming in to give me a kiss before she goes to bed. She does that sometimes. When large arms go around me, I know it's not her. I'm still half asleep, so I don't say anything.

"Shh," he whispers in my ear.

He gets under the covers with me. I'm confused. Dad used to tuck me in, but I haven't needed that for a while. He moves around a little behind me. He rubs my back for a minute. Then he reaches around and touches me. He touches me *there,* and I stiffen.

"Shh," he murmurs again. "It's okay. It's better this way, you'll see."

I want to pull away, but I'm scared, so I pretend to be asleep. That's stupid because he knows I'm awake, but I don't know what else to do. All I can hear is my heart pounding in my head. I can't speak. I can't move.

His hand goes under my shorts and moves on me, and I start to have those same feelings I have when I look at the magazines. But this is different. My insides tighten into something so powerful, I feel like I'm going to explode. Then suddenly, out of nowhere, I do. All over my shorts. Immediately after, I feel something hot and wet on my back as Dad groans behind me.

I'm frozen. My insides feel all twisted, and a sick feeling washes over me. What happened felt good, but I'm frightened and disgusted too.

Dad wipes my back. "You're a man now," he whispers. "I told you it would be better this way. You liked it, or you wouldn't have ejaculated. I knew you would." He sits up, but I don't move. "You're lucky to have a father like me who is willing to show you everything. And Luke is lucky to have someone like me paying his medical bills. Your mom tells me all the time she doesn't know what she would do without me." He gets out of my bed. "Remember, Liam. Men don't talk about the things we do behind closed doors. We're good at keeping secrets. Secrets keep our family safe. They keep us intact. They keep us strong. Don't ever forget that."

He shuts the door behind him when he leaves. I change my shorts and get back in bed. I gaze at the ceiling.

Becoming a man isn't anything like I thought it would be.

Chapter Eighteen

Ella

I lie on a beach towel next to Bria and Katie while the men throw a Frisbee.

"We're glad you could make it, even if it's only for a few days," Bria says to Brad's fiancée.

I roll onto my stomach and face Katie. "Tell me how it happened. How did he propose? Wait, let me guess. Did he take you to the top of the Empire State Building? Or maybe on a romantic picnic in Central Park. Did he do it onstage after a concert?"

She laughs. "None of the above. It was back in December. His family invited mine over so they could meet. We'd just finished playing a riveting game of Trivial Pursuit. Right there at the table, out of nowhere, he asked."

I try not to look surprised. I mean, she's dating a rock star. I thought there might be a little pomp and circumstance. I can't think of a more boring way to get proposed to. "When's the wedding?"

"Beats me. His schedule is up in the air right now. Ronni wants them back in the recording studio by summer. That is if Liam gets around to writing the music. Makes it hard to plan a wedding. Makes it hard to plan *anything*."

My spine stiffens, and I get defensive. "He's writing a lot of music. Has been for weeks."

"Well, good. Maybe we can shoot for later in the summer unless something else comes up."

Katie's phone rings, and she hops up and walks down the beach with it.

"She's … interesting," I say.

"Katie's nice," Bria says. "And I love Brad, but it's almost like the two of them are the piece that doesn't quite fit in the RA puzzle."

I watch Katie briefly before turning back to Bria.

Bria shields her eyes from the sun. "You fit, you know."

I glance at Liam. "We're not—"

"I know you're not, but you still fit."

Garrett strides by, following a group of bikini-clad women. It has me thinking. "You said Garrett's a playboy. But Liam's been staying in his room. How's that working out for Garrett?"

Bria laughs. "Let's just say Garrett is sexually frustrated. I'm not sure he's brought anyone home since we've been here."

"Why doesn't Liam crash with Brad?"

Bria's gaze goes to Katie. "Because those two spend hours on the phone every night."

"I suppose I should feel guilty keeping Garrett from his … hobby?" I snicker.

"Don't. It's good for him to see how normal people live for a change. Some of the guys have strange vices."

"Like Liam's drinking?"

Before I get a chance to ask her more, two men drop on the sand next to us. "You girls don't look like you're from around here."

"How do you figure?" I ask.

One of them gestures a hand up and down my body. "No tan. You're from up north. Are you here on spring break?"

"You could say that," I say.

"Where up north?"

"New York."

Bria keeps glancing at Crew as we chat with the guys. One of them pulls suntan lotion from his shorts and squirts it on my back. *You've got to be kidding me.* I start to stand when suddenly the earth shifts next to me, and a shadow falls across my face.

"Can I help you gentleman with anything?" Thor asks.

The two strangers quickly back away. "We're good. Just looking for our towels."

Thor makes a big show of examining the ground around us. "I don't see any stray towels, do you?"

They hurry off without saying goodbye.

"Ladies." Thor returns to his beach chair.

I lie back down on my stomach. "I forgot he was here."

"Yeah, he's good like that." She looks at the retreating men. "Unless you wanted them here. You can always tell Tom to back off, you know. He's mostly here because of me."

"Why? Did something bad happen?"

"Not to me." She glances at Crew. "He lost someone a while ago. In a bad way. He tries to protect me. Tom's a big part of that. But if you wanted to keep talking to them, just say so."

"I didn't mind talking to them, but when he squirted the lotion, he crossed a line." Someone touches me and I turn, ready to call Thor.

"Didn't mean to startle you," Liam says. "Thought you could use a hand. You have lotion running down your back."

I rest my head on my arms and close my eyes, enjoying the feel of his hands on me. The guy must have squirted a ton back there, because it takes Liam a while to rub it in. He's giving me a massage, and it feels heavenly. I could lie here all day. His hand gets close to the side of my boob, and my eyes open.

"Sorry," he says. "It was running down your side and I didn't want it to get all over your top."

I peek at Bria, who's smiling from ear to ear. Then his hands are gone. I sit up to see him running full on into the water.

Garrett sits on the sand, laughing. "Who gave Pinocchio all the wood?"

I give him a puzzled look.

"You know, like how his nose grows, only it's his dick. And instead of Pinocchio, it's Liam."

I turn bright red.

Bria touches my shoulder. "Ignore him. You'll get used to his crassness."

"You mean my awesomeness," Garrett says.

Bria rolls her eyes.

Someone in the next group says something about a food truck. Garrett perks up. "Food?" he asks our neighbors. "What kind?"

"Tacos."

"Hell, yeah!" He gets his wallet out of his bag. "You guys want some?"

"I'll have to pay you back," I say. "I left all my money in the room."

"No need, I got it."

Ten minutes later, Garrett returns with what I can only assume is half the food truck's bounty. He's got at least eight full bags. I get up and help him. Bria shakes the sand from her towel and lays it back down so we can put the food on it.

Liam comes back, staring at me as he approaches. Did he really get turned on by rubbing suntan lotion on my back? If I'm being honest, I have to admit I did, too.

"Are we feeding the whole damn beach?" Liam asks.

"This must have cost a fortune," I say. "I promise to contribute."

"You think G cares about your ten bucks?" Brad says. "He's a damn millionaire."

Garrett swats Brad. "Shut up."

"My apologies," he says. "He *will* be a millionaire when he collects his trust fund."

"Rich grandma?" I joke.

"Rich parents," Brad says.

"I'm confused."

"His family is rich as shit," Brad says. "But Garrett, for some unknown reason he's never shared with us, hates them."

"Can we not talk about this again?" Garrett asks.

"How about you tell us why you refuse to see them and *then* we'll never talk about it again?"

Garrett throws his taco in the sand and stalks away.

"Brad, stop," Crew says, glancing at Liam. "Garrett isn't the only one with a rich family."

Liam scoffs. "Dirk is not my fucking family."

"Fair enough, but I still think we should drop it."

Katie sighs heavily. "Does there always have to be so much drama?"

Liam shoots her a frigid glare and then runs after Garrett. Crew goes after them both.

Brad gets up too, but Katie latches onto his arm. "They're big boys. They can handle it." He sits back down.

Bria and I share a look. I get the feeling we're both thinking about the puzzle these two don't seem to fit into.

A short time later, I get so hot I go into the water to cool off.

Liam comes in after me. "I'm sorry about all that."

"Doesn't bother me. You're a family. All families have problems."

He murmurs something under his breath.

"What did you say?"

"Nothing. The five of us like to give each other a lot of shit, that's all."

"I get it. And most of the time it's funny. Unless you're asking questions people don't want to answer."

"Ouch, woman. Hitting me where it hurts."

"Just calling it like I see it."

He makes a sudden move toward me, scoops me up in his arms, and throws me into the surf. I get pummeled hard. When I come up for air, spitting water, I gasp, "You're toast!" and lunge for him.

He's too strong for me to dunk. Not only does he stand his ground, he pulls me close, his hand on my back anchoring me against him.

"Liam, what are you doing?"

"El," he says guiltily. "You lost your top."

I instantly stop struggling and look down. My bare breasts are mashed between us. He's not hugging me, he's protecting me.

For a split second, before mortification overtakes me, I glory in the feeling of being skin-to-skin with him. I glance up. He's not smiling. He's not laughing. He's gazing into my eyes, and I feel blood pulsing in my throat.

"Here," a girl says, handing me my top.

"Thank you." I slink down into the water and put it back on while waves lash me. I can't get the back of it tied. "Liam, could you?"

He's still close, shielding me in case I lose it again. He steps behind me and ties it. I make sure it's covering all the right places and stand.

"I'm sorry," he says. "I didn't mean for that to happen."

"It wasn't your fault."

"It was. You should be mad as hell."

"Liam, it was an accident."

"I picked you up and threw you against your will."

I get in his face. "They're just boobs. Half the population has them. I'm over it already. You should be too."

We walk back up the beach and a few teenage boys clap. Liam looks like he wants to kill them.

I put my hand on his arm. "Don't. If I need protection, Thor has my back."

He stops. "What if *I* want to be the one to protect you, El?"

I don't know what to say. Part of me wants that. Part of me doesn't. Part of me thinks it's too soon. Part of me doesn't want to ruin our friendship. *All* of me is confused.

"Forget I said anything," he says. "Let's join the others."

"Epic wardrobe malfunction," Garrett says, bobbing his head.

Liam snaps him with his towel. "Dude."

Garrett holds up his hands in a gesture of innocence. "I can't help it if I have a tit radar. It's like a gift." He turns to me. "Bravo, by the way. I give you a ten."

I laugh. "I'm officially offended, but thanks."

"Crew and I were thinking of going dancing," Bria says. "We should make the most of our night off. Anyone else want to come?"

"I'm game," Garrett says.

Liam looks at me. I shrug. "Why not?"

"Count us in," he says.

"How about you and Katie?" Crew asks Brad.

"She's only here for two days," Brad says. "We play tomorrow, so tonight is our only chance to be alone. Sorry, guys, fiancée trumps friends."

"What else is new?" Garrett grumbles.

Brad gets in his face. "You got something you want to say to me?"

"No, man. Do what you have to do."

"Damn right I will." Brad gathers their stuff, and they head back to the hotel.

"She's no good for him," Garrett says, watching them walk away.

"He loves her," Bria says. "Give him a break. Being apart is hard on them."

"Then maybe she should have come with us."

"Katie isn't like that. She's not going to give up her job and follow us around, and she shouldn't have to."

"Then maybe she should find another line of work," Garrett says. "One that gives her the flexibility to do shit like this."

Liam catches my eye. I know exactly what he's thinking.

"Not everyone wants to live this kind of life," Crew says.

"She should have thought it through before dating someone in a rock band. This is only the beginning. Who knows what will happen next. US tour? International? What will they do then?"

"That's for them to figure out," Bria says. "Not everyone is lucky enough to work with the person they love."

Crew leans over and kisses her. I reach for my phone and snap a picture. I show it to Bria. "I love it," she says and holds out a hand. "How about I take one of you and Liam?"

"Okay."

Liam stands next to me.

"Closer," Bria says. "So I can't see the people behind you."

He closes the gap between us and puts his arm around my waist. His hand lands on my hip. His thumb gently rubs back and forth across my bare skin. Electrified waves pulse through me.

"I think I got a good one," Bria says.

Neither of us moves.

She holds out my phone. "Want to see them? The last one is a keeper."

Liam jerks away, and I take the phone and check out the photos. We're both smiling in the first two, he blinked in the third, but the fourth picture is the one that captures my attention. Liam's head is turned, and he's looking at me. My eyes are closed, and my lip is between my teeth. If I didn't know the two people in this picture, I'd say they were a couple.

I pick up my towel and wrap it around my waist. "I feel like I'm getting burned. I'm going to go back and get in a few hours of work."

I told a lie. Two of them actually. One, my skin is not in the least bit red; and two, I'm almost positive I won't be able to draw a damn thing. On my way back, I tell myself I won't look at the picture on my phone again, but who am I kidding? That would just be another lie.

Chapter Nineteen

Liam

Watching Ella dance is making me hard. She doesn't seem to give a shit who sees her. Half the time, her eyes are closed. The way she moves is so carefree. I envy that about her.

Ella seems to be the perfect specimen of a woman. Strong. Independent. Resilient. From what she's told me about her past, she had the ideal childhood. She's the polar opposite of any girl I've ever been with. Not that I'm with her. And not that I want to be. If I'm being honest, I *do* want to be, but I can't. If I ever showed my true colors around her, that would be it. She'd be gone. Then what would I do? Go back to being the douchebag who can't pull together a decent song if my life depended on it?

Even while we've been touring, I've managed to score two new songs. This afternoon when I came back from the beach, I started working on a third. Shit is flowing out of me like musical diarrhea.

I can't stop watching as she and Bria dance and laugh. Usually at a club, the only thing I care about is how much whiskey is in my glass, but I couldn't care less about that right now. Who needs alcohol when she provides a better buzz than I can get from liquor?

I'm not much of a dancer—never have been—but I'm acting like I know what I'm doing. Garrett and Crew are much better at this than I am. Crew spins Bria around like he's Fred fucking Astaire. I wish I could do that shit.

"Oh, yeah," Garrett drawls. "I think I see my next conquest."

I lift my chin at him, not wanting my eyes to stray from their current position. There's a guy behind Ella, dancing close. He's been trying to butt in, without much success. One of his hands skims her hip. Her eyes are closed, and though it's dim here, I think I see the edges of her mouth turn up. When she doesn't protest, he puts a second hand on her, this time on her stomach. She wets her lips. My heart falls into my stomach. She likes it.

I should turn and walk away. Nowhere in our agreement did we stipulate anything about her not hooking up with men. But I *can't* walk away. I'm glued to the floor, watching them like a goddamn voyeur.

What he does next drives a stake through my heart. He reaches around and grabs her breasts. She does the opposite of what I hoped. Her head falls back against the dude's shoulder. *Fuck.*

I'm about to turn and leave when she opens her eyes. She sees me, and in a split second, her entire demeanor changes. Her eyes widen in shock and terror, her expression turning into a furious grimace. She spins and looks at the man behind her. "What the hell do you think you're doing?" she says, shoving him away from her.

I don't think. I storm over and throw my fist in his face. He hits the ground. I flip him, twist his arm behind him, and plant a knee on his back. I lean down and yell, "Didn't your mother ever tell you not to touch anyone unless you're invited to, you fucking prick?" Immediately Thor is at my side. "Keep him down," I say, standing. Ella is being protectively flanked by Bria and Crew. "Are you okay?"

"I … yeah. I thought …"

"Call the police," I tell Crew.

Ella protests. "I don't want to cause a scene."

I gesture at the club patrons staring at us. "Too late for that."

Club security makes their way over and asks what happened.

"This asshole was groping her," I say.

"Ma'am, is what he said true?"

"He was … you know, it's fine. I'm okay."

I move closer to her. "El, we need to call the cops. You have to press charges. If you don't, the sicko will do this to someone else. He was touching you without permission. He's scum. He should be thrown in jail."

"Let's just go. Can we go please?" She says something to security and walks away. One of them goes over to Thor and has a conversation. Next thing I know, the guy is let go. I lunge for him. Crew and Garrett hold me back. They drag me out of the club, with Ella following, as I watch the fuckwad over my shoulder. He brushes himself off and takes a drink from his friend like nothing happened.

I struggle to break free as we get to the parking lot. "We can't let him get away with that shit."

"Get in the van, Liam," Crew says.

"Fuck that," I say.

"You guys go," Garrett says. "I'll stay and make sure he doesn't go back in. Besides, there's a girl in there who wants me bad."

"You're not coming?" Ella asks.

I shake my head.

"Come on," Bria says to her. "He'll be okay. He needs to cool off. Garrett's got him."

They climb into the van and drive away. I sit on the curb.

"I wasn't kidding," Garrett says. "You are not going back in there."

"Then I'll wait for the motherfucker to come out."

"Remember last year, when Crew asked us to tell him when he was crossing the line to batshit crazy?"

I eye him in disgust. "This isn't the same, G. He was grabbing her fucking tits."

"And she told you not to do anything about it. So don't. If you do, she'll probably be pissed at you. She might even leave. Do you really want to ruin whatever you've got going with her?"

I scrub my face. "Goddammit."

"Go home, Liam."

I nod.

He takes my phone and summons an Uber. Five minutes later, I'm telling the driver to find a liquor store.

~ ~ ~

"There you are," Ella says. "I've been looking everywhere for you. You should respond to your texts once in a while so your friends don't think you're in jail for killing someone."

"I didn't kill him. But I wanted to." I'm sitting on the sand, gazing at the water.

She sits next to me, eyeing the bottle. "Liam?"

"What?"

"Nothing."

"What did you want to say, El? Believe me, I've heard it all."

"Did something happen to a woman you used to date? Is that why you got so mad?"

"I told you, I don't date."

"It's just that your reaction was so intense."

I feel a headache coming on. My hair falls over my eyes as my head slumps. I try to rub the tension from my neck. When I look at her, she seems sad.

"Did something happen to *you*, Liam? Did someone hurt you?"

I look away. The beach is lit by the moon, and I can hear the waves on the sand. I can just make out the sea foam left in their wake.

"It didn't happen to me," I say, grabbing the bottle and standing. I start to walk away and say the words I never thought I'd say. "It happened to the kid I used to be."

I hear the shock in her stifled cry.

"Go back to the hotel, Ella."

She catches up with me. "How much have you had to drink?"

"I wasn't here long."

She takes the bottle from me and examines it to see it's practically full. She wedges it into the sand next to the boardwalk, then takes off her shoes. "Take yours off, too."

"Why?"

"Because we're going on a run."

"Now?"

"Yes. You told me I have permission to stop you from drinking."

"But I've barely even started."

"All the more reason to run. It's cathartic, Liam. It clears your head better than anything I've ever known. Now—when you're feeling like this—is the best time to do it."

I'm wearing dress shorts and a polo shirt. She's in a skirt and blouse. She knows what my next argument will be. She takes off the blouse, revealing a tank top. "I can run in anything. Besides, it's dark and nobody will see us, so who cares what we look like?"

"We don't have our shoes."

"We won't go far. Maybe a mile and back. If our feet start to hurt, we'll walk. What do you have to lose except the possibility of a killer hangover?"

I take off my shirt and drop it on top of her blouse.

As usual, I have to concentrate on my breathing. She's particularly quiet, which gives me time to think. Think about what she's thinking. Think about the fact that I just revealed more to her than anyone other than Crew. Does she think I'm some kind of sicko now?

"Feels good, doesn't it?" she asks when we make the turn.

My lungs burn. My legs hurt. My feet are raw. But, yeah, it feels good. "Don't get cocky."

She laughs and moves ahead.

Returning to the hotel, a million thoughts go through my head, but there is one I just can't shake. I realize what I hadn't before. A man had his hands on her, and she was enjoying it. Then she opened her eyes, saw me three feet away, and her whole attitude changed. Is it possible she thought the man touching her was *me?*

Chapter Twenty

Ella

He's been avoiding me. For two weeks he's made excuses, like he has to work on music. It has me wondering if my presence here is no longer required.

Liam avoiding me has its benefits, however. I've been working so much that I'm almost finished with the illustrations for the first book. They're laid out on the floor of my hotel room. I look at each one, making sure I haven't repeated any of the main elements of the pictures.

I sit and pick one up. I trace my finger across Liam's eight-year-old face. My heart hurts for the boy he used to be. "What happened to you?" The question has plagued me for fourteen days. Something happened to him, but what? Someone hurt him. Who? I used to think it was a bad breakup, but I fear it's something worse.

He hates questions. He's never shied away from telling me this. But then he went and answered the most prying question of all. He answered it and then avoided me.

Is he mad at himself for saying too much? Ashamed at what he thinks I know?

I put away my work and scroll through the recent pictures on my phone. I go to all of their performances and take a picture at every one. Last night they played a small outdoor venue. I was front and center, and got a picture of all five of them. Crew and Bria were singing into the same microphone. Liam and Brad flanked them, both playing their guitars. Garrett was in the background on his platform, one drumstick over his head, the other pounding his snare. I've never seen a better picture of the band. It gives me an idea.

Two hours later there's a familiar knock on my door. I know his knock. It's strong, yet hesitant. Just like he is. I open up. "You ready?" he asks, wearing shorts and running shoes.

I glance at the clock. It's after six. It's their day off, and I forgot we were supposed to meet in the lobby. "Sorry, I lost track of time. Give me a minute to change."

I grab what I need and duck into the bathroom. We've been running almost daily. And he's gotten much better, faster. But sometimes I think he runs fast to keep from talking.

When I emerge, he's got one of my sketches in his hands. "Ella, this is fantastic."

"I'm not finished yet." I try to swipe it from him, but he keeps it. "I still need to color it."

"I have to show this to everyone. This may be our next album cover."

"What? That's crazy."

I scrutinize what I drew. It's a rough sketch. And I took liberties, such as changing the background to something abstract.

"It's not. This is exactly what we need."

I take it back. "Let me finish it."

"No way. It's great as it is."

"You don't have to flatter me, Liam."

"That's not what I'm doing. Can I show this to the rest of the band?"

"Suit yourself." I motion to the door. "Ready?"

At the beach we stretch, then start our run. He comments on the weather. I say something about the sunset. Small talk.

Halfway into it, I do something I never do. I stop. "Liam, do I need to be here anymore?"

"What are you talking about?"

"You never talk to me anymore. You've been avoiding me since, you know. It's awkward. And everyone has noticed. Bria keeps asking if we're fighting."

"We're not fighting."

"Then what *are* we?"

He takes off. I catch up and tug on his arm until he halts.

"I'm here because you thought I inspired you, but now I feel like I'm a burden."

"You're not."

"Then talk to me. About your music, the album cover, your new living arrangements when you get back to New York. Anything but the stupid weather."

His gaze travels to my chest, and he cringes. Is he still upset about what that guy did to me?

"It's going to be dark soon," he says. "We should head back."

He runs so fast, I can't keep up with him. By the time I make it back to the hotel, he's nowhere in sight.

I go upstairs and pack my suitcase.

~ ~ ~

There's a knock on the door. It's a different knock, but it's him. And he's got a half-full bottle of whiskey in his hand. He stumbles into my room, sits on the couch, and takes a swig. He sees the packed suitcase and backpack on the bed. When he tries to stand, he trips over his own feet and ends up on all fours.

He gets off the floor and goes to the suitcase. "I thought we weren't going to Tampa until tomorrow."

"You're going to Tampa tomorrow. *I'm* going to New York tonight."

His eyes are glazed. "What? Why?"

"Why do you think? There's no point in my being here, Liam."

"There is."

"I'm not doing anything for you. I'm not your muse anymore. I've become some groupie who tags along with the band."

"I like having you here."

"Do you? You could have fooled me. You don't even talk to me. You can barely look at me. Are you mad at me for not calling the police on the guy in the bar?"

His attention goes to my breasts, and every line on his face screams of tension. He twists off the cap to his bottle and drinks. "You should have turned him in."

"Maybe. But it was my call to make."

He slams the bottle down on the table and liquid splashes out the top. "He's going to do it again, and you're the one who allowed it."

"So now it's *my* fault?"

"You should have done more."

My blood boils. "I never knew you could be such an asshole, Liam. I think you should leave."

He stumbles to the door, then glances back like he wants to say something. But he doesn't. He walks out. I sit on the couch, a vice gripping my heart. I'm not sure what I expected. I've always been clear that I don't want anything more than friendship from him, so why does the thought of leaving him hurt so much?

His bottle is still on the table. I pick it up and take a drink, feeling the burn all the way from my lips to my stomach. Then I cry.

The doorknob turns. "El, let me in."

I shouldn't open the door, but I do. He sees my red eyes, my smeared makeup, the tears hanging from my lashes. "Did you come back for your booze?"

"It's not your fault," he says. "I shouldn't have said what I did."

I wipe my eyes. "Take your liquor and go. I have to get to the airport. My flight leaves soon."

He comes in and the door shuts behind him. "Don't leave."

I laugh pathetically. "You're not giving me any reason to stay."

He lunges at me and takes me in his arms. His lips collide with mine. I don't even have time to think about it. I have craved this though I've fought my feelings.

His lips are soft and strong and warm, his touch electric. I get lost in the moment and give in to him. He slips his tongue in my mouth and deepens the kiss.

I taste alcohol and pull away. "You're drunk. You don't want this. I'm not sure *I* want this."

He steps back and leans against the door. He pinches the bridge of his nose. "It doesn't matter. Because I can never have this. I just wanted to feel what it's like to kiss you before you walked out of my life." He snatches the bottle and turns to leave.

"It was my dad. He ruined my fucking life. He ruined *me*. He took away any chance I ever had of being with someone like you. And it's my fault he's still out there."

Chapter Twenty-one

Liam

Thirteen years ago

Sitting on the front stoop, I take the guitar back from Crew. "Careful, it's Luke's. I'd hate for you to drop it." I play a tune Luke taught me.

"You're getting pretty good at that," he says.

"That's what Luke says. Dad said he'll buy me one when I turn twelve."

"Cool."

I stop playing. "Do you … miss having a dad at your house?"

"I guess. I mean, doesn't everyone want their dad to live with them?"

"I don't know. Do you feel you can do all the things men do without him there?"

He laughs. "Men? So we're men now?"

I fiddle with the strings, not wanting to look at him. Does he know what I'm asking? Maybe he hasn't done any of it yet. Maybe he never will since his dad doesn't live with him. This is the closest to talking about it I've ever gotten. Crew is my best friend, but I'm not sure what I can and can't say. Dad says men don't talk about it.

He's crawled into my bed a lot over the past few months. Mostly I pretend I'm asleep, even when he does other stuff—like what's in the magazine. He says I'm good at it, better than Luke even, and Luke is fifteen. But I'm not ever allowed to tell Luke that. Luke would get mad and not like me anymore, because big brothers are always supposed to be better. It will be our secret.

He talks about secrets a lot, how they keep our family together. How Mom and Luke and I would have to go back to living in our rundown apartment if we ever told anyone. How Mom would hate me if I ever did anything to change how things are.

"We're almost twelve," I say. "So yeah, we're men."

Crew throws a stone at the mailbox. "I miss my dad taking me fishing. We used to go every Saturday. Now I'm lucky if we go once a month. You're lucky you have your dad to do all that stuff with."

"I suppose."

Luke comes around the corner and spots us with his guitar. I hand it to him. "Nah," he says. "You're better at it than I am. Just put it back when you're done." He goes in the house.

"Your brother is so cool," Crew says. "Kellan's older brother beats the shit out of him if he takes his stuff."

"Not Luke. He looks out for me."

A minute later, Luke is back. "Go home, Crew."

"Why does he have to leave?" I ask.

"He just does. We have shit to do."

Crew whispers, "Guess he was mad after all," and leaves.

I follow Luke inside and set his guitar by the couch. He seems upset, because he grabs my elbow and pulls me all the way upstairs and into the bathroom. He picks up the magazine I accidentally left on the counter when Crew rang the doorbell. The magazine with naked girls. "What is this shit?"

I've never seen him so angry. But I get it. I would have gotten in big trouble if Mom had found it before he did. Luckily she's at the grocery store.

I take it from him, embarrassed. "I … sorry. I'll put it away."

He goes into my room, turning his nose up at my unmade bed. "Who gave it to you, Liam?"

I'm afraid to break Dad's confidence, and I remember what he said about Luke getting mad because I'm better at things than he is. So I lie. "Crew gave it to me."

He sits on the bed. "You sure?"

"Yes."

He runs his hands through his hair. "Fuck."

"What is it? Are you worried about Mom finding out?"

"No. Nothing. It's fine. It's just …" —he lies back and looks blankly at the ceiling— "Sometimes I want to leave. Do you ever feel like that? Would you go with me if I did?"

"What do you mean?"

"You know, leave. Just me and you. Find somewhere else to live."

I look at him like he's crazy. "Why would we want to do that?"

He seems relieved. "Forget I said anything. I was only joking." He springs off the bed. "Want me to teach you a new song?"

I smile. Because Luke teaching me songs on the guitar is my favorite thing to do.

Chapter Twenty-two

Ella

Things are different. Liam and I don't talk about what he said that night. What we did. I never got on that flight to New York. I cried for the boy who was ruined by his father. How that was done, I could only speculate. The next day, when I walked into the hotel dining room for breakfast, I swear I'd never seen anyone so happy to see me.

Things are different, but not in a sexual way. It's like we've become best friends. I know his secret, part of it at least, and that makes him trust me in a way he hasn't trusted many. Except maybe Crew. He and Crew are closer than I've ever seen two men. Maybe Crew knows, too.

We're in the van on the way to Orlando. It's their day off. We got up early because Bria wanted to go to Disney World. Not Universal Studios with all the roller coasters. Not Animal Kingdom with all the exotic attractions. She wanted to go where the little kids go—the Magic Kingdom.

Garrett and Liam are in the middle of a discussion.

"I'm just saying, put a sock on the door handle or something," Liam says.

"What, are we in college?"

"How do I know what the hell people do in college? But walking in on your bare ass humping some chick is not my idea of good porn."

"Maybe you should get your own damn room, then," Garrett says.

I feel guilty. Garrett deserves his privacy.

"We're here!" Bria squeals.

I look out the front window and see a huge arch over the road that reads: **Walt Disney World. Where dreams come true.**

Bruce drops us at a place where we get on the monorail that takes us into the park. He, Jeremy, and Tom are going straight to the hotel. I'm stunned at the number of people making their way inside the park. There must be thousands. I ask Liam, "What would it take to play a concert here?"

"We're playing at Disney Springs tomorrow. It's the next best thing."

We make our way through the gates. Bria runs ahead like a little girl, gaping when she sees Cinderella's Castle.

"Damn," Crew says. "What kind of ride is that?"

"It's not a ride," she says. "There's a restaurant inside. There's also a secret suite upstairs. You can't book it. You have to win a contest or be invited. You can even get married in front of the castle. Can you imagine?"

Crew looks amused. "You trying to tell me something?"

She laughs and grabs his hand, pulling him along.

"I guess we'll see you later!" Garrett yells after them. "I'm not going to some pansy castle."

"What do you want to do?" Brad asks, looking at the map. "There's Space Mountain, the Haunted Mansion, Pirates of the Caribbean—"

"Which one isn't a roller coaster?" I ask. "I'd like to work up to that."

"You've never been on one?" Liam asks.

"I have. It made me sick." I don't tell them it was also the moment Corey declared his love for me. I may have to avoid all roller coasters today. I do not need another reminder of him.

Garrett laughs. "Oh, shit. I'm not sitting next to you then."

"Pirates of the Caribbean looks cool," Liam says.

The sign says it's a thirty-five-minute wait. "Get used to it," Brad says. "It's spring break, and the lines will only get worse throughout the day."

We weave through the ropes, then enter a dungeon-like building. "At least they make the line interesting," I say, glancing at all the Jack Sparrow stuff.

When it's finally our turn, the four of us are seated in the back of a boat. "You're not scared, are you?" Liam asks.

"It's a kid's ride," I say. Five minutes later, I'm eating my words when the boat takes a short but steep plunge. I grab Liam's arm hard. "Uh, sorry."

It's dark, but I see him smile.

Brad and Garrett take off to Thunder Mountain Railroad. Thankfully, Liam doesn't press me into going. I'm not ready for a roller coaster yet. Instead, he has fun humiliating me by making me ride things like Dumbo, the teacups, and the carousel. I'm having fun, though.

We take a hundred stupid selfies. Even one in front of the castle. Bria texts all of us to meet up for lunch and then Garrett makes us go with them to the Buzz Lightyear ride. "You have to try it," he says. "Brad and I have been on it three times already."

"Buzz Lightyear?" Liam says. "Really?"

"Don't give me that look," Garrett says. "Just wait, you'll get addicted to it, too."

I lean close to Liam. "What do you think they'd say if I told them you rode Dumbo?"

He covers my mouth with his hand. I laugh and bite him playfully.

Once we're on the ride, I get why the two of them liked it so much. It's a target shooting game. I score 300,000, beating all of them. Brad and Garrett get right back in line.

"My feet hurt," Bria says. "Can we sit for a while?"

Crew points up. "How about the people-mover thing. Seems like a good place to sit and relax."

We go with them. It doesn't take long to get on, and the four of us get our own car. Liam and I sit facing Crew and Bria. The elevated train takes us all over Tomorrowland, weaving in and out of the building that houses Space Mountain. I hear the screams of people riding the roller coaster.

"No way am I going on that one," I say. "They can't even see where they're going."

"There are lots of other things to do," Liam says.

It's completely dark, so I can't tell if he's upset about it or not. "Are you mad that I don't want to go on roller coasters?"

"No."

"You can go with the others, you know. You don't have to babysit me."

"I like hanging out with you, El. I don't need to ride them."

We emerge from a dark tunnel. Crew and Bria are making out. Bria pulls away. "Oops, sorry."

Crew says, "I think I like this ride the best of all."

I wonder if Liam wanted to kiss me in the dark tunnel. Or hold my hand or put his arm around me. Because it's all I think about. And not just here on this train. It's all I've thought about for days.

But he hasn't touched me since. His words from that night keep echoing in my head. *I can never have this.* What did that mean? Whatever his father did to him made him feel like he could only date women like Ronni. But why?

After five more hours and nine rides—including four more times on Buzz Lightyear, because, come on, I had to defend my title—we're in the van heading to our hotel.

"You're all checked in," Bruce says when we arrive, handing us our keycards. "Tom took your luggage up."

I peek into the bar. Garrett is hitting on a pretty woman. "He doesn't waste much time, does he?"

"Looks like he'll be putting a sock on the door tonight," Liam says.

"Where will that leave you?" I say, feeling guilty again. "You should stay in my room. It's really yours anyway."

"No."

"Liam, we're adults. There are two beds, or a bed and a couch. What's the difference which room you sleep in? We should see if we can switch our room to one with two queen beds. You shouldn't have to sleep on uncomfortable couches anymore."

"Garrett and I switched to queens over a week ago. The couches were killing my back."

"We'll swap with him then. We have both keys; you can give him mine later."

In the elevator, he eyes me speculatively. "Are you sure, El?"

"I'm sure. I feel bad I didn't offer sooner. It's not fair to Garrett."

He hesitates. "I promise I won't—"

"I know." I exit the elevator. "Just make sure to put the toilet seat down so I don't fall in at night."

"I'll do my best."

We get to his and Garrett's room first. "Perfect. Two queens." I see *my* things on the floor and cock my head suspiciously. "Did you tell Tom to put my stuff in here?"

He laughs. "Did I tell him to put your suitcase in here with Garrett's shit? No, El. He must've accidentally switched our bags and put mine in your room."

My stomach growls loudly.

"You're hungry." He checks the time. "It's getting late. We better hit the hotel restaurant before it closes. We can swap things around after dinner. Hey, which bed do you want?"

"The one farthest from the window. I hate morning light."

"Fine by me," he says, leading the way to the elevator. "I don't sleep much anyway."

"What do you mean, you don't sleep?"

He touches a finger to his temple. "My mind is always full of shit."

I smile. "Writing music in your sleep?"

He ignores my question, and I wonder if the shit his mind is filled with is that of monsters, not music.

Chapter Twenty-three

Liam

Crew, Bria, and Brad are sitting at a table in the corner of the restaurant, looking as tired as I feel. "Anyone see Garrett? I need to swap keys with him."

"Maybe he's still in the bar," Ella says.

"We'll check after dinner."

Everyone orders something simple, burgers or salads. It's been a long day.

"Where are we going to run tomorrow?" Ella asks while we eat. "There's no beach nearby."

"There's a trail," I tell her. "I asked the waiter when you went to wash up."

She seems pleased. I'm getting into running, as she hoped I would. I'm keeping up with her for three miles. "There's always treadmills," she says. "I bet this place has a great fitness center."

"Run inside? No way."

She picks at her salad while I inhale my cheeseburger. "It gets super cold in New York in the winter," she says. "What will you do then, or are you going to stop running when we get back?"

"That's up to you."

"Me?"

"Are you going to run with me when we get back?"

She smiles. Maybe she's been wondering what will happen when the tour is over. I've been wondering the same thing. Will she still want to see me? After being with her every day for almost a month, I can't imagine what it will be like going home and not having her with me.

Brad gets a call from Katie and waves goodbye, taking his food with him.

"I can't believe the tour is more than half over," Bria says. "This has been a lot more fun than touring with White Poison."

Crew leans in. "That's because you're touring with the right guy."

"There's never been anyone more right for me," Bria says. She pulls out a notebook and jots something in it, then she shows Crew. He nods and writes something.

He looks at us. "We have to go."

They leave their half-eaten food and go out to the lobby.

"What just happened?" Ella asks.

"They're writing lyrics. It happens like that. You'll get used to it."

"They're really good together, aren't they?" she says. "They're wonderful singers, but as a couple, I've never seen two people more dedicated to each other. They are lucky."

I turn away, not wanting her to see how distant I become when talking about things I can never have. I push my plate aside. "I'm finished."

"Was it something I said?"

"I'm tired, aren't you? It's almost midnight."

"I guess we should find Garrett."

Garrett's not in the bar. I text him but get no response. "Let's get my suitcase out of your room, and I'll text him to pick up his stuff and the key when he gets done doing whatever he's doing."

Her cheeks flush. We both know exactly what Garrett's doing.

In her room, I say, "Good thing we're switching. There's no couch in this one." I pull the suitcase behind me as Ella follows me down the hall. I tap my keycard to the door and open it, letting Ella step through first. She stops abruptly, and I bump into her. We've walked in on Garrett and a woman. She's naked and straddling him on one of the beds. They don't even notice us. Ella backs up, pushing me out the door before shutting it gently. Her expression makes me double over, laughing.

"What?" she asks, mortified. "That was messed up."

I catch my breath. "I don't think I've ever seen anyone turn that shade of red before."

"What are we going to do?"

"Sleep in *your* room, I guess."

"But there's only one bed." She looks at the door, knowing there's no way to retrieve her belongings. "And I don't have my suitcase."

"We'll make do. Come on."

Back in her room, she stares at the king-sized bed. "How is this going to work?"

I get an extra blanket from the closet and throw two pillows on the floor. "There. Easy peasy."

"You're not sleeping on the floor, Liam. If anyone should, it's me. I'm not paying a single penny for this trip."

"Because you're my guest, and guests don't sleep on the floor."

She picks up the pillows and puts them back on the bed. "It's a king. We'll share it."

I try not to smile. "You want me to build a barrier down the middle? Maybe something with a trip wire?"

"We're adults, Liam. I think we can sleep in the same bed. Except …"

"What?"

She peers down at her clothes. "I've been wearing this all day. I can't sleep in these."

I put my suitcase on the dresser and open it. "Pick whatever you want. I'll get your stuff first thing in the morning. Better yet, we'll switch rooms, like the original plan."

She peruses my clothes. I don't miss how her hands linger on some of my favorite shirts. Does she like them as much as I do? She pulls one out and laughs. "I thought for sure you'd have thrown this away by now."

It's the shrimp shirt she made me wear in St. Augustine. I'll never throw it out. I won't ever wear it again, but it will always be in my closet.

"I'll wear this one." She pulls out a pair of my boxer briefs. "And these."

She ducks into the bathroom. The shower turns on. I know she's getting naked, and my dick gets hard. The thought of her in there has so many things going through my head. What makes me go flaccid is when I remember she knows about me. I might have been drunk the night I told her about my dad, but I remember the words. Surely she's filled in the blanks. She's knows I'm dirty. She knows I'm not boyfriend material. Hell, I'm barely fuck-buddy material. Unless that fuck buddy is Veronica Collins. But I don't want Ronni. I never did. I wanted a release. Any time I've ever been with a woman, all I've wanted was a release.

It's different with Ella. I crave more. The problem is, it's something I know I can never have.

She comes to bed with damp hair. My T-shirt goes halfway down her thighs. I swallow hard. Not only will I never throw away that stupid shirt, I might sleep with it under my pillow.

"I'm going to shower, too. You can borrow my phone charger if you need to. It's on the nightstand."

"Thanks."

I pause in the bathroom door. She gets on the bed and crawls over to my side for the charger. Her shirt rides up, and I glimpse my underwear. Holy shit. Does she have any idea how incredibly sexy that is?

She catches me ogling and instantly gets under the covers.

I take the fastest shower in history, not wanting her to think I'm in here whacking off even though I want to. Even though my balls are as blue as the sky at high noon. She's wearing my fucking underwear.

Three minutes later, I cross to my suitcase wearing only a towel. She's doing something on her phone. Her head stays down, but her eyes follow me like the eyes of a woman who wants a man. But how could she after what I told her? Even if she could get past my fucked-up life—*I* can't.

I pull on sweatpants and brush my teeth, then get into bed, making sure to give Ella the vast majority of space. The last thing I want is for her to feel uncomfortable. A sick feeling washes over me. I switch off the light. "You know you don't have to worry," I say, hoping she understands my meaning.

"I know. I trust you, Liam."

She taps on her phone a while longer, then puts it down and settles into her pillow. Her breathing becomes slow and steady. She's falling asleep. I wonder if she knows how lucky she is that she can do it so quickly. Then again, we had a long day.

I'm too hot in the sweatpants, so I remove them, careful not to wake her. I'm glad I put on skivvies underneath. I'd hate for her to wake and find me naked in bed next to her.

Two hours later, I stare at the clock for the hundredth time, wishing I had a bottle of whiskey. Sometimes when I can't sleep, I turn on the TV, but I don't want to wake her. She makes a few noises and turns toward me. I can see her face by the light of the clock. For the next hour I watch her breathe. She's so peaceful that it brings me joy and hurts at the same time. But the best part is that her peace somehow brings me some, and I drift off.

Hours later, I squint against the sun coming through the window and realize the hand on my chest isn't my own. My heart beats rapidly. I've never allowed this before. I don't move, and it dawns on me that it's because I don't want her to wake up and take her hand away.

She's lying on her side, her hair covering her eyes, shielding it from the light. Her pillow is inches from mine. Her face is close, and I can feel the warmness of her breath. But her hand is the only part of her touching me.

I look at the clock, amazed I slept for six hours. I can't remember a time I slept through the night when I wasn't in some kind of liquor-induced coma. I love having her next to me.

I stare at her full lips and remember kissing her. I don't kiss women. I'm twenty-four years old, and she's the only one I've ever truly kissed. I tried a few times in college, but it was awkward and forced—me trying to prove something to myself. I don't kiss women.

Her eyes open. It takes her a few seconds to remember why I'm in bed with her, then she pulls back, embarrassed. "Sorry, habit I guess."

"Corey?"

"Not really. I'm a cuddler, but he never liked it. He said I was too restless, and he's a light sleeper. I guess it's why we never moved in together." She laughs softly. "When I think back, there were so many signs that we shouldn't have been together."

"Then why stay with him?"

"I fell in love. That's what you do, right? Fall in love, get married, have a few kids."

"You want kids?"

"Sure. Doesn't everyone?"

I stare blindly at the ceiling. "Some people shouldn't have them."

"God, Liam. I'm sorry."

"You said kids, plural. You want a big family? Do you come from one?"

"It's just me. I had a sister once. We were twins, but she died at birth. My mom thinks it's why I'm such a cuddler, because I had nine months in the womb with my sister."

"I'm sorry."

"I don't remember her obviously, but my whole life it's felt like something was missing. How can I miss her when I didn't even know her?"

I close my eyes and let my head sink into the pillow. "I miss my brother."

"Is he back home?"

I shake my head.

She sighs. "Oh, no. How old were you when it happened?"

"Almost twelve. Luke was fifteen."

"Twelve. Wow. It's a tough age for any kid, let alone when you lose a brother."

"You have no idea. It was all *his* fault."

She touches my arm to comfort me, but I jerk away.

"Liam, you can talk to me."

"No, I can't."

"I know what happened to you. At least I think I do."

I sit up abruptly, and the sheet falls away, exposing the scars on my outer thigh. I cover up, but she sees them anyway. I turn away. "Then you know how truly fucked up I am."

"If you really think that, you've let him win. He's taken so much from you already. Don't let him take your future."

"I don't even know what that means, El."

"It means you can have anything you desire, Liam. A happy life. Love. If you want it."

I crane my neck around and stare at her. "You don't know what you're saying."

She puts a gentle hand on my back. I flinch, and she takes it away. "I know exactly what I'm saying. I want to know what you're going to do about it."

Chapter Twenty-four

Ella

I all but threw myself at him. For weeks I haven't thought of Corey. I only think about the kiss, and how much I want Liam.

Since that night, we've shared the same hotel room but not the same bed. We sometimes gaze at each other from across the room in the darkness. He wants me, but he's scared. Of what happened to him? Of letting me in?

He runs ahead of me, and I stare at his legs. I want to ask him about the scars. They aren't visible when he's in a bathing suit or running shorts. Is it something his father did? Or did he hurt himself *because* of what his father did?

He's become a fast runner. Some days I have a hard time keeping up with him. "Slow down, Liam."

He jogs backward while I catch up.

I run up next to him. "You need to remember your legs are a lot longer than mine."

"Maybe I'm just trying to impress you."

"You did that a long time ago."

He cocks a brow. "Are we talking about running?"

"Maybe. Maybe not." I smile and run ahead.

"Wait. Just how impressed are you? I mean there's so much of me that's impressive."

"Don't get cocky."

"Well, if you saw my—" He stops talking and shakes his head like he's mad at himself.

"If I saw your what?" I say, teasing.

"Nothing. Let's finish."

The spring in his step is gone. It makes me sad. He was going to joke about me seeing his penis. He jokes all the time with the guys about stuff like that, but not with me. It's like he thinks if he teases me, he'll have to do something about it.

I wish he *would* do something about it. He's holding back big time. It's not like he's never been with girls before. I know about Ronni. And I've heard drunken stories from Garrett about how Liam used to be with the ladies … sometimes more than one.

Used to. Not anymore. Because of me?

After our run, we sit on the sand, enjoying what's left of the morning. I think about how there's only a little more than a week left of the tour. "What are your plans when you go back home?"

"I plan on running five days a week," he says. "You're going with me, right?"

"Of course, but that's not what I meant. What's next for Reckless Alibi?"

"Hard to say. It depends on what happens as the result of all this."

"Do you think you'll go on more tours?"

"That would be the goal. You'll come, won't you?"

I'm unsure what he's asking.

"If we go on tour again, you'll come with me, right? Because it's working. I've got some great material for another album. Bria and Crew are working on the lyrics. We'll probably be in the recording studio by mid-May."

"It depends on what happens as the result of this."

He picks up a shell and throws it. "If you're talking about you and me, you know it can't happen."

I stare blankly at the sand.

"You've become one of my best friends, El. Isn't that enough?"

"Best friends talk, Liam. After more than a month, I feel I hardly know you."

"You don't want to know me."

"That's where you're wrong. I want to know the good stuff and the bad. I want to stay up late and swap stories. I want to know how old you were when you learned how to ride a bike. I want to know who you took to the prom."

"I got a bike when I was seven. I didn't go to prom."

"Come on, Liam. Can't you even try?"

He stands. "We'd better get going. We leave for Tallahassee in two hours."

~ ~ ~

The entire ride up, Liam gazed out the window. He barely said two words to me, let alone his bandmates. I contemplated not even going to tonight's gig at the bar but changed my mind at the last minute. If this is one of the last times I see them play, I'm not going to waste it brooding in a hotel room.

I find a table off to the side and sip a Diet Coke as they play.

"Mind if we join you?" a man asks. Another man hovers at his shoulder. "There aren't any other tables, and I noticed you're here alone."

"I'm not here alone." I gesture at the stage. "I'm with them."

"You know the band?"

"Yes. Go ahead and sit if you want."

"Thanks. Can I buy you a drink?"

I raise my soda. "No, thanks."

"Which one are you with?"

I wish I could say I'm with Liam, but I'm not. "Nobody in particular. We're all friends."

"I'm Paul Julian," the taller one says. "And this is Sam Edenton."

I shake their hands. "Ella Campbell."

Liam stares at the men the entire first half of the set. When they break, he comes over. "Want to introduce me to your friends?"

"Paul and Sam, uh, sorry, I don't remember your last names. This is Liam Campbell."

Paul says, "You're her brother?"

Liam puts an arm around my shoulder. "No."

"But she said—"

Liam pulls me closer. "Does it look like I'm her fucking brother?"

The men are confused but don't press the issue. They probably think one of us is lying. I glance at Liam's hand on my shoulder. One of us *is*.

"Your music is good," Sam says. "What's your band's name?"

"Reckless Alibi," Liam says. He summons a waitress. "Can I get a whiskey?"

I'm upset with his order. I don't like it when he drinks too much.

"Looks like the little woman isn't happy," Paul says.

"Make it a Coke," Liam calls to the waitress. "The wife wants me sober. I perform better that way." He turns to the guys and smirks. "And not just onstage."

I don't know if I should be amused or pissed. I decide this is my chance to test the limits. "Sorry for the deception," I say to the men. "I don't like to brag about my husband. I keep it a secret."

I put my hand on his thigh. He stiffens. I think he's going to pull away, but he doesn't want to break character.

"How long have you been married?" Sam asks.

Liam kisses my temple. "Not long. This tour is kind of like our honeymoon. Isn't it, sweetie?"

"It sure is, baby." I grab his chin and kiss him.

Liam caresses my jaw. "I can't wait to get you home tonight."

What he's doing—touching me, enticing me—is like a fantasy come true. I know it's for show. The second Paul and Sam aren't watching, he'll take his hands off me. And I know how much I'll miss them.

"Well, congratulations," Paul says, lifting his drink when the waitress comes back with Liam's soda. "To the newlyweds."

"I'd better get back," Liam says. He stands and holds out his hand. "Why don't you come with me, sweetie? You can watch from backstage."

"Anything for you, Mr. Campbell."

~ ~ ~

I can't sleep. I keep thinking of what it felt like to be a couple, even if it was only for five minutes and we were pretending. I turn over in bed and glance at the clock. It's 2:25 a.m. Liam is staring at me. I don't say anything. He doesn't either. We just lie here and watch each other.

Minutes go by. My eyelids grow heavy, but they fly open when he speaks.

"I was eleven the first time I played guitar."

I remain silent. I'm afraid if I talk, he'll stop.

"Luke got one when he broke his leg and couldn't play baseball. He didn't want it. I didn't know why until after he died. But because he knew I loved it, he learned how to play and taught me songs." His voice cracks. "Because it was Luke's, it made me feel closer to him after he was gone."

A tear slips from the corner of my eye and is absorbed by my pillow. Other than telling me his dad was the one who ruined him, this is the most personal information I've heard from him. "Thank you."

He turns away without saying another word.

Chapter Twenty-five

Liam

Thirteen years ago

"I hate leaving you when Dad isn't here," Mom says, picking up her jacket.

Luke looks happy. He's been happier this week than I've seen him in a while. Mom is always saying he's more hormonal than a teenage girl. "I'm fifteen," he says. "It's not like I can't look after him."

"I'm almost twelve," I say. "I don't need a babysitter."

"Of course you don't," Mom says. "I just think all kids need a parent around."

Luke snorts. "And some are better off without them."

I don't think she heard him. She dances over and plants a kiss on both our heads. She's happy, too. A huge bouquet of flowers was delivered earlier today. Dad is always giving her stuff. She says it makes her feel special. She leans over and smells them on her way out. "We're lucky to have him, aren't we?"

Luke stomps away.

"Don't worry," Mom says. "He'll be back soon. Don't forget to turn off the oven when you take dinner out."

Luke is playing video games in the living room. "You okay?"

"Better than ever," he says, not looking up.

I sit next to him and watch. It feels strange not having Dad here. Usually when Mom goes to work, he's just getting home. We eat, play games, talk. Luke spends more time in his room lately, but Dad says that's normal. He jokes to me about Luke liking his magazines more than he likes us.

But he's been gone for more than a week. Uncle Dirk sent him to some car conventions. Dirk usually goes, but this year he couldn't because he's helping a politician on his campaign. Dad says Uncle Dirk has political aspirations, whatever that means. He says he wouldn't be surprised if he became president one day.

After eating the casserole Mom left, Luke gets out his guitar and teaches me another song. "I can't wait until I have my own. Dad promised I'd get one next month."

"Don't believe everything he says."

I narrow my eyes at him. Luke has been acting strange ever since he found my magazine a few weeks ago. "What do you mean?"

"Nothing. You can have mine if I'm ever not around anymore."

"You mean when you go to college?"

He bites his cheek. "Yeah, that's what I mean."

It looks like he wants to say more, but he goes back to teaching me the song. I love learning from him, and this week, I've learned more than ever because Luke hasn't locked himself in his room like he usually does. Maybe he thought I was lonely without Dad here.

I stay up past my bedtime again. Luke promises not to tell.

When I finally get into bed, I look out the window at the moon, confused. It's been almost two weeks since Dad crawled into my bed. It's funny, but I've gotten used to the smell of him on my sheets. He wears this cologne that makes him smell like peppermint. But Mom washed them a few days ago, and the smell is gone.

I reach into my sleep pants. I can't help but think about something he always says. "It's better this way, when someone else does it."

The thing is I don't know if it is. It's different, but better? I'm not even sure I like it. But I don't like vegetables either, and I'm still required to eat them. My body craves it, though. The buildup, release, and closeness.

Am I crazy to want him to walk through the door? How can I want something that makes me feel bad inside?

I hear a noise across the hall. Sounds like Luke has gone to bed. I stare at the door so long, I don't know how late it becomes. I get out of bed, the craving between my legs outweighing the warning in my head. I cross the hall and open Luke's door as quietly as I can. My heart races when I sit on the bed and then crawl in next to him, careful not to wake him. I listen to him breathe for a while.

Then I reach around and grab him *there*.

A sound comes from him. It's the sound Sally makes when we leave the house. It's a small, sad howl.

He bolts upright and turns on the light. He glares at me, looking sick and confused. "What the fuck are you doing?"

He's looking at me in disgust. I feel stupid because I've obviously done something terribly wrong. Will Dad get mad? Will Mom hate me? Will we have to go back to the tiny apartment?

I spring out of bed and race back to my room. He follows, ripping open my door and turning on my light. "Liam, for Christ sake, tell me what's going on." He paces in jerky strides. "Does he …" He stops, rubs his eyes, and looks right at me. "Does he touch you?"

I shrug, not knowing what I'm allowed to reveal.

He moves closer, angry. "You know what I'm asking, Liam. Does he fucking touch you?"

I lower my eyes and nod, feeling ashamed.

He falls to his knees, groaning. Then he vomits on my floor.

I hop out of bed. "Are you okay?"

"No, I'm not fucking okay." He takes deep ragged breaths. "I have to clean this mess up before Mom gets home."

He leaves and comes back minutes later with spray cleaner and paper towels. He cleans my floor. He gets up to leave.

"Are you mad at me?" I ask, tears in my eyes.

His shoulders slump. "No, Liam, I'm not mad at you. I'm mad at myself. Go to sleep."

He's mad at himself? Why? For not letting me in his bed? For throwing up?

When I get up to use the bathroom, I hear something across the hall. Then I slide down the wall until I'm sitting on the floor, and I listen to my older brother cry himself to sleep

Chapter Twenty-six

Ella

Every night he gives me another small peek into his past. He told me how he became friends with Crew when he was seven and lived down the street from him. About starting a garage band with him when they were teens. Naked Whale—what a funny name for a band. He told me how they broke up when something terrible happened to Crew's high school girlfriend; and how they formed Reckless Alibi years later.

I'm trying to see Liam from my bed, but I can't. The clock on the nightstand isn't illuminated in this hotel, like it is in most others. The drapes are heavy, and there's no moon. It's almost pitch-black but for a sliver of light shining under the door.

It's like part of my night is missing if I can't watch him before falling asleep.

My bed creaks. My heart stops, then pounds as he lies down behind me. I turn and face him.

"I couldn't see you from over there," he says.

I smile, knowing he was feeling the same as me. I can just make out his face. "Me neither."

"I don't want to keep you up," he says. "I know it's late. I just needed to see you."

Neither of us says another word. Eventually, we drift off to sleep.

~ ~ ~

The bed shakes. It takes me a second to realize Liam's still in it. He's the reason the bed is shaking. *He's* shaking. I touch his shoulder, but he doesn't wake up. I put my hand on his chest. "Liam!"

A pained cry escapes him. "No!" he shouts and pins me to the mattress. It's still dark, but not so much I can't see how angry he is. How afraid. He looks ready to kill me. Then he sees it's me.

I touch his cheek. "It's okay."

I barely get the words out before he leans down and kisses me. At first, it's harsh and demanding, but then it turns into something soft, inviting, incredible. His erection presses into me, and I arch my back. I'm afraid to touch him. It might break the spell.

He moans into my mouth. My body is on fire. Never have I wanted a man this much. His lips graze my chin and up my jaw. They touch me in such a sensual way that every single one of my nerves is hyperaware. It's everything I can do not to run my hands down his back, up his arms, around his neck. When he grinds into me, my willpower fails, and I grab the globes of his ass.

He immediately pulls back and rolls off me, putting distance between us. There is no sound other than our heavy breathing. The tension in the air is suffocating.

"It can never go beyond this," he says.

"Why?"

"Because you'll say what everyone does. That I'm a pervert."

"Why? What usually happens next, Liam?"

"You don't want to know."

I'm afraid and curious at the same time. I've trusted him since we met. He's never given me a reason not to. But what if he hurts women? What if his dad taught him it's the only way? Suddenly, I'm the one who's shaking. "Tell me."

It's still dark. I wonder if that's the only reason he tells me about his past. Maybe it's easier to talk when you can't see the expressions of the person you're talking to.

"I don't kiss girls, Ella. I fuck them."

"You kissed *me*."

He sighs. "You're different."

"So maybe *we* could be different."

"No." He turns away and stares at the ceiling. "I fuck them. Or I watch them do things to each other. But they never touch me."

"I don't understand. How can you make love to someone without them touching you?"

He laughs painfully. "You think I make love to them? No, El. I've never done that. I told you, I fuck. And they never touch me. Nobody will ever touch me again."

I inch closer. "I want to, Liam."

"No."

"But a minute ago, when you were on top of me, we were touching."

"That's different."

"It's my hands you don't want touching you?"

"Yes."

"But that night in Orlando, I woke up with my hand on your chest. Why was it okay then?"

"I don't know."

"Can I put my hand on your chest?"

"Ella," he warns.

I inch closer. "I'm going to do it."

He inhales sharply when I touch him, but he doesn't run away screaming so I leave my hand where it is. I leave it there until I fall asleep.

~ ~ ~

A sliver of light through the drapes wakes me. My head is on Liam's chest, and his arm is around me. I've been touching him all night. I want to wake up every morning with him in my arms.

But he doesn't want that. He doesn't want me to touch him. I lie here and cry quietly, thinking of a boy so traumatized by his father that he thinks he can't have a normal relationship. What did he do to him? Horrible thoughts bombard me as I think of the possibilities. I won't ask him. I can't. It might destroy me having to hear it. Maybe even as much as it would destroy him having to say it.

His breathing changes. "I know you aren't sleeping."

"I didn't want to ruin the moment."

He rubs my arm gently. "I like this, El. I like you, more than any woman I've ever met. But this would be a disaster. You'd hate me and I couldn't bear that."

"But this is okay? What we're doing right now?"

"You'd want more, and I'm incapable of it."

"Maybe eventually—"

"I'm not what you want, Ella. You deserve better."

I lift my head and look at him. "So do you, Liam. You deserve so much more."

He gently pushes me off him. "You're wrong."

He gets out of bed and disappears into the bathroom, slamming the door. The door pops back open a bit. The water turns on. I sit up. I can see him through the crack in the door. He slides down the wall to the floor. His head is in his hands, and he's shaking.

I've never felt more helpless in my life.

Chapter Twenty-seven

Liam

She sits at her art desk, sketching, a sandal dangling playfully off her big right toe. Every once in a while, she'll stop and glance at me. I'm on the bed with the guitar, composing a tune.

"It's beautiful," she says. "Is it new?"

I nod, jotting notes on the sheet music. I play faster and harder to get rid of the feeling of wanting her so bad, it fucking hurts.

"How do you do that?" she asks. "Your fingers move so fast, and you don't even look at them."

"Muscle memory."

"Can you teach me?"

"You want to learn to play guitar?"

"Sure." She sits next to me on the bed. "If you'll trust me with it, that is." I hand it to her, and she smiles. She strums and then laughs. "It's not as easy as it looks." She scoots over and sits between my legs.

"What are you doing?"

"It'll be easier to show me if I can put my hands on yours." She snuggles back against me.

"I know what you're doing, El."

"I'm learning how to play. Now show me."

I wrap my arms around her and put my left hand on the fretboard. She places her fingers on top of mine. "This is an E-minor chord. It's the easiest. Strum like this with your other hand."

I'm instantly hard. The two things that turn me on more than anything else in this world are in my arms.

We play for a while, her strumming and me doing the chords. I teach her each part of the guitar. She seems genuinely interested, but I think she's only doing it to be close to me. Maybe she thinks she'll wear me down or something. I only wish it were that easy.

Someone knocks on the door. "Can you get it?" I ask. "I'll be right back."

I slip into the bathroom and splash cold water on my face until my erection wanes. Ella lets out an excited squeal. I open the door and see her hugging Jeremy.

"Liam! Guess what? IRL is buying my sketch for the new album cover."

"No shit?"

Jeremy nods. "It's true."

"How did it happen?" Ella asks. "Ronni hates me."

"Ronni hates everyone," I say. "I'd be worried if she didn't hate you."

"I didn't tell her it was yours," Jeremy says.

I laugh boisterously. "Nice. I want to be there when she finds out who drew it."

"I'd wait until Ella cashes the check," he says.

"Look at you," I tell her. "Children's book illustrator and now rock album artist. You have quite the résumé."

"It's because of you," she says. "Thank you."

"No, thank *you*. It's going to be a great album. You contributed a whole lot more than the cover."

She turns red. Jeremy clears his throat. "Well, I'll leave you to it. See you tonight." He goes to the door. "Hard to believe we only have two more performances. I think I'm going to miss Florida."

After he leaves, Ella sits on her bed looking sad.

"What is it?" I ask.

"It just hit me that this will all be over soon."

I smile. "And to think six weeks ago you didn't even want to come."

"I've had so much fun. It's going to be strange being back home, where my days will be so normal and mundane."

I want to ask her if she'll miss seeing me every day, but I don't. "Ouch, Ella. It hurts my ego that you think being friends with a rock star will be normal and mundane."

"Is that all we are? Friends?"

I feel the wall go up. "Don't." I get my running shorts and head to the bathroom.

A few minutes later, we're at the beach. It's become easier for me to talk when we run. "You were right, you know. I think I'll be ready for a 10K soon. Maybe we can enter one in New York."

"That would be fun."

It starts raining. Beachgoers quickly pack up their things and jog to their cars. The raindrops make little divots in the sand. The dunes turn a shade darker as the wetness soaks in. "We should find cover."

"Let's run through it."

A dark cloud is approaching. "Ella, it's raining pretty hard to the west."

She gazes at me thoughtfully. "My dad once told me that buffalo instinctively head into a storm."

"Huh?"

"Buffalo. They don't try to avoid a storm," she says. "It's the strangest thing. They don't stand still, and they don't run away from it. They walk right through it. It's almost like they know the storm will be over faster if they face it head on. They know they will come out the other side much quicker than if they stand still or try to run from it."

I stare at the sky knowing she's not really talking about buffalo at all. "I don't want to run through it, El."

"Why not?"

I take a step toward the boardwalk. "Maybe I'm afraid I won't come out the other side."

She takes my hand. "What if I say I want to help you get through it?"

I pull away. "I'd say that's something nobody can do."

I get out my phone and summon an Uber.

~ ~ ~

"Crew's here to see you," Ella shouts through the bathroom door.

I quickly dress and join them. "Hey, what's up?"

"Can we talk?" he asks, motioning toward the door.

"Yeah, sure."

"You're coming tonight, Ella?"

"I wouldn't miss it."

Out in the hall, he leans against the wall. "What is it?" I ask. "You seem nervous."

He reaches into his pocket and pulls out a small velvet box. He opens it, and there's a ring inside.

"Holy shit. You're really going to do this?"

"I want to do it tonight at the show."

"Why not wait until the last performance?"

"Do you remember that day last year when you all confronted Bria and me with the addendum you wanted us to sign because you thought we were having a relationship?"

"Yeah."

He opens his notebook and finds a page. He points to the date on the top. It's today's date, one year ago. I read the lyrics and recognize the song from our second album. "That's the day you wrote this?"

"It's the day I knew I wanted to be with her, but I couldn't admit it to you or myself. It's the day I felt there could be more, when I thought there was a chance of getting past all the shit that happened. That's why I need to do it tonight. I'm going to do it right after this song." He glances behind him to make sure we're still alone. "Then I'm going to sing a new one. Just me on the keyboard. And there's something else. I found out her dad lives in the next town over. They haven't had a relationship in a long time. I reached out to him, and he said he'd come to the show."

I grab his shoulder. "She's going to flip out. I couldn't be happier for you."

"Do you think she'll be okay with me doing it onstage?"

"I don't think she'd want it any other way."

"You'll tell the guys?"

"Sure."

"Don't say anything to Ella, okay? I know how close she and Bria are now, and I wouldn't want her to spoil it."

"My lips are sealed."

"You'll stand up with me, won't you? As my best man?"

My throat tightens. "You know I will, brother."

"I can't believe it's going to happen." He inclines his head to my door. "You know, it's not impossible."

"What's not?"

"You and Ella. I know you think it is. And I get that my shit was different than yours, but maybe one of these days, you'll feel like I did—that there could be more. I really want that for you, Liam."

The door opens and Ella appears. She's surprised to see us standing in the hall. "Oh, hi. Bria called. I'm meeting her at the souvenir shop next door to pick out some things for everyone back home." She looks at me and then Crew. "Everything all right?"

"Couldn't be better," Crew says.

"Bye then. Be back soon."

After she gets on the elevator, Crew snorts. He pats me on the shoulder. "What was it you told me last year? Get over your shit and fuck already?"

"Fucking isn't the problem, man." I rub my chest.

The feeling inside me—it hurts something awful.

"It's everything else."

Chapter Twenty-eight

Ella

I sit on a beach towel on the grass and watch Reckless Alibi play their second-to-last show. It's hard to believe we've been here six weeks. I don't want it to end. While I miss New York and my friends, I know everything will change when we get off the plane at JFK on Sunday.

Crew is especially energetic on stage tonight. I guess he's trying to get the most out of the last few concerts.

What will happen to them after this tour? When they go back home, will they get recognized? Will they be in high demand? Liam told me the whole point of going to Florida over spring break was to garner new fans from all over the country. Millions of young people vacation here, and the hope is they will see Reckless Alibi and then go back and tell their friends.

I see a couple familiar faces front and center. The girls have been following the band, coming to almost every concert. I'm pretty sure Garrett has slept with both of them.

Crew runs offstage after a song, and I straighten. Their set is always the same. He's never done this before.

He returns moments later, walks over to Bria, and sits her on a stool next to the keyboard. She seems confused. The rest of the band is smiling. Liam winks at me.

Crew takes the mic and speaks to the crowd. "What most of you don't know is that this woman is the reason we're on this tour. A little more than a year ago, she joined Reckless Alibi. Before her, we were an all-male band. But something was always missing." He turns to her. "Something was missing from more than just the band."

He pulls a small box from his jeans pocket and gets down on one knee. The audience screams and then goes silent. Bria's jaw drops and she stifles a happy cry.

He takes the ring from the box. "Brianna Cash, you've saved me in so many ways, professionally and personally. Writing lyrics with you is fun, rewarding, and if I might say, a huge turn-on."

The audience snickers.

"You're my best friend, my inspiration, my soon-to-be roommate. We've made incredible memories on this tour, but this is only the beginning. I can't wait to write more songs about our life together and the amazing journey we're about to begin. About the children we bring into the world."

Bria cries. Her hands steeple over her nose and then she wipes away tears.

I expect Liam to be watching them, like everyone else. He's not. His eyes are on *me*.

"After I bought this ring last week, I wrote a song. I want to sing it for you. But first you have to say the one word I'm looking for." He holds the ring out. "Will you please marry me and be my partner in life? My writing buddy. My co-lead singer. My wife?"

She slides off the stool onto her knees in front of him. She puts her hands on either side of his face. "Yes."

Cheers and whistles erupt from the crowd as he slips the ring on her finger and they kiss. Crew helps her back on the stool, picks up the mic, and says, "Bear with me. My hands are shaking, and I promised her a song."

He serenades her with one of the most emotional songs I've ever heard. His voice cracks several times. I'm sure there isn't a dry eye in the place. Even some of the men are surreptitiously wiping their cheeks. Liam is standing off to the side with Brad and Garrett. He glances at me and smiles. But it's a sad smile.

My heart thunders and then falls when I realize I'm in love with a man I've only known for seven weeks. A man who thinks he's damaged beyond repair and can never have a real relationship.

And I cry.

After Crew's song, they finish their set and then he carries Bria offstage. Tom lets me back to congratulate them. I'm hugging her when she stiffens. "Dad?"

An older man approaches. "I hope it's okay that I came. Chris called last week and thought I'd want to be here. I decided I've missed too much of your life already."

Bria runs into his arms. Her dad basically checked out of her life when her mom died on 9/11. Her brother, Brett, practically raised her. She hasn't seen her father in five years, not since the day she graduated high school and he moved to Florida.

A proposal and a reunion on the same day. She's one lucky girl.

The band goes out front to sign autographs. I follow. The two familiar girls are the first to get to them. "Liam!" one of them screams. He walks over. The short blonde girl jumps on him. He has no choice but to catch her. She locks her legs around his waist. "Take me home tonight."

"Uh …" He glances at me.

"Give me something to remember you by," she says loudly. "I promise you'll never forget it."

He puts her down and motions to Jeremy. Jeremy throws him a T-shirt, and Liam gives it to the girl. "How about this?"

The girl eyes the shirt and smiles deviously. Then, right here in front of hundreds of people, she takes her shirt off, exposing her bare chest, and slowly, making sure Liam gets a good look, puts on the Reckless Alibi tee.

She leans close and whispers something to him. He shakes his head, then moves to another group of fans. She pouts and stomps away.

Girl after girl fawns over him, all wanting a piece of him. It dawns on me that I'm one of them, wanting a man I can never have.

~ ~ ~

"There you are," Liam says, easing into a squat beside me. "I've been looking everywhere for you. Mind if I sit?"

I make room for him on my towel. Bright moonlight cuts a path across the water, giving me something to look at other than him.

He elbows me. "That was some show, huh?"

"I'm happy for them."

"They deserve it after everything they've been through."

I dig my toes into the cool sand. "So do you."

"Can we not have this conversation again?"

I lean my head against his shoulder. He doesn't pull away.

"You're emotional," he says. "He proposed and sang her a love song, and they're going to ride off in the sunset or some shit like that. And now you want what they have."

"That's not true," I lie.

"What do you want then?"

"You. I want you, Liam." He lies back, and I lie next to him. "We could be together, you know. I don't have to touch you."

"I won't be with you that way. It's … dirty."

"Even if I say it's okay?"

"I can't, El. Not like that. Not with you."

"Can I just lie with you then?"

A long sigh escapes him, then he moves his arm so I can snuggle into him. I put my head on his chest, then my hand, hoping he doesn't protest.

His heart pounds under my ear as he strokes my hair. We listen to the sound of the waves lapping on the beach. I dare to trace the outline of his nipple. He sucks in a breath, leans in, and presses his lips to my forehead. It's the most sensual gesture he's made. I crane my neck and look up at him. "Kiss me."

He doesn't move.

"Kiss me, Liam."

"Ella."

"You've done it twice. We both know what it feels like. I know you want to, and you think about it as much as I do. I want you to kiss me. I want you to touch me." I take his hand and put it on my breast. "Please."

He pushes me onto the ground and gets on top of me, closing his fingers around my wrists and pinning my hands above my head. He gazes into my eyes, his pupils large and inviting, then he lowers his mouth to mine. When my lips part for him, he growls. It's desperate. It's sexy. I close my eyes, wanting it to last forever. Needing it to be enough. Every time we kiss, it's better than the one before.

He frees my hands so he can touch me, skimming a finger down my side, making me shiver. He puts a hand between us to hold my breast. His touch is as gentle as his kiss. How can he be this caring, this sensual, and be afraid of what comes next?

His lips find mine again. His tongue becomes more demanding. I'm putty in his arms, willing to do whatever it takes to have him. When my fingers weave through his hair, he rolls off me, breaking all contact.

"I'm sorry," I say.

"That's the thing." He scrubs a hand across his stubble. "You shouldn't have to be."

I put my head back on his chest like it was before. "It's okay, Liam."

"Nothing about this is okay. It can never be more than this, El."

I'm careful not to touch him where I shouldn't. "Then this will have to be enough."

His chest rises sharply and then falls, his heavy breath displacing the hair on top of my head. "Until it isn't."

Tears roll down the side of my face and drop on his chest. I wonder if he can feel the wetness through his shirt.

We lie like that for hours. And I fall asleep in his arms.

Chapter Twenty-nine

Liam

Thirteen years ago

Luke leaves me by Uncle Dirk's pool and heads to the house.

"Where are you going? You're the one who asked Mom to drop us here."

"I have to use the bathroom."

"Pee in the pool. We do it all the time."

He shakes his head. "Not this time."

I laugh. "Oh, you have to go number two."

He looks sad. Maybe he's tired from last night. I'm tired too, because I sat outside his door and listened for hours, wondering if he was mad at me.

"Liam, I want you to know …" He stops talking and looks like he's about to cry—but he'd never cry in front of me, he's too big for that.

"What?" I ask.

"Nothing. Just … you're a good brother, is all."

I smile, finally feeling like maybe he's not mad at me after all. "You're a good brother, too."

I work on perfecting my cannonball. I'll never be as good as Luke. He's a lot bigger than I am.

Aunt Sylvia appears when I surface after a really good one. "Hey there, Liam. Do you and Luke want to stay for dinner, or did your mom leave something at the house?"

I try and remember what Mom said but can't. "I think we can stay. What are you having?"

"Helen said she'd make your favorite."

"Cheeseburgers?"

"You betcha."

"We're definitely staying."

"Good. I'll go let her know. When's your dad coming back?"

"Tomorrow."

"I'll bet you'll be excited to have him home."

I think about everything that happened last night. I thought I would be happy to have him back. Now, though, I'm not so sure. I'm all mixed up. He's my dad, and I love him, but a part of me thinks something is wrong, especially after Luke cussed at me. It scared me. But worse, *he* looked scared. My stomach is in knots. "Yeah," I say, because I'm sure it's what she expects.

I sit on the edge of the pool for a long time. Where is Luke? The sun starts to set, and there's a chill in the air. I wrap up in a towel when I see Uncle Dirk walking toward me.

"Where's your brother? Dinner's almost ready."

I shrug. "He went to use the bathroom, but that was a while ago. Maybe he's sick. I don't think he's feeling well."

"Great. That's all I need, someone making me sick."

A loud popping sound draws our attention to the house. I look at Dirk to ask him what it was, but he's as white as a ghost.

He touches my shoulder. "Stay put."

He runs up the path to the house, almost tripping a few times on the stones. I've never seen Dirk move that fast before, so of course I get up and follow him. At the door, I dry off quickly, knowing how he hates us tracking wet footprints on the hardwood floors. I hear screaming like I've never heard. High-pitched, bloodcurdling screams, like in the movies. I'm scared, so I slowly walk toward them.

Someone races into Uncle Dirk's study. One of his security guys, I think. A moment later, he brings Helen and Aunt Sylvia into the hallway. He points at me. "Keep him out of here."

Helen runs the other way down the hall, crying out in Spanish the whole time. Aunt Sylvia drops to her knees in front of me and wraps me in a hug. She keeps murmuring something about how sorry she is. Sorry for what?

I hear sirens. "Where's Luke?"

Dirk appears in the doorway. He shakes his head at Sylvia, and she covers her mouth and sobs. "Go open the front door for them. Then take Liam into the kitchen and stay there until I come for you."

Aunt Sylvia drags me to the door and props it open. A police car and an ambulance pull into the driveway. "Come quickly," she says and takes me to the kitchen.

"Why are the police here? Where's Luke? Is he in trouble? Why is there an ambulance?"

She points to a chair at the table. "Sit. I'll make you something to eat."

"Aunt Sylvia, why are you crying?"

She looks up at the ceiling and says something about God and strength.

A man appears. I've seen him on the grounds. "Mrs. Campbell, you're needed in the front hallway. I'll stay with the boy."

"I was going to feed him."

"I'll find something for him," he says.

I get up to follow her. The man holds me back. "Stay here, son. Someone will be in soon to talk to you."

"Do you know what's going on?" I ask. "Everyone was yelling and crying. Is this about my brother? Have you seen him? Did he get sick?"

"I don't know anything." He opens the refrigerator. "Do you like turkey? I can make you a sandwich."

I don't feel like eating, but I nod. I watch the door Sylvia went through, knowing something must have happened to Luke. Something bad.

Chapter Thirty

Ella

That's it. They're finished. They've given their last performance. Sung their final song. I sit in the audience at the naval station, already in mourning that it's over.

It's over for me, but not for Reckless Alibi. Their lives will soon change forever. Their songs are streaming all over social media. Online fan groups are forming. Radio stations across the country are playing their tunes.

The usual autograph and picture session after the gig is short. Women in the military don't fawn and grope them like the regular fans. Bruce packs up quickly, and we all pile into the van. Jeremy gives him the name of a bar. "Drinks are on me tonight," he says.

Bria is surprised. "You're coming with us, Jeremy?"

"It's our last night. We should celebrate."

Bria sits next to me in the van. "I'm going to miss this."

"I'm sure you'll be going on more tours," I say.

"I'm not talking about the tour. I'm talking about you. It's been fun having another woman around. Sometimes it's hard being the only girl in all this testosterone."

"I'll miss it, too. You've become a real friend, Bria."

"That's not going to end tomorrow. We all live in the city. We can still hang out." She glances at Liam. "And since I'll be living in the same apartment he is, I'm sure we'll see a lot of each other."

Like everyone else, Bria assumes Liam and I are a thing.

"You're all still going to live together?" I glance at her engagement ring. "Even now?"

"We signed a year's lease. We move in next week."

"I'm sure you can get out of it."

"It's okay. I love these guys. I think it will be fun." Garrett farts loudly, and Bria wrinkles her nose. "For a while anyway."

"If you ever need to get away, you can always come over to my place."

"Girls' night," she says. "I'd like that."

"Me too."

We pull up to the bar, and the van empties. Even Bruce and Tom join us. Shortly after we're seated, a few bottles of expensive champagne are brought to the table.

Brad's eyes widen, and he turns to Jeremy. "I'm glad you're buying."

"You won't blink an eye at things like this soon." He passes a glass to each of us. "A toast to a successful tour. I just heard from Ronni. Record sales are up three hundred and fifty percent in the past six weeks." Boisterous cheers issue from everyone at the table. Before we can drink, Jeremy stops us. "There's more." He gives us a brilliant grin. "Reckless Alibi has broken into the top one hundred."

Stunned faces and gaping jaws ensue.

"What song?" Liam asks.

"'On That Stage' is number ninety-two," he says, raising his glass.

Bria and Crew look at each other and scream. Everyone else joins in.

"Things are about to be a lot different for you when we get home," Jeremy says. "Get ready. You're about to live the life of rock stars."

~ ~ ~

It's the dead of night, but neither of us is sleeping. He's still, but I've learned to tell by his breathing when he's awake. I turn toward him and see his eyes in the bright moonlight.

"Can't sleep either, huh?" he asks.

"No. Are you sad because the tour is over?"

"A little, but that's not why I can't sleep."

"Do you want to talk about it?"

He hesitates. He always hesitates when I ask him about such things. "Today is Luke's birthday. He would have been twenty-seven." After a long pause, he goes on to say, "I wonder a lot what he would have been like as an adult."

"He'd probably still be your annoying big brother."

He laughs sadly. "He was never annoying. I think he was the only one who looked out for me."

"You were lucky to have him."

"I was." His voice cracks.

"He would have been proud of you."

He turns onto his back. "He shot himself. That's how he died."

I'm confused. I thought he told me it was his dad's fault that Luke died. Maybe it was his gun or something. I get out of bed and crawl into Liam's. I put my head on his chest. "You were eleven. I can't imagine how it must have felt to lose him. I'm so sorry."

He caresses my arm. "I lied. I'm not sad because the tour is over."

"You're going to miss me." I feel him swallow and nod. I lift my head. "Kiss me."

This time I don't have to beg. As he kisses me, he pulls me on top of him. His erection grows beneath me. I grind my groin into his, causing the most pleasurable friction. My sleep shirt rides up and only my panties and his boxer briefs are between us. It's the closest we've ever been. Oh, how I want him inside me.

He rolls me off him. "Go back to bed."

"It's our last night, Liam. I want you to touch me. I want to touch you."

He shakes his head with a sharp jerk. "No."

I sit up. "Remember when you showed me how to play the guitar? My hand was on top of yours as you created the chords. What if I could touch you like that? Do you think that would be okay?"

He gets on an elbow. "You want to put your hand on mine while I get myself off?"

"If my hand was on yours, I'd be helping you do it, but I wouldn't be touching you. That's allowed, right?"

His head falls back. He's thinking about it.

"Trust me," I say. "I won't do anything more."

He exhales noisily. "Sometimes when you trust people, they hurt you."

My heart breaks for him. "I'm not people, Liam. I'm me."

I fear he's going to say no, so I push my panties aside and put his hand on me. I put my finger on top of his and then put it on my clit. I rub it around. I guide his finger through my wetness. It feels good to have his hand on me.

"Ella. Jesus."

"I want you, Liam. Any way I can have you."

"Fuck." He stares at me for a moment, my eyes are half-open by the feel of his touch. "You first."

I remove my hand from his and take off my shirt. His mouth is on my breast before my shirt even hits the floor. He sucks my nipple into his mouth and releases it with a 'pop.' He licks it, teases it, traces it, then moves to the other one.

I'm writhing, trying to remember not to touch him, but my need for him is extreme. When he slips a finger inside me, I moan. He crooks it, finding the precise spot that drives me insane. My hips rise off the bed. His thumb is on my clit and bolts of electricity shoot through me. I sigh and moan and twist and explode all at once. "Oh, God," I shout.

He doesn't relent until I go completely lax. "Holy shit, El." He looks at me in awe.

"What is it?" I ask.

"I've never seen it happen like that."

"You've never made a woman orgasm?"

"I've heard it, I've felt it, but I've never seen it."

Heat flames across my face. "You were watching me?"

He brushes a chunk of hair out of my eyes. "It was incredible."

His hardness is against my thigh. "Now you."

He stiffens. "I'm not sure I can."

"Show me how you do it."

He snickers coyly. "After what just happened, I doubt I'll last very long."

"Show me, Liam."

He takes off his skivvies. In the dim light, his penis springs up tall and proud. I have to keep myself from reaching out. We've come this far. I can't ruin it now.

He takes hold of himself, and my insides quiver. I've never watched a man do this. We're naked on his bed, and he's stroking himself up and down. I can see out of the corner of my eye that he's looking at me. Does he have any idea how incredibly turned on I am right now? I swear I can feel another orgasm building and he's not even touching me.

His breathing quickens. "El."

Is he going to let me do it or just finish on his own? I hold out my hand where he can see it, then slowly move until it hovers over his. "I want to make you feel like you made me feel, Liam. Can I?"

He stops, and I think that's it. We're not going any further. But then he closes his eyes and nods.

I don't want his eyes closed. I don't know exactly what his dad did to him, but I sure as hell don't want him seeing his dad behind his eyelids. He has to know it's me. He has to know it's safe.

"Open your eyes," I say.

He looks at my face, then down. I gently place my hand over his. He's gone flaccid. He's probably terrified if what I think is true and the only person who's ever touched him before was his father.

I put his other hand between my legs, showing him how turned on I am. He strokes himself again. I don't grip him hard. I let my hand ride lightly on top of his. He thickens again.

I think he's amused that he's hard. He works himself faster. I have to tighten my grip a little to keep up. While I've given my fair share of hand jobs, none have ever been this intimate. This meaningful.

He stiffens. I can tell he's close. He gazes at me with half-closed eyes.

"That's it," I say, wanting it to be my voice that pushes him over.

His hips buck a few times, then he grunts loudly and stills, hot come spurting over our hands.

I lie down beside him, wiping my hand on the sheet. His lips are pursed. He breathes in and out heavily. His hand falls limp on the bed.

He turns his head toward me and smiles.

I bask in the feel of victory. This may have been the oddest sexual experience I've ever had, but I get the feeling it might have been the most normal one for him. In time maybe we can learn to meet somewhere in the middle.

Chapter Thirty-one

Liam

As the sun rises and shines through the window, I gaze at her sleeping next to me. I haven't gotten a lick of shuteye. At first, her head was on my chest. Then she fell asleep and rolled off sometime early. When it happened, I missed her. She was six inches away, but I missed her. She looked so peaceful. She always looks peaceful. It amazes me how some people have such normal lives that they can just sleep.

I haven't had a decent night's sleep in thirteen years.

Today is Luke's birthday. I should be remembering him, but all I can think about is how she had her hand on mine. Through all the years and all the women, nobody ever suggested doing it that way. Then again, I've never let anyone get as close to me as Ella. I can't imagine many women wanting to put up with my deep layers of shit. Why does *she*? I know she's not in it because of the band. Or the potential for fame and fortune—that's not her. What's so goddamn special about a kid from Stamford who's so fucked up he can barely see straight? She could have so much more.

Her eyes open sleepily and her lips form into a lazy smile. "Morning," she mumbles.

"Good morning."

She scoots closer but doesn't touch me. "Last night was—"

"Fucking strange."

Her smile falls.

I lift on an elbow. "I mean, it was okay, but strange."

"I don't want to push you to do anything you don't want to, Liam."

My head falls back on the pillow. "That's what guys usually say to girls. This is so messed up."

She reaches for my hand. "I like being with you. If a little strange goes along with that, I'm okay with it."

"Why, El? Why in the hell would a girl like you ever want to be with a guy like me?"

"Are you asking me why I like you?"

"I guess I am."

"I once heard someone say we don't choose who we fall, um … like."

I sit up and turn away. That's not what she was going to say. Fuck. I run a hand through my hair and swing my legs off the bed.

"Liam." Her hand touches my back, and I flinch. She immediately removes it.

"I don't know what you think is happening here, but you can't fix me, Ella. No one can."

"That's not true."

"Is that why you like me? You see me as some kind of project? Something broken in need of fixing?"

"Of course not."

I get up and pull on my sweatpants. "We have to pack. We leave in an hour."

"Sit down please."

"Why?"

"Because you asked me a question, and I haven't answered yet."

I sit.

"You want to know why I like you? Maybe it *is* because you're different. You're about as far removed as possible from any man I've ever dated. Pretty much the opposite of Corey. You're talented, intriguing, mysterious, but also gentle and kind. When you're performing, whether it's for me or hundreds of people, you're passionate. Maybe I like you because you saved me that day on the sidewalk. Maybe it's because I'm flattered to have been your inspiration. But you seem to forget, Liam, that you've become mine. You've seen my illustrations for the books. The album cover." She moves over next to me. "Do I want to help you overcome your past? Of course I do. I want you to be happy. But damn it, Liam, you have to stop believing I think you're disgusting. You need to separate what happened to you from who you are. *You* aren't disgusting. You need to stop saying a girl like me shouldn't want a man like you, because guess what? A girl like me *does* want a man like you."

I give her a lopsided grin. "You could have just said because I'm hot."

She falls back and laughs.

I spin around and trap her under me. I lean down and let my lips linger over hers. "I'm not promising anything."

"I'm not asking for any promises."

I kiss her. And as she kisses me back, I swear she's breathing life into me.

~ ~ ~

We get settled on the plane. Jeremy was nice enough to switch seats with Ella, who was several rows back.

Garrett squints at first class. "This is the last time we won't be sitting up there."

We look at each other and smile. Jeremy wasn't kidding about the uptick in sales. Our royalty checks from March were deposited yesterday. They were mind-boggling. April's is going to be even better.

I'm flanked by Ella, who has the window seat, and Garrett. Brad is sitting behind us with Crew and Bria.

Ella leans over. "Is everything okay with Brad? He doesn't seem as excited as the rest of you."

"He hasn't been happy."

"He misses Katie."

"It's his own fault. He chose someone who hates rock and roll."

"The heart wants what it wants," she says.

"Are we still talking about Brad and Katie?"

She smiles.

"I can't believe it's over," Garrett says. "I hope we can get back on the road soon."

"Not likely," I say. "They want us in the studio. Jeremy said IRL is expecting two more albums by the end of the year, not to mention more videos."

"Two?" he says. "You think we can do it?"

Crew and Bria have probably written lyrics to half a dozen songs since they got engaged, and I hear music every goddamn time I look at Ella. "I think we can."

"I've got some lyrics that might work with something," Garrett says.

I tear my eyes away from Ella. "Wait—you?"

"You think those two are the only ones who can write them?"

"No, but you've never said anything before. Why now?"

"Wrote them a long time ago. Didn't want to step on anyone's toes. Then when things started to happen, and you got in your slump. I didn't want to pressure you to put them to music." His eyes dart to Ella and back to me. "Now that you're clearly in a different place, I figured it might be a good time."

"Hell yes. Send them to me when we get home."

"We'll be living together," he says. "I can just hand them to you."

I laugh. "I almost forgot. Everything is changing."

The flight attendant stops by with six glasses of champagne. "From the gentleman in 16C."

We stand and toast Jeremy. After we sit back down, Ella holds up her glass and leans close. "To Luke. Happy twenty-seven."

My throat tightens but I drink. Nobody has ever toasted his birthday with me. Crew and I get shitfaced every year in August on the day he killed himself, but I've always suffered in silence on his birthday.

"You're right," she says. "Everything is changing. Things will be different back home."

She looks sad. I have the urge to hold her hand, but I don't. "*Things* will be different, but *I* won't be. Then again, maybe I will. Maybe I'll be better in some way."

"We won't see each other very much," she says. "It'll be an adjustment."

"What are you talking about? We'll run. And we can hang out."

Her attention shifts to the window. "It sounds like you'll be busy."

"Ella." I wait until she makes eye contact. "I will be busy, but that doesn't mean we can't do things. What about the 10K?"

"I guess there's that."

I want to tell her there can be more, but I'm not sure there can be. I've never been one to give false hope.

"Thank you," she says, finishing off the champagne.

"For what?"

"For the invitation. For … everything." She briefly touches my hand. "I'll never forget these six weeks as long as I live."

The way she says it, it's like we're saying goodbye. And something inside me hurts in a way it never has before.

Chapter Thirty-two

Ella

I barely have my things unpacked when there's a knock on the door. Part of me hopes it's him. That he somehow couldn't bear going home without me. On the way to the door, I see a picture of Corey and me on the bookshelf. It was my favorite. I couldn't bring myself to throw it out, not even after what he did to me.

I flip it facedown.

When I open the door, Krista and Jenn fly inside. "Tell us everything!"

"It's not like I didn't give you weekly updates from the road," I say.

"But we haven't heard anything about the last seven days. We need details."

Details.

The three of us are as close as sisters. But I still haven't shared any information about Liam's past. Not that I'd know what to say. I don't know for sure what happened to him. Only what I've surmised and pieced together from the few things he's told me.

I tell them about Crew's romantic proposal. They'd already seen it; apparently it's all over social media.

"We want the 411 on *Liam*," Krista says. "We know you kissed him. There has to be more."

I almost regret telling them about that. It was the day I booked my early flight back to New York. I called them because I was so confused. They're the ones who talked me into staying. They thought he was being the way he was because he was either a narcissistic musician or he'd been hurt by another woman. I didn't enlighten them.

"We're good friends, that's all."

Jenn says, "Oh, come on. You spent six weeks with the guy. You're his muse. He stayed in your hotel room, El."

"In separate beds."

"I'm not buying it," Krista says. "He's hot. You're hot. No way did you keep your hands off each other."

"I'm telling you we're not a couple."

"Not being a couple doesn't mean you didn't have sex."

I look her in the eye. "We didn't have sex."

"You're saying you never touched the man's cock?"

I make the sign of the cross. "I never touched it, Krista."

Technically, it's true. What I don't say is how much I wanted to feel him with my own hands. Taste him with my mouth. Have him inside me. But I can't talk to them about this. It would be a violation of Liam's trust. I get the feeling the only other person who knows about his past is Crew.

They go through every picture on my phone, no doubt looking for evidence proving we're a couple. Jenn stops on the one Bria took of us at the beach. "Girl, if you think this man isn't into you, you haven't seen this picture."

I take the phone from her and look at the photo.

"Oh my God," Krista says. "You're in love with him."

"I am not."

"Ella, you're a big fat liar. We know you too well. You're clearly in love with Liam Campbell."

I close my eyes and sigh. "Okay, so I'm in love with him."

They scream and dance around.

"Stop it. That doesn't mean he's in love with me. Or even that we're a couple. He has … issues."

Jenn sits down. "Fear of commitment?"

I shrug, because I suppose it would be the best excuse.

"He's a rock star," Krista says. "He probably wants to eat his cake and have it too."

"Don't you let him," Jenn says. "I don't care if he's a rock star or the fucking president, you can't let him do what the dickhead did to you."

I give her a sharp look. "I didn't *let* Corey do anything. There's nothing I could have done differently. He cheated on me despite us having a great relationship."

Krista laughs. "Great relationship? Right. Like him dragging you to cooking classes and boring lectures was a great relationship."

"I meant we were happy together, or at least I thought we were."

Jenn smacks her lips. "He came to see me, you know. A few weeks ago he came to my work. Accused me of knowing where you were, and he wanted to go after you. Said he'd made the biggest mistake of his life."

I look over at the bookshelf where I turned down the picture. "You can say that again."

"Are you still in love with him?" Krista asks.

Jenn scoffs. "She just said she loves Liam."

"Doesn't mean she can't love them both."

"I don't think I love Corey anymore. But I'll always care about him."

"We're calling him Corey again?" Jenn asks. "You've done it twice now."

"I can't hold a grudge forever."

"Especially now that she's with a rock star," Krista says. "In your face, Corey Gorman."

"I'm not *with* anyone, Krista."

"But you want to be."

I think of the picture on my phone. "It's way more complicated than that."

"When are you going to see him again?" Jenn asks.

"I'm not sure."

"You didn't make any plans?"

"He's got a lot going on this week. He's moving into a new apartment, and the band is switching rehearsal studios."

They're excuses I've made for him, but deep down I wonder why we didn't make any plans. When we said goodbye at the airport, I didn't want to seem needy by asking what happens next.

"I still can't believe you went on tour with them," Krista says. "No matter what happens, you'll always be able to say you spent six weeks with Reckless Alibi."

I'll always have Florida.

"How about we order pizza and talk about what the two of you have been doing while I was away?"

A few hours later, they leave, and I get out my sketches and organize them. Jimmy's face reminds me of Liam, and I realize I miss him already.

I put the drawings down and fall heavily on the couch. "What have you gotten yourself into, El?"

After wallowing in self-pity for a few minutes, I decide to go for a run to clear my head. It's hard to turn my brain off, though. When did I become this clingy woman who needs to be reassured? What if everything has changed now that we're back in New York? Maybe being on the road together was different—more romantic somehow. Now that we're back, he'll forget about the things we did. The words we said.

"Shut up," I tell myself. "You're overthinking this."

Later, when I'm in bed, my phone pings with a text. It's after midnight. My heart soars when I see who it's from.

Liam: It's strange, isn't it?

Me: What's strange?

Liam: Not being in the same room.

Me: Yeah.

Liam: Goodnight, Mrs. Campbell.

Me: Goodnight, Mr. Campbell.

I smile, put the phone away, and fall asleep.

Chapter Thirty-three

Liam

Moving day is here. I can hardly contain myself. Technically I moved out of Dirk's house the week before going on tour, but it never felt real until now.

Crew picked up the keys this morning. We're in the elevator, riding up to the eighth floor. "Are you sure you want my old bedroom furniture?" he asks. "I mean, you can afford to buy something new if you want. We all can."

"I'm sure. I'm saving my money."

"For what?"

I glance at Bria and Garrett. They wouldn't understand. I shake my head.

"I hope you don't mind. We picked out living room furniture and a dining table yesterday," Bria says. "Everything is being delivered later this afternoon."

"Better not be covered in flowers and shit," Garrett says.

Crew snorts. "I think you'll find them more than acceptable."

The elevator doors open, and Crew leads the way to the apartment. We step inside and stand in silence for a moment.

"This is really happening," Bria says.

Crew puts an arm around her and smiles.

The living room is larger than I thought it would be, which is nice, considering there are four of us sharing it.

"Wait until you see the kitchen," Bria says. "They put in all new appliances. The refrigerator may even be big enough to hold all your beer."

"Who needs beer?" Garrett says. "Where's the liquor cabinet?"

Crew opens a cabinet under the kitchen bar and pulls out a bottle of whiskey and four glasses.

Garrett grins. "Now we're talking."

"At eleven in the morning?" Bria asks.

Crew pours us each a shot. "We have to toast our new place. Reckless on three?"

Bria shakes her head. "Not that. It doesn't seem right without Brad."

"He had his chance to get in on this," I say. "He's probably picking out china patterns with Katie or some shit like that."

"Hey, now," Bria warns. "Crew and I will be doing the same thing at some point."

Crew looks like he'd rather be strung up by his balls. "China? Really?"

Garrett holds up his glass. "You're leaving me hanging, guys. Can we do this?"

"To our new place," Crew says.

"Boring as shit," Garrett says, "but what the hell."

We clink glasses and drink.

"Which room is mine?" I ask.

Crew points to some doors on the left. "You and Garrett can fight it out. Both bedrooms are about the same size. One has a bigger closet and the other has a better view."

I get a guitar pick out of my pocket and turn to Garrett. "The side with the design on it is heads. The blank side is tails. Call it."

"Tails," he says when it's in the air.

Crew grabs the pick before it lands. "You have to assign something to heads, douchebag."

"No we don't," Garrett says. "If I call it right, I get first choice at the rooms. Now you went and ruined it. It was going to be tails. I know it."

"Sorry," he says. "Maybe you should have explained the rules before you flipped."

I slip the pick back in my pocket. "Take whichever one you want. I don't give a shit. I'm just happy I never have to spend another night under Dirk's roof."

"Yeah, but you're still under his control," Garrett says, peeking in the bedrooms. "We all are."

"Not for long."

Crew asks, "Is that what you're saving money for? To buy us out of the IRL contract?"

"I wish. But it's a million bucks, man. Even at the rate we're earning now, I wouldn't have enough by myself. There are other ways to get out from under him."

"Like what?" Bria asks.

"I'm working on it."

Crew eyes me suspiciously, but he knows better than to air my dirty laundry in front of everyone.

Garrett points. "I'll take that one. I couldn't care less about the closet, but there's an adult toy store down the street I can see from the window. Might be interesting to see who comes and goes."

I laugh and enter my new room, stand in the center of it, and turn around. It feels like freedom.

Hours later, after I've finished putting my bed together and the sun is setting, I unpack boxes, starting with the heavy one. I look at each book as I put it on a shelf. I have every autobiography ever written about guitar players I've worshiped, binders full of sheet music, and books about composing.

A piece of paper sticks out of one of the books. I sit on the bed, staring at it. I had almost forgotten it was there. I'll never forget the day I found it. I was fifteen. I was rummaging through Mom's room for the weed I knew she kept hidden there. I smoked a lot back then, and there was only so much I could get away with stealing from Helen and some of Dirk's other employees. After I found the letter, I smoked everything she had. Then I drank so much vodka, I had to be rushed to the hospital, where they pumped my stomach. She had kept it from me for over three years.

I open it hesitantly.

Liam,

I'm sorry. There are so many things I'm sorry for, I don't even know where to start. The thing that upsets me the most is that I couldn't protect you. I thought you'd be safe. If he was doing those things to me, he wouldn't need you. Last night, I found out how wrong I was. And I can't live with myself, knowing that because I didn't say anything, he got to you. I should have realized the day I found the magazine. It's my fault. I just hope you can forgive me. I tried all night to convince myself you'd come out of it better than me. Maybe you wouldn't be so fucked up by everything. Maybe because you're so much younger, things won't get as bad and you'll be able to forget and move on. Those are the thoughts I'll hold onto.

When I'm gone, things will change. I left notes for Mom and Dirk. I told them it's their job to protect you. I was too ashamed before to say anything. No need for that anymore. I'm not sure if people feel anything after they're dead. I hope they don't, because I'm tired of feeling like this. I'm sorry if telling them brings you shame, but I didn't know what else to do. I hope it will help in some way, because it's the very last thing I get to do as your brother. I loved being your brother, Liam. There's no better brother than you.

I wish we could do our handshake one more time.

Love,
Your big brother, Luke

P.S. Don't stop playing guitar. You're good at it. It's the one thing you've always done better than me.

I drop the letter on my bed, go to the kitchen, and pour myself a shot.

"Still celebrating, are we?" Garrett says.

I pour another and down it. "Let's go out, see what kind of bars are around here."

"I'm game." He yells to the others, "Want to check out the neighborhood scene?"

Bria exits their bedroom and carries a box into the kitchen. Crew takes it from her. "Where do you want it?" She points, and he sets it down.

"You guys go ahead. I'd like to get the kitchen in order."

"You sure?" Crew says. "I can stay and help."

She chuckles. "I've been to your old apartment, Crew. You have no idea how to organize a kitchen. You kept your pots and pans under the sink and your plates were where the glasses should go."

Garrett jokes, "Are you going to tell us what time to take a shit, too?"

"Watch it," Crew says. "That's my fiancée you're talking to." He kisses Bria's forehead and turns to Garrett. "*I'm* the one who'll be telling you that."

Garrett mock pouts. "You guys are going to be like our mom and dad, aren't you? The responsible ones. I'm telling you right now, I'm damn well not going to censor what I say or who I bring into my room." He pounds on the wall. "I hope these walls are thick. I wouldn't want you to be jealous of all the screaming."

"You're the one who's going to be jealous," Crew says. "Believe me, there will be no shortage of banging from our bedpost."

Bria's face is beet red. "Crew."

"What? We all live together now. Might as well get used to each other's habits. I'm simply letting them know that one of ours is fucking like bunnies."

She points to the door. "Leave. You're only making it worse."

We go to the door, laughing.

"Seriously, though," Crew says in the hall. "I know we're men and all, but if you can keep any disgusting habits to yourself when Bria's around, I'd appreciate it."

"I don't have any disgusting habits," Garett says.

I give him a pointed look. "Dude, your farts are louder than a goddamn air horn."

"Yeah, that," Crew says.

Garrett frowns. "Are you saying I can't float an air biscuit in my own goddamn apartment?"

"Just be courteous," Crew says. "Get up and leave the room. We all agreed to live together, that's just part of it. I'm sure Bria will have to make some adjustments too."

"What kind of adjustments?" I ask.

He thinks. "For one, she likes to walk around naked."

Garrett and I both raise our eyebrows. "Some guys have all the luck," he says. He closes his eyes tightly, like he's thinking hard.

Crew hits him. "Quit picturing my fiancée naked."

Out on the street, we look both ways. "Where should we start?" I ask.

Garrett points right. "We'll stop at every bar for one drink, working our way down the street and back. That way, we'll get a feel for which ones are the best."

Crew says, "Sounds like a plan."

I couldn't care less about finding the best bar. I just want to get drunk, sleep in my new room, and forget about my miserable fucking past.

~ ~ ~

We wait in line at the fourth bar of the night. "Whiskey still?" Garrett asks. "Or should we switch to beer?"

"You pussies do what you want. I'm having whiskey."

Garrett gets our drinks while Crew and I find a table.

"How long do you think it will last?" I say. "You and Bria living with a couple of certified bachelors?"

He shrugs. "I guess I'll leave it up to her."

"Would you have done things differently? Knowing we'd be raking in money like we are now?"

"I don't know. Maybe. But I'm excited about it. I've only ever lived by myself. I think it'll be fun, all of us together. As long as Garrett can keep his farts to himself."

"I've only ever lived with my uncle, my mom, or, well, you know. I'm pretty happy about it too."

"You're stoked to be out of Dirk's house, huh?"

"You have no fucking idea."

"Earlier today, when you said there are other ways to get out from under Dirk. Were you talking about the video? You still have it, right?"

I nod. "Locked in a safe deposit box."

"Maybe it's time to use it."

"It wouldn't be enough to make any arrests. It's only of Dirk blackmailing my mom."

"Dirk the politician. If you want to hit him where it hurts, release the tape. No way would he be elected governor then. He'd be ruined."

"Maybe, but then everyone would know what happened."

"To Luke, yes. I've seen the video. It doesn't clearly say anything happened to you."

"But it's implied. People aren't stupid, Crew. They'd know. Plus, I'd be betraying Luke."

"You wouldn't. I know why you're getting shit-faced. I saw you reading the letter earlier. You showed it to me when we were sixteen, and you were drunk out of your mind. Luke wrote the letters to protect you. He'd be okay with it. I know he would."

"Dude, I came here to forget about the past. Not relive it."

Garrett puts our drinks on the table. "What'd I miss?"

"Nothing," Crew says. "I was asking Liam about Ella."

"What about her?" I say.

"Have you seen her since we got back?"

"Nope."

"You done with that?" Garrett asks.

I sip my whiskey. "Honestly, I don't know."

"You guys were good together," Crew says. "You should give it a chance."

"What the shit?" Garrett says, becoming rigid as he glares across the bar.

A man is staring right back at him. He tosses back his drink and gets up, not breaking eye contact with Garrett. Although they seem surprised to see each other, Garrett is pissed as hell. The other guy, not so much.

"Let's go," Garrett says, putting his drink down.

We get up and start for the door.

"Come on, Gare," the man says behind us.

Garrett spins. "Stay the fuck away from me."

We exit the bar. The man follows. "Garrett, it's been five years."

"And that's supposed to make everything okay?" Garrett spits.

"You can at least talk to me," he says.

"I told you to stay the fuck away."

"Jesus, man, you sure can hold a grudge." In a split-second, Garrett's fist connects with the guy's face. Blood spatters on the sidewalk. He wipes his mouth. "So this is how it is?"

"This is how it is."

Garrett walks away. We run up behind him. "Who the hell was that?" Crew asks.

He glances back to make sure we're not being followed. "That was my fucking brother."

Crew and I look at each other, surprised.

Crew asks, "What—"

"Don't even ask," he says, quickening his pace.

After we've gone three blocks, he leads us into a bar. We sit and order drinks.

Garrett breaks the awkward silence. "Listen, I know you guys have some messed up shit in your past. I don't ask you about it. So let's just leave it at that."

"Fine by me," I say. "Shit is better left in the past, if you ask me."

Two hours later, we stumble home, having sampled almost a dozen bars within walking distance. As soon as we reach our apartment, Garrett races for the bathroom. We can hear him tossing his cookies. Or more accurately, his whiskey.

Crew stops on the way to his room. "If you ever need to talk, I'm here."

I lift my chin at him, then close my bedroom door. Luke's letter is where I left it. I fold it, thinking about what Crew said.

When we were eleven, Crew and I were already best friends. Sometimes I wanted to tell him what was going on. Ask him if it was normal. But his parents were going through a divorce. He had his own problems. Both of us were avoiding our fathers but for very different reasons. His was having sex with his secretary. Mine was having sex with *me*.

One drunken night when we were sixteen, a guy tried to hit on me. I beat the shit out of him, then broke down and told Crew what I'd never told another living soul, that Luke had killed himself because Don was molesting him.

After that, Crew became my sounding board when I needed to talk about Luke. I spoke of his abuse as if it didn't happen to me, just Luke. But both of us knew I wouldn't have been privy to such details if it weren't from personal experience. He listened. He never judged. Others would have called me sick. Gay. Less of a man. But not Crew. I knew he'd be the only one who would understand.

Or so I thought.

I take out my phone and scroll through the pictures of Ella.

Chapter Thirty-four

Ella

I haven't heard from him in three days. Aside from when he texted me Sunday night, it's been complete radio silence. Maybe I'm being stupid not texting or calling him. But if he wanted to see me, he'd reach out, right?

Or maybe he's saying the same thing about me.

No. He's the one who needs to initiate contact. He's the one who has issues with having a relationship.

I run in Central Park, and someone yells behind me, "Ella!"

My heart soars and then falls. It's Corey. I don't slow down. He goes faster to catch up with me.

"You're looking tan," he says, panting. "Beach vacation?"

"Something like that."

"Were you avoiding me?"

"No." *Yes.*

He slows. "Can you stop and talk for a sec? I've done five miles, and I'm beat."

I stop and stare at him, wondering if the old feelings are going to come back. "What do you want to talk about?"

"I haven't seen you in almost two months. Didn't you miss me?"

"Do we have to keep having the same conversation, Corey? You cheated on me. I broke up with you. End of story."

He touches my arm. "It's *not* the end of our story, Ella. I still love you. We could have a life. Get married. Have kids."

"Married? You barely mentioned the word in the eighteen months we were together. Then you showed up at the hospital and wanted me to go home with you. Now you think we should get married?" I laugh harshly. "Seems to me this is a case of wanting something you can't have."

"I know you want to be a wife and mother," he says. "I saw the magazines you read. I heard what you and your friends talked about."

"Lots of women want those things. It doesn't mean I would settle for someone who cheats on me."

"*Cheat*," he says. "One time. It was a moment of complete stupidity and weakness. I know you can get past it if you give me a chance."

"I have to go." I turn and run.

"That wasn't a no!" he shouts after me.

He's right. I've always wanted to get married and have kids. My parents were the perfect example of a happy couple when I was growing up. He brought her flowers. She rubbed his feet. They kissed every time they saw each other after work. When I go home for a visit, they're still that way, even after all these years. Of course I want what they have.

The irony is that I want it with a man who probably isn't capable of giving it to me. Then there's Corey. He's the safe bet. The stable tax attorney whose idea of risky behavior is to go horseback riding in the summer. What if he's right, and I can get past the cheating? If it was just the one time, would he really risk everything by doing it again?

The truth is I always saw myself with someone like him. Corey is a lot like my dad. Down to earth. A homebody. Pragmatic. He gets along with my parents like he's their long-lost son.

I glance back, and he gives me a wave.

I wonder what Mom and Dad would think of me seeing a musician who won't let me touch him because of something horrible his father did to him as a child.

I run so hard I can't think about marriage, men, or molestation.

~ ~ ~

The next day, fresh out of the shower after another solo run, I race to answer the phone. It's Bria. "Hi. How's the new place?"

"It's great. I'm sure you've heard all about it from Liam."

I sigh. "Actually, I haven't."

After a moment of surprised silence, she says, "Are you telling me he hasn't contacted you since we got back?"

"He texted me Sunday night. Nothing since."

"Four days ago? That jerk. I ought to—"

"Bria, you can't force the man to call me. Pushing him will only make things worse."

"Why are you being so nice about it? He's being a jackass."

"He's probably thinking things through."

"Things? What sort of things?"

I don't respond.

"He opened up to you, didn't he? Of course he did. You guys were practically together twenty-four-seven in Florida."

"He kind of did but only a little."

"I'm glad to hear it. Listen, I don't presume to know what happened in his past. It's not something Crew has shared with me, but if it's anything like what Crew went through, I feel your pain. It was hard on us in the beginning."

"I'm not sure there's an us."

"You need to find out. We're moving to the new rehearsal studio tomorrow. How about meeting me for lunch at IRL?"

"That might be awkward."

"It will be a test. You know, to see how he reacts."

"Maybe I should wait for him to call."

"Ella, do you want to be with him?"

"Yes."

"Come at noon. I'll text you the address."

"Okay, but only because I miss you. Now let's change the subject. Have you and Crew picked a wedding date?"

"Lord, no. We're going to be pretty busy. We'll sit down in a few months and try to figure it out. I'm not in any hurry. I've got the ring on my finger, and that's all that matters."

"Are you going to change your name?"

"Good question. While I love the thought of being Mr. and Mrs. Rewey, my music career has been built on me being Brianna Cash."

"So become Mrs. Rewey legally but keep your maiden name for the band."

"Maybe. You do realize you wouldn't have to change your name if you married Liam. I mean, how often does something like that happen?"

As if the thought hadn't ever crossed my mind. "I'm not sure he's the marrying type."

"I think you're wrong. I see the way he looks at Crew and me. He wants what we have."

"Somehow this conversation turned back to Liam and me."

"That's because it's the most exciting thing going on."

"Oh, come on. You have a new apartment and a new rehearsal studio. You're going to make another album soon. You just got engaged. My love life is hardly exciting compared to all that."

"Liam is one of my best friends, Ella. I want good things for him. And you're a very good thing."

"I hope you're right, otherwise I might end up doing something stupid, like marrying a tax attorney."

"Corey? He's not still calling you, is he?"

"I ran into him yesterday. He actually brought up the word marriage."

"You're kidding?"

"I wish I was."

"Girl, we need to go out for more than lunch. Better make it drinks, too. Will you have time?"

I laugh. "I think I can manage that."

I get dressed and go downstairs to check the mail. In my box are a few bills, a padded envelope from Corey (eye roll), and a letter from IRL. I rip open the one from IRL even before I get back to the elevator. It's my commission check for the album cover. It's more money than I usually see in two months. I still can't believe Liam made it happen. Between this and the money I'm making from the books, this year will be my best one ever.

It's nothing like what Liam is making now. He showed me his bank account when they got their most recent royalty check. It's staggering. I don't know what I'd do if I had that much money coming in every month.

Back in my apartment, I handle the envelope from Corey as if it's kryptonite and I'm Superman. He sent it by overnight mail.

Another token of his guilt, I'm sure. What will it be this time? I tear it open and turn it over, emptying the contents: a note and a small black box.

> Ella,
>
> Maybe this will show you how serious I am.
>
> I love you,
> Corey

Surely he didn't.

I open the box and my jaw goes slack when I see the ring. It's not just any ring—it's *the* ring. Although I never told him rose gold was my favorite band, nor did I ever say I prefer oval-shaped diamonds, it's evident what he said yesterday is true—he *was* paying attention to the magazines I used to read.

I snap the box shut and go to the kitchen for a drink of water. Then I go to the bedroom, where I don't do a thing. Trying to ignore the box is somehow making me feel claustrophobic. I return to the living room, open the box, remove the ring, and slip in on my finger. It's fits perfectly.

What am I doing?

I immediately take it off, put it back in the box, and shove it across the table.

Chapter Thirty-five

Liam

We move equipment into the new rehearsal space. "It's not as big as the barn," Garrett says.

"Not many places are," Bria says.

"It's not as cool either."

Crew carries in a stool. "We'll get used to it. Famous bands don't practice in barns."

"Who says?" Garrett asks.

I step forward. "*I* say."

Garrett twirls a drumstick. "I get that you hate Dirk and all, but I'm going to miss that old barn."

"Good fucking riddance," I say.

"Good riddance to whom?" Ronni asks.

I haven't seen her since the day she left Florida, and it's been the best five weeks of our contract. "We're going to need boundaries, Ronni. You can't just burst in here whenever you want."

She pulls out a business card and reads it. "Veronica Collins, Independent Talent Agent, Indica Record Label." She shoots me a triumphant look. "I work here, and I'm your rep, so I think I can burst in here whenever I damn well please."

Bria lets out a huff and leaves to get another load.

"Seriously, Ronni?" Crew says. "We know who you are and what you've done for us, but we need some space. We want to be able to work or even goof off sometimes, without everyone breathing down our necks."

"What do you propose? That I make an appointment every time I have to see you?" She laughs as if it's a preposterous idea.

He thinks on it. "We only got together with you once a week before. When we're not recording, how about we schedule a time, say every Monday afternoon or whatever works for you. We'll have a meeting and go over anything you need to talk about. Otherwise, maybe do us the courtesy of sending a text to see if we're available."

"Who appointed you leader?" she says to Crew. "You're rehearsing here for free. When I need to talk to you, I'll come in. There's nothing to discuss."

I brush past her. "Unless you want to get dirty, I suggest you steer clear. Either that or help us. We still have a lot to unload."

She follows me into the hall and steps close. "I may want to get dirty, but not unloading your gear." She gives me her fuck-me eyes.

It takes me two seconds to realize what a colossal fool I was to sleep with her. She's nothing like Ella. Nobody I've slept with is like Ella. "Not gonna happen, Ronni."

"That's what you said after the first time."

"Whatever." I leave her inside and head out to the van. I do a double take when I think I see Ella standing on the sidewalk talking to Bria. It *is* her.

Crazy shit happens to my body. It hits me like a gut-punch how much I've missed her. Suddenly I feel like a real dick for not calling. I join them, tail between my legs.

"I'm not here for you," she says shyly. "Bria and I are going to lunch."

Bria thumbs to the door. "I have to get my purse. Be right back."

Ella and I are alone on the sidewalk.

"I should have called," I say. "I promised we'd keep running."

"You don't owe me anything."

"That's where you're wrong. I owe you a lot. You helped me compose again."

She looks at the ground. "You'd have done it with or without me."

"On that we'll have to agree to disagree."

"What are we disagreeing about?" someone says behind me. My nostrils flare. It's Dirk. He looks Ella up and down. "And who do we have here?"

When I don't introduce him, she says, "Ella Campbell."

Dirk's eyebrows shoot up as his gaze darts between Ella and me.

"No relation," she hastily adds.

He offers his hand. "Dirk Campbell. Nice to meet you, Ella. I apologize for the rudeness of my nephew." I step towards him and he holds up a hand. "Easy, boy. I came around to see how the new rehearsal space is shaping up."

"In case you didn't notice, we moved out of the barn to get away from you."

"Yet you moved into another building I own. If you recall, I own the entire company, so in a way you could say I own *you*."

"Fuck off, Dirk."

I start to walk away, and he grabs my elbow. "Is that any way to talk to your boss?" He turns to Ella. "Again, you'll have to excuse Liam. If he were younger, I'd give him a good knock on the ass to teach him some manners."

I look down with a mutinous glare. "Want to get your goddamn hand off me?"

"You don't like it there?"

It takes me half a second to pin him to the wall. Fury burns deep inside me. "I could ruin you."

He laughs in my face.

"Remember Lance Holloway?" He looks at me blankly. "Of course you don't, because you don't give a shit about the people you employ. He was part of your security team for ten years. You really fucked the pooch, Dirk, because right after you fired Lance, he slipped me a flash drive with footage from your house that I'll bet would be interesting to a lot of people."

"You're lying," he says. "You'd have done something before."

"I was waiting for the right moment. Guess what? That moment is coming." I clench my jaw. "Now leave."

"Everything okay out here?" Garrett says.

I let Dirk go and glance at Ella, who is put off by what just happened.

Dirk brushes himself off ceremoniously. "I'll see you inside then. Have to make sure everything is running properly. I didn't get rich by accident, you know." He scowls at me. "With wealth comes lots of important connections. Don't forget that."

Crew and Bria come out, passing Dirk. "What'd we miss?" Crew says.

"Same old shit." I kick the side of the building. "Maybe moving here was a mistake."

"He won't be around much," Crew says. "He's got way more to do than babysit us. He's only here to rile you up."

I go over to Ella. "I'm sorry you had to see that. My uncle and me … it's complicated."

"I can see that. He owns the record label?"

I snort. "He bought it after we signed with them. He thinks he can control me."

"Oh, God." Her eyes say it all. She thinks he's like my dad.

"No, he doesn't … he's not."

She looks relieved but still very confused.

Niles joins us. "You settling in okay?"

"Yes. Thanks. Ella, this is Niles Armentrout. He runs things here."

Niles whispers. "Don't tell that to Dirk."

"Ready?" Bria says to her. "Sorry, Liam, we'd invite you, but this is a girls' only lunch."

Crew comes up behind her and gives her a hug. "You bailing out so the rest of us have to do all the heavy lifting?"

She spins and kisses him. "I think you can handle it. See you later."

"Bye," Ella says over her shoulder.

"Maybe I'll see you sometime?" I feel like a prick the second the words leave my mouth. I don't know how to do this shit. Of course I want to see her. But everyone is standing here. And Dirk is inside. Also Ronni. We should never have agreed to rehearse here.

"Maybe," she says before turning the corner.

Crew goes by, carrying two of Garrett's cymbals. "Smooth."

"Shut up."

Brad walks up and looks inside the van to see what's left. "Hey, Liam."

"Nice of you to show up," I say, heavy on the sarcasm.

"I didn't realize we were moving ourselves," he says. "You know, since we have Bruce and all. I was in town and wanted to check out the new space."

"Bruce isn't here. You should check your email once in a while."

"Been a long week." He picks up a box. "You're lucky I'm here at all. We were supposed to have the whole week off to recover from the tour."

Garrett appears. "Lucky? We're *lucky* to have you here? Who died and made you king?"

"Fuck off," Brad says.

Garrett and I share a look. Brad doesn't usually curse.

"What's wrong with you?" I ask. "You look like death warmed over. You okay, man?"

He looks guilty for snapping at us. "It's nothing. Let's just get this stuff inside."

I hang back and sit in the open van. I stare up at the IRL sign. It's a huge gold record emblazoned with the company name. Everything we've wanted is happening—I glance at Dirk and Ronni as they talk inside the main doors—but at what price?

I'm beginning to understand that getting what you want doesn't come easily. Why should Ella be any different?

Chapter Thirty-six

Ella

A knock on the door wakes me. I fell asleep on the couch. My head is still fuzzy from the three margaritas I had at lunch. There's another knock. The room is dark. How long did I sleep?

I turn on a lamp, stumble to the front door, and put my eye to the peephole. Nobody's there. I open the door and look down the hallway. Liam is walking away. "Hey, I'm here."

He spins around, a slow smile spreading across his face.

I motion inside. "Want to come in?"

"Sure."

He walks in and spends a minute checking out the room. "I forgot you've never been inside my apartment," I say.

He laughs. "Kind of strange, considering how well we know each other."

I cock my head. "Do we? Know each other?"

"Can I sit?"

"It's a free country."

He sighs. "I should have called."

"You said that earlier."

He sits on the couch and rubs a hand across his jaw. "I don't know how to do this, El. On the plane it was almost like you were saying goodbye. I don't know what you want. I don't know what I want either."

I sit in the chair next to the couch. "I wasn't saying goodbye. I was pointing out that things were going to change. We went from living in the same hotel room and eating all our meals together to returning home and going back to reality. But it doesn't change how I feel. I told you before what I wanted."

"So you still want to—"

"Run together? Yes."

He blinks, clearly confused. "I, uh, yeah."

"I'm kidding. Yes, Liam, I still want to."

Relief washes over him, but I also sense a hint of fear.

"What did you mean when you said you don't know how to do this?" Realization strikes. "Have you *ever* had a girlfriend?"

"Girlfriend?" He chokes on the word. "Who said anything about girlfriend?"

"Answer the question."

He shakes his head. A chunk of hair falls over one eye, and he pushes it aside.

"You need a haircut."

"Haven't had time."

"I could do it. I used to cut … well, I can cut hair. Want me to?"

He hesitates. Is he thinking I'll have to touch him to cut his hair?

"Surely you don't cut your own hair," I say.

"No."

"Then what's the big deal if I do it?"

"Fine."

I stand. "Pull one of the kitchen chairs under the light over there. I'll get my stuff."

I'm practically giddy, knowing I'm going to touch him again. It's been five days. Five long, drawn-out, lonely days. When I return with the haircutting kit, he's standing at the table, gazing at the ring. I run over and take it from him, close the box, and put it away.

His eyebrows draw down as he scowls. "What the hell is that?"

"What does it look like?"

"A goddamn engagement ring."

"I think Corey might have proposed."

"You *think*?"

"I ran into him at the park a few days ago, and it came in the mail yesterday."

"He *sent* it to you?"

"I think he was trying to prove a point."

"Which is?"

"That he loves me."

He paces behind the couch. "What did you say?"

"I haven't said anything."

"Why not?" He studies me. "Is he what you want, El?"

"Of course not."

"Then why haven't you sent it back?"

"Haven't gotten around to it." I motion to the chair. "Are we going to do this or what?"

He sits, clearly brooding which pleasures me to no end. I wrap the smock around him, but it gets caught on the chair post and rips. I make a disgusted noise.

"What's wrong?" he asks.

"The smock is useless now."

"I don't need it."

"Hair will get on you, and it will be itchy."

"I think I can handle it."

I fetch a dishtowel from the kitchen. "Use this to catch any drips."

I use a spray bottle to wet his hair, then I comb through it, speculating how I should attack it. I part it down the middle, and section by section, work my way from front to back and top to bottom, cutting only little bits at a time.

"Don't be afraid to cut," he says as small wisps fall to the ground. "It's only hair."

"It's not just any hair. You're in a rock band. It has to be perfect." I take a step back. "What if I screw it up? Ronni will have my head on a platter. Maybe we didn't think this through."

He pulls me between his legs, and suddenly this has become much more than a haircut. "It'll grow back. I trust you, El."

My heart flutters. Does he have any idea how powerful those words are, coming from him? I doubt he's trusted many people in his life.

I go back to cutting. I'm so close to him, I can feel his breath on my chest. I'm all too aware that he's left his hand on my leg. I can feel the heat of it through my jeans. I need to move to do the sides, but I don't want to. I like the way his hand feels on me.

Eventually, I'm forced to change position or the front will be too short. He's a rock star. His hair needs to be long and roguish. I can't take off too much.

When I finish, I run my fingers through the back of his hair. He grabs my hands. "What are you doing?"

"Checking to see if it's even."

He releases me. I come around front and do the same thing. I'm acutely aware that he's breathing faster, and I'm pretty sure there's a bulge in his pants. I try not to smile.

"All done." I pick up the hand mirror and hold it out. "What do you think?"

He doesn't even look at it. "It's fine."

Our eyes lock. Flutters rise in my belly.

He stands abruptly. "I … you were right. It itches. Can I jump in your shower and rinse off?"

"Sure." I point. "Right through there."

He disappears without another word. I hear the water turn on. And all I can do is stand here and think about him naked in my shower.

A knock on the door pulls me from my fantasy. Without even checking to see who it is, I open it. Immediately I realize my mistake. It's Corey, with a dozen roses. "Well?"

I glance back at the bathroom. "This really isn't a good time."

He steps around me and into the room. "You got the ring, right?"

"I got it." I pick it up and hand it to him. "And now I'm giving it back."

"Don't, Ella. We belong together."

"If that were true, you'd never have cheated, and we'd actually still be together."

"How many times do I have to say I'm sorry?"

"You don't have to anymore. Just walk away."

A noise comes from the bathroom. Corey looks around the apartment. He sees the hair on the floor. "Is someone here?"

"Yes."

"Who?"

"No one you know."

"A man?"

The bathroom door cracks open. "Did you say something?" Liam asks. When I don't respond, he sticks his head out and sees Corey.

"This is—"

"I know who it is," Liam says, coming out with only a towel around him.

"Aren't you going to introduce us?" Corey asks through gritted teeth. When I don't, he steps forward and holds out a reluctant hand. "Corey Gorman."

Liam doesn't shake. "Liam Campbell."

Corey's surprised. "Campbell?" He looks hopeful. "Are you related?"

Liam puts an arm around my shoulder. "I hope not, because we'd probably get arrested in some states, eh, El?"

I'm shocked by what he said. Liam smiles and kisses my head.

Corey's lips are pinched. "So you two …?"

Liam pulls me tightly against him. "Pretty much."

Corey eyes the box in his hand. He's clearly devastated. I feel bad for him. I still care about him despite what he did to me. "Corey, I'm sorry, but I've tried to tell you for months it's over."

Defeated, he starts for the door, pausing to put the flowers on the credenza. He glances back at Liam. "Liam Campbell. Where have I heard that name before?"

Liam shrugs. "Beats me."

"Goodbye, Ella," he says. "I hope you'll be happy."

I hold back tears.

The door closes, and Liam lets me go, confused by my reaction. "Why are you crying? Did you *want* to marry him?"

"No, but he was a big part of my life for a long time, and now it seems so final."

"This was a good thing, then. He knows you're unavailable. Maybe now he'll be able to move on."

"Am I unavailable?"

He nods to the hair on the floor. "We should clean that up. I'll get dressed while you find me a dustpan."

He comes out of the bathroom as I throw the hair in the trash. "Do you want a drink?" I ask from the kitchen.

"I was going to clean up the floor."

"It's no big deal."

"You did a great job on the haircut. Can I buy you dinner as a thank you?"

"I'm not very hungry. I ate a lot at lunch."

"But you need to eat something. How about I order in? Pizza?"

I point to a drawer. "Menus are in there."

He peruses them and places a call. Then he opens the fridge. "You have beer?"

"I'm not a prude, Liam. Of course I have beer."

"But I've never seen you drink much."

"I drink."

"One drink is not drinking. Sometimes you have to relax and let go."

I raise an eyebrow. "Are you saying you want to get drunk with me?" Then I realize I shouldn't be fighting it. Maybe drinking together will loosen him up. Maybe the alcohol will make him more amenable to my touch. I motion for a beer. "Hand one over."

He smiles. "Have you ever played drinking games?"

"I played quarters in college a few times."

"Quarters? What are you, fifty? I'm talking beer pong. Flip-cup? The dice game?"

"Nope, sorry. I was the good girl."

"You've got a lot to learn. Do you have a ping-pong ball?"

"Why would I?"

"Right. Dice then?"

"I'm not playing a drinking game with you, Liam. Especially not one I know I'll lose."

"Fine. Quarters." He searches my cabinets until he finds the appropriate glasses. "These will do."

"Are you serious about this?"

"Hell yes."

"What are we playing for?"

He laughs. "You don't play *for* anything, El. You play to get drunk."

"Fine, but I get a mulligan."

"A what?"

"A mulligan. You know, I get to try again if I miss."

He looks confused.

"My dad's a big golfer," I explain. "You've never heard of a mulligan?"

"Whatever, let's play."

I take several practice shots realizing playing quarters is like riding a bike. Though I haven't done it in years, I'm not half bad. We play and joke and laugh. By the time the pizza gets here, I'm three beers in and ravenous for more than just food.

"I thought you said you weren't hungry," he says when I take my second slice.

"I'd forgotten how well pizza and beer go together. I can't tell you how many nights Jenn and I did this in college."

"What were you like back then?"

"Pretty much the same as I am now."

"Did you always know you wanted to illustrate books?"

I shake my head. "I loved creating things. Drawing, painting, sketching. I knew I wanted to do something with it, but I didn't know what. I kind of fell into the children's book thing during my senior year when a friend of a friend was looking for an illustrator, so I showed him some of my stuff."

Liam drops his slice of pizza.

"What is it?"

"I'm figuring out how much I don't know about you."

"Because you rarely ask questions." I put my hand on his. "It's okay. I get it. If you ask me questions, you're afraid I'll ask about your past."

"Some things are okay to ask."

I perk up. "Really? What things?"

"I don't know. I'll let you know at the time." He nods to the quarter. "Your turn."

Two hours later, Liam stumbles out of the bathroom. "It's late. I should go."

"You're drunk. You can sleep on the couch."

"I'm not driving, El."

"You still shouldn't go. Riding the subway drunk is a bad idea."

"So I'll take a cab." He tries to focus on me. "You *want* me to stay."

"I didn't say that."

He gives me a smug little grin. "Admit it. You missed me."

I roll my eyes. "Fine. I missed you. Is that so bad?"

His eyes dart to my bedroom. He sighs. "You're drunk, too. If you think—"

"I don't think anything, Liam. I just want you to stay. Don't you want to?"

"Yes. But not on the couch."

I'm shocked. "You want to sleep in my bed?"

"I miss sleeping next to you. I haven't slept well since coming home."

I don't tell him I haven't slept well either. For the first time in my life, I've laid awake night after night, thinking about a man. Now he's here, asking to climb into my bed. I'm practically giddy, and not from the alcohol. "Okay. I'll clean up and be there in a minute."

By the time I put away the pizza and brush my teeth, he's passed out on the bed. I change into my sleep shirt and crawl in next to him. Part of me is relieved he's asleep. I thought drinking together might make it easier for him to allow *more*. But now I know that's not what I want. If he lets me touch him, it shouldn't be because he's drunk. It wouldn't be real.

I watch him sleep. I've missed this.

Hours later, I'm startled awake by a scream. "Luke!"

I touch his arm. "Liam, it's okay."

His eyes fly open. It takes him a moment to orient himself. He blows out a long breath.

"Bad dream?"

"I dream about him a lot. I still hear the gun go off like it was yesterday."

"Can I ask you something?"

He hesitates. "Maybe."

"You said Luke killed himself, but you also said he died because of your father. I'm confused."

"Don't call him that. The bastard's name is Don. He was never my father. He adopted us when I was seven. Luke might have pulled the trigger, but it was Don who killed him."

"I'm so sorry."

"Me too."

"If Don wasn't your real dad, then Dirk isn't your real uncle. Is that why you hate him?" He's quiet, and it makes me think I've crossed a line. "You don't have to answer."

His breathing evens out. I think he's gone to sleep.

"Are you still awake?" he asks a few minutes later.

"Yes."

"I hate Dirk because he blackmailed my mom and me." He sighs heavily. "And I hate myself for letting him."

Before I can ask anything else, he gets up and moves through the moonlight to the bathroom. I lie here watching him cross the room, realizing I've never met a man who makes me so happy and sad at the same time.

Chapter Thirty-seven

Liam

Thirteen years ago

The past week has been the worst of my life. Luke is dead. Dad is gone. Mom is a basket case.

We're at Dirk's house. We haven't left since the night Luke died except for today, when Mom went to collect some of our things. Helen sends me to find Mom for dinner. I hear her and Dirk talking in her bedroom. I stand outside and listen. Nobody has told me much. Only that Luke shot himself with Dirk's gun. They think I'm too young to be a part of their adult conversations, so no one talks to me. Dirk is always on the phone. Sylvia cries every time she looks at me. Mom gets drunk.

"You read the letter, Dirk. It was clear as day. It explains why Donny didn't come back after Luke died. Luke says right here that he called Donny and told him to stay away from Liam." She cries in agony. "He put his hands on Luke. He molested my son. He ran when Luke told him he was going to tell me everything. I'm calling the police."

"Hold on, Colleen. Don is gone. He hasn't contacted me or been to work. He didn't show up at the funeral. As far as I know, he's never coming back. He can't hurt Liam now."

"Maybe …" There's a long pause. "Maybe he already has."

"The letter doesn't explicitly say that."

"It does in the one he left for Liam."

"He left a letter for Liam? I'd like to see it."

"No, and neither will Liam. Luke said he couldn't protect him," Mom says. "What else could that mean?"

"Maybe he meant he didn't know how he *would* protect him if it came down to it. Right now all we have are a few letters from a messed-up kid, who may or may not have accidentally killed himself."

My stomach tightens into a ball. How could they think it might not have been an accident?

"Are you saying I shouldn't go to the police with this?" Mom asks.

"And put yourself and Liam through hell? I promise you this letter isn't enough evidence to put Don away. All it will do is prolong your suffering."

Mom cries some more.

"Let me pour you another drink," he says.

I hear glasses clinking.

"Donny has to pay for what he did," she says, sobbing.

"I think he'll be doing that the rest of his life. Think about it, Colleen. He'll get nothing from me. Not a penny. We both know the only reason he was able to provide for you was because of me. For all we know, he'll be living on the streets. Lord knows, if what Luke claims is true, he deserves that. But you know what I'm willing to do? I'll take care of his family. You won't be able to give Liam a good life, not now. You lost another job because they wouldn't give you time off. What if you can't get another one? Do you want to go back to living in squalor? Stay here, live in the east wing. You and Liam can have the run of the place. You won't have to worry about where your next paycheck is coming from. Hell, you don't even need to work if you don't want to. Liam's college—paid for. Whatever you need, ask and it'll be done."

Her voice is thick. "As long as I never say anything."

"It's your choice, Colleen, but before you decide, you should ask yourself what's better for Liam. Being put on the stand and through the wringer by prosecutors who will say horrible things about what might have been done to his brother? Or growing up here and not wanting for a single thing. He's already lost Luke. He's lost Don. If you drink yourself to death, he might lose you, too. Who will take care of him then?"

I've heard enough. Nothing they are saying makes sense. Why would Dad need to "pay for what he's done?" Why would Mom go to the police? What was that word she used? Molested?

I return to the kitchen and tell Helen I couldn't find them. She ladles soup into a bowl for me. "Looks like it's just the two of us, *mijo*."

She eats with me. She's done that a lot lately, when the others don't show up for dinner.

Halfway through the meal, she asks, "Don't you have anything to say? You're usually a chatterbox."

I put down my spoon. "Helen, what does molested mean?"

Her face loses all color. She closes her eyes and mumbles something in Spanish, then she gets up from the table.

"Is molested a bad word?"

"Maybe you should ask your mother."

"I don't want to make her more sad."

Helen sits back down. "Molested means that someone has been touched on their private parts by a person who shouldn't be touching them."

"So it's bad."

She nods. "It's very bad."

"Can people go to jail for it?"

"Oh, yes."

My hands shake. I try not to cry in front of her.

She pulls her chair next to mine. "You're safe here."

"But what if they take me to jail?"

Tears come to her eyes. "I promise you won't go to jail. Only the one who does the bad touching goes. None of this is your fault, mijo."

Bad touching. My stomach turns. Is that what Dad did to me?

I feel like I've been punched in the gut. I crawled into bed with Luke and touched him. That makes *me* bad. Is that why he's gone?

I run to my room.

I want to go where Luke has gone.

I want to die.

Chapter Thirty-eight

Ella

"I'm happy to see you can still keep up with me," I joke as we finish our run.

"I ran three times this week."

"Without me?" I pout.

"Yes, but it wasn't the same."

"Running alone sucks. Are you doing anything later?"

"Why?"

"I was thinking we could grab something to eat."

He slows. "That sounds a lot like a date."

"Liam, we've gone out to eat together a hundred times."

"With other people."

I stop at my usual place and stretch. "Okay. We won't go out to eat."

"We can go. No white tablecloths or fancy shit like that, though."

I raise a snarky brow. "Tacos on a park bench?"

He laughs. "How about something in between?"

"Okay. What time do you want to meet?"

"Can you shower and come back to my place? There's something I want to show you."

"Sounds good. I'd love to see your new apartment."

A while later, we're entering his building. Two police officers get in the elevator with us. We ride up in silence and get off on the eighth floor. The cops follow us out and down the hallway. Liam and I look at each other and shrug.

Liam fishes keys out of his pocket. One of the cops asks, "Is this your apartment?"

"Yes."

"Were you the one who called about a break-in?"

"No." The door opens, and Garrett stands there, looking pissed. "What's going on, man?"

"Someone ransacked the place," Garrett says.

"Shit." Liam rushes in, and the rest of us follow.

"Looks like your room got the worst of it," Garrett says.

One of the officers inspects the door. "Doesn't seem to be any damage. Whoever did this didn't force their way in. You should check to see if anything's missing."

Liam makes a beeline for his bedroom.

Their place is nice, or it would be if it weren't for all the upended furniture and emptied drawers.

"The door was unlocked when I got here," Garrett says. "I called Crew. He and Bria left around noon. He's sure he locked the door."

"Whoever it was had a key," the officer says. "Or is one hell of a locksmith."

"Nobody else has a key," Garrett says. "We only moved in a few days ago."

"We'll check with the super and see if the locks were changed. If not, it could be an angry ex-tenant. Maybe they got evicted."

Crew and Bria run in. Bria covers her mouth in shock. "Who would do this?"

"You live here, too?" the tall cop says.

"Yes, both of us," Crew tells him.

"Can you check to see if anything was taken?"

A few minutes later, Bria comes out with her jewelry box. "It was scattered on the floor, but everything is here. Even my mom's wedding rings."

Liam returns, carrying a guitar. "We weren't robbed."

"What do you mean? Look around. Of course you were."

He ignores me. "You missing anything, Garrett?"

"No."

He turns to Bria. "How about you?"

She shows him the rings.

"Whoever did this wasn't searching for money or even shit to pawn. This guitar is worth almost ten thousand bucks."

"But … why then?" Bria asks.

Liam shoots Crew a look. "This has Dirk written all over it."

"Your uncle?" I ask. "Why would he do this?"

"Fuck!" He rights a chair and sinks down on it. "Yesterday outside IRL, I told him I had video on a flash drive that could ruin him."

The shorter officer frowns. "Something was taken, then. A flash drive?"

Liam says, "It's not here. I keep it in a safe deposit box."

"So nothing was stolen?"

Liam looks at Garrett, Crew, and Bria. They shake their heads. "Not as far as we know."

Crew picks things up off the floor.

"Stop," I say, turning to the cops. "Don't you have to take pictures and dust for prints?"

"You watch a lot of TV," the tall one says. "Nothing was stolen. There doesn't even appear to be any damage. Count yourselves lucky. Most places that get tossed don't look so good."

"You're not going to do anything?" I say, appalled.

"We'll fill out a report. If you have any additional information, call us."

"But we know who did it," Bria says.

Liam makes a rude sound. "Dirk wouldn't have done it himself. There'd be no way to prove it."

The police get statements from them and leave.

An hour later, we're all sitting in the living room. On top of the coffee table are the only two casualties: a broken dish and a splintered picture frame.

"You really think Dirk did this?" Garrett asks.

"Who else?" Liam says. "Looters might not know about the guitar, but Bria's rings—they'd be gone. I'm one hundred percent sure it was him. Fucking asshole."

"How did he get in without damaging the lock?" Bria asks.

"Dirk knows lots of shady people. They either picked it or bribed the super."

"Maybe the super will talk," she says.

"You don't know Dirk. Do you think he's that stupid? He's perfected the art of covering his tracks. It's pointless to go after him."

"What's on the video?" Garrett asks.

Liam and Crew get shuttered looks.

"What?" Garrett says, glancing between them. "I know there's stuff you don't want to talk about, but this is getting serious."

"Blackmail," Liam says. "The video shows him blackmailing my mom."

"Why did he do that?"

I stand abruptly, knowing Liam doesn't want to answer him. "Does it really matter? I'm going to the kitchen. Anyone want anything?"

Nobody responds.

"You keep it in a safe deposit box?" Garrett asks him. "Must be some pretty damning evidence."

"It is."

"Is this why you wanted to get out of his house?"

"Yeah."

"Does this have anything to do with why he bought IRL?" Garrett is like a dog with a bone.

"It has everything to do with it. If he can't control me, I'll destroy him."

"Then we need to get out from under him."

"You got any bright ideas?"

"I don't know. There has to be something. Isn't he running for governor next year?"

"Not if I have anything to say about it."

"Dude," Garrett says. "This is fucked up."

Liam glances at me. "You have no idea."

~ ~ ~

Liam isn't talkative at dinner. "Listen," I say. "Maybe we shouldn't have done this, considering what just happened."

He sips his beer. "I know I'm shit company."

"You have every right to be. You got robbed."

"But I didn't."

"You know what I mean. What happened to you is scary, Liam. What if he comes after you some other time?"

"Let him. He'll never find the flash drive."

"What if he hurts you?"

"He won't."

"But you said he knows shady people."

"He's smart enough to know if he touches me, I'll end him. I should have driven out to Stamford and confronted him."

My heart falls, knowing that could put him in danger. "You were smart not to. You don't know how far he'll go. You should definitely cool off before you talk to him."

"You don't think I'll be this mad tomorrow?"

"Maybe not. Please tell me you'll be careful."

"I won't do anything stupid, so don't worry. Can we not talk about this anymore? It's really putting a damper on my appetite."

"What do you want to talk about instead?"

"How are your illustrations coming along?"

"Good. I'm about to start on the third book."

"Wow. You got through the second one fast."

I shrug. "Didn't have much else to do this week."

He looks guilty.

I remember something. "You wanted to show me something at your apartment. What was it?"

"It wasn't show as much as hear."

I straighten. "You wrote another song?"

"Garrett wrote the lyrics and gave them to me Monday. I didn't work on it until this morning."

"Until this morning, huh?"

"Like that should surprise you, Mrs. Campbell. I did sleep next to you last night."

Why is it every time he calls me Mrs. Campbell, tingles shoot through me? It's pretty much my name, but when he says it—oh lordy.

"*Garrett* wrote the lyrics?"

"That's what *I* said. But they're good. I wanted to run the tune past you. See what you thought."

"I'm sure it's great. Everything you compose is perfect."

"You're biased."

"I'm not. Liam, I thought your music was great even before this."

This. Us. We. Boyfriend. Girlfriend. Couple. Exactly what are we? It's the question that has plagued me for weeks.

"I'm glad you feel that way, but I still want you to hear it."

"I can't wait."

A man at the next table kisses his companion. Liam sees it too. He looks at my hand like he wants to hold it. Like maybe he longs to be that couple.

"Has Corey contacted you?"

I take a drink, eyeing him over the rim of my glass. "Since you ran him off last night? No."

"Good."

I suppress a smile. "Are you jealous?"

"No."

I glance around to make sure no one is listening. "Liam, do you want me?"

"That's a stupid question."

"But one I'd like you to answer."

"Of course I do, but—"

"I'm tired of your *buts*. You want me, and I want you. So let's go have each other." I slip a shoe off and run my foot up his leg. His eyes widen in surprise. "What? You never said anything about my feet touching you." I can't reach the place I was aiming for, but I know he's turned on. "Can we go back to my place and try?"

"Try what?"

"I don't know. Something. Anything."

He looks out the window for a few long seconds, then back at me. "I can't make any promises."

"I don't expect any."

He motions for the check and I smile.

Chapter Thirty-nine

Liam

Ella comes out of the bathroom wearing a T-shirt. I had a taste of her a week ago. It was the most vanilla experience I've had. In many ways, that made it the best.

She keeps the lights on and stands in front of me as I sit on the edge of the bed. She works her way between my legs. "You have too many clothes on."

I smile up at her. "What are you going to do about it?"

She untucks my shirt and pulls it over my head. "Can I sit on you?"

I nod.

She climbs on my lap. I'm already getting hard, and feeling her on top of me has my dick pulsating. She removes her tee, revealing her breasts. All that remains are her panties.

Her wavy hair falls to where it almost touches her nipples, and her eyes, well, I swear I'm under their spell. I hope the enchantment is strong enough to get me through this without running away like a fucking scaredy cat.

I touch her face, absently brushing my thumb across her cheek, and then I kiss her. Before her, I never dreamed of kissing a woman. Now it's *all* I think about. But in my dreams, she touches me. In my dreams, I'm normal and we do all the things other people do when they get intimate.

I put my hands on her breasts. They're as nice as I remember. It's like they were made to fit perfectly in my hands.

Ella touches my shoulders, and when I don't protest, she weaves her fingers through my hair. I try hard not to flinch. I don't want to scare her away. But sometimes when people touch my hair, it reminds me of *him*. How he used to grab onto it right before he blew his load into me.

As I start to go flaccid, I get pissed at myself for letting him into my head. I look at Ella, intent on thinking of nothing and no one but her. *She's* the one touching me.

I lick her nipple. She inhales sharply and arches into me. The more demanding I am, the tighter she grips my hair. I reposition us so I'm lying down and she straddles me. "You're beautiful, do you know that?"

Her cheeks pink.

"I've never said that to anyone before. You're the first."

She smiles. "I want to be the first to do a lot of things with you." She leans down until her breasts squish against my chest. "I want you."

I tense. "I want you too, but not until we can do it the right way."

"We don't have to do everything." She rolls off me. "Take off your pants."

"You do it."

"Are you sure?"

"Do it, Ella."

She unbuttons my jeans and pulls them down, careful not to touch me. It makes me both happy and sad at the same time. She's respecting my boundaries. But damn it, I wish there weren't any boundaries to have to respect.

She drops my jeans on the floor. "Can I touch your feet?"

I nod.

She watches me as she caresses my foot for a few seconds before moving higher to massage my calf. It feels great. Maybe I can do this after all.

"Can I put my lips here?" she asks, touching the inside of my knee.

I swallow hard and nod again.

She kisses the spot, flicking her tongue against my skin. I'm getting hard again. I want to touch her, but she's too far away.

She accidentally grazes the scars on my thigh, and I flinch. "Jesus," I say, embarrassed by my reaction. "Sorry."

She stares at the scars. I know she wants to ask me how I got them, but she won't. She never asks me about anything. Unlike most people, she understands that my past is private. And nobody's business but mine. "It's okay, Liam. I won't touch you there if you don't want me to."

"I want you to, El. I want you to touch me *everywhere*. But when you do, sometimes I can't help but think of other shit I shouldn't be thinking of."

She straddles me again, undulating on top of me, two scraps of fabric the only things between us. I'm instantly hard. If I pulled aside her panties, I could slip right in. I don't even think she'd object. But I can't do it quick and dirty, not with her.

I fondle her breasts. Her head falls back, and the sexiest little noise comes out of her mouth. Not a moan. More like a chirp. Holy shit.

I work a finger under her panties. She's so wet. I slip it inside her and work the wetness up around her clit. She arches her back again and braces her hands behind her on the bed, opening herself to me. I work my fingers harder. She pushes down on me. I can tell she's close. I reach up and pinch her nipple, then release, then pinch again. She cries out, and her walls clamp down on my fingers.

"Put your hands on me," I say.

She opens her eyes. "Where?"

"Here." I point to my chest.

She carefully works her fingers over my pecs and nipples but doesn't go any lower. She won't test my boundaries without asking. I've never met another woman like her.

I move her hand down to my abs. I keep my hand on top of hers as I move it around. It feels good. Somehow this seems okay, like I'm the one in control. I wonder if—

We have the same idea at the same time. "Could we try it like this?" she asks, glancing lower.

I shrug.

"You can stop me any time."

I think about it. "We can try."

She takes my boxers off, careful to only touch the fabric. Then she straddles me again, sitting on my thighs. "Show me."

I cup her hand in mine and put it on my dick. It's such a foreign feeling. My eyes close, and he's here, telling me how much I like it because I get hard. Because I come. My heart races and bile burns my throat. I swallow over and over, trying to push him away. "No!"

Suddenly, I'm alone on the bed. My eyes fly open to see Ella next to me. Tears coat her lashes.

"I'm not going to do it," I say.

She moves for the edge of the bed. "You don't have to."

I grab her arm and pull her back. "That's not what I meant. I meant I'm not going to let him ruin this for me." She looks hesitant as I guide her back on top of me. "I want this, El. You have no idea how much."

I put her hand back on me. I'm completely soft, so I rub up and down, her hand under mine, like how we did it in Florida, only in reverse. So many emotions bombard me. The feel of her hand is amazing and terrifying at the same time.

I focus on our hands, mine rough with calluses, hers as soft and smooth as the finest silk. Then her breasts, her face. I get hard again. She smiles and bites her lip when I grow in her hand.

It's sick and twisted to have to do it like this, but at the same time, *her* hand is on me, and I never thought this could happen.

She puts my other hand on her breast. Oh, yeah. That makes it even better.

"You feel so good," she says.

I love her sultry sex voice. "So do you."

My balls tighten. Her hand moves faster. I make sure not to lose my grip on her, as I don't know what would happen. I try hard not to close my eyes. I focus on her. *She's* doing this to me. *Ella.*

I shout as come spurts across her chest. Our hands fall away. She gets on all fours and hovers over me, giving me a smug little grin.

"Don't get cocky," I say, as she lies on top of me, smushing jizz between us. I chuckle. "Now I need a shower."

"Me, too. Let's take one together." I'm hesitant, so she adds, "I'll use the loofah. It'll be okay."

"You're kind of bossy." She looks taken aback, so I pull her closer. "But I fucking like it." I lean up and kiss her. "I like it a lot."

Confident again, she hops off the bed, leading the way to the bathroom. And suddenly, I get the feeling I'd follow this woman anywhere.

Chapter Forty

Ella

I'm hot. I go to take the covers off and realize I'm trapped. Liam's arm is around me, and he's spooning me. I hold still, wanting to keep the connection as long as possible.

Last night was incredible. It felt like a real date, with real intimacy, and a real sleepover. I know he said no promises, but the way he looked at me in bed after our shower, it sure as heck felt like one.

He shifts behind me and inhales deeply. *Is he smelling my hair?*

"I know you're awake," he says.

"I was just enjoying lying here."

He chuckles. "It's new for me, too. But it's nice."

"I'm glad you think so. Not to scare you off, but you do realize this is the second time you've slept over."

"Kicking me out already, Mrs. Campbell?"

My insides flutter. "Hardly."

He quickly pins me beneath him. He circles my wrists with his long fingers, locking my hands to the bed. I can feel his erection. "How can you be so different from every other girl?"

"I don't think I am. Maybe I'm just different from the girls you've been with."

"It's not that. You're *different*, El."

"As long as it's a good thing."

His lips almost touch mine. "It's a great thing."

He kisses me. All sorts of feelings course through me. I want this. I want it every morning. How can I feel like this after only two months? I knew Corey for eighteen months and still wasn't ready to move in with him. With Liam, every time he leaves, I feel like a part of me is missing. Every time I see him, I become whole again.

He hops out of bed. "I should get going. I have to drive out to Stamford today."

My happiness sours. "I wish you wouldn't."

"He tossed my apartment, Ella."

"And what is confronting him going to accomplish?"

"It's going to show him he can't control me. I want to see his face, knowing he didn't find what he was looking for. It's not often Dirk Campbell doesn't get his way."

"You want to go there to gloat?"

He pulls his pants on. "You wouldn't understand."

"If you insist on going, take me with you."

He stills and turns, a frown snapping between his brows. "No fucking way."

"Why not?"

"One, because Dirk is an asshole. And two, I don't want you anywhere near that part of my life."

I run a finger along his arm. "Am I part of your life?"

He stares at the bed. I wonder if he's thinking about what we did last night. He looks back at me. "Yes, of course."

"Then take me with you."

"It's not a good idea," he says.

"Neither is you going alone."

He sits on the chair and pulls his socks on. "Why do you want to go? Tell me the truth."

I get up, put on my robe, and sit on his lap, straddling him. "Because you're part of my life, Liam. You are important to me. I want you to be safe."

"And you think you can keep me safe?"

"I'll be your buffer. Neither of you will do anything stupid if I'm there. Besides, you're trapped. I'm not letting you go without me."

"You can't keep me from going, El."

I open my robe and expose my breasts. "I suppose not, but I can do everything in my power to make you stay."

He outlines my breasts with his fingers, sending chills through me.

"Take me with you."

"God, woman, you're demanding."

I shimmy on top of him. He's going to say yes.

He appraises me like a starving man in front of a steak dinner. "And after last night, I think I trust you more than anyone I've ever known."

My heart leaps, and it takes all my willpower not to tell him how much I love him.

~ ~ ~

I fiddle with the radio as we drive to Stamford in Crew's old Nissan. "You don't have your own car? Or did you sell it when you moved to the city?"

"I used to drive one from Dirk's car lot. He took it back when I moved out. Since Crew and Bria live and work together, they only need one car, so he lets me use this one."

"I'm surprised it still runs."

"He's taken very good care of it. Do you have a car?"

"I don't even have a license."

"You're twenty-three, El."

"I've lived in the city all my life. There's never been a need."

"Everyone should know how to drive."

"I know how to drive. I learned from watching TV."

"You can't learn how to drive from watching television," he says.

"Want to bet?" He exits the highway even though we're nowhere near Stamford. "Where are you going?"

"To win the bet."

"You want me to drive?"

"Why not? It's an old piece of shit. What better way to start?"

"You're crazy."

"Don't think you can do it, eh?"

"Oh, I can do it."

He pulls into a large empty parking lot, parks in the middle of it, and turns off the car. "Prove it," he says, smiling ear to ear.

We get out and switch seats. I put my seatbelt on and turn the key. It makes a god-awful grinding noise. Liam laughs.

"Shut up."

"Sorry. When the car starts, stop turning the key. Okay, go ahead."

I place my hand on the gear shift, determined to do this without any help. I put it in drive and press on the gas. We surge forward and almost run into a light pole.

"Ella!" he screams.

I slam on the brakes, and Liam has to brace himself or hit the front window.

I turn to him. "That'll teach you for not wearing your seatbelt."

He puts it on. "We're in a fucking parking lot. I didn't think I'd need one. Are you trying to kill me? This time *ease* your foot off the brake and the car will move forward slowly. Then lightly touch the gas, don't stomp on it. I thought you said you knew how to do this?"

"Well, they don't show some of that stuff on TV."

"There's a reason you have to take a test to get a license, you know. Can you imagine if every Joe Schmo who thought they could drive was out on the streets?"

I give him a pouty look.

He flicks a wrist. "You gonna do this or what?"

I ease off the brake and gently press on the gas. I drive through the massive lot, speeding up and slowing down. I turn to him. "This is fun."

"Eyes on the road."

"This isn't a road. But maybe I should go out on one."

"I think that's enough for today."

I raise a brow. "Meaning you'll let me drive again?"

"Sure."

"So who wins the bet? I think I should because I did actually drive the car."

"Yeah, right into a pole."

"Shut up. I didn't hit it."

"We'll call it a draw."

I turn off the engine and jut out my bottom lip. "I was kind of wanting to know what I'd win."

"What did you want?"

I give him a sultry smile.

"God, woman, you *are* going to kill me."

"What did *you* want if you won the bet?"

"To turn around and drop you off so you wouldn't go with me."

My smile falls. "Really?"

"Yes, really. This is going to be uncomfortable as shit, Ella."

"Then don't go. Turn around and we'll both go home. Then I'll collect my winnings."

He thinks about it. He thinks hard. "This has been a long time coming. We're going."

We switch seats again, and he gets back on the highway. A song I like comes on the radio, and I turn it up and dance in my seat.

"You like this band?"

"Who doesn't like White Poison?" Then I feel guilty, remembering Bria used to be their backup singer. "I forgot we're not supposed to like them."

"They're real pricks."

"So you've met them? Of course you did, you opened for them. How many times?"

"Four. We never met them though."

"Never? How can that be?"

"We were explicitly told never to even look at them unless they addressed us."

My jaw drops. "You're not serious."

"We weren't allowed at their after-parties either. They'd sometimes let us eat from the buffet before shows, but only after everyone on their crew, plus their groupies, had their share. And we barely got paid enough to cover our hotel and expenses."

"That doesn't seem fair."

He shrugs. "It's how it works. Opening for them was our payment. It got us a lot of attention."

"And it's starting to pay off for you big time. Maybe you can upgrade the car soon."

"I won't be buying a new car."

"Then what are you going to do with all your money?"

"I'm saving it."

"For what?"

"Never mind."

I scan the radio stations and stop when a Reckless Alibi song comes on. Liam smiles. "What does it feel like to hear your songs on the radio?"

"Probably the same as it feels to see your illustrations in books."

"No way. It's totally different. People hear your music and they seek you out. They buy your albums. They come to your concerts. It must be surreal."

"It's everything I've ever dreamed of."

"You're lucky in so many ways. You're in a successful band. You have incredible friends. Maybe all that can help make up for the bad stuff."

He grips the steering wheel so hard, his knuckles turn white. "Nothing can ever make up for the bad stuff."

"I didn't mean to downplay anything."

He's quiet, and I feel terrible for saying what I did.

We pass the welcome sign for Stamford. He turns off the road and onto a driveway lined with trees. He stops at a gate, punches numbers on a keypad, and it opens. "I'm surprised he didn't delete my code."

"Why would he do that?"

"Because he hates me as much as I hate him."

"Then why did he take you in?"

"I told you, it was blackmail. He kept me and my mom around for insurance."

"Insurance for what?"

"So we would never tell anyone what happened to Luke."

I touch his hand. "And you."

He pulls away.

We approach the house, and I'm stunned. It looks more like a hotel than a single-family home. "You lived *here*?"

"Only as long as I had to and not a second more."

"When did you move out?"

"Right before the tour."

"How come you lived here for so long if you despised him?"

"I had to. The band wasn't making enough money for me to support my mom."

"Where is she now?"

"In the ground next to Luke."

I gasp. "Oh, no. I'm sorry."

"Don't be. In a lot of ways, she's better off. She never got over Luke's death. She drank a lot. It's ultimately what killed her."

"Liam—"

"I said stop it, El. I don't need you feeling sorry for me."

"Your mom died. So did your brother. I'm not feeling sorry for you. I'm sad for you. There's a difference."

He pulls up in front of the house, looking at it as if he'd rather be anywhere but here. We get out and go to the front door. He stops before ringing the bell. "You're not going to say anything, right?"

"What would I say? I'm only here for moral support."

He rings. Even the bell sounds rich. A woman opens the door and smiles. "Mijo!" She pulls him into a hug.

"Helen, this is Ella."

"How nice to meet you," she says.

I'm confused. Why is he getting such a good reception? "Hello, Mrs. Campbell."

"Helen isn't Dirk's wife. She's the housekeeper."

Heat crosses my face. "Oh, I'm sorry."

Helen laughs. "To be mistaken for Ms. Sylvia. Oh, the fun in that. Thank you, child."

"I'm here to see Dirk," he says.

Helen gestures to a room on the right. "If you'd like to wait there, I'll find him. Can I get you something to drink? Tea? Water?"

"We won't be here long. Thanks, Helen."

She walks away, and we go into the room. "I feel so stupid. Of course your aunt wouldn't answer the door." I glance around. It's one of the most ornate rooms I've ever been in. "I've never seen any place like this. It's like a castle."

"And Dirk is the fucking king."

Helen hurries back. "Mayor Campbell will see you in his office."

Liam glares. "Fuck no."

"Mijo, watch your tongue."

"Sorry. Helen, can you please ask him to come here?"

She gives him an apologetic look and looks like she's about to cry. "He said he will only see you there. Nowhere else."

"That's how he's going to play this?"

"I'm sorry," she says.

"What's so bad about meeting in his office?" I whisper to him.

"I don't ever go there. It's where Luke died."

My mouth drops open. "That fucking prick." I turn to Helen. "My apologies."

Liam's eyebrows hit the ceiling. "I didn't think you had it in you, El."

"I call 'em like I see 'em."

"Maybe you should stay here with Helen."

"What do you think, Helen? Should I stay here with you or go with him while he talks to Dirk?"

"If you go with Mr. Liam, I think there's likely to be less shouting."

I shoot Liam a smug look. "See? Helen's a smart lady. You should listen to her."

He tugs on my elbow. "Come on then, let's get this over with."

We turn down a hallway that seems to go on forever. I wish I could get a tour, because I'll never again be in a house like this. Liam stops at a door on the right. He glares at it. How cruel must his uncle be to make him take the meeting in the place his brother died?

He sucks in a deep breath and knocks.

"Come in."

Dirk sees me and stands. "Ah, Miss Campbell. How lovely to see you again so soon." He turns to Liam. "I wasn't aware you needed a chaperone."

"Did you really think I'd have kept it on me, Dirk?"

He goes to the bar and pours himself a few fingers of whiskey. "What are you referring to?"

"Don't be so fucking obtuse."

He gets in Liam's face. "Don't disrespect me in my home."

"How about we sit, Liam?" I walk to the couch and stare him down until he follows.

"I'd offer you a drink, but I hate to encourage an alcoholic," Dirk says.

Liam's jaw tightens. "I'm not an alcoholic."

"Well, the apple can't fall too far from the tree, now can it?"

"I'm only here for one thing, Dirk. Sell the company."

"Surely you're not talking about IRL." He holds up his glass. "Best investment I ever made."

"Sell it, or I'll release the video."

"Bullshit," he says. "Like I said yesterday, you'd have done it by now if you have it."

"I was living under your roof. I had my mom to think about. I couldn't do it until now. Everything I said is true."

"You're bluffing."

"Maybe I am. Or maybe you have no fucking idea what's on the video. You're old. I'm sure your memory isn't what it once was. You can't possibly remember all the conversations you had in this house or how damning those conversations might have been."

He walks over and hovers above Liam. The guy is intimidating if nothing else. "Are you threatening me?"

Liam laughs. "I am, and there's not a damn thing you can do about it."

He backs away and gestures to me. "You want your little friend here to know how disgusting you are?"

"He's not disgusting," I say.

Liam puts a hand on my arm. Dirk watches the motion. "Yes, keep your little lap dog quiet, why don't you."

I open my mouth, but Liam shakes his head at me. I'm beginning to realize what he had to put up with all these years.

"You want her knowing how your father put his hands on you? You want her knowing how much you liked it?"

My heart races when Liam explodes off the couch and goes after Dirk. But before he can touch him, a large man appears in the doorway and loudly clears his throat.

"Right," Liam says, stopping. "Because you hire people to do your dirty work. Is he the one who broke into my apartment?"

"I have no idea what you're talking about."

Dirk looks at me like he expected some kind of reaction. I don't give him one, and I can tell it pisses him off. I cock my head and raise my brows wanting so badly to say, *"Thought you could hurt him, did you?"*

Liam retreats to the couch. "Sell the company, Dirk, or I promise I'll end you. By the way, several other people know about the video. If anything happens to me, they'll be sure to publicize it."

He finishes off his drink. "You can't blackmail me."

"You mean I can't blackmail a blackmailer?"

Dirk motions to the guy in the doorway. "Mike will escort you out. Then he'll change the gate code. You won't be returning."

"As if I'd ever want to."

Dirk looks purposeful as he crosses the room to his desk. "His body was found right here, you know. It was pathetic really. He wasn't even man enough to live. Took the coward's way out."

Liam lunges for Dirk, and Mike intercepts him. "This way," he says.

I turn back to Dirk. "How can you live with yourself?"

He laughs. "Quite nicely, as you can see."

Back in the car, Liam's head meets the steering wheel.

"That was intense," I say.

"Every meeting with him is intense."

"I'm sorry it went so badly."

"It went exactly how I expected it to go. I delivered the message. It's up to him what to do next."

"Do you think he'll sell the company?"

"Hell no, he won't. Especially after I told him to do it."

"Then why ask him to?"

"It's the only thing I could ever get from him that would benefit me. I'm releasing the video no matter what. I thought if there was any chance to get him out of IRL in the process, I had to take it."

"Can what's on the video really hurt him?"

"If adults have knowledge of the abuse of minors and don't say anything, it's a crime. My mom was guilty of it too. They both knew and didn't go to the police. I don't blame her for keeping quiet—Dirk didn't give her a choice—but everything he did, everything he's always done was to further his career and earn more money. Even if the video doesn't result in him being arrested, it'll ruin his chances at being elected governor or staying on as mayor."

"Why not go after your dad, uh, Don? He could still be charged for what he did."

"I have no idea where he is. He fell off the planet. If I had to guess, Dirk had something to do with that too. Besides, the bastard lives in my nightmares. I don't need to go dredging that shit up in real life. If I never see him again, it'll be a day too soon."

As we drive away from the palatial estate, I look back, and it seems smaller somehow. Not so grand. "You live one complicated life, Liam Campbell."

He takes his eyes off the road for a second to lock gazes with me. "Does that scare you?"

I smile. "Not even a little."

Chapter Forty-one

Liam

Bria knocks on my door. "Hurry up. We don't want to be late for our first rehearsal at IRL." She pokes her head in to find me still in bed. "Liam, get up."

"Is this how it's going to be? You ordering us around?"

"Someone has to crack the whip."

"Who gives a shit if we're late anyway?"

"Ronni, for one. She texted this morning. She wants to meet with us first thing."

"Screw Ronni."

"I feel the same way, but we need to stay on her good side to keep the studio."

"We can afford to rent space now." I regret the words as soon as they're out of my mouth. The truth is, I don't want to spend a penny I don't have to.

She comes in and opens my curtains. "Why rent one when we can have one for free?"

I want to argue. I want to say Ronni will be watching our every move. Maybe Dirk too. "You'd better leave unless you want to be introduced to my morning wood, Bria." I move to get out of bed, and she covers her eyes and runs out of the room.

"We're leaving in ten minutes!" she yells from the hall.

After a quick shower, I go to the kitchen, fill a bowl with cereal, and dig in. "Anyone hear from Brad?"

Garrett looks up from his phone. "Not a peep since we saw him at IRL."

"Don't you guys think it's strange that he crawled under a rock after coming back from Florida?"

Bria takes my empty bowl and rinses it out. I kind of like having her around. Even though she's a little bossy, she does pick up after us.

Bossy. I think of Ella. We've gone out to dinner twice since going to Dirk's. She wanted me to go back to her place. Maybe sleep over again. But after being in his office, shit came back to me in a bad way. I've needed a minute.

"Brad's never been in constant contact," Bria says. "Before the tour, we only talked to him at rehearsals and gigs. He's not as social as we are. Could be you're noticing his absence more now that the rest of us are living together."

"It's not that," I say. "Something's changed."

Crew joins us with wet hair. "Who used all the hot water?"

Garrett raises his hand. "That'd probably be me. Got a sexy text from this chick I met last night. Had to rub one out in the shower."

"Ew." Bria rolls her eyes. "I did not need to know that."

Crew says to her, "There's one way we could save on hot water. Shower together."

"Yeah, baby," Garrett says, giving Bria a wink and a thumbs-up.

"You guys really have no boundaries, do you?" Bria asks.

Crew laughs. "You agreed to the living situation."

"Living with us means you have to put up with all our shit," Garrett says. "Hey, speaking of shit, I was wondering if you guys drop duces in front of each other."

"Oh my God, stop," Bria says.

The rest of us are laughing.

Crew grabs his notebook and we head for the door. "To answer your question, no. There are some things you shouldn't watch your lady do."

"Yeah, that's what I thought," Garrett says. "And the tampon stuff?"

Bria looks shocked. Crew discreetly shakes his head at Garrett.

Garrett continues teasing Bria the entire way to IRL. He gets some funny looks on the subway because of his vulgarity. Bria's a good sport, though. She's learned to put up with us after a year of being the only girl in RA.

We stop laughing when we walk into IRL to see Ronni brooding. She glances at the clock. "You're late."

"We're artists," I say. "We don't work on a schedule."

"I expect you to be on time when we have a meeting."

"Then you'd better not tell us about it the morning of."

"Come," she says, like we're dogs that obey her command. "Jeremy and Brad are waiting in the conference room."

Garrett raises an eyebrow. "Ooooo, the conference room. Fancy."

"I'm already missing the barn," Crew says.

We sit around a large table, and Ronni hands us each a packet. "What's this?" I ask.

"Our new business plan."

I glance at the others. "We're a goddamn rock band, Ronni."

"And you think that's not a business? Until now, all you've had to do is play your music, sit back, and let me do the rest. Not anymore. Your brand is growing, thanks to me. You've seen the royalty checks, and they're only going to get bigger."

"She's right," Crew says. "This is a business. Now let's get this over with so we can get to rehearsal and do what we do that makes them money."

Ronni sits at the head of the table. "Open to page one. It's the schedule I've set for you. It covers six months. We'll need to cut two more albums and make a whole lot of music videos. You're getting a lot of airtime, but we don't want the songs to get stale. We need to freshen things up. On page two is a list of all the clubs I've booked. We're in a different league now. No more bars and taverns. High-end dance clubs only from here on out. I predict that within a year, you may not be playing clubs at all. Tours and appearances only, that's the goal."

"We're going to need more security," Crew says, talking to Ronni but looking at Bria.

"We'll deal with it as needed," Ronni says.

Crew pounds a fist on the table. "We'll deal with it now, before we have a situation."

"Crew's right," Jeremy says. "In Florida we needed event security more than we ever have."

"Fine," she says. "It's your money. The first one was on us. Any additional security is your responsibility. Read the contract. Can we move on please? I don't have all day."

I turn to the next page and skim it. "Dancing? What the hell, Ronni?"

"I've hired a dance instructor and choreographer. I saw video of some of your performances in Florida. You were all over the place. Uncoordinated. We need to clean it up."

"We're not NSYNC." Everyone at the table complains but Garrett. He's laughing because he's the drummer and drummers don't dance. I point at him. "Shut up."

He pulls his sticks from his back pocket and beats them on his thigh.

"We're not dancing," Crew says.

Ronni arches a mocking brow. "Think of it more as having synchronized movements to the beat of the music."

"What's the difference?" I say. I pull the page out of the packet and rip it in half. "I'm not fucking dancing."

Ronni comes over and puts an authoritative hand on the table in front of me. "You'll dance if I say you dance."

"Are you guys hearing this shit?" I stand and cross to the other side of the room, not wanting to hit a woman.

"Sit down," Jeremy says. "No one is going to make you dance. Especially if you're terrible at it."

Ronni glares at him like he's her worst enemy. "Really, Jeremy? Now they'll be bad on purpose."

"Noooo," he says melodramatically. "They wouldn't dare." He turns to us, smiling. "Would you?"

It still amazes me how Jeremy went from being Ronni's lackey to being on our side.

"Either way, it's a done deal," Ronni says, her lips forming an uncompromising line. "Let's move on."

"What the hell is this about imposing fines?" Garrett says, leafing through the packet.

We all turn to the page he's referring to.

"Oh, yes," Ronni says. "In order to keep you from pulling any further stunts that will damage your brand, we've instituted a system of fines."

"You're kidding!" I say.

"You may not realize it," she says. "But stunts like what Crew pulled in Florida—proposing on stage—hurt you. I understand you thought it was romantic, but that has no place here. You shouldn't be airing your dirty laundry in front of the fans."

"You think us getting engaged is dirty laundry?" Bria says defensively.

"Obviously not if you were bank tellers, but you're rock stars. There is a certain reputation you need to uphold. You have to keep the fantasy alive for the fans. If they think you're taken and will live happily ever after, they have no reason to worship you."

"Haven't we been over this a hundred times?" Crew asks.

"And we'll keep talking about it until you hear me. You're on the cusp of being famous. Years from now, when you're established and bringing in serious money, you can have some latitude. Until then I'm your rep. IRL handles your PR, and you'll do as we say."

"You can't tell us how to act," Garrett says.

"I suggest you read your contract, because it clearly says we can."

"No," Crew says. "That's how *you* interpret it."

"And right now mine is the only opinion that matters." Ronni's fake smile becomes a smirk. "You're free to hire an attorney at any time. If you don't like what you hear, write us a check for a million dollars, and we'll gladly part ways. Until then, you'll do things *my* way."

"How much longer are we stuck with IRL?" Crew asks.

"Two years, one month, and thirteen days," I say flatly.

Jeremy laughs. "But who's counting?"

Ronni shoots him a traitorous glance.

"Listen, people, it's imperative I have my finger on the pulse of Reckless Alibi, or I won't be able to help you. Crew and Bria, have you considered what a messy divorce would do to the band? Have you thought about children? What will you do with them when you're on the road?"

"Plenty of musicians have kids," Bria says.

"And they have a spouse to take care of them when they go on tour."

Crew takes Bria's hand. "We'll work it out."

Ronni turns to Garrett. "What about you? Anything I need to know?"

"Uh, I masturbated in the shower this morning, thinking about a hot chick I met last night."

"See?" She motions to Garrett. "*This* is how rock stars behave." She looks in my direction. "What about you?"

"Fuck off, Ronni."

"Do you deny being in a relationship with that awful girl I was tricked into paying for an album cover?"

"Ella is none of your business."

She puts her hands on her hips. "I'll take that as a yes. Wow, rarely do things surprise me, but Liam Campbell having a girlfriend is definitely one of them."

"I don't have a girlfriend."

Ronni looks to the others. "Does he?"

They shrug.

"People, keep your personal shit out of the limelight." She points to the packet. "Read the rules. Follow them, and we won't have a problem. You're awfully quiet, Brad. You good with all this?"

He clears his throat. "There's something you should know."

"Oh, for Christ's sake, what is it now?"

"Katie's pregnant."

Ronni sits down and her head falls back. "Will you people ever learn?"

It all makes sense now, why Brad has been distant. Why he seemed pissed the other day.

"How far along is she?" Bria asks.

"Three months."

"Good," Ronni says. "Not so far along you can't do something about it."

Anger flares in Brad's eyes. "I know you're not suggesting we get rid of the baby."

"It happens all the time. Some women practically use abortions as birth control."

"You really are a bitch, Ronni," I say. "I swear to God if I had a million bucks, I'd write you a check right fucking now."

"We're keeping it," Brad snarls through gritted teeth.

"We?" she asks.

"Yes. We. We're getting married."

"Then congratulations are in order," Jeremy says.

Ronni slaps the table. "Just fucking perfect." She gets up and stares out the window for a minute. "Okay, fine. Here's what we're going to do. Brad will be the family man. Every band has one. The clean-cut, untouchable bassist. The rest of you will play the part of being desirable rock stars. Got it?"

I get up. "If you're done being a dictator, we have to get to practice."

"I expect you to put in a full day. You had your week off. It's time to get back to work."

"Give it a rest, Ronni," Jeremy says. "They know what they have to do."

She strides over to him and jabs a finger in his chest. "Don't forget, everyone is replaceable. Especially you."

He holds up his hands in surrender, and she leaves.

We swarm Brad. "A baby, wow," Crew says.

"I'm still wrapping my head around it. She told me last week when I got home."

"Congratulations," Bria says. "I know you didn't plan it, but it will be fantastic all the same."

"Thanks. I can't believe I'm going to be a dad."

"Did you and Katie talk about having kids?"

"All the time. She really wants to be a mom, but I thought that was far off in the future."

Garrett steps forward. "You think she's trying to trap you, man?"

"Trap me?" he says, angrily. "We're engaged. She doesn't have to trap me. It was an accident."

"She hates RA," I say. "Could be she's trying to get you to quit."

He gets in my face. "It was an accident."

"Whatever you say."

"You don't get it, do you?" he says. "When you find the person you're meant to be with, you'll do anything for them."

"What the hell does that mean?"

"Nothing. Let's go rehearse."

We practice for seven hours, but I'm not sure any of us are into it. Brad's concerned about the position he's in. Crew and Bria are worried about the ridiculous restrictions Ronni wants to put on them. Garrett—well, I don't know what the hell Garrett is thinking about. Maybe the girl from last night.

Me—I'm thinking about the one person I know I'd do anything for.

Chapter Forty-two

Ella

I pick up my chirping phone. "Hi, Mom."

"Hi, sweetie. How are you?"

"Good."

"Are your illustrations coming along well?"

"They are. Even faster than I thought they would."

"And the boy? What was his name again? How's he?"

"It's Liam, Mom. I've told you a dozen times."

"Right. How are things going there?"

"Good, I think. I don't know. It's complicated."

"Things were never complicated with Corey."

"Right up until he cheated on me."

"Hasn't he apologized? He still calls us, you know. We even had lunch with him the other day."

"I wish you wouldn't see him. He's not a part of my life anymore."

"He said he wants to marry you."

"He *cheated* on me."

There's a long moment of silence. "Things like that can be overcome. It doesn't have to mean the end of a relationship."

"Did Dad cheat on you?"

"No."

"Then how can you sa—"

"I'm the one who cheated, Ella."

I sit on my bed, floored. Everything I thought about my parents is a lie. They aren't the perfect couple with the perfect marriage.

"Say something," she says.

"I … I can't. I'm shocked. When? How?"

"It was a long time ago. I never truly got over losing your sister. I was delighted to have you, and I loved you with all my heart, but a piece of me was missing. I guess I went looking for that piece."

"And Dad forgave you?"

"Not at first. But you weren't even two years old. He stayed for you and eventually we worked it out."

"Wow, okay."

"My indiscretions were far worse than Corey's."

"How so?"

"I had a long-term affair. It lasted almost a year."

"You cheated on Dad for a year?" Did New York City just have an earthquake, because it feels like the ground shifted under my feet.

"In my whole life, it's the thing I'm most ashamed of."

"Did you love the other man?"

"I thought I did, but in the end, no. He was a replacement for Ava. He was shiny and new and exciting. He made me feel like I wasn't the mother of a dead baby."

"Mom, that's awful."

"I know. But it's how I felt about myself. When I was with your father, I was the sad woman who'd lost a child. But with *him*, I was just Ann."

"How did it end?"

"Your father found a letter the man wrote me. He confronted him, even told his wife."

I gasp. "He was married, too?"

"We were young and stupid. Your father hated me for a while. I begged him to go to counseling. He resisted for months. I went on my own. I learned a lot about myself. I finally wore him down. And now look where we are, twenty years later."

"I always thought you and Daddy were perfect together."

"We are, but it took a while for us to get back there."

"Still, I'm not sure how this all applies to me. I love Liam, not Corey."

"You *love* him?"

"I do."

"Does he share the sentiment?"

"I don't know. I haven't told him. We don't talk about that stuff."

"You have only known each other for a few months. Are you sure you're not with him to get over Corey?"

"Mom, drop it. I'm not getting back with Corey. Even if Liam and I don't work out, I still won't go back to him." As I say the words, a weight lifts off my shoulders. I realize I'd rather be alone than with someone I can't love and trust fully.

"If you're sure."

"I'm sure."

"When can we meet this new man then? How about tonight? Can we take you out for dinner?"

"Tonight?" I try to think up a quick excuse, but my mind fails me. "I'll have to check with him. He's pretty busy."

"I'm sure he's not too busy to meet your parents."

Would he agree to meet them? It's a big step. I'm almost afraid to ask him. Our relationship is fragile at best.

"We won't bite, Ella."

"You promise not to come on too strong?"

"I'll wait to plan the wedding until our second meeting."

"Mo-om."

"I'm kidding."

We hang up. I text Liam with the dinner invitation. While I wait for his reply, I think about Mom's revelation. She told me so I'd reconsider things with Corey, but it did the opposite. Her telling me makes me think Liam and I might be able to overcome his past. They went to therapy. What if Liam did too? I could go with him. It's far too early to bring something like that up with him, but the thought of it gives me hope.

~ ~ ~

"So," Liam says, leaning in the doorway. "Meeting the parents. You know I've never done this before, right?"

We're on the way out. I pull the door closed and lock it. "I figured. It doesn't mean anything. I talk about you sometimes, and they want to meet you, that's all."

He raises a brow. "You talk about me? What do you say?"

"I had to tell them *something*, Liam. I did go to Florida with you for six weeks. I told them about Reckless Alibi and the tour."

"What did you say about me specifically?"

We get on the empty elevator. "That you're super talented, and nice. And … hot."

He traps me in a corner. "You told them I'm hot?"

I swallow and look up at him. "I think I may have used the word handsome."

He kisses me. I wish we could ride back up and go to my bedroom.

"What else did you say?"

I shrug.

"Do they think I'm your boyfriend?"

"I didn't put a label on it. Don't worry, I don't think they'll call you that."

"What do you call it when the guy you're with doesn't want to be with anyone else, and *you* don't want to be with anyone else?"

I suck my bottom lip into my mouth. "You don't want to date anyone else?"

He whispers, "I don't want to do *anything* with anyone else. Do you?"

"No."

"Good."

The elevator doors open. I'm reeling. Did we just enter into an actual, adult, committed relationship? He holds my hand as we walk down the street. I can't stop smiling.

He glances at me. "Cat got your tongue, El?"

"I'm happy, is all."

"Happy," he muses, like it's an emotion he's not familiar with.

"There is something I should probably warn you about, though."

"Oh, shit, is your dad a huge motherfucker? Is he going to talk to me about safe sex or some shit like that?"

I laugh. "You're bigger than him and no, he won't talk about sex. But you should know they really liked Corey."

"Great. They love your ex. So what you're saying is I don't have a snowball's chance in hell to impress them."

He wants to impress them? This night is already going better than I expected.

"I didn't say that. I just wanted you to know. Maybe don't cuss a lot around them. You know, tone down the rock star."

"You don't think they'll like me the way I am?"

"They will eventually. You're an acquired taste, Liam. I don't want them to get the wrong impression."

"Fine. I'll be on my best behavior."

"There they are." I point ahead.

Mom pulls me into her arms. "Sweetie!"

Then Dad gives me a hug. I hug him extra tight and long, feeling bad for what Mom did to him.

When I finally let go, I make introductions. "Mom, Dad, this is Liam. Liam, my parents, Ann and Peter."

They shake hands.

"Our table is ready," Dad says.

We are seated and place our drink orders.

"Liam, what's your last name?" Mom asks.

Liam looks at me, surprised I hadn't told them. "Campbell."

Dad glances between us. "You don't say?"

Mom chuckles. "Have you checked to make sure you aren't related?"

"We're not. I'm a Campbell by adoption," Liam says.

"What are your parents' names?" Dad asks him. "Maybe we know them."

Liam tenses. "Colleen and … Don."

"Hmm," Dad says. "Can't say that I do."

I don't like where this is going. I pick up the menu. "What's good here?"

As my parents go over the entrées and tell me what they like, Liam squeezes my knee. I put my hand under the table and give his a pat. He traps mine and holds it.

"The broiled scallops sound good," I say. I turn to Liam. "What about you?"

"I'm going for the sirloin."

"Ah, a fellow carnivore," Dad says. "A boy after my own heart."

Mom scolds him. "Liam's hardly a boy. What are you, twenty-five?"

"Twenty-four, ma'am."

I raise my brows at him. I don't think I've ever heard him be so formal. I can tell he has no idea what to say or how to act. I feel bad for agreeing to this.

"Pish, stop with the ma'am," Mom says. "Call me Ann."

After the waitress takes our order, Dad quizzes me about the books I'm illustrating. Then he turns to Liam. Here we go.

"Ella tells us you're in a rock band."

"Yes, sir. I play guitar."

Sir? I give him a sideways glance. He mouths, *"What?"*

"And this band is the reason my daughter followed you to Florida? What's it called, Reckless something or other?"

"Daddy, you promised."

"I'm just making conversation, pumpkin."

"She didn't follow me," Liam says. "She came because I invited her. We weren't, um, together or anything. But she inspired me."

"Liam writes music for Reckless Alibi. Not the lyrics but the melodies."

Dad's eyebrows shoot up. "A composer?"

Liam nods.

"Impressive," Dad says.

I squeeze Liam's hand.

Dad tops off his glass of wine. "Where do you see yourself in the long term, Liam?"

"Still with Reckless Alibi."

"Kind of a pipe dream, don't you think? Wanting to be in a rock band in your thirties and forties? What kind of life can that be? Do you expect your wife to support you?"

"Daddy," I warn.

"It's okay," Liam says to me. He looks my dad straight in the eye. "The average record sells just over 11,000 copies. The average record from an indie label, like ours, sells less than 2,000. Reckless Alibi's first album has sold more than 50,000 copies in under a year. We've got two others and are about to cut our fourth. My bank account is fat, and I don't expect that to change anytime soon. We're only at the beginning of being famous. So I plan to be in a rock band until the day I die." He glances at me to see my surprise. Then he turns back to my dad. "Sir."

Dad stares him down. There is a lot of tension in the air. Finally, his palm meets the table. "Okay, I stand corrected."

I let out a breath of relief. I think I see the hint of a smirk on Liam's face. God, it's so sexy the way he just handled my dad.

The rest of dinner is fairly benign. Dad asks Liam a lot of questions about the music industry. It's almost as if he envies him. Mom listens to them and smiles at me. She nods her approval at me. I can tell she's smitten with him.

Dessert comes, and with it, the question that makes Liam crush my hand like he's drowning and I'm his life preserver.

"What kind of work does your father do?" Mom asks.

"Liam's parents aren't with us anymore. Can we please talk about something else?"

"Oh, I'm sorry," Mom says to him. "We're no stranger to loss. I'm sure Ella told you about her twin sister."

"Mom, that is *not* not talking about it."

Liam clears his throat. "Did Ella tell you she created the cover for our next album?"

"She did indeed," Dad says. "Now that I know how successful you are, I'm even more impressed with her."

The check comes. Liam reaches for it. "I'd like to get this."

"Son, I don't care how fat your bank account is," Dad says. "We invited you. We tortured you with our questions. We're paying for the meal."

"Thank you."

On our way out, Dad and Liam walk ahead. Mom pulls me close. "You said he was handsome, but I didn't expect this. Well done, sweetie. I approve."

"Good. So no more talk about Corey?"

"No."

I hug my parents at the door. Mom hugs Liam. He looks completely awkward when he pats her on the back. I try not to laugh.

Dad extends his hand. "Liam, it's been a pleasure. You two don't be strangers now."

Liam shakes. "Nice to meet you too, sir, and we won't."

They walk away.

Liam rolls up his sleeves and loosens his collar. I don't think he means for it to be sexy but it totally is. He's just happy to be done with the third degree.

I slump against the side of the building. "I am so sorry for subjecting you to that."

His gaze sweeps over me. "Just how sorry are we talking?"

I question him with my eyes.

"I'm only saying, if you think you owe me something, I'm willing to collect."

My insides tingle. "Let's go back to my place so I can pay up."

He takes my hand and leads me away. I love the feeling of his hand holding mine. I glance around. Does anyone recognize him? How long will it be before he can't stroll down the street without girls chasing him?

"You really stood up to my dad when he was grilling you."

"Is that not how guys talk to the fathers of the daughters they're dating?"

I smile. "So we're dating?"

He doesn't answer, but he tightens his fingers around mine.

"It was sexy," I say.

He stops and looks at me sideways. "The way I talked to your father?"

"Corey agreed with everything he said. He was such a kiss-ass."

"And you don't want that?"

"No. I want you."

For a second, I think I see fear in his eyes. Then something changes. Our gazes lock. I wish he could know what I'm thinking. If he did, though, he'd probably run away. Because I love every part of him, the damaged and the good. I want to be with him every day and sleep next to him at night. Love him the way he deserves to be loved.

He runs a finger across my cheek and pulls my bottom lip from between my teeth. "I want you, too."

Chapter Forty-three

Liam

We're alone as we ride up in the elevator. I stand behind her and pull her close. I gently wrap a hand around her neck and maneuver her head to the side so I can kiss her along the top of her shoulder. She shudders and presses into me as I work my lips toward her ear. I make sure she can feel my erection through my slacks.

The elevator doors open. Ella tugs me down the hall. The way she wants me is amazing. Other women have wanted me, but only for sex. After they had me and knew how messed up I was, they didn't want me again. The way Ella wants me is different. She wants my heart. My soul. And I'll be damned if I don't want to give it to her.

As soon as we're inside her apartment, she kicks off her shoes, leads me to the couch, pushes me down, and straddles me. She looks at me with such heat, reverence, and intensity, I almost can't breathe.

She pulls off my shirt. Her hands feel exquisite as they explore my chest. I'm hungry for her to do more, but I can tell she's hesitant. "Lower," I say.

She's surprised. "Are you sure?"

"Lower," I growl.

Her eyebrows shoot up. "Who's being bossy *now*?"

"God, woman. Just do it."

I lean my head back and close my eyes.

"Not unless you look at me," she says.

She's always been right about that. I have to watch so I know it's her touching me. She runs a hand down my stomach. I draw in a quick breath, and she withdraws. I take her hand and put it back on me.

She caresses my lower abs and runs a finger under the waistband of my pants, teasing me with her light touch. She grazes the head of my cock and pulls back. "I'm sorry."

I stand up with her in my arms. "I don't want you be sorry, El. I want you to fucking touch me." I set her next to me and strip off the rest of my clothes. "I want you to touch me like I'm a normal guy, not some freak."

Her gaze runs up and down my body. The way she strokes her neck as she peruses me makes my cock stand at full attention. "You've never been a freak, Liam."

"That's not what everyone else says."

She skims her hands down my arms. "I'm not everyone else. Now sit."

I do what she asks, then watch as she undresses in front of me. Her blouse falls to the floor, followed by her pants. Only small scraps of pink fabric remain. She moves between my legs. "You do the rest."

I unclasp her bra. Her breasts are right in front of my face, so I take one in my mouth. She moans. I reach around and knead the soft globes of her ass as I lick her nipples.

I rip off her panties to find her soaking wet. When I slip a finger inside her, she says my name. It's one sexy, sultry, throaty word. One I want to hear her say every day for the rest of my goddamn life.

She climbs onto my lap and rubs her clit on my dick. *Ho-o-ly fuck*. I could slip inside her so easily, but I can't.

"You have to touch me," I say. "I won't do this with you unless you touch me."

She scoots back onto my thighs, looks down at my hard, slick cock and then back up at me. She's nervous. I'm fucking terrified.

I put her hand on me. Like before, my hand is on top of hers, and I leave it there when she starts to move. But then I take a deep breath and pull my hand away. She stops moving when I tense. I swallow and nod.

Then my whole goddamn world changes.

Her hand moves up and down my shaft. I cup her breasts. We gaze at each other. Her eyes half close, and her teeth capture her bottom lip as the motion of her hand quickens.

I've never been so scared yet deliriously happy at the same time. She's touching me. And I'm letting her.

I'm watching in fascination as she gives me the first real handy a woman has ever given me. When I feel thoughts of Don start to creep into my mind, I push them aside. Ella is nothing like him. Her hands are soft and gentle. And more importantly, I invited her to do this. *I'm* the one in control.

"God, Liam, you feel so good."

My insides burn as she tells me how she likes doing this to me. Her voice pushes me over the edge, and I grunt as I come amazingly, gloriously, and unabashedly.

Holy shit. I sit, stunned at the incredible way I feel after she flew solo. The sick bastard was right about one thing, it *is* better when someone else does it. But it has to be the *right* someone. Not some pervert pedophile.

I shake my head—tossing him out of my thoughts. Because after what she just did for me, there's only one thing in this world I want to do.

We switch positions so she's on the couch and I'm kneeling before her. I get my shirt off the floor and wipe the come off her chest, then I stick a finger inside her and lower my head between her legs. "You have no idea how long I've dreamed of doing this to you."

Her head falls back as soon as my tongue touches her clit. She grips my hair and holds me close, and I realize I don't even mind it. Because the smell of her, the taste, is beyond anything I've ever experienced. She's all woman. And right now—she's fucking *mine.* As if there's any chance I'd stop. Every other time I've done this, it was for my pleasure, not theirs. Her mouth is open, and her eyes are closed. I've never given two shits how I made a woman feel. I'd give anything to make her feel like this every second of every day.

I push two fingers inside her and find the spot that drives her wild. She says my name again. I suck on her clit, lashing it with my tongue, grazing it with my stubble. She bucks into my face and tenses every muscle, then has the most spectacular orgasm.

Her pussy is pink and swollen. I get hard again looking at it. I want to be inside her so bad. I want it more than a gold record. More than any amount of money.

I pull her closer to the edge of the couch. She knows what I'm doing. She reaches between us and runs her hand along my erection. This time I don't flinch. I don't tense. I don't do anything but enjoy the feel of her hand on me. I inch closer and she guides me inside her.

She's warm and slick and tight. "God, Ella."

A tear rolls from her eye. I wipe it away. I kiss her as I make love to her. Hell, I almost cry myself. I'm making love to a woman. Not fucking, making love. It's the most intimate thing that's ever happened to me. And suddenly I feel free.

I pull away from her lips, needing to see her face as I pump in and out of her. "Liam, I …" She pauses, and I panic. Maybe she doesn't want this after all. But she grabs my ass and holds me inside. "I love you."

Something inside me shifts. Nobody has said those words to me since I was little. Even my mother rarely said them. This woman—this angel—loves me? How can that be?

I realize she's holding my ass. And I'm letting her. I've never allowed anyone to touch me there, but she is. And I'm not stopping or running away. I'm not even moving her hands.

And she loves me.

I start to move in her again. I frame her face with my hands and kiss her. I can't say the words. I'm not sure I even know what love is. But I can kiss her. Will she know there are things I want to say but can't?

She wraps her legs around me. The noises coming from her throat make my balls tighten. I thrust one last time and shout as I come inside her.

I collapse on her. "Shit, I couldn't wait for you. I'm sorry."

"It wouldn't have mattered," she says into my hair. "I've never come twice."

I sit up and look at her, surprised. "Never?"

She shakes her head.

"You realize you've issued a challenge, right?"

She gazes at me sweetly. "So you're not running away?"

"After that? Are you kidding? El, I never thought … I just … No, I'm not running away."

I sit on the couch next to her and cross my feet on the coffee table, going over in my mind what just happened. It's unbelievable.

"I'm on the pill, in case you were wondering."

"I know. I've seen them in your bathroom. I've never gone without a condom. At least I don't think I have. There may have been one or two drunken nights where I blacked out and didn't know what happened. Shit, we should have used one. I'll get tested."

"We'll both get tested. I've gone without them myself." She thumbs to her bedroom. "Do you want to stay over?"

"If I do, I can't promise I won't take you up on your challenge."

The edges of her mouth turn up. "I was kind of counting on it."

I stand, pick her up, and carry her to the bathroom.

While she turns on the shower, I see her toothbrush on the counter and remember something Crew said to me not long ago. I pick it up and squirt toothpaste on it before sticking it in my mouth.

Ella sees me. "I can get you your own if you want."

I smile because, like Crew, I don't want my own. If she only knew what a monumental moment this was. If only I could find the words to tell her.

Thirty minutes later, the lights are off, and we're doing one of my favorite things—lying in bed, gazing at each other.

"So you're good?" she asks. "*We're* good?"

"Yeah."

"I got carried away. I blindsided you. I shouldn't have said it."

I rise on an elbow. "Are you saying you didn't mean it?"

"I meant it. I mean it. But I shouldn't have said it. It's too soon."

"There's a timetable for this sort of thing?"

She snorts. "No."

I brush her hair back. "I want you to always be honest with me."

"The same goes for you."

I roll her on her back and pin her to the bed. "I honestly want to give you two more orgasms."

She shimmies beneath me.

"I want you to touch me everywhere, El."

When I lean down to kiss her, I can feel her smile.

I pull away and stare into her eyes. "As long as we're sharing, there *is* something I want to tell you. This. You. Us. It's making me feel something I've never felt before."

"What?"

I lean down so our lips almost touch. "Happy."

Chapter Forty-four

Ella

Strolling down the sidewalk to meet Liam for lunch, I can't help my smile. He said he's happy. Hearing that delighted me more than hearing him say I love you would have. He's happy. I didn't scare him off. He spent the night. He met and exceeded the challenge.

Last night may have possibly been the best night of my entire life.

I'm approaching IRL when I see the one person I didn't want to run into. She gets a sour look on her face and stomps over. "You're here for Liam, I presume."

"Hi, Ronni. We're meeting for lunch."

She looks me over. I dressed for the occasion, but you'd think she was staring at a pauper. "You're doing more harm than good, you know."

For a second, I think she's talking about Liam's past. But then I realize there is no way he would have told someone like Ronni about it. "I don't think Liam sees it that way."

"You being around him all the time ruins their image, especially given the unfortunate circumstance of you both having the same last name."

"We could be brother and sister," I say with a smirk.

"Are you trying to make a joke? Because this isn't a joking matter. This is business."

"You say you're worried about their image, but what you mean is you don't want Liam having a girlfriend."

She laughs cattily. "Girlfriend? You think you're his girlfriend? Liam doesn't have those. He hops from woman to woman, taking what he wants and leaving them in his wake."

"Sounds like you're jealous."

She's surprised. "Why would you say such a thing?"

"He told me he hooked up with you a few times."

"You think that makes me jealous of you? Think again, honey. Believe me, if I wanted him, I'd have him."

"Wow. You really think a lot of yourself, don't you? Now if you'll excuse me."

"Where do you think you're going?"

"Inside, to meet my *boyfriend*."

Her jaw drops. It's exactly the reaction I was going for. "They're in rehearsal. You'll have to wait out here."

"Seriously?"

"What is it about me having the upper hand that you don't understand?"

The door opens and Garrett appears. "Hi, Ella. You here to see Liam?"

"Yes, but Ronni doesn't want to let me pass."

"Fuck off, Ronni." Garrett takes me inside, closing the door on her. "Sorry about her. She likes to think she can control everything we do. I was using the bathroom and saw you two talking. Figured you might need rescuing."

"Thank you. She's a real piece of work."

Garrett opens the door to the studio, and I'm bombarded with music. I'm amazed at how soundproof the studio is. Liam's back is turned to me, and he's playing guitar. Even in rehearsal, he's giving it everything he has. His head bobs up and down, and his back tenses, punctuating the high notes. My insides melt. Watching him is like foreplay for me.

He stops playing. "I want to go again. The last part wasn't quite right. It needs something."

Crew gestures, and Liam turns. He smiles when he sees me. My heart flutters. *Happy*.

"Give me ten minutes," he says. "I need to nail this down."

"Sure."

I sit on a stool in the corner. The others stand around and listen. He gazes at me while he plays. I recognize the tune. It's the one he wrote for Garrett's lyrics. It's even better than when he played it for me last week.

He finishes and waits for a reaction. "Fucking yeah," Garrett says, twirling a drumstick.

"Perfect," Crew says. "Do it again, exactly the same way. Brad, let's add you this time."

Bria comes over to me. "He's been working on this all morning. I thought it was great all along, but then you walked in and *poof!* It's gone from great to amazing."

I whisper to Bria, "I accidentally told him I was in love with him last night."

Her eyebrows shoot up in surprise. "So that's why he's been in such a good mood today."

"He has?"

"Oh, yeah."

"He didn't say it back."

"Neither did Crew at first."

"Really?"

"These guys are dark and mysterious. It takes a certain kind of woman to get to them. Don't worry, I can see how he feels about you. He's never looked at a woman the way he looks at you."

"He doesn't think he deserves me."

"That's why you're the one for him."

"Do you really think so?"

"Just listen to him, Ella. Since you came into his life, he plays better than he ever has."

They stop, and Liam puts his guitar down and comes over. "What're you grinning about?"

"Nothing. Girl talk."

Garrett joins us. "Ronni was trying to keep Ella from coming inside."

Liam stiffens. "Are you kidding me? What did she say to you?" When I tell him, his jaw tightens. "That bitch." He stalks to the door, anger emanating from every pore.

I go after him. "Liam, don't. You'll only fuel the fire."

"I'm sick of her shit, El."

"Maybe there's another way to get back at her," Bria says. "A more passive-aggressive way."

Liam stops. "I'm listening."

"She's coming to our show on Saturday. Remember those stunts she said we shouldn't pull? Why don't you do one?"

"But we'll be fined," Liam says.

"Stunts? Fines?" I say. "What are you talking about?"

"Ronni's trying to keep us on a tight leash. She didn't appreciate Crew's public proposal. It wasn't the first time he's done something like that. She said we were going to be fined if anything similar happened again."

I can only imagine what kind of "stunt" he might pull. He doesn't love me. We're not even technically a couple. But the thought of him doing something publicly has me tingling all the way down to my toes.

"It's bullshit," Crew says. "There's nothing in the contract about fining us if we don't behave a certain way. Just because she said that shit and wrote it into the so-called business plan, that doesn't make it legal."

"What are you suggesting?" Liam asks.

"I'm not sure," Bria says. "I'll think of something. We have all week."

"Do you want to join us for lunch?" I ask them.

Bria takes Crew's elbow. "We're meeting my brother."

"How about you?" I ask Garrett and Brad.

"I'm good," they each say.

I turn to Liam. "I guess I'm all yours then."

He grins. "Exactly the way I like it."

More tingles ensue.

We pass Ronni on our way out. Liam gives her the evil eye. She looks at her watch. "I trust you'll be back in an hour."

"You're not my mother, Ronni. We'll be back in two."

Bria and Crew, walking up ahead, snicker.

Ronni scoffs and turns on her heels, stomping away.

As we walk down the street to a nearby bar and grill, I say, "I don't want you to get in trouble because of me."

"Are you kidding? Irritating Ronni is one of our favorite things to do. As long as we're stuck with IRL, we might as well have a little fun."

"What kind of control does she have over you? She can't really tell you not to date someone, can she?"

He takes my hand. "Hell no. She likes to think she can. Because we're new at this, she attempts to dictate our every move. Believe me, IRL is making a lot of money off us. She'd be a fool to do anything to jeopardize that."

I blow out a breath of relief. He doesn't fail to notice.

"She really got to you, huh?"

"She said I'm ruining your image. She explicitly said, since we have the same last name, people might get the wrong idea."

"Fuck her, El."

I tell him what I left out earlier. "She said you weren't the kind of guy to have a girlfriend."

"I wasn't."

"I might have provoked her by calling you my boyfriend."

He stops and laughs. "Oh shit, I would have loved to have seen her face."

"You're not mad?"

"It's strange," he says, skimming a finger down my arm. "I never thought I'd be anyone's boyfriend."

"So what are you thinking?"

"I'm thinking I might like the sound of it."

Before I can react, a woman trots up next to us. "Are you Liam Campbell? Like, from Reckless Alibi?"

"The one and only," he says proudly.

I've never been around him when a random person recognized him. It's happened to Crew and Bria. Understandable, because they're out in front, singing.

I back away, giving him space. He shoots me a glance that says I'm being ridiculous.

The woman is beyond excited. "Do you mind if I get a picture with you?"

I hold out my hand. "I'll take it."

"Oh, would you?"

I point. "Stand there, so the sun isn't behind you."

Liam puts his arm around her, and they smile. Then he winks at me.

"Thank you," the woman says. "I just love your music." She turns to me. "Are you his girlfriend?"

"Uh, no."

Liam pulls me close. "Yes."

"You're so lucky," she says to me. She holds up her phone. "Thanks for this."

"No problem. Thanks for listening to our stuff," Liam says.

"Oh, my God!" I squeal quietly. "That was awesome. Has it ever happened before? I've only seen girls fawn over you after concerts."

"It's happened once or twice."

"There will come a time when you might not be able to go down the street unnoticed."

"Will that bother you?"

"It will be amazing."

"I'm not sure you know what you're saying, El. You saw those crazy fans in Florida."

"You'll always have to deal with fans like those." I glance behind us. "But I think most of them will be like her. And if you want to be successful, it goes with the territory. I understand that. And I want you to get everything you want in life."

He looks at me like I'm one of those things. "That woman was wrong, you know. *I'm* the lucky one."

Chapter Forty-five

Liam

My phone chirps. I roll over in bed and grab it off the nightstand. It's a text from Crew, telling me to check my bank account. I open the app and my jaw hits the floor. Sitting up, I rub my eyes, not sure I'm seeing straight. I look again. The numbers are clear as day. I run into the living room to see three people smiling at me.

"Is this for real?" I say.

"I've been telling you all along," Garrett says, "we're gonna be millionaires."

"We're not even close yet," Crew says.

"Yeah, but it's a good start."

I have enough now to do what I planned.

"What did Brad have to say?" I ask.

Crew checks his phone. "He hasn't gotten back to me."

"He's so far up Katie's ass, he probably can't even read the text," Garrett says.

"Give him a break," Bria says. "He's going to be a dad. He needs a minute to grasp that."

Garrett shakes his head. "He's had two weeks."

"It's a kid, Garrett, not a new haircut. It might take him a tad longer."

"You guys want to celebrate?" Crew asks. "Maybe go to the place Bria always talks about?"

Her eyes light up. "The one with the hundred-dollar hamburger? Let's do it."

"You guys go ahead," I say. "I have other plans."

"Bring Ella," she says.

"The plans aren't with Ella."

Garrett looks around. "But everyone else you know is in this room."

"I can do shit by myself, you know."

"What kind of shit?"

"Shit that's none of your fucking business. Now go eat your hundred-dollar burger and leave me alone. And why the hell would you want to eat there anyway? Didn't you grow up eating that stuff?"

"You act like my family is the Rockefellers or something. So they have money. A lot of people do."

"A lot of people don't have a trust fund."

"It's not as much as you think, it's only a m—" Garrett stops talking mid-sentence, suddenly deep in thought.

"It's only what?" I prompt.

"Nothing."

"Are we meeting back here before the gig?" Bria asks. "Or at the club?"

"Didn't you hear what Ronni said yesterday?" I say. "We're arriving in a limo again. We're meeting at IRL."

She rolls her eyes. "At least we can afford it now."

I start toward my room. "See you there at seven."

"You're really not going to tell us where you're going?" Garrett asks.

"I'm really not."

~ ~ ~

"Ella's not coming?" Bria says when I arrive at IRL.

"She'll be there, but she's not riding with us."

"I should think not," Ronni says, appearing around the corner. "She's not part of the band. It wouldn't be allowed."

I wish I would have insisted she come with me just to irritate Ronni.

I hear a familiar voice and curse under my breath. I gesture to Dirk. "No way is he going with us."

Ronni laughs. "I can hardly tell him no. He owns the company."

"Why in the hell would you want to come?" I ask him. "It's not like you haven't heard us play a dozen times."

"Making sure my investment keeps paying off. Thanks to me, you all got a substantial payment this morning." He leans into me. "You're welcome."

"Like you have anything to do with it, Dirk. You can't even claim I got my talent from you. We write the songs. We play the music. You coming in and buying a company we already work for doesn't make you responsible for our success."

"How easily you forget everything I've done for you. The barn, Jeremy, the White Poison gigs. None of that would have happened if it weren't for me. So suck it up, why don't you, and give credit where credit is due."

Garrett steps between us. "We're grateful for what you've done, Dirk. Thank you."

"Now that's more like it," Dirk says and climbs into the limo.

"What is it between you and Dirk?" Garrett asks.

I glare at him. "What is it between you and your brother?"

"No way could it be as bad."

"I promise you, it's a whole lot fucking worse."

I can feel Garrett's eyes on me as I walk away.

"You should tell him," Crew says.

"No."

"He's one of your best friends. You said you were going to release the video. At least tell him about Luke. It doesn't have to be about you."

"I said no."

"You've decided not to release it then?"

"Right now, I'm going to get through tonight."

He puts a hand on my shoulder. "You know I'll support whatever you do."

"I know."

Brad comes over. "I'll sit next to Dirk so you don't have to."

I stand on the sidewalk until everyone else is inside. Jeremy pokes his head out. "You coming?"

I climb in and sit next to Bria, then put my earbuds in so I don't have to listen to Dirk.

Twenty minutes later, we pull up to the venue. As always, Ronni has the driver wait until a crowd forms. We exit and sign some autographs on our way in. I look around, disappointed I don't see Ella.

We're guided into a back room set up with food and drink. I pull Jeremy aside. "Can you see if Ella is out there? I need to know where she's sitting."

"Sure thing."

He returns a minute later. "Table to the right of the stage, about fifteen feet back. She's got two friends with her."

"Thanks."

He cocks his head. "You're not going to do anything stupid."

"Depends on how you define stupid."

He shakes his head, laughing. "I love my job."

Ronni shows up. "Okay, people. This is your first show since the tour. Fans are taking notice. Sales are up. You're rock stars now. Go out there and give them what they came for."

If one of the five of us had given that little pep talk, we'd be fired up, but we look at her as if she announced we're getting a tax audit.

"Thanks, Ronni," Bria says. "We've got it from here."

She pouts and leaves.

"She may be the devil's whore, but she's right," Garrett says, pouring us each a shot. "We're on our way up. Let's go out there and enjoy the goddamn ride. Bring it in, guys. On three."

We each take a glass and huddle around him as he counts it off.

"Let's get reckless!" we scream.

During the first song, I locate Ella right where Jeremy said she'd be. She's with Krista and Jenn. I've met them both several times over the past few weeks, and I'm pretty sure they couldn't care less if I'm a douchebag or a cheater. They want their friend to date a rock star.

Sometimes I wonder if she's told them about me. I didn't tell her she couldn't, but I don't think she has. Most people look at you differently if they know you're a freak.

She doesn't, a voice in my head says.

The lights pointing at the stage aren't as bright as at some of the other venues, and I can see Ella's face. She's singing along with every song, chair-dancing to the beat. I can't wait to be between those legs again.

We have a short break, long enough to get some water, but not so short Ronni can't come backstage and piss us off a little. "Will you stop staring at her?" she says.

"Who?" I ask innocently.

"Don't pull that shit with me, Liam. Women notice that sort of thing. They want you to look at *them*. Do you want them to buy your records?"

"Of course."

"Then for Christ's sake, throw them a goddamn bone."

Bria pulls me aside as we return to the stage. "Give Ronni a little of what she wants. She'll be happy for about two minutes before you go rogue."

As I play, I make eye contact with several women. They give me their fuck-me eyes. Three months ago that might have made me hard. I might have taken them backstage and fucked them quick and dirty. Then they would leave, mumbling about what a pervert I am. Some of them are beautiful, but there's not so much as a tingle going on down there. Not unless I'm looking at Ella. It's torture keeping my eyes off her.

I glance at Ronni. She gives me an approving nod. Bitch.

I try to make eye contact with more women, but my gaze never strays far from Ella. There's not a doubt in my mind—I play better when she's around. My fingers move effortlessly along the frets. My pick never misses a single string. I lock eyes with her during a long riff, feeling like I could play forever.

When the riff is over, I glance at Ronni again. She's not happy. She points two fingers at her eyes and then gestures to the audience. If looking at Ella is pissing her off, wait until she sees what's next. It's nothing big, no grand gesture like what Crew has done, but I'm one hundred percent sure she's going to lose her shit.

The third song ends, and like Bria told me to, I stand behind Crew and tap his shoulder. He turns around, pretending to be surprised when I reach for the mic. "Hey, man, you trying to take my job?"

I speak into the mic. "I wanted to talk to the bartender for a second."

"You thirsty?" he jokes.

"I'm going to ask him to send a drink to the most beautiful girl in the room."

Gasps are heard in the audience. I look at Ella. I can't see the color of her skin, but I'd guess it's bright red.

Crew puts an arm around Bria, another stunt sure to piss off Ronni. "Dude, she's already taken."

I laugh. "Sorry, Brianna. You're hot too, but you're like my best friend. I was talking about the girl at the table over there, with the brown wavy hair." I point at Ella. "She looks like a champagne kind of girl. Bartender, can you send her a glass of your finest?"

All eyes in the room are straining to see who I'm sending a drink to. The bartender gives me a thumbs-up. If looks could kill, Ronni's dagger eyes would have me dead on the stage. She says something to Dirk and storms off.

"Mission accomplished," Crew says into the mic, as if getting Ella a drink was the mission. "Mind if we play now?"

"Send *me* a drink!" a woman shouts.

"I think one's all he can afford," Crew jokes.

Garrett counts us off on the drums, and we finish the set. Ronni's gone. And good fucking riddance. She can yell at me, sue me even, but there's nothing she can do to keep me from spending the next ten songs staring at the only woman I ever want to look at.

Chapter Forty-six

Ella

The past month has been incredible. Reckless Alibi recorded another album, the one with my sketch on the cover. A few of the new songs are already on the radio. I've finished two more books of illustrations. And Liam and I are practically inseparable.

But I can tell he's keeping a secret. He's happy yet distracted. He sometimes leaves the room to take a call. There's something going on he doesn't want me to know about. He's not cheating; nothing about his behavior hints at him feeling guilty. Something's going on, and I wish he would tell me what it is.

"Turn left at the light," he says. I do it perfectly. "You're getting a lot better."

This is the fourth time he's taken me driving. He thinks I'll be ready to take a test by the end of summer.

"I have a good teacher."

"Eyes on the road."

"Where are we going?"

"Garrett told me about a good restaurant. I think he grew up around here."

"He doesn't like to talk about his past either, does he?"

"No."

"You don't think—"

"No, I don't. It has something to do with his brother. He hasn't talked to him or anyone in his family since I've known him, and that's over four years."

"I don't know what I'd do without mine."

"Your parents are different. They're nice, and supportive. You're lucky."

"I wish everyone had parents like mine."

"Some people shouldn't have kids."

I stop at a red light. "Do you want kids?"

"I can't have them."

"Oh, Liam. Did he … damage you somehow?"

He belts out a painful laugh. "You could say that, but not in the way you're thinking. I assume I'm capable of having kids. What I meant is I won't."

"Why not?"

"Why do you think, El? Because, well, what if I …" He stares out the window.

"You're afraid of doing what he did, aren't you?" I put a hand on his arm. "Liam, you won't. You're much stronger than that. You're incapable of hurting a fly."

He nods to the street. "Light's green."

I turn down a residential street and pass several driveways with entry gates. "Wow, swanky area. Some of these rival Dirk's house."

"Stop!" he shouts.

I slam on the brakes, heart pounding. "What?"

He points to one of the driveways. The gate is closed and large gold letters span both sides of it that spell YOUNG.

"You don't think this is Garrett's house, do you?"

The gate opens, and a Porsche drives out. He waits for me to go, but I wave him on.

"It's his house all right," Liam says. "That was his brother."

"I thought you've never met."

"Saw him at a bar last month. Garrett punched him."

"You guys really are full of secrets, aren't you?"

Ten minutes later, we're seated at a Mexican restaurant. "Drinks?" the waitress asks. "We have two-for-one margaritas."

I raise an eyebrow at Liam, who says, "Not if you plan to do any more driving."

"I'll have water," I say, trying not to pout. The waitress leaves. "Since when did you become so responsible?"

"Since I have something to lose."

He gazes at me intently. It's like he's shot an arrow into my heart, claiming me as his. I lace our fingers together. "Same."

"Ronni told us something this morning."

I pull away. "Way to ruin a good moment."

"I was actually trying to make it better."

"How so?"

"They're trying to schedule a tour for next year. A US tour. As in the whole country."

"Really? That's incredible." I narrow my eyes. "I can't believe you waited two whole hours to tell me."

"I was waiting for the right time." He cracks his knuckles, something I've seen him do when he gets nervous. "Come with me."

My bottom lip is pulled between my teeth.

"You know you want to, El. Say yes."

"Next year is a long way off. You have no idea what will happen between now and then."

"You mean between us." He leans back. "You think I'm going to dump you?"

"I don't know."

He lets out a sigh. "You think because I haven't said the words, I don't plan on keeping you around."

"It's not that."

"Then what? Is it what I said in the car about kids?"

I shake my head.

"Tell me, Ella. We said we'd be honest with each other."

I want to call him out, tell him I know he's keeping something from me, but I don't. "It's a big commitment to make for something that's not happening until next year."

"You think I'm afraid of commitments, don't you?" He takes my hand. "But asking you to go on tour should prove I'm not."

Food is placed on our table.

"Say yes, El."

The waitress says, "Honey, I don't know what he's selling, but look at that face. You'd be crazy not to say yes."

"I'm not giving up my career to follow you, Liam. I love what I do and don't intend to stop."

"I would never ask you to. Come on," he says, his mouth twitching into a wry grin. "Even the waitress thinks you should."

I finger my necklace, deep in thought. "Yes."

The lady glances at me, then him. "Did you just get engaged?"

Liam chokes. "Uh, no."

"Darn," she says. "You know what? I'm going to give you a free slice of pie anyway. You seem like a nice couple."

She walks away, leaving us speechless. We're practically drowning in awkwardness. Then Liam starts laughing, and I join in.

"Just so you know," he says. "If I ever ask anyone to marry me, it sure as hell won't be at a Mexican restaurant over a glass of water."

"In front of a waitress," I add.

"At least we get a free slice of pie," he says, and we laugh harder.

He seems carefree and happy. He's joking about proposals. This man, who was so deeply hurt by his father that he believes he's a freak of nature, is joking about proposals.

He's still holding my hand. My left hand. As his thumb rubs up and down my ring finger, I wonder if he's thinking that someday it could be possible.

Back in the car, we talk about going on tour again.

"Do you think you'll play stadiums and arenas?" I ask.

"It would be surreal to play for a huge audience, like when we opened for White Poison—only *we'd* be the main band. I've dreamed about it since I was a kid."

"I'm happy for you."

He puts a hand on my leg. "I'm glad you're going to be there."

"Separate hotel rooms, right?" His expression makes me laugh. "I'm kidding."

He blows out a breath. "Don't do that to me."

I feel the heat of his hand through my thin skirt. His finger drawing circles along my thigh makes my insides all melty. "If you're going to do *that* to me, you should be the one driving. It's distracting."

I stop at a light, and he grabs my hand and puts it in his lap so I can feel his erection. It may be two o'clock in the afternoon, but I want him. When the light turns green, I turn onto a side street and pull into an empty parking lot. "You drive."

He gives me a heated stare. “I don’t think either of us should drive.”

“Liam, we’re in a church parking lot.”

“So?”

“Kind of inappropriate, don’t you think?”

“Why? God made our bodies to do this very thing.”

My jaw drops in surprise. “You believe in God?”

“Sometimes.”

“When?”

“When I look at you.”

I turn off the engine, climb over the console onto his lap, and kiss him. What he said to me might be the single best thing anyone has ever said in the history of the world.

Chapter Forty-seven

Liam

I walk into IRL with a spring in my step. Not even Dirk's car parked out front can keep me from thinking about the past few weeks with Ella. Not to mention the deal I've been working on finally came through. Everything in my life is coming together. When I pass Ronni's door, it occurs to me getting rid of her would make everything perfect, and I wonder how I can make that happen.

Her door unexpectedly opens, and we're face to face. Her lipstick is smeared. She pulls the door shut behind her. "Liam," she says curtly.

She walks past me to the restroom. Without thinking about it, I open her office door. Hatred sears my gut when I see Dirk buttoning his pants. "You've got to be fucking kidding me." I belt out a maniacal laugh. "Why should I even be surprised?"

He puts on his suit jacket. "What I do is none of your damn business."

I stride over and get in his face. "It's been six weeks. Plenty of time for you to sell IRL. Why don't we have a new owner yet?"

"You don't get it, do you?" he says smugly. "Even if you have a video, you won't release it. People will know you're a victim. You have too much pride. You won't do that to yourself or the band. There's too much at stake."

"You're wrong."

"Am I?"

"Go to hell." I walk out, catching Ronni as she's returning. "You really have hit an all-time low, haven't you? I knew you were a slut, but he's an old man."

"An old man with power."

"I'd warn you to watch out for him or you'll get burned. But I think I'd enjoy seeing the flames."

"Aren't you late for practice?"

I stomp down the hall, my morning ruined. When I enter the studio, I announce, "Ronni's sleeping with Dirk."

Nobody seems surprised.

"We know," Crew says.

"And you didn't say anything?"

"What's to say? You already hate both of them. Didn't think I needed to fuel the fire."

Garrett gets off his stool. "I found out last week. Thought maybe it had been going on all along, and that's part of the reason you hated Dirk."

"I hated him long before Ronni came into the picture."

Crew motions for me to sit. "And that's not even the *bad* news."

I take a seat next to him. "What do you mean?"

He looks at Brad. "Do you want to tell him or should I?"

Brad looks guilty as hell. "I'm leaving the band."

The looks on everyone's faces tell me this is no joke.

"I'm sorry," he says. "It's something I've been thinking about since I found out about the baby."

I get up and pace. "Brad, musicians have kids all the time."

"I know, but if we go on tour next year, the baby will only be a few months old. I can't do that to Katie."

Garrett laughs bitterly. "So this is Katie's decision, not yours."

"We decided together."

"Do you realize what you're doing?" I ask. "Have you checked your bank account lately? Once you leave, that's it—no more royalty checks."

"This was never about the money," he says.

"Maybe not, but you love playing bass."

"That hasn't changed. I'm going to keep playing. Maybe I'll find someone local who plays a few gigs a month. And there's always the church band."

Garrett rubs the back of his neck. "The *church* band? Are you shitting me?"

"Listen," Brad says. "I'll stay on until you get a replacement. I'll even help you find one. I'm not walking out today and saying sayonara. You guys mean too much to me."

"Apparently not enough to keep playing with us," Garrett says.

"I love you guys," Brad says. "But I love my family more."

I turn to Crew and Bria. "You're awfully quiet. You don't have a problem with this?"

"Of course we have a problem with it," Bria says. "We like Brad. We like the way things are, but he's getting married. He's having a baby. His priorities have changed. We need to respect that."

"You can marry and have kids and still go on the road," I argue.

Brad stands and places a hand on my shoulder. "I'm not going to miss my kid's first smile and first steps. I don't want to miss a single day of his or her life."

"Bring them on the road with us."

"Katie doesn't want to."

"You'll resent her," Garrett says. "Maybe not at first, but it'll happen."

"It won't. Like I said, this wasn't only her decision. I want this too."

"That's it?" I say. "There's nothing we can say to change your mind?"

"I don't want to hurt you guys, but hey, I'm *just* the bassist. Easily replaceable, right?" he jokes.

Bria hugs him. "That's not true. Somebody will have big shoes to fill."

"When are you going to tell Ronni?" I ask.

"We're not telling her," Crew says. "I don't want IRL having anything to do with finding a replacement. We'll do it ourselves. We don't talk about it with anyone else. Agreed?"

We nod.

"Okay, then," Crew says, walking to the mic. "We've still got our jobs to do."

We rehearse for hours, but it's not the same, knowing things are changing. So much for everything in my life coming together.

After practice, Crew pulls me aside. "Is everything okay?"

"Why wouldn't it be? Dirk still has me by the balls. We're losing our bassist. Everything is wonderful."

"I'm not talking about what happened today." He makes sure no one is listening. "You've been getting some official-looking envelopes in the mail lately. Is there something I should know about?"

"Nope."

"You're not plotting anything against Dirk?"

"Not yet."

"What is it then?"

"It's nothing. You're going to have to trust me on this."

"All right, but I'm here for you. Whenever and whatever. I've got your back."

He walks away and I bite my tongue, wanting to tell him but knowing he could never understand.

~ ~ ~

"Hey, slow down!" Ella shouts. "Why are you running so fast today?"

I let her catch up.

"You've been quiet, too. Is something wrong?"

"Brad quit the band this morning."

She tugs me to a stop. "Seriously? Why? Oh—the baby."

"I don't think it's the baby. It's Katie. She wants him at home."

"What does *he* want?"

"He claims he wants the same thing she does, but I'm not buying it."

"What'll you do?"

"Find another bassist."

"As in put an ad in the paper or something?"

"It doesn't work like that, and we have to keep it quiet. Ronni and IRL don't know, and we don't plan to tell them."

"Why not?"

"Because they'd find someone and force him on us. They did it last year when Bria almost quit the band."

"Oh, right. She told me about that. So how will you find a replacement?"

"Brad's going to stay on until we hire someone. We can take our time, scout out other bands."

"You'd take a bass player from another band?"

"It happens more than you know. If you look at a lot of the famous guitar players of our time, many of them played together in one band or another early in their careers."

"How does it work?"

"We invite them to play with us and see if they're a good fit."

"You invite them to your rehearsal studio at IRL? The one Dirk owns and where Ronni works?"

"Shit. We didn't think that far ahead. More good news, Ronni and Dirk are fucking. They were in her office this morning."

"They really have no boundaries, do they? So he's still at IRL? Maybe now is a good time to release the video."

I start running again.

"Liam, wait. Did I say something wrong?" She draws even with me. "You do want to release it, don't you?"

I think about what Dirk said this morning about me being a victim. "I'm not sure I can."

"Stop. We've done five miles already, and I want to talk about this."

I slow to a walk and turn in the direction of home. "There's nothing to talk about."

"Why aren't you sure you can do it? Are you scared of what people will think?"

"Of course I'm scared, El. You think I want people knowing what a freak I am?"

"Please stop calling yourself that. You're stronger than he is and a far better man."

"Maybe you don't know me at all."

She grabs my hand. "You're not being fair. I do know you, Liam. I love you. You may not want to hear it, but it's true. I wouldn't want you to do anything that could hurt you. But you need closure. Releasing the video might be how you get it."

"It's not. I know how I can get closure."

"How?"

"I'm not ready to talk about it yet."

She eyes me suspiciously. "Something's going on with you."

"Something *is* going on." I pull away from her. "My band is falling apart, my uncle is fucking my label rep, and my goddamn girlfriend won't leave me the hell alone about the video."

"You want your girlfriend to leave you alone? No problem."

Chapter Forty-eight

Ella

He didn't come after me yesterday like I thought he would. Bria called to ask if I knew why he was moping around the apartment. I found little solace in that. I'd rather he was with me, working through whatever it is together.

I debated not going to their show at the club tonight, but Bria talked me into it. "You can't give up that easily on a man like Liam," she said.

I'm not giving up on him. Giving him space maybe, but not giving up.

I had to go. I haven't missed a performance since that first night in Florida. Sometimes I miss the flurry of activity we experienced when they were on tour. Part of me is excited at the possibility of doing it all again. Only this time, they will practically be a household name.

I want to see him, make sure he's okay. Make sure *we're* okay.

"You go get a table," I tell Jenn. "I'll be right back."

"Tell the hottie I said hello!" she shouts as I walk away.

I find the door I think leads backstage. It's locked. I knock a few times but realize it may be too loud out front for anyone to hear me. I'm about to give up when it opens. A big guy stares me down. "This area is closed to bar patrons." He points to the sign on the door. "You can read, I assume."

"I'm looking for Liam Campbell. He plays guitar for Reckless Alibi."

"And you are?"

"Can you tell him Mrs. Campbell wants to speak with him?"

He gives me a dismissive glance and closes the door. I contemplate texting Liam, but before I get my phone out, he appears.

He's surprised to see me. "You're here."

"I wanted to see you before your set."

He lets me back and leans against the wall, thrusting his hands into the front pockets of his jeans. "I thought we were over."

"Liam, I walked away because you said something hurtful, not because I wanted us to be over."

He looks at me sideways.

"You really don't know how to do this, do you?"

"Do what?"

"Have a relationship."

"I told you, I've never had a girlfriend."

"Having a fight doesn't mean we can't be together. Couples fight. Then they make up."

"But you didn't make up with Corey."

"That wasn't a fight. He cheated. Are you cheating on me?"

"No."

"Good, because cheating is the only thing you could do to make me leave for good."

He steps toward me and traps me against the wall. "I really thought you were gone."

"You could have called."

"*You* could have called."

"You're right. I'm sorry."

"I'm sorry, too."

Someone clears their throat. "You're on in ten," Jeremy says.

Liam lifts his chin. "Give me a minute."

I stand on my toes and give him a peck on the lips.

"So we're good?" he asks, his hand lingering on the curve of my neck.

"Yes."

"Can I come over after? I think I like the idea of making up."

I bite my lip and nod.

"Jesus, El. You can't do that right before I have to play."

I giggle.

"Where are you sitting?"

"I'm not sure. Jenn went to get a table."

"I'll find you. I'll always find you."

I give his hand a squeeze. "I'll always find you too."

He puts his lips to mine. "Promise?"

I smile. "I thought you didn't like promises."

"A guy can change his mind."

"Then, yes, I promise. Now give us an amazing show."

I start for the door, but he pulls me back and kisses me. He more than kisses me—he claims me, ruining me for anyone else.

When I find Jenn, she says with a smirk, "Quickie backstage?"

"Better."

"What's better than a quickie with the hottie?"

I take a selfie of Jenn and me and send it to Krista.

"She's going to be so pissed she had to work tonight," Jenn says.

"It's not as if she'll never see them. Don't you ever get bored being dragged along to watch their shows?"

She looks at me like I'm crazy. "Bored? I'm waiting for Garrett Young to ask me out."

"You don't want to go out with him. He's not boyfriend material."

"Who said anything about a boyfriend? I want to know what those tattoos taste like."

"Ew."

The waitress delivers our drinks, and I raise my glass. "To Reckless Alibi."

A man bumps into our table, spilling Jenn's drink. "Sorry, miss. I'll replace it. What was it?"

Jenn and I sneak a peek at each other. No way is this old guy getting her a drink. He must be twice our age, and he looks creepy with his baseball cap pulled low.

She says, "I'm good."

"I insist."

"And I said I'm not thirsty."

He gestures to the stage. "Have you seen this band before?"

"We have," I say.

"Are they any good?"

"They're the best."

"You have an empty seat. Can I join you?"

I put my hand on it. "Sorry, it's saved for our friend."

"Maybe I'll keep her seat warm until she gets here."

He's really creeping me out. What kind of old man comes to a club alone? The perverted kind, that's who. I pull the seat close to me. "Not a good idea."

He growls angrily. "Who made you queen of the barstools, sweetheart?"

Jenn stands in a display of aggression. "You should leave."

"You heard the lady," a deep voice says behind me. I've never been more relieved to see Thor.

The man sizes him up. Is he really thinking of taking Thor on?

"I was just looking for a place to sit."

"Sit somewhere else," Thor says, getting in the guy's face. He points to the back of the club. "Plenty of seats back there."

The man glares at us, pissed, and walks away. "Bitches," he says before he's out of earshot.

I release a deep breath. "Thanks, Tom."

"Anytime, Ms. Campbell."

Jenn is grinning ear to ear. "Oh, the perks of dating a rock star." She nods at Tom as he leaves. "Is *he* single? The guy is huge. I can only imagine what he's like down there."

"That's Thor."

"*That's* Thor? As in the one in Florida you told us about?" She fans herself with her hand. "Tell him he can use his hammer on me anytime."

I'm laughing when the lights dim and the spotlights turn on. Reckless Alibi run out on the stage. Liam picks up his guitar and scans the room. He finds me. I put up my hand and give him the "rock on" sign. He smiles. Then I add my thumb to the sign, changing the entire meaning. He winks at me.

Jenn sighs. "Must be nice to have a rock star in love with you."

"I'm not sure he is."

"Did you see the way he looked at you? Everyone in the club knows he's in love with you."

Several people are looking at me—a few like they might want to see my head on a platter.

The band plays, and I get lost in the music. Doesn't matter how many times I see or hear them, my heart still pounds when they're onstage.

The audience sings along to the chorus when they play their most popular hard-rock song, "Sins on Sunday." Men punch their fists in the air, chanting the words. Women dance between the tables. Fans crowd the stage, vying for the best position.

When Crew and Bria sing a love song, Liam watches me, his attention never straying. It amazes me how he can play without looking at his guitar. He truly is the most talented person I've ever met. And he's mine. At least I think he is. He wanted a promise, and I'm willing to give him anything he wants.

During the break, I race to the bathroom. I'm standing in line when Creepy Guy walks by. He stops. "Do you know the guitar player?"

I don't answer.

"He was looking at you. You his lady or something?"

"I don't know what you're talking about."

"You're lying," he says. "Like you lied about saving the seat for a friend."

"Can you move please?" a lady says to him. "You're blocking the way."

He continues down the hall. He made me feel dirty.

When I come out of the bathroom, I'm super aware of my surroundings, not wanting to get cornered by the man again. I rush back to the table and tell Jenn what happened.

She's irritated. "After the show, we need to get Thor to walk us to a cab."

I laugh. "You want to get his number, don't you?"

She shrugs. "If it turns out I do, well so be it." She grabs my arm and squeals. "They're coming back on."

She fangirls over Reckless Alibi. It's strange being here while women, and some men, ogle the man I love. I'm going to have to get used to it. He's becoming a musical icon. A star. Maybe someday he'll even be a legend. But I don't love him for any of those reasons.

"Oh, God," Jenn says, looking like she swallowed a bug. "He's back."

Creepy Guy has taken his hat off. At least it doesn't seem like he's going to bother us. He only seems interested in the band. He did ask me about Liam. Maybe he's a talent agent or something.

The song the band is playing sounds funny. Liam has stopped playing. The rest of the band is trying to get his attention, wondering why.

Then everyone sees what I see. Liam is gazing at Creepy Guy in horrific disbelief. And Creepy Guy is staring back at him.

Liam's face turns red, and his neck is corded. He throws his guitar down and jumps off the stage, hands balled into fists, right onto Creepy Guy. He tackles him to the ground and punches him.

"Liam!" I yell. Is he doing this because Creepy Guy was talking to me earlier?

The crowd clears a space around them. Thor runs over and reaches for Liam. "Don't!" Crew yells, jumping to his side. "Let him."

Thor holds back anyone who tries to intervene. I'm appalled by what Liam is doing to the man. Over and over, he punches him in the face. Creepy Guy is pinned to the ground, but still gets in a punch. Liam's blood spatters all the way to my legs. "Do something!" I yell.

Crew pulls me behind him, protecting me from the fight.

I try to break free. "Crew, help him."

"He doesn't need help," Crew says. "Let him do this, Ella. He needs to."

"What?" I stand here and watch, horrified. Why is Liam beating up this man? He only talked to me. He didn't touch me. I think of the stories Bria told me about how Crew would punch men who came close to her. Other than the guy who grabbed my boobs in Florida, I've never seen Liam become violent. The only time he's ever angry is when he's talking about— "Oh, God." I grab Crew's arm. "Is that Don?"

I'm not sure if he's surprised or relieved I know about Liam's father. He doesn't need to say anything. I know the answer is yes.

Club security finally makes it through the crowd and not even Thor can keep them from breaking things up. Liam stands, his fists bloody, not taking his eyes off his dad. He lunges for him again, but is held back. Thor says something to security and then leads Liam backstage.

Garrett, Brad, and Bria get off the stage and join us. Crew picks something up off the floor—a wallet maybe, and I wonder if Liam lost it in the scuffle.

"Dude, what the fuck just happened?" Garrett asks. He touches my arm. "Did that asshole attack you or something?"

I shake my head.

He looks at Creepy Guy, who's being helped up to his feet. "Then why did he beat the shit out of him?"

"Only Liam can answer that question," Crew says. "Come on, let's make sure he's okay."

Jenn tags along as we go backstage, all of us trying to process what Liam did. Thor comes up the hallway alone. "He's gone. Took off out the back door."

I run to the end of the hall and throw open the door, looking up and down the street for him.

Crew comes up behind me. "Give him time, Ella."

My voice cracks. "What if he's hurt?"

"He's strong. He'll be okay."

"But what if this is the thing that breaks him?"

Chapter Forty-nine

Liam

Twelve years ago

Molestation.

I type it into the browser's search field. Helen once told me what it was, but I didn't want to believe it. For the past year, I've denied it could be anything as bad as she said. I've pretended Luke's death was a freak accident and Dad disappeared because he was sad over losing his oldest son. I've blocked out any conversations I overheard that would indicate it was anything different.

But I'm almost thirteen. I hear the way my classmates talk in the school locker room. They joke about boys touching other boys. They call them homos, faggots, and sickos.

What I read on the screen doesn't give me much explanation: sexual assault or abuse of a child up to the age of eighteen.

I type in another search term. *Child sexual abuse.*

What I read are terrifying, disgusting, horrible words. *True* words. And it one hundred percent describes what my father did to me. Why didn't I stop him? Deep down I knew it was wrong, but he's my dad. Is he still, I wonder?

Victim is a frequent word on the pages. I see it over and over, and every time I read it, I feel myself becoming more of one.

"Put down your phone," Aunt Sylvia says. "You kids spend too much time on those silly things."

I put it in my pocket, not wanting her to see what I was searching. "There's nothing else to do."

"That's ridiculous. You can go swimming. It's a beautiful day outside."

"I went swimming yesterday."

What I don't tell her is I have to force myself to go in the pool. It's the last place I saw Luke. Every time I'm there, I see him looking sad. I hear him telling me I'm a good brother. No way would I go in it today, on the anniversary of his death. Not one person has said anything about it either. It's like they've completely forgotten him.

"How about playing that guitar of yours? I heard you the other day. You're getting quite good."

"Okay," I say and shuffle away.

I go to the east wing, where Helen and a few of the other servants stay. I can't complain much though. This room is way nicer than my old one, and I get my very own bathroom. Mom's door is open. She's sitting in a chair, watching soap operas. It's all she ever does. Well, that and drink. She used to tell me it was soda, but I know better now. She stumbles a lot and slurs her words. She's so thin I can see her collarbone jutting out. One day a few months ago, I said something about how skinny she was. That was the last time she ever sat by the pool with me. She hardly ever joins us for dinner anymore. When I bring her food, she throws it away.

It's almost like I lost her too. Helen is the one person here who seems to like me. And maybe Gus, the man who drives me to school and activities. I guess Aunt Sylvia does too, but I think she wanted kids of her own, not someone else's. She's nice to me, but she always seems sad.

I've learned to stay out of Dirk's way. He grumbles a lot when he sees me. Thankfully he's not home much, and I pretty much have the run of the place. But it's not the same without Sally. Dirk said Aunt Sylvia is allergic to dogs, so we couldn't bring her, even though I begged and said I'd keep her in the east wing.

I really miss Sally.

I stop in the doorway. "Hi, Mom."

She holds up a finger. "Shh, this is the good part."

I wait in silence until a commercial break, then go in and sit on her bed. "I was going to play guitar. I've been learning a new song if you want to hear it."

"Oh, baby." She sips her drink. "Today isn't a good day. You understand. Why don't you come back tomorrow?"

At least *she* remembers.

"Yeah, sure." I leave, knowing full well she'll be passed out on the bed by nightfall.

Helen appears. "Your friend Chris is here."

My eyes light up. "Can he come to my room?"

"Of course. I think Ms. Sylvia called his mother. She worries about you, mijo. I do, too. We want you to be happy."

I glance at Mom's door and know that will never be possible. I feel small moments of pleasure sometimes, fun even, but not happiness.

When Crew comes to my room, he's carrying a large rectangular black case. "What's in there?"

"My mom got it for me. It's a keyboard."

"Cool. Let me see."

He sets it on the desk. "You can make it sound like a piano or an organ or even a guitar. Here, listen." He plays a few random notes.

"Can you play any songs?"

"Not yet. Mom said she'll get me lessons."

"Maybe you could learn some of the songs I know, and we can play together."

"That would be fun. Hey, we should start a band."

I call him crazy.

"I'm serious. You've been playing your guitar for hours every day since … Well, you're really good. I can get good on the keyboard. And you know I can sing. We're halfway there."

"You want to be a rock star, don't you?"

"Hell yes. Don't you?"

I have no idea what I want to be, if anything.

I hear glass breaking across the hall and run to Mom's door. She's on her knees, cleaning up a broken bottle. "I'll get it."

"Thanks, sweetie."

I pick up all the large pieces. "I'll ask Helen to sweep in case I missed any."

"Good boy. On your way back, be a dear and get one of Dirk's bottles from the bar that looks like that one did."

"Sure, Mom."

Crew is in the hallway. He knows she drinks a lot, but I still make excuses. "Today is hard for her. It's been one year since Luke died." I nod down the hallway. "Come on, I have to get her some more."

After finding Helen and telling her about the glass, Crew and I go into the room Dirk calls the salon. Bottles line one wall. I find one resembling the one Mom broke.

"He won't care if you're in here, taking his stuff?"

"Mom does it all the time. Then more magically appears. You'll never find an empty spot."

Crew gets a devious grin on his face and grabs one of the fancy brown bottles labeled Crown Royal.

I give him a look.

"What? You said he doesn't care if anyone takes it. We're going to be rock stars. Rock stars drink alcohol."

"You're crazy."

He goes to my room, walking fast in case anyone is around. "Come on," he says over his shoulder.

I deliver the bottle to Mom and then join Crew, locking the door behind me.

"Do you have any glasses?" he asks.

"Yeah, I keep glasses in my room to drink stolen bottles of my uncle's alcohol."

He twists off the top. "We'll drink out of the bottle." He raises it. "To Luke."

He takes a drink and starts coughing. I grab the bottle from him and take a whiff. It smells like gasoline. "To Luke, the best brother anyone ever had."

I swallow a large mouthful and almost puke it back up. Crew laughs. He swipes the bottle back. "I could be your brother, you know."

"I wish."

"Let's make a pact right now. It'll be like we're blood brothers, only without the blood. We'll never leave each other. We'll be in a band, get famous, and tour the world. And every day on this date, we'll drink whatever this shit is and toast Luke."

"Let's do that."

"Not some pansy drink. Take a big gulp, like a man."

"You mean like a rock star."

Three hours later, after throwing up so much I doubt I have any more insides, Crew is passed out on my bed. I hope he meant what he said. But I wonder if he'd still mean it if he found out about me. Would he call me a fag? A homo?

I get my phone out. It's still on the website I was looking at earlier. My head is spinning, but I read it anyway. My stomach turns again when I read the part about the physical signs, such as blood and bruising, and behavioral signs like nightmares and bedwetting. Things I hid from everyone, even my dad.

There is one sign I don't understand: self-harm. I dig deeper and read that some victims of abuse cut themselves. Kids often do it because it makes them feel better. It gives them relief from the pain of strong emotions and desperate feelings.

I keep reading about how, why, and where they do it. The article goes on to say why it's a bad thing, but I don't read that part. I go across the hall to Mom's room. She's passed out, like I thought she'd be. I pull a large piece of glass out of her trashcan, run back to my room, and lock myself in the bathroom.

I push my shorts up near my crotch and graze the jagged glass across my outer thigh. I put more pressure on it, until it pierces the skin. The pain makes me flinch. Blood beads along the cut. I like the way it looks. And even though it hurts, I like the way it feels, because this kind of pain—it's different. *I'm* in control of it. And that makes it exhilarating.

I do it again. And again.

Chapter Fifty

Ella

I nervously knock on the door to Liam's apartment.

Crew opens the door and cocks his head. "Hey, Ella." He glances down the hall.

"Is he here?"

"I thought he stayed with you last night."

My heart pounds. "I haven't seen him since he left the club."

"Shit, me neither." He moves aside. "Come in."

He gets his phone and texts Liam.

"He hasn't been answering my texts or calls," I say. Tears flood my eyes. "Crew, what do you think happened to him?"

"Out clearing his head is my guess."

"But where would he go? I have to find him. I need to know he's okay. I was already worried about him. Even before last night, he was acting strange, like he had a secret." Dread crawls up my spine. "You don't think he's with another woman, do you?"

He vehemently shakes his head. "No fucking way."

"Then where could he be?"

He takes me to Liam's room. "I get what you're saying about him having a secret—I mean more than the regular shit he keeps from everyone. He's gotten a lot of mail lately. Maybe we can find something that will give us a clue." We stand in Liam's room. "You check over there, I'll start here."

I hesitate before opening his nightstand. "This feels like such a violation."

"He's missing, Ella. After a traumatic experience, no less. If I'd known he wasn't with you, I'd have done this last night."

I open the top drawer. There's about a hundred guitar picks in it, along with two unopened packages of condoms and several pages of sheet music in various stages of completion. My heart stops when I see the title on one page: "Ella's Song."

"Anything?" I ask Crew as he riffles through the dresser.

"No."

In the bottom drawer are a few envelopes. I open one and pull out the papers. They are legal documents. It's a final settlement statement from a title corporation. Next to the property address, it lists Liam Campbell as the buyer. It's dated last week. I show it to Crew. "I think he might have bought a house or something."

He races around the bed, takes it from me, reads it, and sighs.

"What is it?" I ask.

"He bought a house, all right. It's his childhood home. The one where he lived before he moved in with Dirk."

"The one where …?" I sit on his bed. "Why would he do that?"

Crew sits next to me. "He once told me he wanted to burn it to the ground."

I look at him, terrified. "Do you think he would?"

"Honestly? Yes."

I hop up. "I have to go there."

"I'll drive you. I know where it is. I lived a few doors down from him."

Along the way, I keep trying to call Liam, but he must have turned off his phone. "What if we're too late?"

"Let's hope we're not."

"Do you think he knows he can get arrested for burning it down, even if he owns it?"

"At this point, he might not care."

"Was last night the first time he's seen Don since Luke died?"

"Yes."

I swallow tears. "What that must have done to Liam, seeing him after all this time."

"I'm sorry I held you back last night, but Liam needed to do that. It was the only time he had the upper hand with that man."

"But it wasn't enough. He'd have come home if it was."

Crew glances at me. I've never seen him look so scared.

An hour later, we pull into a neighborhood, and I look at the sky. "Well, there's no smoke. That has to be a good sign."

He turns down a street. I immediately see the old Nissan parked in front of a brown house. Crew parks behind it. He starts to get out, but I stop him.

"Crew, will you do something for me?"

"You don't want me to go inside with you? What if he—"

My heart gets stuck in my throat thinking of the implication, then I see movement on the front porch. Jean-clad legs stick out from behind a trellis. I recognize the shoes. "Look." I point.

Crew lets out a relieved breath.

"He's alive, and the house isn't burning. I have an idea. Can you make a trip to the store?"

"What do you need?"

I tell him and exit the car, then go slowly up the walk. When I get closer, I see a can of gas sitting next to his legs. I climb the steps and round the corner. Liam's perched against the wall, sleeping, an empty bottle of whiskey on the floor a foot away.

I touch his shoulder. "Liam?"

He jerks awake. "El?"

I sit on the porch next to him, not caring how much dirt will get on my clothes. "I told you I'd always find you." I carefully touch his split lip. "You're injured."

His eyes close. "It's not the worst thing he's ever done to me."

My throat becomes thick with tears, but I swallow them, not wanting him to think I feel sorry for him.

"It was him last night."

"I know."

"How did you know where I was?"

"When you didn't come home, we got worried. We found the closing documents in your room. Crew drove me here."

"Where is he?"

"He had to run a quick errand." I look at the gas can. "You know you'll get in big trouble for that."

"It's my house."

"It's still arson, Liam."

"I should be able to do whatever the fuck I want with it."

I get up and peek through the window. "What a coincidence the house was for sale when you had the money to buy it."

"It wasn't for sale."

"Then I'm confused."

"I contacted the owners a few months ago, when the money started rolling in. I told them I wanted to buy it. They weren't interested in selling, but I kept upping the offer." He laughs sadly.

"I paid them way more than its value, but it'll be worth it to see it burn."

I cringe and hope I can change his mind. "Where did you sleep last night?"

He pounds the floorboards next to him.

"You haven't gone inside?"

He shakes his head. "I haven't been inside since the day Luke died."

I hold out my hand. "How about I go in with you."

"I'm not taking you into my nightmare, El."

"In my experience, things aren't as scary when you do them with a friend."

He picks up the empty bottle and looks at it as if he wishes it were full, then throws it in the yard. He stands and reaches for the gas can.

I intercept. "Let's leave it here for now."

"Maybe you should go."

"I'm not leaving, Liam. Not unless you force me to."

He looks sick. "I'd never force you to do anything."

I take his hand. "I know."

He fishes around in his pocket and pulls out a key, letting it dangle from his finger. I take it from him and unlock the door and push it open. He doesn't move.

"It's only a house, Liam. It can't hurt you. Not anymore."

He takes a step inside, squeezing my hand so hard it hurts. We stand in the living room, and he glances around. "It seems a lot smaller." He takes me into the kitchen. "They painted it. It used to be yellow." He lets go of my hand, moves to the sink, and puts his mouth under the faucet, drinking for a long time.

I follow him as he walks through the dining room and back into the living room. He looks at the stairs for a drawn-out moment, then puts a reluctant hand on the banister. His knuckles go white as he climbs the first steps. On the landing, he looks down the hallway, the skin around his eyes bunching. I instantly know which room is his, because he looks ill as he stares at it.

He touches the wall to the right, running his hand along it. "This was Luke's room."

He stands in the doorway to the room across from Luke's. His breathing becomes heavy and labored. His jaw gets tight. Squaring his shoulders, he punches a hole in the door. Blood trickles from his already bruised and battered knuckles.

Slowly, quietly, he crosses to the center of the room and collapses on the floor. He shakes violently and sweats. I fear he's on the verge of a panic attack, but when I go to him, he pushes me away. "Don't touch me," he says scathingly. "Not here."

I step back, horrified at the memories that must be assaulting him.

"Dirk was right. I'm fucked up. I'll always be fucked up. I-I allowed it to happen. I even liked it in some sick and twisted way. I never said no, never asked him to leave. I"—his head slumps into his hands—"I fucking got off."

I fall to my knees next to him. "You were eleven, Liam. It's not your fault."

"I should have known it was wrong. What kind of sick kid thinks his father doing those things is okay?"

"You loved him once. He was an authority figure. It's normal to do what our parents tell us to do, even if we don't think it's right."

"I was a victim then, and I'm a goddamn victim now. I'm too much of a coward to stand up for myself."

"You stood up for yourself last night."

"I mean the video. I was kidding myself. I can't release it. I can't have everyone *knowing*."

"I think it will be the opposite. People will commend you for being strong."

"But they'll look at me differently. The poor kid who was fucked by his father."

I try not to react. Is he speaking literally or figuratively? He hasn't provided details, so I don't know the extent of the abuse he suffered. I was hoping it didn't go further than touching, as horrible as that is in itself. What kind of monster could do that and more to his child? I want to embrace him, tell him he's even stronger than I thought, but I can't. Not here.

His watery eyes focus on me. "They'll look at *you* differently too. They'll wonder what kind of woman wants a man with my twisted history."

He gets up and punches the wall, his fists getting bloodier.

"Liam, stop. You need your hands to play."

"Fuck my hands." He hits the wall. "Fuck Don." He hits it again. "Fuck my pathetic life."

I helplessly watch the man I love completely fall apart. With each punch, he utters dark, hateful words punctuated by sobs so painful, they make me want to kill Don with my bare hands.

Liam stops and leans against the windowsill in exhaustion.

My phone vibrates. It's Crew; he's outside. "I'm going downstairs for a minute. Promise me you won't hurt your hands while I'm gone."

He grunts and sits on the floor. "Bring the gas up with you."

I meet Crew at the door. "Thank you for this," I say, grabbing his purchases.

"Want me to come with?"

"I'm not sure. Do you think you can wait outside? Maybe guard the gas can, just in case?"

"I'll put it in my car and be right here if you need me."

I shut the door, go back upstairs, and put the things in the hallway.

Liam says, "Where's the gas?"

"I have a better idea. Something that might be just as satisfying but won't land you in jail."

I show him what I brought: a crowbar, an axe, and a sledgehammer. I hold out the axe. He lunges toward me. "Hell yes."

"Wait," I say and give him a pair of work goggles before putting on mine.

He swings the axe into the wall with a satisfying crack of wood and drywall. He does it four more times before switching to the sledgehammer. He pounds the wall and swings at the ceiling fan, sending it to the other side of the room, shattered.

He uses the crowbar to pry up some of the floorboards and then the axe to splinter the rest. By the time he's finished, we're in a shell of a room.

"Which one do you want to do next?"

He crosses the hallway to Luke's room. "Want to take the first swing?"

I pick up the axe. "You bet your life I do."

We spend the next hour tearing out every piece of drywall from the three bedrooms upstairs. Every light fixture is smashed, each cabinet desecrated. Even the studs are mostly gone, except the ones supporting the roof. All that's left are wires, pipes, and dust.

He returns to what was his room and sits in a pile of rubble. I remain close, not touching him, like he asked, but he pulls me into his lap and removes our goggles. I brush dust out of his hair.

"Your life is not pathetic," I say. "You have Reckless Alibi, and friends who would do anything for you. And you have me. You can go to therapy to fix whatever it is you think is broken. I'll come with you if you want."

He hugs me tightly and doesn't speak. His cheek rubs against the top of my head as he holds me like I'm his lifeline.

"*You're* my therapy," he says after a long silence. "I can do anything as long as you're with me."

"Then I'm never going anywhere."

A tear blazes a clean trail through the dirt on his cheek. He cups my face. "Marry me, El."

My heart thunders. I desperately want to say yes, but not in this house. He also has work to do to become the man he thinks is worthy of me. What he doesn't know is he was worthy the day we met. He was perfect then, and he's perfect now. But my knowing that and him understanding it are very different things.

"We can't, Liam. It's too soon."

"I'll never want to be with anyone else."

I smile. "Me neither."

"So marry me."

I kiss him because I need him to know my answer isn't no, but it's not yes either. "Promise you'll ask me again another time. When you're really ready."

"Knock knock!" Crew yells from downstairs.

"Up here!" I yell.

He runs up the stairs and stops, taking it all in. "Holy shit." He asks Liam, "You okay, man?"

Liam doesn't look at Crew. He runs a finger down my face. "I think I'm okay now."

Crew kicks some boards aside on his way to us. "What are you going to do now? Need some help with the downstairs?" He picks up the sledgehammer and gives it a swing.

Liam and I stand. "I think we're done here," he says.

"So, the gasoline?"

"Ella was right. I'd probably go to jail for arson. I don't need that shit hanging over my head too."

As we step over the rubble, I ask, "What now? You're not going to live here."

"I'll pay someone to refurbish it, then I'll sell it." He laughs. "I'll never get near what I paid for it."

"Was it worth it?" Crew asks.

"Destroying the walls, tearing through the doors, pummeling the wood? Every swing was another punch to the bastard's face." He glances around. "So yes, totally worth it."

Crew pats him on the back. "I'm glad, brother."

Liam holds out a hand. "Thanks for having my back."

Crew pushes Liam's hand aside and brings him in for a hug. "Always."

We exit the house and go to the cars. Liam doesn't look back. He catches my arm and spins me against his chest. "Thanks for finding me."

"I'll always find you."

He kisses me. "Thanks for saving me too."

I shrug. "Conjugal visits just wouldn't be the same."

He laughs, then sobers. "I'm not only talking about today. You've saved me, Ella, in so many ways."

"I'll do it as many times as you need me to."

He traces my bottom lip. "The same goes for you. I promise I'll always find you. I'll always save you. I'll always be there for you."

His words sound like promises—vows even. I've never been more confident that one day, I'll be his wife.

Chapter Fifty-one

Liam

Ella and I enter the bar and look around for the others. "There they are," she says, pointing to a corner. I carry the gift we're giving Garrett—a charcoal sketch of him sitting at his drums. Ella drew it, and I built the frame.

Someone brought balloons, probably Bria. She's always doing that sort of thing. A huge helium **25** floats behind Garrett.

"Happy birthday," I say, shaking his hand.

"Thanks. Glad to see your knuckles are healing nicely. He hasn't bothered you again since that night, has he?"

I shake my head. Garrett, along with the rest of the band, now knows my father is a scumbag, and Dirk was covering for him. I didn't share details, but they can put two and two together.

Many drinks are brought to the table as Garrett opens his gifts. He opens ours last. "Holy shit, Ella, this is fantastic."

"My girl is talented, isn't she?"

"Hell yes, she is, but we already knew that." He pulls out an envelope. "I have something for you. Well, it's for everyone, but mostly you. I'm no stranger to family bullshit. I hope this will make things better for you."

"But it's *your* birthday. You're the one who's supposed to get gifts."

"This will benefit me too. Go on, open it."

I slip a finger under the seal, rip it open, and pull out a check. It's made out to Indica Record Label, and it's for a million dollars. My eyes snap to his. "What are you doing?"

"I'm buying us out of the contract."

"But this is your inheritance."

"Every damn penny."

I hand it back to him. "You can't do this."

"I can, and I will. Everyone at this table knows we'll all be making this kind of money in a year or two anyway. This way we can get out from under Ronni and Dirk. We'll find a label that wants to work with us on our terms. We have a lot of leverage now. Anyone would kill to represent us."

I can't believe this is happening. "Are you fucking serious?"

"As serious as the numbers on that check."

I turn to the others, who are all smiling. Thoughts fly through my head. No more of Ronni's bullshit rules. And Dirk—I'll finally be free of him, once and for all.

I hug Garrett. "You have no idea what this means to me. I don't even know how to thank you."

"You can thank me—you can *all* thank me—by playing the best damn music anyone has ever heard."

"You got it, man." I call the waitress over and ask for shots, then hand one out to everyone. "On three." I count off, and we all yell, "Let's get Reckless!"

Ella giggles. "That was fun."

"You like that?"

"I do."

"You'll have to come backstage and join in when we're on tour."

"Do you think there will still be a tour?" Bria says. "I mean, if we're not with IRL anymore, all bets are off."

Crew says, "It might take a while longer, but we'll go national. Maybe even international."

Bria seems sad. She puts her drink down.

"What is it?" Ella asks.

"Everything's changing. Brad's leaving. After tomorrow, we won't have a label, and who knows when we'll go on tour."

I hold up the check. "We don't have to do this, you know. I don't want you all capitulating because of me."

"Are you crazy?" Crew says. "First thing tomorrow, we're marching in there and giving Ronni the check." He laughs. "I can't wait to see her face."

"Jeremy will find us another label," Garrett says. "I'll bet they'll be fighting over us."

Brad straightens. "Liam, your uncle just walked through the door."

Dirk is coming straight for me. I stand. "What the hell are you doing here?"

He pulls a chair over and sits. "I have a proposition for you."

"How'd you know where to find me?"

"Ronni may have overheard you talking about Garrett's party."

I sit and pick up my drink, tossing it back in a single swallow. "You're not invited. You should leave."

"Don't you want to hear what I have to say?"

"Anything you needed to say to me, you could have said at IRL earlier." He shifts uncomfortably in his chair, something I've never seen him do. Dirk always has an air of superiority about him, but not today. "This has something to do with Don, doesn't it?"

He doesn't respond.

I laugh. "Holy shit, you heard about the fight. You're scared. Don turned up, and now you think he's going to ruin your shot at being governor. Is that it? Or maybe he's blackmailing you. He needs money, right?"

"How much will it take?" he says sternly.

"For what?"

"For the video. How much for the video?"

I laugh again. "Dirk, there isn't any amount of money that would make me give it up."

"What if I sell the company?"

"I'd say you're too late."

"I'm a businessman, Liam. If I know anything, I know it's never too late to negotiate."

"Hold on a sec," Crew says. "What if there was something in it for both of you?"

I cock my head at him. "How so?"

He picks up the envelope and drags me out of Dirk's earshot. "Dirk can sell the company to Garrett, and you give Dirk the flash drive. You never wanted to release the video anyway. This way, you both win. He'll be off your back, and we can run IRL the way we want. We wouldn't have to find another label. We could go forward with the tour." He smiles deviously. "We could fire Ronni."

I don't even have to think about it. "Okay, let's negotiate," I say to Dirk and sit down. "You'll sell the company to Garrett."

Everyone is surprised to hear me say it, especially Dirk, who says to Garrett, "I didn't realize you were in that sort of position."

"He'll give you a million dollars for it," I say.

Dirk sneers. "IRL is worth ten times that."

"Maybe so, but it's what we're offering. And that part is non-negotiable. How much do you think the video is worth? Or your career in politics—what's the price tag on that?"

He rubs his forehead. "It's not even close to fair."

I push a shot across the table to him. "Then I'd say drink up, because tomorrow the world will see exactly what kind of man Dirk Campbell really is."

"You wouldn't."

"Try me." I get in his face. "After facing your asshole brother on Saturday, you have no idea of the rage inside me." I glance at Crew and Ella. "Ask these two what I did to Don's old house. It'll never be the same. Just like you won't be when the media gets wind of what a lowlife you are."

I see the tremor in his hands. I've got him over a barrel, and he knows it.

He stands angrily, his chair toppling over. "Be at IRL at ten tomorrow morning. Bring the money and the video. You'll be asked to sign an affidavit, stating it's the only copy, and a non-disclosure agreement concerning anything on the tape or overheard in my home. Got it?"

I raise a glass. "See you at ten."

He leaves, and the rest of us stare at each other, stunned.

"What the hell just happened?" Ella says.

"What happened is Garrett is about to become the owner of IRL. We're out from under Dirk's dirty paws, and Ronni will get the boot before the goddamn ink dries."

"I'll drink to that," Crew says.

Ella leans close and whispers, "What about Don?"

"Don can go to hell. I doubt he'll bother me anymore, but if he tries, I'll know about it. His wallet fell out of his pants at the club. Crew looked at his license and found the name he's been living under—Curtis Wingate. Something I'm sure Dirk helped him do. I hired a private investigator to keep tabs on him. He won't be able to make a move without me knowing."

"But you won't be able to release the video. I know you were hesitant, but if you sign the papers, that's it. He could go on to be governor, and no one will ever know the kind of man he is."

"Sooner or later his past will catch up with him. If bad people do enough bad things, eventually they get caught." I kiss her. "Let's forget about all that for now. We have a lot to celebrate. And later, we're having our own private celebration."

For the next few hours, I tease her under the table. By the time we're in a cab on the way back to her place, we can barely keep our hands off each other. I put my hand beneath her skirt and tantalize her. She strokes my inner thigh. I whisper things in her ear that have her squirming in the seat next to me. By the time we get to her place, my body is humming.

We strip off our clothes on the way to the bedroom. She jumps up on me. I'm already hard, and she rubs against me as I carry her to the bed. I put her down and gaze at her gorgeous body. The lights are on, as usual. We never turn them off. I take in every inch of her. We're not even touching each other, but a sexy moan escapes her throat, and I swear I'm about to come.

I stand naked before her, and she takes my cock in her hand. She doesn't have to ask permission anymore. She knows I trust her. She leans forward, and I can tell she wants to put her mouth on me. It's something she's never done before. I've never asked her to; it's always been off limits. She licks her lips. I see her waiting for my reluctance, the repulsiveness, but it's not there. For the first time in my life, I crave it.

"Are you sure?"

I give my answer by inching closer.

Her tongue swipes across the cockhead, tasting me for the first time. I shudder, and she pulls away. "Don't stop." I hope she knows I'm shaking because I like it, not because I don't.

She runs her tongue along the side, then takes me in her mouth. My breath hitches. I put a hand on the back of her head, guiding her, setting the rhythm. I don't let go, knowing I'm in control this way, like I need to be. I didn't know it could be like this. I become unsteady on my feet.

She grabs my ass, holding me against her. I think I see the hint of a smile. It must be damn difficult to smile and give a blowjob at the same time. I almost say something about it, but I don't want to ruin the moment. Besides, the feeling of her lips on me is a thousand times better than I imagined. I grip her shoulder as my thighs tighten and I come, shouting her name.

A few deep breaths later, I collapse on the bed next to her and apologize. "I should have pulled out. I've heard a lot of girls don't like it."

"I didn't mind. I've never been a fan of the taste, but with you, it didn't bother me at all."

Her saying that makes me feel like fucking Tarzan. "That was pretty much my first time."

Her eyes become glassy. "You allowed me to do what no woman has ever done before. The trust you place in me is incomprehensible. It's a gift you give me every time we're together. I'm honored to have been the first. I hope you liked it enough to let me do it again sometime."

"Sometime?" I say, laughing. "How about *every* time? It was incredible." I climb on top of her. "Then again, everything you do to me is incredible."

"I feel the same way."

"Good." I flick her nipple with my tongue. "Then you're going to love this."

I lick every inch of her chest and stomach, working my way down to the place that makes her squirm uncontrollably. I put two fingers inside her as my tongue lashes her clit.

She fists the sheets when I bring her to a quick and intense orgasm. Watching her come has to be my favorite thing to do. "I think we set some kind of record. I doubt you lasted a minute."

"What did you expect after you let me do what I did to you?"

I flash her a devilish grin. "Give me a few minutes, and I'll be ready for round two."

~ ~ ~

Bria, Crew, and I arrive at IRL at 9:45.

"Why do you think Garrett left so early this morning?" Bria says.

"Beats me. He said he had to take care of some things, and he'd meet us here."

I open the door to a flurry of activity. I've never seen so many people here at one time. Niles greets us before we're two feet inside the door. "Lots of changes happening today," he says cheerfully. "Can I get you anything before you start?"

"I think we're good." I whisper to Bria and Crew after he leaves. "See that? He's kissing our ass so he can save his job."

Bria looks at me. "Is his job in jeopardy?"

"Guess it will be up to the new boss."

Crew laughs. "Garrett Young, owner and CEO of Indica Record Label."

"What does that make *us*?" I ask.

"Friends of the boss, I guess. Not a bad position to be in."

Dirk comes through the front door, followed by a suit that must be his lawyer. He doesn't make eye contact with me on his way to the conference room. How the tables have turned. It's delicious.

Some guy sticks his head in the hallway and sees us. "If you're ready, we'll get started."

"Who's that?" Bria whispers.

"Hell if I know."

"Should Crew and I wait out here?" she asks the stranger.

"Mr. Young would like all of Reckless Alibi present."

"Mr. Young?" I mumble in amusement. "But Brad's not here."

"Brad Templeton is parting ways with Reckless Alibi. His presence is not required."

We enter the room. Garrett's already inside, sitting next to the guy who called us in.

"This is Joe Perry, my lawyer," Garrett says.

My brows shoot up. "Since when do you have a lawyer?"

"Since yesterday, when I met with him to collect my inheritance. I called him late last night and asked if he'd represent me in this deal. We've been at it since seven o'clock this morning."

"Been at what?" Crew asks.

"You're about to find out. Sit."

We take seats across the table from Dirk and his lawyer. Dirk sips his coffee so he doesn't have to look at me—as if that will somehow protect him.

"First thing's first," the suit says. "I'm Jason Kutcher. I represent Mayor Campbell in the sale of the company and the matter of the video Liam Campbell will be forfeiting in exchange for the transaction."

He pushes papers across the table to me and Garrett's lawyer. "Sign these, Mr. Campbell. They're all straightforward. It says the copy you are surrendering is the only one and you've not made a backup or duplicate. The non-disclosure agreement states you'll not discuss any conversation, situation, or meeting, whether in person or overheard by circumstance concerning my client, Dirk Campbell."

Mr. Perry quickly reads through them and nods. I sign all the copies and pass them back.

"Now to the sale of Indica Record Label," Mr. Kutcher says. He passes us each a packet.

"Why do *we* need these?" Crew asks.

"You're all named in the purchase agreement," Mr. Perry says. "Mr. Young is putting up the capital to buy the company, but he, along with Brianna Cash, Christopher Rewey, and Liam Campbell, will be equal and controlling partners."

The three of us look at each other. We're surprised, to say the least. Bria's mouth opens and closes repeatedly, but nothing comes out.

"What? Why?" Crew asks.

"We're a team," Garrett says. "I don't want my being the boss to come between us. Now pick your jaws off the table and sign. I want this. I don't give a shit about the money. I just want to be a rock star."

"None of us know how to run a company," I say.

"But Niles does. We'll keep him on as president."

That makes sense. "Okay. Where do we sign?"

Thirty minutes later, Garrett hands over the check, I surrender the flash drive, and then my uncle and his suit leave. Dirk doesn't say a word or look at me. The motherfucker knows I've won.

"So that's it?" I ask. "We own the company?"

"That's it," Mr. Perry says. "I'll file the paperwork with the state." He shakes our hands. "Good luck."

We sit in the conference room, not knowing what to say. Then Crew's face breaks into a brilliant smile. He gets up and runs a victory lap around the conference table, then lifts Bria and spins her around while the rest of us holler and whoop.

I pick up Dirk's coffee cup and slam-dunk it into the trash. This has to be one of the best moments of my life. Man, I wish Ella were here to see this.

"Do we go practice now?" Bria says when we calm down.

Garrett laughs. "Not so fast. There are a few personnel decisions we have to make."

My smile almost cracks my face. "Oh, please let me be the one to toss Ronni out on her ass."

There is a knock on the door. Niles sticks his head in. "You wanted to see me?"

Garrett waves him in. "Have a seat."

Niles looks mildly ill, like he thinks he's about to get the axe.

"Let me introduce you to the new owners of IRL," Garrett says, gesturing to us.

"All four of you?" Niles says.

"That's right. We'd like you to stay on if you're willing. None of us know how to run a record label, and as far as we can tell, you've been doing a good job of it."

He looks more than a little relieved. "I'd be happy to. Thanks."

"Now can I fire the bitch?" I say.

Niles appears concerned. "Can I speak freely?"

"Please," Crew says.

Niles stands and paces. "I know you all have your differences with Ronni, but I've been in this business for twenty-five years, and

I've worked with a hundred reps. Believe me when I say Veronica Collins is one of the best, if not *the* best. She's brusque, demanding, and unconventional at times, but she also gets the job done. She gets more airtime for her clients than anyone I've known. She got you the tour in Florida when nobody knew who Reckless Alibi was. She has a brilliant mind for this business."

I give him a hard look. "Be straight with us. Are you sleeping with her?"

He chokes, pulls out his phone, and shows me the background picture: two little girls and a woman. "These three are my entire life. That woman out there may be sleeping with half of New York City, but not with me. You asked me to stay on as president because you trust I know what I'm doing. I'm asking you to trust me on this. Ronni will take you where no other rep can. You're her boss now. She has to answer to you, not the other way around. All I'm asking is you give it a chance. Will it be difficult? Maybe. She can be hard-headed and heavy-handed, but in time, I think we can make this work. I promise it's what's best for Reckless Alibi. And as the owners of IRL, you need to do what's best for business."

I'm tempted to pound my head on the table. "Fuck."

"He's right," Bria says. "As much as I hate to say it, we need to keep her on, at least for now. We're only getting started. If we go with another rep, it could set us back. We don't want to lose this momentum. It's a small price to pay for success, don't you think?"

"Are we all in agreement then?" Garrett asks. "Ronni stays?"

Everyone nods, albeit reluctantly.

"What about the others?" Niles asks. "There are six more on staff."

Crew says, "If Ronni gets to stay, I doubt we can fire anyone else."

Niles shakes our hands. He doesn't appear to look down on us. He doesn't even seem intimidated that a bunch of twenty-somethings are now his bosses. Maybe he's impressed that we managed to get the company out from under Dirk. "So it's business as usual?"

The four of us glance at each other. "Guess so," Garrett says. "Go do whatever it is you do."

"I appreciate the vote of confidence," he says.

"Hey, Niles?" I say before he leaves. "Can you send Ronni in? We have a few things to go over with her."

He chuckles. "Sure thing."

Garrett crosses his arms in amusement. "This is going to be fun. Liam, you have the floor."

In usual form, Ronni saunters in five minutes later, letting us know we work according to her timetable, not ours. She's annoyed. "Will somebody please tell me what the hell is going on around here? Dirk left in a huff, Niles is practically giddy, and the four of you look like a bunch of kids on Christmas morning."

Crew gives me a nod. I've waited for this moment for a year.

"There are a few things we need to discuss with you." I motion to an empty seat at the end of the table.

We're all trying to keep straight faces. Ronni examines us one by one and crosses her arms in front of her, refusing to sit. "Is this an intervention or something?"

Chuckling, I say, "Or something. Take a good look, Veronica. The four people sitting at this table are now the owners of IRL."

Her face contorts into an ugly, mutinous expression. Then she laughs. "This is a joke, right?"

I push my copy of the sale agreement over to her. She leafs through it, disgust emanating from her every pore. She looks up. "How?"

"It doesn't matter how. The four of us own the company and that's a fact."

With a flick of her wrist, the contract is flung across the table. "I suppose I'm fired now?"

"Believe it or not, no. You have Niles to thank for that."

"So you're keeping me around to torture me? Some kind of payback?"

The corner of my mouth twitches into a wry grin, because there's nothing I'd like more. "Not exactly, but if that's what floats your boat."

"Maybe I'll just quit then."

"You won't. You're making a killing off us. Nobody in their right mind would give that up."

Her eyes perk up. "So you admit you need me."

"We need each other, Veronica."

Her lips pucker. She's hates it when we call her that. "If you wouldn't mind, I prefer Ronni."

My insides are bursting with laughter, but I hold it together. I swear to God saying those words was like eating a forkful of dog shit for her.

"No problem, *Ronni*."

"I'm not going to kiss your asses, you know."

"We don't expect you to. But you will treat us with respect, as you do Niles. Just as you would any superior. And we won't tolerate you telling us whom we can and can't look at, date, marry, or fuck. Is that clear?"

"If you think I'm calling you Mr. Campbell, think again." She's trying not to show it, but I know this is killing her. She takes another look around the table. "Why isn't Brad here?"

"He's leaving Reckless Alibi," Garrett says.

Her eyebrows shoot up. "Since when?"

"He told us a while ago."

"And you're just telling me this *now*?" She turns her back to us and gazes out the window. She's obviously trying to hold it together.

"He's staying on until we can find a replacement," Crew says. "We'll start looking soon."

"I have a list of candidates for every single one of your positions in a folder in my office."

The four of us shake our heads. "Of course you do," I say. "You are free to submit names to us, but we'll be the ones choosing Brad's replacement. You're welcome to a vote. But let's face it, it won't hold nearly as much weight as it would have yesterday."

I watch her throat as she swallows hard. "Is that all, or do you want me to fetch you coffee?" she says sarcastically.

"I think that's it for now," Bria says. But before Ronni reaches the door, she adds, "Oh, and you can call me *Bria* from now on. No more Brianna unless we're in public."

Ronni exits without another word. I twirl my chair around a few times. She was right. This does feel like Christmas.

Chapter Fifty-two

Ella

Watching Liam onstage is my favorite thing to do, but he's been different this last month. Since the incident with Don, he scans the audience for more than just me. He's looking for him. Even though he's paying a pretty penny for round-the-clock surveillance, he's afraid Don might show up.

Tonight is one of Reckless Alibi's last club performances. They have two songs in the top 100, and their albums are getting more popular every day. From here on out, they'll only play larger venues or make special appearances. Despite Ronni being a royal pain in the ass, she has come through for them, and they've gone ahead with planning another tour. Although I'm less than pleased they kept her on, they've assured me she's the best at what she does.

I sit at a table in front with Jeremy, wondering what it will be like when they play for thousands of fans, not hundreds. When they won't be able to walk into a restaurant without being recognized. When my greatest claim to fame will be that I'm Liam Campbell's girlfriend.

Sometimes I wish things could stay the way they are. I worry about what fame could do to someone like Liam, with his sordid past. He's no stranger to drugs and alcohol. On the other hand, I want him to get everything he's worked so hard for. I made a promise to save him if he ever needs saving.

He gazes at me during the final song, and I wonder if he's having the same thoughts I am. This may be the last time I get to see him play from the floor. I flash him the "rock on" sign. He winks at me.

"You're good for him," Jeremy says.

"I hope so."

"I've seen a lot of musicians in my time. Rarely have I seen one get tamer as they gain popularity. It's usually the opposite. He's changed since Florida, and I know you have everything to do with it."

"What do you think is going to happen to them, Jeremy?"

"Honestly? I think you're listening to one of the next best new artist nominees. They're the most talented group I've seen in the past ten years. I believe they're going to reach levels beyond even that. I wouldn't be surprised if they become one of the classics, like Aerosmith or the Eagles."

My heart beats wildly. "You're kind of scaring me, Jeremy."

"Don't worry, Ella. I've got their backs. In addition to being talented, they have good heads on their shoulders. And Liam has you to keep him grounded."

"Everything's going to change, isn't it?"

He puts a fatherly hand on my arm. "Are you ready for that?"

Liam is at home onstage. It's exactly where he belongs. "I think I could be ready for anything as long as we're together."

The music stops, and the audience cheers loudly. Jeremy takes my elbow. "Let's go backstage."

Liam spots me and smiles, his grin full of hungry anticipation.

I hug him. "Great performance."

He kisses me. "Thanks."

"Are you going to miss playing places like this?"

"I think I am. I love being able to see the people—their faces, their excitement." He brushes my hair behind my ear. "I love being able to see *you*."

Ronni comes in a side door. "They're ready for you on the sidewalk," she says. "The limo leaves in fifteen minutes. Try to sign as many autographs as you can." She walks over to me. "You can wait in the limo if you want. I can have someone escort you."

I try not to smirk. I know how hard it's been for Ronni to be nice to me. I can see in her eyes that she still doesn't like me. She doesn't like Bria either, but she's been smart enough to swallow her pride and make nice. My guess is she goes home and screams into her pillow, because she's no longer calling the shots. But she's willing to put up with it because Reckless Alibi is not a band she wants slipping through her fingers.

I watch from the limo as the five of them pose for pictures and sign autographs. Security holds back women who try to breech the ropes and grope the guys. Five months ago I was this heartbroken girl with an ordinary life. I was one of those women. Then I fell through the ropes into Liam's world. How did I ever get so lucky?

Thor opens the door and everyone piles in. Liam checks his phone, as he always does after a show. He gives me a look.

"What is it?" I ask.

"The private investigator left a message. He wants to see me as soon as possible."

I check the time. It's almost eleven o'clock. "It's pretty late."

"He texted me half an hour ago." He types something, sends it, and almost immediately gets a reply. "He wants me to come by his office."

"Now?"

"Will you come with me?"

"Of course."

The driver drops everyone else at IRL and then takes us across town.

"What do you think he wants?" I ask.

"I have no idea, but it must be important to have me come in this late on a Friday night."

"Do you think Don left town?"

"That's something he could have said in a text." He holds my hand tightly, clearly bothered.

"It's going to be okay," I tell him. "Whatever it is, we'll deal with it."

We arrive at our destination and are buzzed into the building. We take an elevator up, and someone meets us when we step off. "Liam, thanks for coming."

"Hi, Mr. Stone. This is my girlfriend, Ella."

"Nice to meet you. Come on in, and please call me Ethan."

He leads us through an immaculate reception area, down a hallway, and into a large office. The whole way I'm thinking how expensive this must be, though Liam doesn't seem to care.

"I was surprised you wanted to meet this late," Liam says.

Ethan motions us into the two chairs opposite his desk. "I thought you'd want to know the latest developments. I wasn't sure how quickly it would hit the news, and I wanted to brief you first."

Liam looks scared. I have to say, I'm a bit terrified too.

"Tell me," Liam says.

"I'm not sure how to say this, so I'll just come out with it. Curtis Wingate—Don Campbell—is dead."

My hand flies to my mouth to stop a gasp. Liam is stunned.

"Dead?" he asks. "How?"

"We've kept tabs on him continuously. At six o'clock tonight, there was a shift change between two of my investigators, Kirk and Neil. As circumstance would have it, that's exactly when things went down. Kirk followed Don home from a midtown bar, where he drank alone for two hours. Don parked but didn't exit the car. He was clearly drunk. Kirk parked behind Neil, who had recently arrived. A man came out of the bushes, fired two shots into Don's car, and took off down the street on foot. Since Neil had a better view of the crime, he called 911 and stayed on the scene while Kirk discreetly followed the perp, saw him get into a car one block over, and then tailed him for over an hour to his destination."

I say, "He was murdered?"

"He was," Ethan says. "Does the name Michael Scarbucci mean anything to you, Liam?"

Liam shakes his head.

"He's in the employ of Tri-Camp Enterprises."

Liam stiffens. "That's my uncle's company. Dirk Campbell."

Ethan nods. "Mr. Scarbucci drove all the way to Stamford after the shooting, straight to Dirk Campbell's house."

Liam is in utter disbelief. "My uncle?"

I take his hand. "Remember the guy in Dirk's office when you went there a few months ago? His name was Mike."

Liam's expression changes from confusion to realization to pure amusement. "My fucking uncle put a hit on Don?"

"It's too early to say," Ethan says, "but my sources tell me Dirk Campbell is a major person of interest. There is a warrant out for his arrest. Could be Scarbucci was quickly persuaded to turn state's evidence. It was an incredible stroke of luck that we were on the scene when it happened. If Kirk and Neil hadn't been there, he'd have gotten away with it."

"It makes sense," Liam says. "Dirk needed insurance."

"Insurance?"

"My uncle and I had a falling out a long time ago. I'm sure he was protecting Don, but after he came to the gig last month, Dirk has been scared. He didn't want anything to ruin his chances at running for governor. With Don out of the picture, he wouldn't have a problem. It also ensured I'd never go to the authorities for the abuse I suffered as a kid."

Ethan looks sad. "I'm sorry for whatever he did to you, Liam."

"He's really gone?" Liam asks. "Are you sure he's dead? They didn't revive him at the hospital?"

"Neil stayed at the scene. Don was pronounced dead there."

"And Dirk could go to jail for it?"

"If they determine he ordered the hit, it doesn't look good for him. Even if he does get off, he can take being governor off the table. People don't recover from the kind of press he's about to get."

Liam is having a hard time suppressing a smile. "Don's dead. Sorry, you probably think I'm a douchebag for being happy about it."

Ethan holds up his hands. "It's not my place to judge. My wife went through something as a kid. Her mom dying was one of the best things that happened to her. Whatever baggage he saddled you with—don't carry it around. Let it go. Your life will be profoundly easier."

Liam stands and shakes Ethan's hand. "I don't know how to thank you."

"You can thank me by paying my rather substantial bill. And by referring me to your friends."

"You got it."

Out in the hall, Liam leans against the wall. "It's over. Don's dead. Dirk is going to jail or at the very least, his life will be ruined."

"Looks like you're getting everything you ever wanted."

His eyes burn into mine. "I think I am."

I take his hand. "Let's go celebrate." I realize what I said. "Oops. That's probably not the right word to use on this occasion."

His lips turn up in a sultry grin. "That's exactly the right word. What did you have in mind?"

"It's up to you."

He thinks on it. "You might be surprised at what I pick."

"Tell me. You can have anything."

He tugs me against him. "I want to lie next to you in bed and talk like we did in Florida. All night."

"You do?"

He laughs. "You were imagining something more along the lines of chocolate and whip cream?"

My eyebrows shoot up. "I might have been totally on board with that."

"Tomorrow then." He pulls me toward the elevator. "Tonight we're going to learn everything about each other."

My heart is already racing with anticipation.

An hour later we're in bed doing just what he wanted—looking at each other in the light of the moon and talking. A *lot.* He opens up to me more than he ever has, though I can tell it's hard.

"There's no hurry," I say. "We have all the time in the world."

"Do we?"

"Yes. I'm not going anywhere, Liam."

I have no doubt he's thinking about the events of tonight and how they will affect the rest of his life.

He traces a line up and down my arm. "For years I've wished him dead and prayed my uncle would go down in flames. Now that it's happened, I realize it's not even important. What's important is *you*. Nothing else matters."

"You're not like Don, you know. You'll never be like him. You're a good man. And someday you'll be an amazing father."

"I didn't understand that until now. I'm not scared anymore—about anything." A happy tear rolls down my cheek. He catches it with his thumb. He rises on an elbow and gazes thoughtfully into my eyes. "You can say it, you know. I want to hear it. I want to hear it every day."

I run a finger along the stubble of his jaw. "I love you."

He sighs as if I've opened the gates to heaven, then he feathers the most sensual kisses up my neck. He whispers in my ear, "I love you too, El."

My eyes fly open in surprise. It's the first time in his life he's ever said the words. My heart is so full, it's about to explode. This man is everything I want in life. He's my best friend, my soul mate, my love. The look in his eyes tells me he feels the same way. And I know. Suddenly, I know for sure that wherever life takes us, we'll go together.

He cups my face. "Someday I'm going to ask you to marry me again, Mrs. Campbell."

I smile. Because … how could I not? "Someday I'm going to say yes."

The End

My dear readers,

Most of you have come to expect an epilogue at the end of my books. However, like Crew and Bria, Liam and Ella's relationship is just beginning. You'll see much more of both couples in the next book, so to have an epilogue at this point would be premature. I hope you understand. If you're eager to see more of them and the rest of Reckless Alibi, you can read the next book in the series, Reckless Reunion.

Thank you all so very much,

Samantha

Acknowledgments

Liam's story was hard to write at times. It was also very rewarding. The subject of male sexual abuse is often discarded, but some sources claim its prevalence is almost as high as female sexual abuse, so I knew it was a story worth telling.

It's not always clear to children that they are being abused. And if *they* don't know, it can be tough for the adults in their lives to see it as well. If you are being abused, or think someone in your life is, please call the national sexual abuse hotline at 1-800-656-4673.

As always, there are many people to thank.

To my special editor who has been with me since the beginning, Ann Peters, thank you for your continued support. Also, a great big shout out to my copy editor, LS, at Murphy Rae Solutions.

To my beta readers, Shauna Salley, Joelle Yates, Laura Conley, Jeannie Hinkle, and Tammy Dixon—you ladies all have unique ways of finding things that have slipped past everyone else.

Thank you to Susan Phelan of the Denver-based band, Ryan Chrys and The Rough Cuts. You've helped me get inside the heads of rock stars.

And finally, to my Facebook reader group, Samantha's Sweethearts. The first thing I do each morning and the last thing I do every night is pop into the group to share in the love and encouragement you fine ladies give one another.

About the author

Samantha Christy's passion for writing started long before her first novel was published. Graduating from the University of Nebraska with a degree in Criminal Justice, she held the title of Computer Systems Analyst for The Supreme Court of Wisconsin and several major universities around the United States. Raised mainly in Indianapolis, she holds the Midwest and its homegrown values dear to her heart and upon the birth of her third child devoted herself to raising her family full time. While it took time to get from there to here, writing has remained her utmost passion and being a stay-at-home mom facilitated her ability to follow that dream. When she is not writing, she keeps busy cruising to every Caribbean island where ships sail. Samantha Christy currently resides in St. Augustine, Florida with her husband and four children.

You can reach Samantha Christy at any of these wonderful places:

Website: www.samanthachristy.com

Facebook: https://www.facebook.com/SamanthaChristyAuthor

Twitter: @SamLoves2Write

E-mail: samanthachristy@comcast.net

Made in the USA
Monee, IL
14 July 2022

99678507R00240